LOSING GRAVITY

by
Kamala Ramy

Word Wrap Press
PO Box 7362
Somerset, NJ 08873-9998

LOSING GRAVITY

by
Kamala Ramy

Published By:
Word Wrap Press
PO Box 7362
Somerset NJ 08873-9998

First Edition

Library of Congress Catalog Card Number:
97-60120

Printed on Recycled Paper

Non-Profit Organizations, Education Enterprises:
Quantity discounts are available on bulk purchases
for educational purposes, or fund raising.
For information, please contact
Word Wrap Press, PO Box 7362
Somerset NJ 08873-9998

LOSING GRAVITY

It begins as a trickle of molecules tentatively dissolving, a fizzling at the fringes of the fingers, at the ridges of the toes. Within the conduit marrow, the rampaging blood settles to a wadding calm, releasing the anima from its imprisoning current. Consciousness begins to leak out. There is a sensation of lightness, of letting go, as the body increasingly empties. Eventually too little is left to pervade the ego. The endorphin-numbness stiffens to paralysis; subverting vibrations shatter the soul from its cellular bonds. Finally, the causal head bobs forward. Scarcely restrained to its spinal bindings, it anxiously wavers. Suddenly, there is a quantum leap — followed by the disquieting realization that the quintessential stuffing has escaped.

At this point in the equation, Grace finds herself floating past her bedroom bookcase, its shelves precariously stacked with how-to guides on astral adventures. Belatedly, she recalls the instructions for righting herself as she crashes into the ceiling. With great effort, she maneuvers from where spiders have woven their webs. Unable to project to more exotic environs, Grace contemplates the disheveled bed sheets and her face, tenaciously buried inside the pillow. It is a wonder she does not suffocate. According to the illuminated clock, it is already 5:45 a.m. An alarm will shortly waken her. In the meantime, Grace scrapes along the ceiling and counts the cracks. Occasionally she collides with a wall, a sensation less painful than disconcerting. Being measurably less dense, she dissolves into the yellowing stucco, only to get stuck half-in, half-out.

Purportedly, out-of-body adepts can astral-project themselves into other dimensions. Thus far, Grace cannot extricate her north from her south, or, for that matter, extract her embedded elbow. Should worse come to worse, she can waken, or slip into a conventional dream. Hoping to set her astral wings aloft, Grace undertakes suggestion three from chapter four in astral guide number nine. Diligently, she fine-tunes her visualization, conjures rising tides of angels. Almost immediately, the image is smudged by a misgiving thought: perhaps such beatific beings will find her astral incursion presumptuous. Stymied by such terrestrial doubts, Grace ends up engulfed in gulls, pleating waxy wings within a down-draft sea of wings, one hundred thousand strong.

Unable to escape the panting stream, Grace collaborates with her confederate gulls as they overtake the incoming tides. Delightedly, Grace recognizes the serpentine shoreline, the ribbon ridges, and frost-fog sky of Alyeska Bay, so often drawn by mystic dreamers, so rarely seen. Owned by the Qwaquiwei tribe, it is considered the original Eden from which humankind was expelled. So supremely sacred, not even Qwaquiwei may inhabit it. Whether wistful dream, or astral incursion, Grace cruises the lucid vision in her stowaway sea-bird guise. Opalescent sea crests sizzle atop glistening waves of sapphire; coral-striped slitherslanks flash their iridescent fins. Like a triumphantly cresting wave, the winged flotilla surges over the praline peaks of varnished snow. Suddenly, they break formation, spill into the sheltering valley, dispersing like unraveling clouds. Swept within the entangling updrafts, Grace separates from her companion gulls as they chaotically scatter into their separate eddies.

Meanwhile, off shore, off course, a poisonous web of toxic ooze leaks from a listing tanker. Guilelessly unaware, Grace dives into the baiting waters. Seconds after impact, she begins to drown. Thrashing within the tumultuous spin, Grace attempts to orient herself towards the surface. Rummaging the murky waters for a directing ray of sunshine, Grace tangos with another panicked pair of wings beneath the obfuscating mousse. Grace tries to waken, only to realize she is awake. Desperately, she probes for the golden cord which links her astral stuffing to its custodial flesh and bones. She can spool it like a tow rope, reel herself back to her comfortable bed. But where is it? Her ungainly wings are in the way. Meanwhile, the listing tanker leaks oil and more oil, transforming once virgin waters into an ever condensing grave. A sliver of light seeps through an opening whirlpool. Grace splashes towards the saving portal. Upon breaking the surface, she is blinded by a caustic veil of petroleum grease. Noxious fumes scald her lungs; searing toxins scour her skin; her saturated wings cleave to her body like down-rushing anchors. Again, she begins to drown.

Ta-ring! Ta-ring! A low-voltage augury from a travel alarm attempts to coax Grace from her goose-down covers and thickening nightmare. *Ta-ring! Ta-ring!* Her drowsy arm periscopes the area, then slaps down and misses. Reassessing its coordinates, her arm adjusts, then slaps down and misses, then readjusts, slaps down and misses, then — slam! Having deactivated the persistently ta-ringing mechanism, Grace cautiously opens one eye. But of course: it was only a dream. The golden cord cannot be broken. That is what the good book says. Assured she lies safe in her bed, one sock off and one sock on, Grace wrests the comforter over her head, then floats back to the ceiling. Again she maneuvers around the spiders. Again she over-projects.

This time, she finds herself lost in a desert, clumsily clutching a child in each arm. After scouring an abandoned cliff dwelling for water, for food, she concedes: not a drop of rain, not even a scorpion to eat. Suddenly, there is a terrible explosion. Pulsing lava rages from the vacuous eyes of the vacant dwelling. Ignited rocks rain down, leaving nowhere to take shelter. Amidst her children's wrenching screams, Grace scurries to dig a saving hole. As she claws the desiccate ground, her fingers fracture digit by digit. Eventually her tears melt the hardened clay. Instinctively Grace molds a tribal wedding basket. Faithfully she fashions the customary conjugal spouts. As the sky peremptorily shatters, Grace pours her children into one spout before crawling into the other. Deep inside the mud-bakcd womb, she comes upon an unexpected clearing: a garden of Eden surrounded by trees and streams, and Aaron Mushkin brushing his teeth in her bathroom — meaning the back-up alarm has sounded.

Placed strategically out of reach, the radio-alarm clock entices Grace with the whir and whirl of worldly events. At ten minutes past the hour, it duly notifies Grace of a jam-up on Route 27, along with a sixty percent chance of rain. The morning light has amassed sufficient photons to pierce the diaphanous curtains. Grace shields her eyes from the encroaching sunrise. The intensifying rays, compounded by the radio's pestering chatter, inhibit a smooth transfer out-of-body. The causal body squiggles and squirms in its quest to float back to Eden. Finally, an unexpected wave washes Grace ashore. It is a pleasant respite. Grains of sand chaff her webbed toes. The shoreline ripples with blossoms of seaweed. The breeze hints of honeysuckle. Grace plays tag with the incoming tide and hand-shadows with her outstretched wings. Grace waltzes forward as the tide creeps in. Grace tiptoes backwards as the tide seeps out. Grace prances sideway, then hopscotches headlong into the swash, first four steps, then five steps, then eight, nine— something is wrong. Fish squiggle helplessly in the mysteriously exposed bay. Judging this an ill omen, Grace hoists her wings.

Unfortunately, unaccountably, her feathers have molted from her limbs, leaving stranded forearms of barnacle crusted bone. Resigned to this twist of fate, Grace dutifully examines her lifeline. Unable to make out where it begins or ends, she realizes her life is not an actual line but the resultant shadow from an ever-shifting dune. Meanwhile, rushing towards her at hundreds of miles per hour, wave upon wave converge wave upon wave. So this is where the sea has gone: tsunami, assaulting with an eerie twist, its crest ablaze with the burning tanker from her previous nightmare. Flaming refuse studs the climaxing waters. Like tongues from hell, they lash apocalyptically. Grace bolts upright in a rude awakening.

Shivering convulsively, wringing with sweat, Grace assesses her bedroom, innocuously secure. Her wakened eyes assert it was only, only a dream; however, her heart continues to pound hysterically as if still pinned beneath the fiery deluge. Aaron, his mouth full of paste suds, teasingly tosses Grace a wet washcloth. "I warned you about those peppered pickles.

And it wouldn't hurt to cut down on your caffeine, darling."
Aaron kisses Grace's tousled hair, then turns up the radio
before returning to the bathroom. As Grace mentally attunes
to WBMX on the FM dial, she realizes there was indeed an
accident at Alyeska Bay. Grace has been inter-splicing
fragments of the morning's news into her subconscious dreams.

Roving reporter Tim Tinkerton relates the actual
details. "Like casualties of war, they lay in drums of death by
the thousands. Officials estimate one-quarter million are
already dead. That's fifty percent of the indigent wild life.
Spokespersons for the Olie Oil Corporation assert the 250
million gallons of crude oil which leaked into the pristine bay
was a tragic accident. Bad karma, you know, but initial
inquiries lead us to believe the captain and crew were more
than mildly intoxicated. How else could they have rear-ended
an exposed, clearly demarcated reef. The facts are not all in,
but it is rumored a corporate board meeting took place in the
captain's cabin the prior evening. Chairpersons were
celebrating their multi-million dollar bonuses with belly dancers
and booze. Such unbridled revelry may have contributed to the
grounding. The last such spill, one-twentieth the size, spread
toxic havoc one thousand miles before dissipating.
Environmentalists claim this calamity will impact every inch
of shoreline around the globe. Others disclaim these
'exaggerations of political proportions', but the mounting
bonfires of oil-doused bodies dampen their credibility. Perhaps,
when the ashes..."

Grace lowers the volume. She has more pressing
problems. A lawyer's life is lucrative but not easy. As Grace dots
her face with the warm, wet washcloth, she outlines her agenda
for the day. Her blood pressure refuses to rise to the occasion.
She has been working long days, frequent nights, and too, too
many weekends. Times like these, she wishes she had a more
elementary job, like Aaron's. Instead, she has Aaron.

Aaron is what her first and second husbands were not.
Her first husband was an alcoholic with no sense. Her second
husband was a genius with no heart. After her first husband
died, she vowed never to marry in the heat of passion. After

divorcing her second husband, she vowed never to marry. Grace Ivanosky determined to raise her twin sons by herself and accumulate enough money to retire to an island paradise. But island paradises proved hard to come by. So did Aaron Mushkins. How could she resist the sweet, simple forest ranger and his long, lingering kisses. Though she dated him on and off for years, she is not much past the biblical knowing. Perhaps that is the key. Familiarity precedes contempt. Grace had known her first husband since they were children. She met him at his lemonade stand. They had their first argument over the number of lemon slices in her paper cup, and the amount of change on her dollar. Her second husband was an intellectual celebrity. She knew him well before she knew him, having viewed him countless times on television as he resoundingly debated his ideas. She read his writings, pondered gossip columns detailing his lost loves and financial assets. She was certain she knew every "thing" about him. After years of icy anguish, she realized a curious aspect of the human heart: you can come to know it in a single second, or never know it in a lifetime.

Grace lowers the blinds, turns on the bed light, then rummages through her pouch for a newly purchased toothbrush before entering the bathroom. Aaron exits the bathroom, raises the blinds, cracks open the window, shuts off the bed light, then re-enters the bathroom. Grace exits the bathroom, turns on the bed light, slams shut the window, rummages through her pouch for a newly purchased roll of floss, then re-enters the bathroom. Grace turns on the sink faucet while she polishes her front teeth. Aaron retrieves his razor from the medicine cabinet, dots on some shaving lather then turns off the sink faucet while Grace brushes her back teeth. After Aaron exits the bathroom, Grace turns on the sink faucet, rinses her toothbrush, switches the shower head to its steamiest setting, then rummages her pouch for a newly purchased jar of conditioner. Meanwhile, Aaron, lathered with shaving lotion, re-enters the bathroom. Firmly, he switches off the sink faucet, shaves his morning stubble, turns on the faucet, rinses his razor, rinses his face, turns off the sink faucet, returns his razor to the medicine cabinet, then switches the shower head to a cooler setting. Finally Grace locates the conditioner, climbs into the shower, turns the temperature to hot and the shower setting to full blast. Dutifully, Aaron screws the top back onto Grace's oozing tube of toothpaste, scratches the price sticker off her roll of floss, then returns her toothbrush to its holder. Having done his ritual part, he switches off the light, then exits the bathroom. Left alone in the dark, conditioner dripping into her eye, Grace screams for a towel.

Neither Grace nor Aaron has progressed beyond separate but equal lives with some notable areas of interference. Aaron insisted they cohabit after their baby was born. He loves Grace. He loves her twin sons. He loves his child. He wants to marry. Grace loves Aaron but she knows better. She has been married twice, is a few years older, has a higher intelligence quotient, and more substantial income. Besides, Aaron is the perfect man. That automatically makes him suspect. Grace decided it best for their marriage if they didn't actually marry. Grace works the long hours and manages the money. Aaron tends to a small park in his care and to Webster, their baby daughter.

The twins, from Grace's second marriage, look after themselves. Always treated like adults, Rom and Reem can not be broken into family life with its concept of inter-dependency. Though barely twelve, they have outgrown parental guidance. They inherited their father's genius but Grace believes they harbor her soul. Scrutinizing their identical faces, she,is hard pressed to tell where their father's genius ends and her soul begins. They don't look much like Grace, reflecting their father's oriental features and jet black hair. There is one token resemblance to Grace: their gravel-gray eyes. The color suits them. It is the color of inner resource so perhaps they are more like Mom than Dad after all.

Initially, Grace was intrigued with her identical twins. It was fun confusing people until those people began to include herself. It was then Grace remembered a friend's fateful warning: never buy a second parakeet. When you have the one, it will perch on your finger, chirp on your shoulder, learn to say, "Hello, I love you." Put a second parakeet in the cage and they will look to each other and shut you out. Like peas in a pod, Rom and Reem perfectly complement each other. They have no friends; they have no need. They never ask about their father. If they have a problem, they discuss it with their assigned counselor at the Gifted Children Institute. For most things, they consult their local library or personal computer. Grace faithfully puts out the food and writes any requisite checks.

As Grace descends the stairs, brushing back her overhanging bangs, relishing the aroma of maple syrup and fresh brewed coffee, she notes: she should be pleased. Her sons have developed despite her absences. Pausing at the kitchen entrance, Grace considers her perfect family. Under the beamish kitchen lighting, Rom pokes back his wire-rimmed glasses with his left hand, while manipulating the hand-held electronic game with his right hand; Reem pokes back his wire-rimmed glasses with his right hand, while manipulating the shared hand-held electronic game with his left hand. At the tiled breakfast counter, Webster lies burping over Aaron's shoulder. For a wistful moment, Grace wonders what it would be like to be a mother.

"Pignoli pancakes?" Aaron proffers his frying pan with its four golden offerings. Grace rarely eats this early. To avoid rejecting a feast prepared so lovingly, Grace takes a few bites then asks Aaron to bag it. After cheerily removing Grace's uneaten portion from its plate, Aaron turns to Rom and Reem. Before Aaron can pose the question, the twins respond one after the other without glancing from their game monitor.

"No!"

"No!"

"Of course, of course." Aaron has taken to answering twice. "You boys don't like pancakes, don't like tofu omelets, or blueberry blintzes. No frivolous fare, so I will keep it simple: cereal and fruit."

Grace borrows Webster for a good-bye hug before kissing Aaron's nutmeg-dusted lips. While tickling a responsive Webster, Grace counter-checks. "No, dear. Just milk in a glass with two separate straws. Rom and Reem must be able to hold their food in one hand, preferably while standing, so they can continue doing whatever nonsense they are doing with the other."

"Nonsense?"

"Nonsense!"

The twins erupt at the accusation. Rom exhorts, "You seem to think this is just a game, Mother. You know how many points we get for finding where the Wizard keeps the Holy Lantern?"

Reem elaborates. "This is mental gymnastics, preparation for the future. Sooner or later, we will be forced to redesign the world. Besides, Cindy Jacobs has acquired the key to the Secret Cavern and is mere man-hours from breaking the code. We can't..."

Rom assents. "No, we can't let her beat us. Not us!" "Not us" is proclaimed in emphatic unison, as a force not to be challenged.

Grace instructs Aaron. "We've been over this before, sweetheart. Just give them their box of Captain Munchies. They can crunch them down on the bus. Throw in a few chewable vitamin tablets and they'll be fine, right guys?"

Aaron seems distressed. "No fruit? No fiber! Where are you going to get your potassium — and what am I going to do with all these talking bananas?" Aaron yanks a banana from the bunch. "You can't mean you prefer Munchies to conversant bananas?"

Grace furtively prods her twins to humor the ranger and his forest ways. Aaron catches her covert wink. "I see. You don't believe me."

Rom turns to his mother. "Perhaps Mr. Mushkin doesn't realize we are fully twelve years old, that twelve-year-olds know bananas cannot talk, know how to procreate."

Reem hastily amends, "Or rather how absolutely not to procreate, as well as how to make nuclear bombs from common household items."

Aaron is undaunted by their doubts. "Yes, yes, you boys are precocious beyond your years so don't take my word."

Reem rolls his eyes and cracks, "All right. But just this once." Reluctantly, Reem faces down the yellow fruit. "So answer me, banana creature. If a train is traveling fifty miles per hour at a ten degree westbound angle..."

Rom further compounds the complexity. "Yeah, yeah, and a second train, five miles due west, is traveling thirty-five miles an hour at a fifteen degree westbound angle, how long will it take for the second train to intersect..."

Aaron waves his banana in alarm. "Well, no, no; they don't do numbers. They can only handle yes-no questions, but of course."

The twins disdainfully assess their step-guardian and his dull-witted banana. Trying to salvage Aaron's dwindling credibility, Grace valiantly poses. "In your estimation, Mr. Banana, does Aaron Mushkin still love me?"

Aaron waves his hand nervously. "You can't..."

Reem insolently interjects, "Now what? I thought you said it could handle yes-no questions?"

Aaron lamely defends. "But love is complicated. Don't know if a banana, even a talking banana can..."

"So it can't really communicate, can it Mr. Mushkin? Well, that is just what Rom and I..."

"Yes, we said it couldn't."

"And it can't!"

Apprehensively Aaron slices the end knob of the banana. Embedded in the knob core is the letter Y, or rather the shriveled vein whose cuneiform impression might be interpreted as a Y.

Grace giggles delightedly. Discounting this sketchily drafted Y as sufficient proof of higher intelligence, the twins snootily pack their box of Munchies before departing for the bus.

Animatedly shaking the banana, Aaron privately reproves Grace. "How could you ask such a— What if the banana said no?"

"Why would it say no? Don't you still love me?"

"Of course, but I could have sliced the banana to unmask the letter O, or rather a little undeveloped Y which kind of looks like an O which indicates 'no'. That's how it works."

"I see." Grace pouts teasingly. "So this banana is not speaking out of any firmly held conviction. You may not love me after all."

Propping Webster on his shoulders, and consigning the feckless banana to his jacket pocket, Aaron pledges. "Can't speak for the rest of the bunch but I swear I love you, will always, always..." As Aaron smothers Grace in an assuring embrace, she sighs as she reckons the time. To leave such a perfect man at such a perfect moment attests that life, however cleverly created or well intentioned, is often poorly executed. Perhaps that is why salmon forgo their weary flesh to lay their glittering dreams within the fatal waters.

EYE - WITNESS FROGS

Grace raps her curdling stomach, hoping to induce last night's dyspeptic pickles into suspended digestion. Her case is not going well. Again, she prompts her expert witness. "So in your estimation, Dr. Diego, there was nothing, absolutely nothing to..."

Complying to her drift, Dr. Diego extracts his air quality report from his fraying air quality report folder. Monotonically, he summarizes: "The air quality tested negative, meaning there were no contaminant particles." Carefully reinserting the air quality report into its respective folder, Dr. Diego extracts his water quality report from his fraying water quality report folder. Without raising or lowering or varying his voice in the least degree, he again summarizes: "The water also tested negative, meaning there were no chemical pollutants." Carefully reinserting the water quality report into its respective folder, Dr. Diego extracts his food quality report from his fraying food quality report folder. True to his fatiguing facts, he summarizes: "And last but not least, the samples of celery, scallions, and broccoli-rabe garnished from the garden tested negative, meaning no unnatural toxins."

Striving to elicit a more impassioned proclamation, Grace prods her witness. "So in your estimation, Dr. Diego, there is absolutely nothing to support these hypochondriac imaginings."

Despite Grace's baiting, Dr. Diego does not digress from the inner sanctums of his fraying folders. Monotonically, he summarizes: "As I stated, the air quality tested negative, meaning there were no contaminant particles. The water tested negative, meaning..."

Grace peremptorily waves. "So, in summary, Dr. Diego?" Grace stresses *in summary* as if posing a concocted cue.

13

Abruptly out of character, Dr. Diego simulates a smile to indicate his expert sincerity. "Oh, in summary as in 'in summary'. Well, yes, in summary, I can only say that after careful and repeated testing, repeated and careful, careful testing, we found nothing to substantiate these hippo— hypochondric— driac..." Nervously tripping over the ill-rehearsed word, Dr. Diego takes great pains to ensure his lips and teeth remain in static alignment. The resultant displacement of his facial features makes clear that his sincerity has been pre-recorded.

Reluctantly Grace takes inventory. The jurors' sympathies are with the Wallabys. It stands to reason. The Wallabys, an elderly couple in economic straits, foreshadow the fate of the average citizen and now-judging juror. Unable to keep up with rent increases on their urban apartment, the Wallabys retired to their family estate. Fortuitously, a distant cousin had died and left them a modest country cottage. Unfortunately the gift had a trojan lining: back taxes. Happily the Wallabys negotiated a payment plan. Unhappily, it was designed to work in the best of times, at best. Consequently, when Mr. Wallaby's truck got stolen, when Mrs. Wallaby's hip dislocated, when the quaint but dilapidated septic system began to leach into the county well, the Wallabys found themselves on the verge of foreclosure. Just when it seemed there was no way out, Mr. Wallaby contracted a mysterious disease which has no medical basis — which is the basis of this case. The Wallabys are suing the local textile mill for environmental assault. Coincidentally, they are suing for the amount of their debts. "Environmental assault" is the latest variant on the mental cruelty theme. Grace has defended a number of business concerns against these nebulous allegations leveled by increasing numbers of distressed citizens struggling against a slumping economy, worsened by a series of natural disasters and an epidemic of political misadventures. Though personally sympathetic with the unfortunate Wallabys, Grace cannot condone their desperate con. Initially no reputable attorney would take the case. Luckily for the Wallabys, Iroquois Jefferson is out on bail.

Iroquois Jefferson, the opposing attorney, is an old friend, or rather lover. Known for his outlandish antics, he is as frustrating to befriend as to defend against. Tall, muscular, and tawny, Jefferson approaches the bench like a championing warrior. Swiveling abruptly, his loose jacket and dangling tie whirl rapturously like dancing dervishes.

"Your Honor, I would like to thank the estimable Dr. Diego for his almost human-like rendering of shamefully partisan data. So shameful and partisan, why waste the court's valuable time disputing anything he has said?"

As usual, Judge Corbin has dozed off. This lapse of interest on the Judge's part does not diminish Iroquois's fervor. Like a train without brakes, he careens down his winding oratory tracks. "Instead, I will call my next and only credible witness. In all fairness, we should discount Dr. Diego's paid professional testimony along with my own clients' testimonies. The Wallabys are clearly trying to bilk the textile mill for the balance on their mortgage, so they can retire to raise winnebeagles or something equally senile."

These last comments register in Judge Corbin's subconscious. Immediately, she wakens to her defense. "I am not senile! Who said that?"

Iroquois pounds the Judge's desk emphatically. "These clearly biased witnesses should be struck from the record." The Wallabys fidget uneasily as their attorney seemingly distances himself from their cause.

"They are an affront to the respected judicial process — unlike my next witness who has nothing monetary to gain, no special interests to please, no possible stake in the outcome of this case. On the contrary, my next witness is present solely to bear witness to his own simple truth."

In vain, Grace monitors the back door in anticipation of this highly-touted witness. Instead, Grace overhears the quizzical remarks of the Judge. "Oh, isn't he cute? Does he eat worms? I happen to have some worms."

Iroquois Jefferson has just placed a yellow-bellied bull frog on the stand. Poignantly, he explains. "Your Honor, this is Bill Bialy. He lives in the pond behind the Wallaby cottage.

Until recently, he resided there with his wife Milley along with her twenty-seven tadpoles by another mating."

Grace bolts to her feet. "Your Honor, this is an outrage! I demand you dismiss that witness. I further recommend that Mr. Jefferson be held in contempt of court!"

As her Honor searches her pockets for worms left over from a previous court session, Iroquois feigns indignation. "I'm disappointed at Ms. Ivanosky. Perhaps she hasn't read recent recommendations regarding cultural diversity. I see no reason why Mr. Bialy's testimony should not be considered."

Grace cites an elemental law. "Mr. Bialy is a frog."

"Your point being?"

"That Mr. Bialy is a frog!"

Iroquois amiably counter-cites. "Who, as such, can personally attest to the environmental degradation. Why five years ago, that pond behind the Wallaby cottage was overrun with yellow-bellied bull frogs like himself. But today: not one. Not even Bill Bialy whom I rescued from a cosmetic research lab; there he lay, waiting to be dissected so that women like Grace Ivanosky can immerse themselves in ode-de-pheu, sacrificing scores of virgin males along their maniacal career paths."

"Your Honor, I object to this very personal slander. I realize recent overhauls in the judicial system give due-process greater leeway, introduce an element of informality. However, I doubt our esteemed colleagues meant to include eye-witness frogs. Nevertheless, I shall defer to the moment, concede the frog scenario. Will the court please note." Grace accusingly approaches Bill Bialy. "By the attorney's own admission, his witness has lied. Mr. Jefferson stated that Bill Bialy never resided at the Wallaby pond so no matter how you interpret the current fine print, this case should be thrown out of court!"

It is.

Iroquois has trouble keeping pace with Grace. "Why are you so upset? I'm the one who lost, Again. Don't you care what happens to that poor couple?"

"I'm a lawyer not a social worker and you? You're a —
I don't know. I do know if you tried that stunt on anyone but
the doddering Judge Corbin, you would have been disbarred.
In fact, I thought you were disbarred."

"Suspended temporarily, unfairly, due to my affiliation
with that mild-mannered lobby group, SOIL."

While quickening her steps, Grace incredulously
narrows her eyes. "Mild mannered? Soilists are borderline
terrorists. Still under investigation for kidnapping loggers and
sabotaging tree trunks with exploding pipe bombs. Neither the
logger or tree survive the demonstration. Of course, such
shenanigans suit the warped mindlessness of Iroquois
Jefferson."

"Give them credit for being passionate. These days if
you don't rant and rave on the side of caution, you end up with
ill-designed oil tankers spilling 250 million gallons of toxic..."

Grace instinctively defends. "If you are speaking about
the Olie Oil incident, no one could have anticipated..."

"No, no, no, no, no. When the first oil tanker spilled 50
million gallons, it was: no one could have anticipated; it will
never happen again. It didn't. Next time, it was 100 million.
Now, it is 250 million, half of it in Alyeska, of all places.
Qwaquiwei must be on the war path. How, oh how will Olie
Oil squirm out of this one? If only I could get my hands on their
defense."

"Serve under false pretenses?"

Iroquois skips several steps ahead. "But of course, I will
do my best to defend them, explain to our good citizens how
Olie Oil wanted to apply chemical dispersants but were
prohibited by bureaucratic red tape. So what if dispersants are
poisonous. At least, they make oil sink to where no one can see
it. And, oh yes, I will gladly reveal how Olie Corp. is cleverly
utilizing oil-eating microbes. So what if the microbes have to
be fattened on phosphorus and nitrogen fertilizers. So what if
this artificial injection triggers ill-conceived effects elsewhere
in the ecosystem. So what if the unsuspecting workers handling
the hazardous fertilizer urinate blood."

Grace hastens down the stairs, testily mumbling. This sudden downswing fails to derail the soliloquy. For every three steps Grace takes, Iroquois counters with four, all the while decrying. "I will dutifully explain how Olie Oil cleaned up their last spill, how they hosed down miles of beach with super-heated water, blasting the oil off the surface of the shoreline rocks along with the crabs, barnacles, and any living whatnots. Big deal if these shorelines are now biologically sterile and continue to leach underlying crude. At least, they are 'environmentally stabilized'. That's oil man talk for — take your picture from a distance."

Grace abruptly halts. "Don't you ever stop to breathe?"

Circling Grace like a ferret-hound begging to be petted, Iroquois regales. "Not until I apply my infamous illogic to vindicate their savagery, rationalize that with a spill this size, Olie Oil has effectively killed every life form in the food chain, so we don't need to worry if the death of the phyto-plankton will impact the mating cycles of the sea lion, or if the poisoning of the slitherslanks will cause tumors in swamp otters. Since the entire chain of events has been wiped out, there is no one left to be negatively impacted. It's really quite a blessing."

Grace takes this opportunity to critique. "Always the figments before the facts, eh Iroquois?"

"Since I can't say you've grown old and ugly, I can say you have lost your innocent after-glow. You have certainly lost your mutinous edge. Doesn't it bother you that individual rights are being sacrificed in the name of the collective comfort zone? Ever since you left me..."

Grace agitatedly interjects, "Being a disbarred, suspended, lawless lawyer, you cannot appreciate the fine art of being impartial. And stop with the ever-since-you-left-me routine. Every time I defeat you in court, you dredge up our past — and very brief liaison. What happened between us happened twenty years ago. When does the statute of limitation on that relationship expire?"

"That all depends. How is your third marriage working out? Hear you're going to have another child."

"She was born seven months ago."

"Ah, and to think she could have been ours."

Grace maliciously chuckles. "If I had conformed to your hellish idea of the heavenly life. As I recall, my part of the equation involved the rising at dawn to milk the goat, to churn the butter, to harvest the grain, to grind the grain, to cook the grain, to clean the stove, to thatch the roof, to lug the water, to wash the clothes while you lounged on that river raft waiting for the riverbed to dry up so you could simply pluck the guppies off the muddy bottom. Correct me if I'm wrong: we never did have fish for dinner."

"I object. Would the witness please answer this question. Is her life any different now? It is the way you are, Grace. No one can stop you. I never told you to milk the goat. Until you told me, I thought it was a coyote. And I hated when you harvested the fields of grain. You ruined the porch view. And what's your point? Are you saying that I drove you to marrying this sapless forest ranger? I must know him. He must have attended the Solar Energy rally. Kind of short, right?"

"Tall."

"But pudgy."

"Lean."

"Graying at the temples? Losing his hair?"

"Iroquois, you never met him, and don't expect to be invited for dinner."

Hauling bull frog Bill from his jacket pocket, Iroquois makes a precipitous plea. "Not even if I bring the frog legs?" As Grace exits the building, Bill utters a disquieting croak. Milley had warned him: you can't trust lawyers.

WRONG FUNCTION KEY

Grace crosses the wide street between the courthouse and the corporate suites of her most colorful client. Connery Deloy is a technocrat of some ill-repute. He has the enviable reputation for creating empires in a single day, but the regretful knack for destroying any indigent ant in his path. Grace is certain she can resolve the impasse in his latest real estate coup — if Deloy stays out of the negotiation. Though he legitimately purchased a worthless tract of land from an authorized representative of the Qwaquiwei tribe, a respected elder, Sadu Qwa, is trying to prohibit development. Apparently, beneath the layers of sand, gravel, and parched clay rest the sacred bones of their honored ancients. Grace does not believe in ghosts. Her lawyer instincts reckon the Qwaquiwei simply want a better deal. Perhaps they are hoping to obtain more firma-terra from Deloy's bevy of properties. If so, Grace will higgle-haggle, then induce Deloy into relinquishing one of his farmable parcels. In the end, all parties will be satisfied. Deloy will add the Southwest to his empire, and the Qwaquiwei will grow jojoba for the prospering shampoo conglomerates.

Reluctantly Grace enters Deloy's infamous archway. An unnerving electrostatic buzz raises her skin hairs. Leerily, Grace presses her palm against a computerized palm reader. After it validates her identity, a hidden door cracks open. Initially, Grace was impressed by these trendy gadgets. She now finds them obstructing. The worst component is Deloy's receptionist, Tootsie Rustbottom. Grace dreads confronting the gangly robot with its exposed microchips, dangling wires, and rusting plates of steel. Tootsie was given to Connery Deloy as a joke, a reminder that all that digitizes is not high-tech. For some reason, Connery kept the contraption. Today, the anatomically in-question robot is wearing a neon-orange negligee. Besides appearing anything but provocative, Tootsie is in serious need of an upgrade.

"Good morning, Tootsie. What an atrocious outfit." Grace sees no point being kind.

"Thank you, in·com·ing per·son. I pick·ed it my·self. Are you an out·side dis·rup·tive, or pay·ing cust·o·mer?"

"Mr. Deloy's lawyer. I have an appointment, remember?"

"What is your name key·word?"

"Grace Ivanosky."

"Oh boy. A big one. I·van·o·sky? Are you in the da·ta·base?" Tootsie inflects the next to the last syllable in each sentence: the result of a programmatic bug or perhaps the designer's attempt to impart a characteristic tonality. While Tootsie types Grace's keyword, Grace testily interjects.

"You added me last time, remember?"

"One mo·ment, whi·le I go to." Tootsie presses several buttons on her dented chest. "Yes. Your law·yer func·ti·ons are due at four·teen hun·dred. It is thir·teen fif·ty-se·ven. You are ear·ly. Please must wait." With this, Tootsie powers off. Grace is forced to sit out the next three minutes. At precisely fourteen hundred, Tootsie reactivates and again queries, "Hell·o? You are who?"

"Grace I·van·o·sky." Grace inflects the 'o' exactly as Tootsie had previously. Nevertheless, Tootsie mis-inputs.

"Oops! Wrong func·ti·on key. I hate these e·lec·tron·ic de·vi·ces. Just look at my nails. I will have to re·place them du·ring my lunch ho·ur." Her nails, eraser tips at the ends of pencil fingers, have long worn off. Before Grace is reduced to chitchatting with the digitally impaired, Connery appears from his office sanctum. As usual, his suit is crumpled, his brassy hair static with agitation.

"Stop dawdling, Ivanosky! That crazy tribal woman is due any minute. We've got to discuss our strategy. My God!" Connery is taken aback by Tootsie's neon negligee. "Toots? You look..."

Tootsie creakily cranks. "A·tro·ti·ous. Yes, I have been in·form·ed. Ne·on makes me look fat, but it was: buy one, get free bat·ter·ies. Not to re·fuse such cost ef·fec·tive rea·son·ing."

Connery shrugs despairingly, having repeatedly tried to reprogram the dysfunctional areas of Tootsie's personality. Unfortunately, every time he alters one of its modules, he seems to dislodge neurotic subroutines embedded deep within its micro-code. Consumed by the crisis at hand, he drags Grace into his office by her briefcase. Unfortunately, Sadu Qwa is already sitting at his desk, in his chair.

"What the— How did you get past my security? And my secretary?"

Sadu Qwa scornfully peers into the receptionist alcove where Tootsie cross-checks her accounting subroutines with a pocket calculator. She tactically observes. "I see no secretary. I see no people. How can a man who has no people tell a nation of people how to worship their dead?" Sadu Qwa, master shaman of her tribe, commands Connery's desk like a reigning royal. A legend to devotees of indigenous tribes, she appears remarkably young for one who has weathered generations.

Connery cantankerously defends himself. "I don't need actual people. I have technology, infrastructure — credit." A mosquito mischievously buzzes his ear. Connery petulantly waves it away as he asserts, "Well, you're here, you're here. Makes no difference. I can say anything in front of you that I can say behind your back. Facts are facts. I have the means to take your people out of the dark ages, feed them, house them, qualify them for high-paying factory jobs. You name it; I have the technology." The mosquito isn't biting. He nibbles at Connery's nose while Connery bluntly presents his case.

"I don't understand your objection. I am taking a desert and turning it into condominiums and schools and jojoba processing plants. This land we're arguing over is dust. There aren't even insects to exterminate." As if to dispute this claim, the mosquito comes in for a dive. Peripherally monitoring the nuisance, Connery stealthily snatches a device off his desk. Zap! The mosquito dissolves into a puff of smoke.

Connery stomps in joyous victory. "Isn't this great? Lets off a miniature laser beam just strong enough to sizzle those pesky pests. I'll send you one, as a thank-you for that stunning gift you sent me. Nice token gesture. Now where did I put it? Wait till you see this, Grace. Plush pink petals. Best quality silk. Waxy green leaves with golden edges so skillfully threaded you can't detect the seams. Brilliantly crafted, but where is it? I remember showing it to Tootsie the other day. Hey Toots!"

While Connery searches for his errant secretary, Sadu Qwa locates the misplaced offering. Its succulent petals have shriveled and fallen into a ring around the vase. Its bright waxy leaves, now dried and crinkled, layer the hardened soil. One yellowing leaf still hangs precariously, in silent testimony to Connery's suitability as caretaker. Grace tries to squash the damage. "Mr. Deloy was away on business. Apparently, the maintenance crew neglected to..."

Connery belatedly fathoms, "You mean, the thing was alive? You sent me something biodegradable? Like a child? Well, that was rather negligent."

Grace correctively counters. "What Mr. Deloy means to say..."

Connery flails his arms in genuine astonishment. "I never suspected a thing so flawless could be a living organism. I figured silk, plastic — polyurethane. Well, not to worry. Leafy things are hardy. A little liquid and it will bounce right back." Connery precipitously pours his cold, curdled coffee into the plant. Straight-away, the last leaf separates from its disfigured stalk. Connery becomes momentarily silent before stubbornly alleging. "This proves my point. I'm going to show you something totally unrehearsed. Really, I had no intention of showing you what I'm going to show. I just happened to stop by my research lab this morning. It's top secret but clearly this situation calls for something." Like a trickster uncle plucking a quarter from behind a toddler's ear, Connery yanks a tomato from his right drawer. Or something like a tomato. It is four inches high and five inches wide. It is crimson and lacquery and utterly freakish. Proudly, Connery announces. "The *tomatop*! Much more than a tomato: a genetically re-engineered, partially cloned, negatively ionized, strategic mutation." For comparison, Connery extracts a small, misshapen tomato from a local grocer's bag. Confidently, he places it beside his man-made monstrosity. The tomatop superciliously dwarfs the naturally grown tomato. From one perspective, the naturally grown tomato looks pathetic, as pathetic as the deflowered plant to its right. From another perspective, the diminutive green tomato, with its distinguishing rot spots, has a certain dignity. Despite its cultivated comeliness, the tomatop lacks credibility. However, when Connery slices the two tomatoes, the naturally grown tomato drools into a puddle of over-ripened seeds. In contrast, the tomatop remains lusciously poised.

Connery plucks another naturally grown tomato from the grocer's bag. "You buy a naturally grown tomato: it's too soft, it's too hard, it's too ripe, it's too raw." Connery drops the naturally grown tomato. It spatters upon impact. After dispatching his mutant tomato to the same fate, even minus a slice, like a cat, it lands on its feet. The impact does not dislodge a single seed. As Grace plucks the seeds splattered by the mere mortal tomato from her stockings, Connery brags. "This tomatop is designed to be firm enough on the outside to withstand shipping, yet ripe enough on the inside to ensure a scrumptious fruit. We have deleted the gene which triggers the enzyme responsible for the mush property, thereby eliminating a culinary flaw."

Sadu Qwa rises. Connery and Grace hinge backwards as she dubiously circles the tomatop. Finally, she turns to Connery. "You dare judge God? You say: this is too hard; this is too soft. We cannot create a tomato, yet we declare we can make one better?"

Connery questions God's agrarian intentions. "Hey, if God didn't want us to reinvent the tomato, he wouldn't have invented us because this is what we do. It is our nature to improve upon an idea. The tomato was a good concept; now it's better. It's bigger. It's tastier. Has a longer shelf life."

"It has no vitamin C."

Connery apprehensively twitches. How could she know this? Distractedly tugging his earlobe, Connery confesses.

"Minor trade-off. More than made-up by the fact that we inserted a gene which acts like a chemical insecticide to repel the dotted wiggly worm. As a result, I can grow this tempting delectable in a field infested with ravenous wiggly worms, and not one will bite."

"Proving my point." Sadu Qwa impersonates Connery with uncanny irreverence. "If the dotted wiggly worm with its scanty brain matter refuses to ingest that impostor, what fool am I?"

"To·may·to? To·mah·to? That's not the issue." Grace diligently defends her client. "Mr. Deloy is not trying to challenge your shaman authority, however, with respect to this land deal, there was no subterfuge. Agents for Mr. Deloy purchased the property in question from a lawful representative of the Qwaquiwei tribe. Since then, Mr. Deloy has invested in blueprints, paid subcontractors, hired staff, committed sub-plots. Preventing him from moving forward will cause him financial distress, cost jobs, impact..."

Sadu Qwa interrupts Grace. "I am surprised how you speak. I was with your husband last evening. He is of a different nature."

"Aaron? You must mean someone else. He was..."

Sadu Qwa explains. "He travels the underworld. He is much honored by the spiders. They are weaving him a shield. You have a daughter."

"Yes, I..."

"Also a son."

Politely, Grace enumerates, "Two. Twins. Identical."

"A son can have many names, many faces. I have three syllables, one body. Everything is evident but nothing revealed." Seeing Grace and Connery's confusion, Sadu Qwa explains. "I have not come to stop you. That is not our way. I have come to warn you. I have been to Alyeska."

Grace suspects that Sadu Qwa has not actually been to Alyeska, only traveled there via the underworld. It is how she knows what she knows. No one outside the Qwa way gives credence to this purported plane of consciousness in which telepathic powers emerge, subtle energies manifest, mystic wisdom reveals. Nevertheless, many revere the words of Sadu Qwa. She is too often right, whatever her purported sources.

"Many brothers and sisters have died. Many more are dying. I have seen their oil-soaked bodies packed in drums like sardines for export. The raging barn fires cannot burn bright enough to release their tormented qwa. It is not the thickness of petroleum ooze, but the walls of hardened hearts which damn their spirits."

Straining to understand her drift, Connery gestures time-out. "Not quite following you. I don't trade sardines. Ivanosky, please explain to Madam Shaman here that I don't export perishable commodities or deal in petroleum or..."

Sadu Qwa attempts to clarify. "Qwaquiwei must name their dead. How else can the great Lord Mother receive us into her womb. A cat does not suckle a rat; a swan does not cradle an asp. A mother must know her child. But these dead are unrecognizable."

Before Grace can explain as directed, Connery clamors. "Oh, oh, the Tim Tinkerton version of the Alyeska fiasco. You're concerned about industry directions, ethics. Now I get it. Lady, don't believe what you hear. The man is stuck in overdrive. These days, reporters refuse to confine themselves to facts. Instead, they've taken vows of prophesy, replaced their degrees in journalism with poetic licenses. Not that any of them can rhyme or reason. So Olie Oil made a mistake. Sue them. Take your cut and get over it. Hey, if I stopped ticking every time someone put in their thumb, pulled out a plum and said what a bad boy am I, well, I wouldn't be here and you'd be arguing with the wall."

Sadu Qwa calmly persists. "Again, you do not follow. I am giving you to see what I saw. Such horrors. Otters blinded, listlessly moored to the waves. Their oil-matted fur had lost its buoyancy, any ability to retain body heat. Many froze before they starved to death. Alyeska has been touched, has been tainted."

Connery scornfully scoffs, "Does it matter? No one is allowed there, not even you, by Qwaquiwei decree. Perfectly good land no one can develop. You can't be doing well on that arid reservation. In Alyeska, your people could be harvesting manna from the heavens. You refuse to inhabit it because of some preposterous yarn your forefathers spun about a lost paradise. One can't even hike there. What a waste. What a pointless, pointless taboo."

"Where is your heart?"

"It has nothing to do with my heart. I'm just saying, 'How stupid'. I mean, not even the Nature Channel is allowed to encroach on their tippy toes to document for posterity. What's the harm in looking? You tribal people are too..."

"No. Listen to what I am saying: where is your heart? Mine beats inside my chest. I feel no need to cut it out, to examine it. Some mysteries must remain."

"Not if you intend to sue. In order to estimate the damages, surveyors will need to..."

"You are seeing ghosts. I have only said what I have only said. I am trying to tell you, to warn you: when the heart is damaged, the tributary breaths, the ebbing exhale, the flowing inhale no longer course their tranquil depths. And so I know what I know: eagles feeding on tainted fish, becoming, as you say, 'neurologically' impaired. Instead of scaling their sheltering cliff faces, they smash..." Sadu Qwa abruptly turns to Grace. "Didn't you see their twisted wreckage?"

Misinterpreting the meaning of the message, Grace dutifully maintains. "But Mr. Deloy had nothing to do with the Olie Oil spill. He has no stock in the company, no ties to the implicated executives. He has not purchased any Alyeska land. The Cliff of Ancients is in your southern territory. I fail to understand how Alyeska relates to..."

Sadu Qwa's tone becomes suddenly harsh. "I thought you were here to hear. Forgive me. I have paths to go before I join my son on the Cliff of Ancients."

Presuming she understands at last, Grace nods. "But of course, you have a son buried on this disputed cliff."

Connery hikes a dissenting eyebrow. "Well, bury is not the word. Let's not mince cultural differences: Qwaquiwei feed their dead to the vultures, hack them into bite-size pieces so each scavenger gets his fair share. Kind of barbaric but hey, do what you do. But don't whine about burial ground. What's left to bury?"

Sadu Qwa gently strokes her misplaced offering. "Yes, we give back the husk, return what remains to the soil. The body, without its motivating qwa, can bear no seeds. What use is it? From bird, we have taken eggs and feathers; from coyote, we have taken flesh and fur. When the time comes to take down our tent, we make peace with those who have fed us in our time. We absorbed their spirit. They should absorb ours. It binds us ever closer to our common mother."

Grace supposes. "So your burial ground is symbolic. No one is actually..."

Sadu Qwa lowers her eyes in deference to the dead. "We send watchers to guard the qwa as it emerges into the spirit world. Patiently we wait while our fellow creatures take what they need. Before all trace of our beloved are gone, we beg for one vestige, a bone fragment, a tooth, a lock of hair. In this way, we remain connected. Some relics are placed in the ground; others are kept for ceremonies. This is our way."

Grace eagerly conciliates. "Then of course, of course, we will relocate your ancients, or perhaps erect a park in commemoration. We are not without feelings, or sympathy."

Grace's mistaken notions confound Sadu Qwa. "I do not mourn my son dead. I celebrate his ascension. He was called by the Lord Mother to do the work of the Ancients. He exists as I exist, merely elsewhere. Our seeming dead await us on the other side. But only after we have finished our allotted chores. Often, they speak to us, guide us. That is why Qwaquiwei sleep facing forward, do not prop pillows against our ears, always alert to the whispers of our Ancients."

Connery rails, "Exactly what I'm talking about. We're on the same wave length. You're just coming at it from the wrong end of the spectrum. Look, if you just leave me to my devices, your people can avoid all this mythic hokum. Let me build schools where your children can grow wise in comfort, with heaters and air conditioners and high-tech gymnasiums to monitor their cholesterol counts. They'll learn science, math, object-oriented programming, and jojoba extraction."

Sadu Qwa says nothing, neither offended by what he has said, nor the least surprised. "You do as you do. I have come not to stop you. That is not my place. I only make one request. On behalf of the prophesy. Perhaps you know: Qwaquiwei worship an untroubled God. Unlike your vengeful Father, our Lord Mother does not try to trick us into hell. Rather, she leads us towards the light. You catch more flies with honey.

"Every 22 years, Qwaquiwei celebrate the Inner Lightning. The only year we may trouble our God for her grace, the only time we pray the way you pray. What you call prayer, we call beseechment. You pride yourselves on prayer, but there is no pride for beggars. Qwaquiwei must earn the right to implore the Lord. Only after years of paying homage, performing sacrifices, adhering to the Qwa way, may we kneel in supplication.

"We honor Lord Mother's forests, plains and rivers. We respect Lord Mother's children, whether human or wolf. While we are on this planet, we are Lord Mother's guests and must behave as such. We are transients, like the element fire. It can shine so brightly, so warmly, yet so quickly it can go out. For this reason, we maintain the fire of Qwa until the morning of the Eve of Inner Lightning. Only then is it extinguished, to allow the pause between breaths. Within this pause, we may die, or be reborn. Qwaquiwei will either continue here, or we will face extinguishment. Only if lightning flashes, do we prepare another fire to..."

Connery patronizes. "To symbolize your resurrection. Yes, we all fear death, concoct comforting rituals to assure our children of the continuing good life. You see how you and we..."

"How you misunderstand. Qwaquiwei do not light the fire for joy; we re-light the fire in obedience. It is not our wish to continue here. According to the Ancients, if we have pleased Lord Mother Earth during our years of effort, she will breathe her being into us, make us one with Herself. There will be no need to rekindle the Qwa flame. Our days of embodiment will be over. This is what we pray for 22 days and 22 nights. We drum, we dance, we sing *qwaquiwei, qwaquiwei, qwaquiwei.*"

As Sadu Qwa slips into trance, Grace leans towards Connery. "According to weather records, it thunderstorms, thunderstorms ferociously every Eve of Inner Lightning. According to eye-witnesses, the lightning never starts until after the propitiatory chant. Even on a cloudless day, as dry as bone, thunder clouds will suddenly encircle the Qwaquiwei reservation. Always thunder and lightning, but thus far, no aliens from outer space and no sign of their Lord Mother Earth."

Sadu Qwa abruptly opens her eyes. "As we chant, we listen. We are listening for the breath of Lord Mother. Upon hearing that divine breath, we become transported. To hear the breath is to become the breath."

Connery slams down his hand. "Exactly what I'm talking about. You have turned planet physiology into spiritual myth. You are trying to explain in supernatural terms a very natural phenomenon. During this planet's formation, it was dense with clouds. The surface was so hot, rain would sizzle into steam. In turn, the steam would rise then condense into rain; then the rain would fall and vaporize. Meanwhile, inside this test-tube of tumultuous clouds, thunder would follow lightning crash, bam, boom. This went on for millions and millions of years. When the ocean was forming, the atmosphere was predominantly hydrogen, water vapor, methane, ammonia. Lightning helped transform ammonia and methane into molecules that recombined to form proteins which eventually erupted into living substance. It's all a matter of record, of scientific data. Data, data, data."

Sadu Qwa grins lovingly, as a mother for a child who has taken a first step. "Exactly what I am saying. You have corrupted divine physiology into scientific myth. You are trying to explain in natural terms, a clearly supernatural phenomenon." With this, Sadu Qwa rises without having obtained Connery's blessings or haggled for compensatory acreage.

As she slowly paces towards the door, Connery offers. "I get it. You want to play out this Lightning thing one last time. Well, I'm no rock in a hard place. I can make adjustments.

31

Seems a reasonable request. Why risk potential protests? I can hold off development, accommodate this day of reckoning, so yes, tell your..."

Sadu Qwa does not turn as she, in turn, answers. "I have already told my people. I only came to tell you."

THE AMBASSADOR IS DEAD

Grace arrives home earlier than usual. When she parks her car in its designated location, her front wheels end up squarely in the cabbage patch. Grace surmises Aaron has once again extended the range of his vegetable garden, in keeping with their conjugal agreement. After committing to cohabit, the deal was: Grace would make the interior house decisions. Aaron would make the exterior house decisions. Grace would be the final authority for all matters relating to the twins. Aaron would have dominion over the ants and spiders. They would mutually govern Webster.

Grace enters via the kitchen where Aaron is meticulously chopping his vegetables. After kicking off her pumps, Grace offers Aaron an expeditious kiss. Without removing her blouse, she wriggles out of her bra then tosses it over the banister as she ascends the stairs. Once inside the bedroom, she removes the remaining irritants, yanking off her stockings before snuggling into a pair of stretch pants.

Grace re-enters the kitchen in her bare feet. After repositioning jars in the refrigerator, she retrieves an open bottle of wine from the rear. Grace pours a glass, takes several sips, then sets the glossy tumbler next to Aaron's juicer, fresh with carrot drippings. While Aaron chops and slices, carefully measuring teaspoons of ginger and chili into his vegetable mosaic, Grace throws together her standby meat and potatoes. Brutishly, she pounds her filet with a bulky meat mallet, dousing the marinating flesh with daring dashes of salt and pepper. While Aaron gently sautés his vegetables on the right range, Grace sears and sizzles on the left range. Bits of sputtering meat fat drizzle onto Aaron's meekly simmering vegetables. Grace apologizes. Aaron smiles, "never mind".

The twins prepare their own Burrito-Bangles. Rom removes the frozen entrees from the freezer. Reem plunks them into the microwave. Rom sets the power to two minutes, eleven seconds. Reem pours milk into their respective mugs. Rom checks the batteries in their hand-held Wizard game. Reem sets their single, shared plate.

As Grace and Aaron discuss the events of the day, Rom munches his Burrito-Bangle with his left hand while Reem munches his Burrito-Bangle with his right hand. In between bites, they alternately type secret algorithms into their electronic dinner companion. When they instigate an erroneous move, the Wizard objectionably sirens. Being the final authority for all matters relating to the twins, Grace commands Rom and Reem to deactivate the rankling sound until dessert is served.

The telephone rings. Grace leans back in her chair to pluck the receiver from the wall. "Hello— Yes, he's right here— Okay, but he's right— Well, of course I can, but he is sitting— Yes, I have it. Thank you." Grace hangs up the phone. "I guess time is money. That was for you. Something to the effect of: your crustacean pipes are ready."

Aaron's eyes excitedly widen. "So soon? Well this is great. My crustacean pipes! You remember." Grace shrugs "of course not", leading Aaron to patiently explain. "That drainage project I couldn't get funding for. Metal piping has become so expensive, I asked a friend to..."

Grace prepares for something complicated and clever. Part of Aaron's appeal is his uncanny ability to create silk out of seeming sand. Grace's ample salary allows them to contract any expert for any task. Nevertheless, Grace finds comfort in the fact that Aaron can simulate modern conveniences should civilization fail. Perhaps it has to do with her recurring nightmare. The scenario is always the same. While vacationing on a desert island, the local volcano erupts. Hot lava careens towards her sleeping condo, sizzling everything in its path. In one version, she calls to her first husband, the alcoholic, for help. He waves, pulls a cork from a bottle, then begins to drink. Grace is left to watch Reem and Rom expire in searing pain. In another version, she calls to her second husband, the ponderous thinker. He waves, then debates at length the pros and cons of each solution. While he deliberates, Grace watches

Rom and Reem suffer horrible deaths. Shortly after Webster was born, Grace agreed to move in with Aaron to await the final cut. Is he or isn't he the one? So far, Aaron has not turned up in her dreams smiling and waving while her children bake to a crisp. For this reason, Grace is reluctant to marry. She needs to know what Aaron will do when the prophetic volcano explodes. As if reading her subconscious concerns, Aaron pulls out a sample piece of crustacean pipe.

"So, in actuality, this pipe is composed of shells: not metal, shells. Anyone can do it. Just take wire mesh, drop it into the sea, run electricity through it, attracting calcium ions from the sea water which combine with carbon dioxide to form calcium carbonate which attracts shell-bearing invertebrates. They're the target market. Since shell-bound invertebrates need calcium, they hang out on these mesh cylinders generation after generation. They are born then die, born then die, over and over, layer upon layer, until that skeletal mesh becomes a solid working pipe."

Grace raises an eyebrow. "Sounds ingenious, but won't those cold-blooded invertebrates put a lot of warm-blooded metal workers out of business?"

"Initially, but eventually those industrious invertebrates will evolve, unionize, then refuse to shell-out."

Grace peers at Aaron warily. "Sarcasm from the mild-mannered forest ranger? Sounds like you've been spending too much time in the underworld with that medicine woman, Sadu Qwa."

Aaron hangs his head in self-reproach. "But of course! Today was the eventful day. And here I am going on and on about my crustacean pipe dreams. How did it go? What is she like? My grandfather met her before she was Sadu, before she was shaman. She was only a child, but he was much impressed. What did you think?"

Grace chews reflectively before remarking. "Your typical shaman, adorned in prayer beads and magic potions, spouting apocalyptic claptrap, though I couldn't help feeling for her. Her son is dead and unfortunately buried on that disputed cliff. I don't think she relishes the idea of his 'qwa' decomposing beneath a Burger Blaster concession."

Rom looks up from his game. "A quark? That's a type of subatomic particle, isn't it? Did you bring one home? Can I see it?"

"No, darling, I said 'qwa'. Qwaquiwei believe the essence of a person resides not in their physical bodies but in their 'qwa', a kind of—" Grace defers to Aaron.

"What we call our soul, Qwaquiwei call qwa, though they're not quite the same. The qwa, as I remember, is the leftover essence of angels. Qwaquiwei believe they descended from angels — indeed were once themselves angels until they committed some kind of misdeed. As punishment, they are no longer born of angels but of Lord Mother Earth. They therefore owe their allegiance to this planet. So long as they are here, they are no better than any other creature. For this reason, Qwaquiwei believe all life forms have a qwa. Humans, foxes, slitherslanks."

Reem speculates. "Is that why you won't eat meat or fish, Mr. Mushkin? Because if you eat the flesh of an animal, you will incarnate its sins?"

Rom further elucidates. "Because you used to be Qwaquiwei, until you defected, or got expelled or something."

"No, no, no. My great-great-grandmother was Qwaquiwei. They do eat meat but only small, necessary amounts. Certainly, they are less wanton in their consumption. I don't eat animal flesh because of the way I was brought up. I'm a vegetarian. I'm not afraid of ingesting anyone's qwa. In fact, according to Qwaquiwei, even rocks are imbued with qwa. I don't eat meat because, well, I don't like the idea of slaughtering helpless animals."

Aaron makes this rather forceful statement just as Grace thrusts an unwieldy slice of steak into her mouth. After swallowing with decided effort, Grace notes to Rom and Reem. "Vegetarians don't slaughter helpless animals when they can so easily hack to death legless, leafy things."

As Grace mischievously smiles, Aaron nervously chuckles. He cannot help himself. He grew up on his grandparents devotedly organic farm after his parents died young, of atypical cancers. He was reared on Mother Earth stories passed down from great-great-grandmother, to great-grandmother, to grandfather. A wonder Grace took such hold of his heart. She eats meat. She supports a political ideology biased towards humankind's vices and devices. She fails to recycle. She purchases on whimsy and discards the same way. According to all calculations, he and she should not be sharing the same table. But nature often draws opposites to the bed in order to spike the gene pool. So, if nature has brought them together for higher purposes, the union is not to be questioned. As Aaron and Grace lean over their opposing food stuffs for a conciliatory kiss, the twins retreat in disgust. Uncertain if they are out of range, Grace whispers to Aaron. "Ready for the weekend? Two whole days of trial-father and sons."

Aaron chooses his words carefully. "Well, their bags are packed." Grace construes this to mean one pair of underwear between the two of them and as many boxes of Captain Munchies as will fit into their knapsacks. Aaron gently interrogates Grace. "They said you told them they had to go." True. Grace felt this was the least she could do for Aaron, and certainly the twins will be none the worse for wear. However, she wishes Aaron had chosen a more appropriate setting. A field trip to an organic farm seems ill-considered, considering the electronic age from which her sons derive.

Aaron assures. "I think they've warmed to the idea. When I showed them where the farm was located, they requested a side-trip to the Animal Research Center. Since Rom is so interested in mammal psychology and Reem so taken with anatomical similitude..."

Grace shakes her head despairingly. "No, Rom is interested in aberrant psychology and Reem likes to break things apart in search of raw materials for his electronic game empire. They have been hounding me to take them to the Animal Research Center ever since Cindy Jacobs did a report on the psychotic animals unit. Rom and Reem just want to heckle the schizophrenic gerbils."

Disheartened by this revelation, Aaron clears the table on a down-note.

Preparing to tuck in for the night, Aaron asks Grace once again. "So, you think it's a bad idea?"

Grace agitatedly adjusts the bed sheets. "For the last time, darling, whatever it takes to bond with them. Just don't get your hopes up. Rom and Reem are a pair of cactuses. They don't need anything, anyone. Don't take it personally." Grace administers another assuring kiss before locking herself in the bathroom.

Aaron retreats to the edge of their bed to contemplate his onerous undertaking. Not long into his contemplation, he encounters a fellow life traveler, of the genus formica, of the order hymenoptera, more commonly called an ant.

Aaron peers between his toes. "Hey, I thought we had an agreement. Remember the agreement? You can graze all you want around the perimeter of the refrigerator, though not inside the refrigerator. You have exclusive rights on all the crumbs under the stove, but not inside the stove, or on the counter tops." Aaron whispers conspiratorially. "And never, never, never in the bedroom. You know what Grace will do if she..."

Grace exits the bathroom. "Were you talking to me?" Aaron feigns puzzlement then implicates Webster. As Grace investigates, Aaron darts into the bathroom. Webster gleefully gurgles. Grace crinkles her nose critically. "Not another poop! Are you trying for a record, Webby?"

The telephone rings just as Aaron exits the bathroom. Grace cedes Webster then hastens into the hall. Aaron suspiciously sniffs. When Grace returns, Aaron re-deposits Webster into Grace's arms, then hastens into the bathroom. Grace places Webster on the changing table. After removing the dirty diaper, she struggles to locate a fresh one at the bottom of an empty box. "Drat! Webby, you go through disposable diapers faster than your brothers go through batteries."

Grace re-enters the hall. A moment later, Aaron re-enters the bedroom, waving a cloth diaper like a triumphant flag. A tuck here, a pin there, and Webster is dry and ready for bed. Grace re-enters the bedroom, lugging a new box of disposable diapers to the now empty changing table. Before she can protest, Aaron pledges, "Not to worry. I'll do the laundering. Who was on the phone?"

"Cindy Jacobs, returning Rom's call. He wanted to confirm the trigger word for sending the lobotomized lemurs into a frenzy. As for you? You are perfectly free to do what you like with your half of the baby." Grace knows Aaron will launder as promised.

Again Grace enters the bathroom. Again, Aaron encounters his trespassing traveler. "Hey, weren't you listening? You realize what Grace will do if she—" Aaron crouches more closely. "Oh, oh, I see. You're a brown agriculus from the local bog, unfamiliar with house rules. Well, you can't come in here, and I doubt the backyard ants will cede any of their prime crumb tracks. The best I can do is offer the front porch or the bottom shelf of the pantry. I suggest you act as ambassador, return to your ant hill to offer your family one of those designated areas. You see, we believe in peaceful coexistence here. We..."

Grace exits the bathroom, unexpectedly entering — then ending the negotiations. Examining the ambassador's remains on the bottom of her slipper, Grace scolds, "Not another ant, Aaron? What's going on? I had to swat bunches last night, not counting the ones that escaped."

"That's the idea. Some have to escape in order to deliver the message to the others. Otherwise, they will continue to traipse through, unaware of house rules. It's worked for the spiders. The one in the hall has stayed inside the closet. The pair on the ceiling never move from their corner. That group in the living room never stray from their crevice, except to collect the dead flies. That's because we have an arrangement."

Twirling her hair over her head, Grace acknowledges. "Perhaps spiders can keep an agreement. I can't say the same for ants. I don't trust ants. To be perfectly honest, I don't like spiders. Why do they have to be here?" Grace tries to knot her twisted lock into a bun. As it unravels, she snaps, "You don't find me napping in the petunias. I can't sleep some nights knowing one is dangling over my head. What if a sudden breeze rips apart his web. He could end up on my pillow. He'll hatch babies in my hair. It's a terrible thought." Remembering Sadu Qwa's allegations, Grace admonishes. "Of course, I don't expect you to take my side. The spider lobby has you wrapped inside their webs. I heard about that shield they've been knitting for you. Well, I have my own connections to the underworld." Grace hauls her briefcase onto the bed to extract the plant discarded by Connery Deloy. "A gift from Sadu Qwa. It has dark green leaves with golden edges, and luminescent petals. Smells just like lilac."

Aaron skeptically, but dutifully, sniffs the dry brown stalk. Grace inescapably grants. "Well, I realize it needs tending."

Aaron delicately observes. "It's dead."

"It is not dead. It's hibernating. Plants do that."

"No, they don't. Bears hibernate. Plants die. This plant is dead."

"It is not dead. It just needs a little water, a little..."

Touched by Grace's combative will to nurture, Aaron offers to assist. "Okay, I'll see what I can..."

Grace refuses to release her laurel. Aaron has diapered her daughter in soft cotton, and no doubt, will launder the cloth in rain water with his bare hands. Tomorrow, he intends to lead her twin cactuses into the desert, inspire them to forsake their electronic ways. Rom and Reem will return home flowering in Aaron's organic image. Where will that leave Grace? Alone on her desert island with the forever erupting volcano? And then what? Grace watches her fate unfold: a clam washes ashore. Hoping to find a morsel for sustenance, she pries it open. Aaron has returned, decked in pearls. Alongside him, Rom smiles, Reem waves, Webster gurgles "Daddy". As she climbs inside, to take her rightful place, the cultured foursome merrily fly away on a magic diaper, leaving her to her predestined place in the Animal Research Center, alongside the schizophrenic gerbils.

Hoping to forfend the inevitable, Grace resolutely clutches the disputed stalk. "I can handle this. I'm a mother, you know. Just like you."

The doubt in Aaron's eyes reflects the doubt in Grace's heart. Not wishing to concede, Grace retreats to the bathroom cradling the leafless plant in her arms. As Aaron secures an extra blanket around Webster, he hears Grace obdurately running water over the conspicuously unresurrectable blooms.

IN DAYS OF OLD

First stop on the weekend tour is the Animal Research Center, a non-profit animal rights foundation. Aaron and the twins arrive at 8:56 a.m., just as a busload of senior citizens disembark. When the gates open a few minutes later, the seniors jubilantly pass through the turn-stile. Entry is free. Consequently, the seniors tour exhibit to exhibit, meticulously reading all the signposts and taking one of every brochure. At lunch time, they unfold their handkerchiefs to remove parsimonious halves of cheese sandwiches. They depart, certain they have secured their money's worth. They have seen everything twice, except for the psychotic animals unit which houses the psychological remains of animals used, or rather misused in the names of science, progress, and doctorate degrees.

For the majority of tourists cajoled to the center by pre-teens in search of their hormonal roots, the free admission proves expensive. The pass to see psychotic animals costs twenty-seven dollars. Schizophrenic gerbils do not come cheap nor do pre-teens forethinkingly pack cheese sandwiches into their knapsacks. Worse, they run out of Munchies. The food concession charges four dollars for a hot dog, two dollars for a six ounce bag of Munchies, and three-fifty for a super-slush. Aaron reasons the Center needs to support its worthy endeavors. As importantly, Rom and Reem seem to be enjoying themselves.

Attempting to transform the lurid curiosity of the psychotic unit into an educational experience, Aaron dutifully decries the cruel experiments that drove the convalescing boarders to their current states. In one cage, a hyena poises on a ledge with his back to the visiting humans. He cackles as he sways back and forth, back and forth. Occasionally, he falls off his asylum ledge. After hauling himself back up, he paranoiacally peeks over his shoulder to assess the incrementing pairs of peering eyes. The twins whistle their approval each time the hyena takes a spill.

In another cage, a parrot stands at attention, intrepidly facing his audience. Over and over, he repeats, "A is for apple, B is for baby, C is for catfish, D is for— A is for apple, B is for baby, C is for— A is for apple, B is for baby, C is for catfish, D is— Damn it!" Unable to remember the sequence, the bird tips over to a book and mechanically turns its shredding pages. Needless to say, the parrot cannot read. He has, however, been drilled to perform the meaningless task by some postgraduate in search of a thesis theme. Each time the parrot returns to his perch to begin at the beginning in an effort to fulfill his prime imperative. Unfortunately, he never reaches Z so he never gets to end.

The monkey marked "Fred" refuses to perform his routine. Steadfastly, he maintains his dignity as he squats on a tree trunk casually peeling a papaya. Aaron attempts to dissuade the twins from teasing the recovering primate. Rom and Reem allege they are conducting research. To demonstrate their scientific sincerity, they proceed to emit bizarre noises as they strike comical flamingo poses. Rom totters on his left leg while Reem quivers on his right. Or does Reem totter on his left while Rom quivers on his right? Aaron cannot tell them apart or get them under control. Fortunately for Aaron, Fred tires of the adolescent antics. Presenting his derriere to the boys, the monkey provocatively smacks his fanny and shrieks a shriek that needs no translation.

Just in time for lunch. Aaron stakes out a picnic table adjacent to a beaver cage. Aaron chomps through his tofu omelet with as much relish as the beaver chomps through his logs of wood. In contrast, the twins covet their bags of Munchies from a gang of wild birds soliciting crumbs. Against his better judgment, Aaron pinches a bit of tofu, then tosses it to the avian beggars. Eagerly the birds sample the offering — then forthwith spit it out. After sniff testing his day-old tofu, Aaron instructs the twins that human food is too refined, too over-processed to be of nutritional value to creatures of the wild. Compelled to confirm this theory, Rom parts with a handful of Munchies. Black birds descend from trees; sparrows dart from bushes; glade-gliders desert their nests to inspect the tendered treat. Within seconds, not a single saccharin-coated flake is left. This time, Aaron's explanatory comment is the lateness of the hour, and their need to leave as soon as possible.

As Rom deposits their empty bags into the receptacle by the beaver cage, Reem curiously queries. "What's his problem? We don't get it."

Rom reiterates. "No, we don't. Looks like a beaver building a dam. Not so peculiar." Aaron dutifully reads the inscription while Reem speculates.

"Unless he intends to blow it up."

Rom further enflames. "That must be it. He is just waiting for some unsuspecting fisherman to sink his line. Like those killer porpoises. They say the government has trained porpoises to drop torpedoes onto enemy submarines."

Reem nods knowingly. "Yes, yes. That's what I heard. In fact, some porpoises defected to the enemy and are laying mines inside our harbors at this very moment."

Aaron waves his hand assuringly. "No, no; this is Harold from the Ecology Exhibit." Aaron strains to read the rain-washed words on the sun-baked plaque. "According to this narrative, *Harold hails from Grover Ridge where over-logging whittled away the indigenous trees so severely the seasonal buildup of twigs in the nearby streams failed to create natural dams to hinder the flow of water after the winter snow melt. Consequently, the streams ran rampant, carved deep gorges that eroded the surrounding habitat. Local beavers tried in vain to correct the problem. Valiantly, they built dams along the raging streams. Unfortunately, without appropriate materials, they could only manage flimsy replicas out of brush which washed away in a matter of days. Noting the beavers' endeavors, the human community decided to subcontract the beavers by providing them with enough decent wood. The beavers dutifully cut, cleaned, built, and maintained the dams* — as I take it, Harold is demonstrating here."

Not exactly. After swimming to the dam, Harold drops the twigs into the water, almost despairingly. He then dives to the bottom of the muddy pond, then proceeds to blow bubbles to the surface in erratic sequences like some classified code. While Aaron re-reads the caption for clues, Rom cynically notes. "Maybe he's not really a beaver. Maybe he's a porpoise disguised as a beaver."

Reem suspects a bleaker purpose. "Unless he's a psychotic beaver preparing to blow up his own dam to protest lack of payment for his services."

Rom yawns. "Well, he better do something because this is getting boring. Maybe we should go home. Can I drive?"

Aaron balks at the proposition. "Of course not!" Sensing Rom's disappointment, Aaron consoles. "Perhaps, when we get to the farm, Old Man Jones will let you steer his tractor."

Rom gasps, "The farm? We're not actually going to go there, Mr. Aaron?"

Reem blurts indignantly, "No, we didn't think you were really serious, Mr. Aaron."

"Mr. Aaron" is their way of saying: you are not our father; you are not our mother; you are not even our guidance counselor: therefore you have no right to exert any undue influence. Despite these taunts and threats, Aaron persists, though somewhat testily.

"Yes, because the purpose of this outing is to visit the organic farm where I was raised so I can share my life experiences, impart the wisdom of the ages. It is important for each generation to witness how the food chain progresses from grass to grasshopper to Burger Blasters smothered in onions and peanut brittle. If you don't understand how we got from the grass to the peanut brittle, you may become like that bird in the psychotic ward trying to get to Z by mechanically leafing through a book of blank pages. Calculus and astrophysics aren't going to bake your bread. You've got to get in touch with gravity, grasp the critical environmental issues plaguing our day." Aaron hasn't the slightest idea what he is talking about. He just wants to bond. Why won't they cooperate?

Reem politely grants. "Sounds very educational, Mr. Aaron, but couldn't you just show pictures from your yellowing scrapbook at some later date?"

Rom politely concurs. "Yes, because we didn't bring enough underwear."

Reem adjusts his wire-rimmed glasses then confidentially confirms. "No, we didn't."

Fortunately, civilization, like an obstinate weed, has seeded itself everywhere. A jaunt to the Hasty Mart for refueling, another case of Munchies, and extra underwear, puts the threesome back on track, unswervingly heading towards Mercery Farms. The twins remain grumpily quiet as Aaron regales them with childhood remembrances: crimson poppies in scrub-grass meadows, wheat stalks glimmering in afternoon sunsets, wild game scampering about the unfenced yard. Aaron paints a pastoral collage of muffins baking in the oven and herbs drying on the clothes line. Scrupulously, he describes the buttery smoothness of unpasteurized cream, the juicy outburst of vine-ripened tomatoes, and the confectionery redolence of wild strawberries.

Unfortunately, these poetic words don't fit the visuals. Aaron checks his map. He must have taken a wrong turn. The cross streets match but not the memories. In place of a white-washed barn and ponds thick with cattails, stands a windowless aluminum monstrosity amid a matrix of electric lines. The sounds of coyotes and crickets is drowned by buzzing transport vehicles, grinding machines, and static electrons coursing through the ungainly wires.

Aaron locates the nearest refuel station to confirm his coordinates. He is informed that Mercery Farm has gone virtual. Aaron's grandparents, now deceased, had sold Mercery Farm to long-time friend, Old Man Jones. Last he heard, Old Jones was having a good season. According to the station attendant, that good season was followed by years of drought. After defaulting on a loan, Jones sold Mercery to a conglomerate specializing in high-tech solutions. Aaron never thought to call, favoring the delight of surprise. A surprise indeed: the organic homestead is now a farm factory. Aaron is devastated.

The twins are ecstatic. The farm factory is a mechanistic masterpiece. At Hydroponics Incorporated, plants are grown from seed to harvest product, untouched by man, sun or soil. Seeds are robotically inserted into test tubes, kept at constant temperature and humidity while lamps suspended overhead douse the germinating seedlings with thousands of watts of simulated sunshine for unvarying hours each day. A precise blend of nutrients and trace elements are administered intravenously, forcing the plants to maturate just in time for market. Farmer Jacques, the current CEO, smugly proclaims, "So, we never worry about droughts or tornadoes or cloudy days. Had one blackout in '94 but our back-up generators kicked in within the hour. We didn't lose a single vegetable. I can't say the same for the local hospital."

Aaron gives credit where credit is due. "You seem to make efficient use of water."

"Efficient!" Farmer Jacques bristles at the inadequacy of the word. "It takes only six pounds of water to grow one pound of border-lettuce. Compare that with the forty-eight pounds you need in an open field. Look at this place: a mere hundred square feet. It nevertheless produces as much as ten acres of land. As population increases, land decreases, the demand for factory farms will rise. I'm telling you guys, this is a great investment. Get in on it while you can."

"And no bugs." Reem cautiously sifts through the lettuce heads as soothing harmonics serenade the coddled veggies.

Farmer Jacques nods. "Since the farm is enclosed, insects are excluded from the process. Foodstuff is gathered in mint condition. There are no soils to rinse off, no pesticides to wash away, no bruises from intrusive farm machinery, injurious pests, pelting winds, drying sun."

Reluctantly, Aaron samples an ear of corn. "Admittedly, this is delicious. Mind if I purchase a bushel or two?"

"Oh, you don't want this crap. This is filler ingredient." Farmer Jacques hustles the threesome into the next room where the noise, in contrast, is deafening. Straining his vocal chords, Farmer Jacques trumpets how the corn is husked, desiccated, powdered, dyed, then reconstituted into reams of multi-colored strings. Enthusiastically jiggling the garish strands, Farmer Jacques screechingly instructs. "Just drop these strings into boiling water and they're done. That's all it takes. The same filler that makes the strings, makes the sauce. We just put the filler through a different set of grinders and flavorings. And these strings are handy. Just tie them around your kids." Farmer Jacques drapes several strands around each of the boys. "When they get hungry, they just have to unknot and nibble. You never have to pull off the road or wash a pot. The red ones are cherry flavored; the green ones are lime-lemon, the brown are candy caramel."

Horrified, Aaron stutters. "But, but— Well, what,what if you just want corn as corn."

Farmer Jacques has trouble comprehending. "What would be the gimmick? Where's the value added? The profit?"

The tour ends with a table displaying the extent of reconstituted wares. Broccoli has been turned into sugar-coated broccoli flakes. Potatoes have been fried into donuts. Radishes have been shellacked into earrings. Farmer Jacques zealously hands out brochures and free samples.

"Try our bean jerky. No cholesterol. No fat. Tastes just like jalapeno sausage. Snuggle by the fireplace while you digest our investment strategy. All visitors get a coupon entitling them to discount shares of common stock."

While Reem venturesomely fills a bowl with sugar-coated broccoli flakes, Rom pops open a new box of Captain Munchies. At last defeated, Aaron pats Rom — or is it Reem? "Let me know when you guys are ready to leave. I'll be reminiscing by the fireplace."

With this, Farmer Jacques hands Aaron a brochure along with several quarters. Aaron sardonically inquires. "Towards my first shares of stock?"

Helpfully, Farmer Jacques plucks two quarters from Aaron's palm, then deposits them into a slot by the fireplace. The apparently wooden logs are actually fluorescent tubes; when properly coin fed, they blink on and off, off and on like cheap motel lights. Aaron is dumb struck. Suspiciously, he examines the remaining quarter. Mistaking this distress for curiosity, Farmer Jacques transfers the last quarter. "For the buttered popcorn".

Aaron brightens. Popcorn? From real corn kernels? Not quite. As recorded snapping, crackling popcorn teasingly echoes in the background, a mysterious packet is ejected. Farmer Jacques foreknowingly rips the free sample open, then intrusively dabs a pinch of its crystalline substance onto the tip of Aaron's tongue. Earnestly he divulges, "Amino-crypto-chemozine. Can pass for the hot-buttered thing."

Churlishly retracting his affronted tongue, Aaron introduces a moot point. "Leading one to wonder why you didn't simply go with the hot-buttered thing. After all, this is a genuine, working farm."

Jacques is momentarily miffed. "But where would the absolute cleverness come in? Don't you understand? This is my dream. You think I earned a BA in advanced mathematics, a Masters in marketing, a Doctorate in hydroponics just so I could rise at dawn to milk a bunch of stinking cows?"

Apparently not. Unable to restrain an exasperated exhale, Aaron unintentionally scatters the lithesome amino-crypto-chemozine. Like wafting dandelion seeds, the microscopic crystals embark upon their predatory voyage to supplant the crimson meadow poppies, the ponds thick with cattails, and the confectionery redolence of days of old.

SCALING DOWN

Aaron searches for the remains of Old Man Jones. According to the local barber, Jones migrated over the border to run the Cachoo Cafe along an adjacent farmstead. Aaron locates his long lost friend forty miles south and five miles west. The twins resist entering the dubious establishment. The building appears unenduring, held temporarily in place by flimsy planks of wood, irregularly cut and precariously nailed.

Reem asserts. "Doesn't look sanitary. I don't think Mom would like it."

Rom concurs. "No, Mom wouldn't like it."

Neither cares what Mom would like. Clearly, they don't like it. It reeks of the physical universe and the possibility of bugs. Snatching their knapsack buckles, Aaron prods them forward. Once inside, the cafe looks surprisingly perky. The walls are decorated in bright tropical colors. Exotic birds freely fly from perch to perch. In one corner, a young couple sips pungent cider as they mull over blueprints. In another corner, a white-haired native man slumps over his shot glass, asleep or unconscious. Old Man Jones chuckles delightedly at the sight of Aaron. His white teeth sparkle against his pitch-black face. His salt and pepper hair bristles in eddies of kinks and curls. "Well I'll be. How did you— but of course. Not quite the old farmstead. What'd you think?"

Aaron gropes to articulate. "That depends what you have to drink."

"Mango-mayhem: one big fat mango, a jigger of rum, and daring pinch of lemon-pepper."

As Jonesy pours a frothy mug of mayhem, Aaron politely chides. "If only you had written, I would have been prepared. Granted, I should have called. Of course, I should have called. How juvenile to expect you to be living up to my past. Sorry."

Jones apologetically shrugs. "Thought I could buy it back. Thought I'd pay off my debts, thought— Hell, thought I'd drop dead stuffing beans into their trenches, living out your past and mine."

Aaron nods sympathetically before generously gulping the fomenting beverage. A few seconds past ingestion, Aaron winces. "Little less lemon-pepper and a pinch more rum, and — everything has it's season. So, you had to sell, and you sold to the big guys. Mind you, I have nothing against technology, it's just, why produce corns that taste like cream puffs. Either produce the corn or produce the cream puff — or manufacture soap."

Diluting the excessive pepper with a pinch more rum, Jones pinpoints the culprit. "Heavy metals poisoning. Making everyone crazy. Look at the statistics. Years ago, someone woke up with a great idea, the world went to bed a better place. Today, someone goes to bed with a great idea, the world wakes up with a hole in its head. Only one explanation: low-level lead poisoning. Speaking of which, what in blazes are those things?" Jones insolently indicates Rom and Reem sitting at the farthest table with their hands folded, silently staring through their wire-rimmed glasses like mirror images of each other.

"Those are Grace's sons, Rom and Reem. We're living together. In fact, Grace and I have one of our own: a little girl named Webster."

"What's wrong with them? They look exactly alike."

"Well, they're identical twins."

Jones rears his head incredulously. "When they were first born, maybe, but they should have diversified by now." Belligerently, Old Man Jones approaches the undifferentiated pair. "Okay, who's Rom and who's Reem?"

When Rom dutifully attempts to identify himself, Jones waves silence. "It's a rhetorical question like, 'What's the sound of one hand clapping?' Know anything about heavy metals poisoning?"

Pausing to assess the rhetorical intent of the question, Rom answers less swiftly but not less surely. "Well, the body doesn't need the metals but will absorb it in varying amounts. Some people tolerate it better than others."

Reem further elucidates. "It can't be excreted so it's stored in the tissues, chiefly in the bone from which it is released back into the bloodstream."

Rom continues. "Where it wreaks psychological, neurological, and kidney damage."

Reem summarizes. "It can also cause blood abnormalities, hearing loss, hyperactivity, impaired ability to metabolize, lower IQ scores, and decreased muscle tone."

"Speaking of which—" Old Jones examines Reem's biceps, "looks like you guys can use some blueberry pie."

Rom defensively declares. "Oh, no thank you. We don't..."

Reem aggressively concludes. "Don't like blueberry pie."

Dismally nodding, Jones makes his final diagnosis. "First sign of low-level lead poisoning: a slowness to comprehend." Turning to the twins, Old Jones admonishes. "Didn't ask if you *liked* blueberry pie. Didn't ask if you *wanted* blueberry pie. You obviously weren't paying attention because I didn't ask. I *said*: looks like you could use some blueberry pie. It was a rhetorical statement." Without further ado, Jones serves the necessary portions of pie. He hands Rom a fork; he hands Reem a spoon. This time, Jones examines Rom's biceps. "Light-weights. Even if you add them together. Why don't you kennel them here for the summer, Mushkin. I'll fatten them up, stiffen their backbones."

Aaron plays bad cop stepfather. "Sounds like a great idea." The twins freeze. Trying not to laugh, Aaron quickly excuses. "But I don't think their Mom would like it. What about you, Jones? What are you up to here?"

"Farming the old-fashioned way. Cows give milk when they're ready; hens lay eggs if they feel like. We never slaughter an animal until it has developed a personality. Not like Lickin' Split Chicken where the poultry eat, shit, and die in the same square footage. What kind of protein could they make? Meat with no spirit. Like eating carrion."

Jones plucks pods from a pot, then skillfully pries out the peas as he recounts. "After I foreclosed on Mercery, I set out for some hole in the wall where I could meditate myself into a transcendental stupor. I came here, coincidentally, just as the main industry was closing shop. Next thing I know, me and some local folks pooled our brain matter, came up with the idea of applying appropriate technologies, you know, designing and deploying simple tools and machines that fit rather than overwhelm the environment. Don't need big tractors for small plots. Can't kill a fly with an elephant gun. So we scaled down the technology, scaled down the local economy. After all, there were people living here one thousand years before Dingo Dog tossed them a bone. Now that Dingo Dog shares aren't worth a pooper scoop, what's an economy to do? Basically, we bought the town. Windmills provide all the energy we need. Got a simple but efficient manual pump. Keeps the pumper in shape. Got a pedal-powered sugarcane press. That's the sugarcane peddler over there. When she's not looking, take a peek at her gams." Jones winks good-naturedly then shrugs. "Nobody's rich but everyone is clothed, fed, and reasonably educated. No metals poisoning here. In fact..."

A commotion from a corner table interrupts the heavy metals dialogue. A bottle, tumbling along a slanted table, has hit its mark. The assaulted man wakens spasmodically. After confusedly rubbing his banged noggin, he shakily rights the bottle in order to pour another shot. Though directing his accusations at Jones, he doesn't take his eyes off his trembling tequila. "Is that Old Jonesy yabber-dabbering? Thinks he's gonna power the whole damn country with those wishful windmills."

Lowering his voice to a whisper, Jones confides to Aaron. "Forgot he was here. Hardly ever conscious. That's Quincy Qwa: half Qwaquiwei, half devil. Our citizen group waylaid his plan for a nuclear facility. Quince tried to sell tribal territory to a nuclear power consortium, hoping to fund his retirement and booze. But someone has to look out for the children. Speaking of which—" Old Jones demands, "You boys finished those pies?"

The twins half-heartedly pick at their portions of blueberry. Rom mopes. "It's kind of gloppy."

Jones raises his arms in wonderment. "It's very gloppy. It's as gloppy as I can make it. And it's organic, you know."

Intentionally raising his voice, Old Jones reprimands Quincy. "Not like those nuclear plants. How can you call yourself Qwaquiwei, Quince? Qwaquiwei, of all people, know that nuclear don't biodegrade. Life ain't life unless it biodegrades, decomposes beyond recognition, past remembrance. That's what makes death so sobering. To dust to dust. Not like those nuclear plants; they can't be turned off, have to be 'decommissioned' like a ghost that won't release its hide. Ever see one of those things put to rest? Have to build unwieldy enclosures to trap the radioactive dust. Have to pulverize the radioactive concrete with special devices which in turn get contaminated, which in turn have to be buried. Ever been to their sacred burial site? Want to get really spooked? Travel north on a cold, sunless day and count the brass headstones marking where their gargantuan steel pressure vessels lie in wait like evil genies, hoping to be regurgitated so they can revive their nuclear mayhem. Why those damn reactor vessels ain't officially dead for a zillion years. Takes a lifetime just to count that high. People guarding them will themselves be ghosts. Ghosts guarding ghosts. Positively ain't natural."

Rom deferentially raises his hand. "Excuse us sir, but could we have something to drink."

Reem respectfully waves. "Yes, something to wash this down."

Old Man Jones indicates the distiller. "No snow melt down here. No clean drinking water. See that distiller? Works like a green house. Muddy water evaporates under the heat of the sun, condenses on the glass roof, then drips into side receptacles, perfectly pure. Isn't that amazing?"

Reem plaintively queries, "Does it come carbonated?"

Jones turns to Aaron suspiciously. "You sure they aren't space aliens?"

Aaron loyally insists, "No, just gifted."

"Wouldn't be so sure. Normal child shouldn't take more than three minutes to chow down a fruit pie. The Pitskys had an invasion of aliens last June. Said they came from Zicculi Reticuli. Promised to save the world then, as so often goes, left without paying their rent."

Quincy slams down his bottle. "You yammer, yammering about me? Calling me a space alien, you, you— terrestrial toad! Trying to reach the sun one lily pad at a time when I know a short cut. At any moment, I can activate my enchanted wings and rise, rise." Realizing, he isn't rising to the occasion, Quincy revises. "Fortunately, Qwaquiwei are forsworn to keep our wings hidden from you qwaless heathens. Hell, I don't have to shit here with you, you parasitic— parasitic— parasite! Least Qwaquiwei tread lightly, hardly daring to breathe the painstakingly amassed ethers. You rake this planet, contributing nothing, mining the land with your toxic toys, voraciously consuming the treasured archives of departed life forms in one greedy sitting. The nerve of peoples like you trying put one over on peoples like me. Never— Never did want no nuclear facility. Just trying to break out of this relentless orbit. Only wanted that facility so I could short-circuit the rod regulation program or something. Planning to sabotage— set the world ablaze in celebration of the Inner Lightning. Was just a scheme, just, just a—" Quincy starts to cackle maniacally like the psychotic hyena at the Animal Research Center.

"Can you believe such fungus thinking?" To confirm this, Jones pounds his palm over his daily news. "How someone can plant a bomb in a baby carriage, then set it off in the middle of a market — with the baby still in it? Damn these mal-contents, and those entitled Qwaquiweis. Why don't they vote? Why don't they participate in the governing process? Stop hiding behind some religious taboo, deferring to some Lord Mother Earthdom."

While the politely listening Aaron spoons the excessive lemon-pepper from his Mayhem, Jones unleashes his political frustrations. "And these members of SOIL? Why don't they put their hand to a plow if they care so much about organic produce? Stop posting a tonnage of unedifying material designed solely to provoke. Mark my words: we are sowing the seeds of disaster."

Reeling from the extra helping of rum, Aaron cheerily cajoles, "But of course! Your seeds? Last time we corresponded, you were experimenting with a variety of wild grains. Anything of interest?"

"Didn't I write? Yes, I did. No, I didn't. I started to. About a hybrid. Not my personal discovery but, well, it's called mazing, because it is amazing. Grows five times faster than ordinary maize. Popco Industries is developing it in a big way. Planted several fields myself."

Aaron puckers contemplatively. "Not becoming a one-grain man, are you? Remember the last corn blight? Millions of acres of triplelux corn were planted, then the woolly mold struck. Struck the triplelux hard. No other strains were planted so the entire crop failed three consecutive years. What a disaster! Little enough variety as is. Don't back yourself into a corner."

"No need to warn me, Mushkin. Those were my parting words to you, remember? Why I got seeds under my toenails, falling out the flaps of my jammies. I'll be sure to sustain a variety, to..."

"Liar!" Quincy, wobbles from his chair. "Liar, liar, tale's on fire. Variety is against our nature. Like mindlessly impregnating bulls, we sow our seed, our seed only. We see things with one myopic eye. Our mind cannot comprehend complexity. We take a wild jungle and we turn it into millions of acres of triplelux corn as unvarying as—" Roguishly indicating Rom and Reem, Quincy forewarns. "Imagine them not two, but two by two, then four by four, then eight by eight by sixteen by thirty-two until they are no longer a curiosity but an infestation." Worn from counting, Quincy falls to the floor, insensate.

Despite his seeming somnolence, the twins cautiously creep around him. Even more cautiously, they submit their blueberry-smeared plates for inspection. Old Man Jones pats them on their respective heads. "Good, good, little doggies."

Rom drops his plate as a burly bug scrambles up Jones' arm. Old Jones expounds cheerily. "Nothing like real bugs up your sleeve, right boys? Don't use pesticides here. Get the native insects to do their bit. This here fellow is an antiantnoid. Eats the aphids off the blueberry buds."

"You, you let them loose on purpose? But might not one, or two—" Reem hesitates calculating as he proposes, "get stuck inside a blueberry?"

With an increasingly attenuating voice, Rom nervously chimes. "Yes, isn't there a chance one will end up..."

Leaving the twins to contemplate their potentially adulterated plate, Jones explains his cooperative farming philosophy. "Well, what do you suppose gives the pie its distinguishing crunch? Antiantnoids are low in cholesterol, contain absolutely no fat, provide the suggested dosage of trace minerals. Why, antiantnoids are the most essential ingredient in the recipe."

For a moment, Aaron frets that Rom and Reem will faint, but worse, their Mom won't like it.

OIL AND WATER

When it comes to insects, Grace sides with her squeamish sons. She doesn't mind grasshoppers or damsel-flies who abide playfully outdoors, and she concedes the benefit of bees. However, mites and fleas and grubs and silverfish — all insects of that irritant ilk have less convincing roles. Certainly they curry no favor as they cower under dank rocks, conspire behind concealed crevices, mine sweater pockets with gluey nests, feast on slowly sloughing skin cells. Perhaps, it is the discourteous notion that, to these least of God's creatures, the human body is just another rotting organism on which to lay their maggots. As Grace places her briefcase on the floor, a millipede darts from a dusty shadow. Rather than gooking her expensive pumps, Grace whacks the hapless bug with an abandoned oxford.

The spare shoe is no lucky coincidence. Hurling shoes at government hearings has become an accepted form of protest. An enterprising woman sells half pairs on the Senate steps. This expropriated oxford was jettisoned on behalf of a frustrated ecologist decrying the wasting effects of acid rain. The Senator interrogating the matter was being unnecessarily antagonistic. Unfortunately, the objecting oxford landed one balcony short.

Grace is attending these hearings at the behest of Deloy Enterprises, to ensure radical environmentalists do not muddy the black and white facts with their emotional colors. Economic growth is sluggish; already too many people are out of work. Grace could have spared Deloy her fees. This hearing on environmental trends is taking a decidedly pro-industry stand. Grace is not necessarily pleased. Her intent has always been to negotiate the extremes, to coax environmentally hostile corporations into environmentally conscious modes of operation by citing the success of pro-environment groups litigating against industry offenders, and by pointing out the liabilities of recent climatic trends. Floods, droughts and unexplained epidemics have become more pervasive, more destructive. Scientists and politicians, long oil and water, are desperately seeking consensus. Unfortunately, problems seem to be getting more complex, more unsolvable. Ordinary citizens prospecting for heroes invariably dig up villains. Politicians, trying to avoid both the fire and the frying pan, have simply stopped functioning. Meanwhile the planet continues to erode revolution by revolution.

Having pulled the lowest card from the deck, Senator Grady reluctantly presides over the proceedings. Her no-nonsense approach does not seem to be working. Expert witnesses are not cooperating; no one is giving the same answer, and no one is putting their absolute certainty on the line. Returning to her original dilemma, Senator Grady pleads, "But you still haven't answered my question, Dr. Vanetsky. Is it good or is it bad? Is the ozone deteriorating beyond recognition or what?"

Dr. Vanetsky cautiously ponders. "Well, the components of the ozone are certainly changing."

Senator Grady jots a significant word in her notebook. "So it's bad."

"Not necessarily. These changes could represent naturally occurring, seasonal fluctuations."

Slowly erasing her last entry, Senator Grady hazards, "So, it's okay."

"Not exactly. While seasonal fluctuations per se may be natural, the fluctuations we are currently experiencing may not be so natural, so let's just say, it is cause for concern."

Hurling her pencil in despair, Senator Grady uncharacteristically snarls. "That does it! Can't any of you scientific types calculate whether one and one amounts to anything? How are politicians supposed to pass laws? We need to make conclusions. To make conclusions, we need facts, but not thousands of intertwining facts knotted into unrelenting 'ands', conditional 'ifs' and lily-livered 'but-buts'. That's just too many facts and figures going into too many damn directions."

Dabbing the beading sweat from his forehead, Dr. Vanetsky sheepishly confesses. "What can I say? The atmosphere is not a controlled system. We cannot put it into a test tube to analyze it."

Senator Grady petulantly notes. "Since when? Didn't you unflinchingly propose how the universe was created? Haven't you presumptuously described behaviors of life forms on undetected planets, in stellar systems billions of light years from here, lectured extensively on quirky little quarky things no one can see, hear, or locate on the head of a pin? So don't tell me you cannot answer a simple question like: will the use of chloro-fluoro-carbons, hydro-chloro-fluoro-carbons, hydro-fluoro-carbons result in the thinning of the ozone layer causing deleterious consequences or not?"

"Well, the ozone is indeed being reduced, and CFCs, HFCs, and HCFCs do degrade the ozone, cause skin cancer, cataracts, crop damage as well as..."

"Not that old line?" Senator Seerington juts his lower jaw derisively as he raps his puffy fingers on his sagging double chin. "So the world is evolving into different elementary particles. The price of progress. Stop whining and apply more sunscreen. Wear bigger hats. Invest in factory farms. If you can't take the heat, get out of the kitchen. That's what my mama used to say."

Dr. Vanetsky dutifully instructs. "Unfortunately, Senator Seerington, these carbon compounds remain in the atmosphere some hundred years. Enough has already been released to eat away the ozone for the next century, even if we stopped all production as of this very moment."

"And it is not just cancer." Senator Fingerstein cinches his shoulders at the cowering prospect. "Sadly, cancer may prove as hokum as the common cold if this auto-immune shutdown syndrome continues to escalate."

Senator Seerington catapults from his seat. "We are not debating ASD, Senator Fingerstein. This is a hearing on environmental trends, not a medical symposium on freak diseases."

Senator Fingerstein splays his arms defensively. "ASD is not— not a freak disease! The medical community is decidedly alarmed. The immune system goes haywire, treats neighboring cells like foreign bodies, loses sight of its own self. Imagine losing sight of one's own self. Researchers are suggesting that environmental tampering has disrupted the planet's electromagnetic fields. Since these fields may control the electric body, the subtle layer beneath the grosser nervous system, common to all species— Well, by damaging this vital foundation, we have essentially switched off our antennae. The auto-immune subsystem is no longer getting good reception. We have disconnected from our guiding mind."

Senator Seerington narrows his scoffing eyes. "Only you, Senator Fingerstein, are disconnected from your misguiding mind. ASD is a peculiar syndrome affecting a peculiar stratum of peculiar people. To my knowledge, it only affects that mutant evolutionist cult. I am hardly surprised. They were bound to die *en masse* of something. Trying to mutate faster than the next guy, skip a millennia or two of evolution. I've read about the unsavory rituals they employ to shock their genetic material into warp drive. They only come out at night, lie naked on their roof tops absorbing moon beams, consume mummified food products and mega doses of vitamins, sleep in tanks filled with salt water. They don't exercise or have intercourse, trying to entice energies up their spinal columns into unmapped sections of their cerebral cortex. Naturally, they don't talk. Talking raises the blood pressure, diverts necessary nutrients from their power chakras. Frankly, I am glad they don't talk so we don't have to hear from them, so I don't want to hear from them — from you!"

In the brief, ensuing silence, Senator Grady resumes her inquiry. "Getting back to your last statement, Doctor, it is definitely bad, real bad. Why didn't you say so in the first place?"

Dr. Vanetsky leerily hedges. "I didn't explicitly say that. After all, when chlorofluorocarbon was introduced, it was considered the ideal product: non-toxic, odorless, nonflammable, chemically inert. Those characteristics on paper made it appear fail-safe, so considering where we've been, and where we may be going, I would hate to act precipitously."

Senator Seerington supports the prudently politic scientist. "Stop badgering him, Grady. You heard the man. You cannot put atmosphere into a test tube. The chemistry and dynamics are a chaotic interaction of..."

Senator Mungus abruptly bellows into his microphone. "Of very complicated stuff. Very, very complicated." With each emphatic "very", Senator Mungus raises his shoulders as if preparing to take flight. "So let us tread with sore feet. We don't want to set a match to a burning building, leave a dying sponge cake out in the rain."

Reluctant to set the treacherous precedent of removing a colleague for mental incapacity, the Senate indulges Mungus' increasing stupefaction. The assumption, the hope is, one day soon, the brain tumor responsible for such gnarled reasoning will fatally detonate. Oblivious to these ill intentions, Senator Mungus adjusts his reading glasses. "If you lookie here, the Klink study says that methane has increased by ten percent, but the Burgess study insists methane has increased by twelve percent. Well, is it ten percent, or twelve percent? If we reduce methane by twelve percent and it turns out to have been ten percent, we end up two percent short. We don't want to add more salt to the ocean. No point making a big black hole out of a little side pocket."

Gingerly, Senator Fingerstein interjects, "The crucial point, Senator Mungus, is not the debatable two percent but the irrefutable direction. The percent of methane in the atmosphere is increasing. *Increasing* is the operative word. Everyone agrees it has to come down. Unfortunately, current laws ensure it will continue to rise."

From the back of the hall, a member of SOIL belligerently appends, "As will carbon dioxide and nitrous oxide and nitrogen oxide and carbon monoxide and hydrogen fluoride and bromine and don't forget those chlorine waste products polluting our breast milk and semen."

Senator Seerington dastardly refutes. "There they go again. Can't sing, can't dance, can't zip down my pants. So we've spilt a little milk and semen along the winding road to Oz. What did you expect? We can't return to the Stone Age. We've evolved from that point on the pinwheel. It's a *fait accompli*. Face facts, folks: we can't crawl back into the womb, can't grow hair on our backside, and Rhett Butler will never return to Scarlett, so get over it. Don't know about the silent majority, but my father didn't gnaw on raw wilderbeasties and my mother doesn't masticate tree bark. I don't care how many trace minerals it contains, if I consistently regurgitate, it won't count. You don't see wild antelopes cajoling their fawns to eat. They eat what they eat. They don't have to think about it. We spend too much time contemplating involuntary ticks. Learn to ignore them. Too many anguishing experts. Remember when they claimed Burger Blasters increased cholesterol? They compared a test tube here to a test tube there, then said, 'Hold the Blasters. Switch to salmon!' All well and good until they came upon a dissenting test tube that suggested a properly prepared burger has enough good cholesterol to counterbalance the bad cholesterol and that salmon, though theoretically preferable, in actuality is tainted with mercury. Unfortunately, your local burger concession went out of business after receiving the perfidious press. Meanwhile, the theoretically good salmon is poisoning you to death. Worse: I ruined an entire holiday season nibbling kiwi fruit and bristle-sprouts. When my hair started to fall out, my nutritionist warned I was not getting enough selenium. Seleni whom? Never heard of it before yesterday; will be out-of-fashion or in disrepute tomorrow. Got a medication for systolic; got a medication for diastolic; got a medication for hyper-flux; got a medication for hypo-flam; got me juicing bags of celery and carrots to boost my vitamin A. Suddenly, I'm not feeling so well. Only then do these so-called experts apologetically footnote: oh, by the way, too much vitamin A can kill you — except now it's too late. I'm already dead."

Still very much alive, Senator Seerington wields his fist threateningly. "Well I say these so called experts are a bunch of witch doctors, putting whole industries out of work on the say so of a blundering test tube. Now, they are going on and on about a few marauding molecules. Do we want to see another thousand citizens out of work? And you of all senators, Senator Fingerstein! Didn't you help Senator Mungus defeat legislation that would have reduced hazardous emissions by twenty percent?"

"It wasn't strong enough. Twenty percent isn't good enough. Senator Mungus voted against that bill because he doesn't believe in reducing man-made emissions at all. I voted against it because the bill didn't go far enough. We defeated it for very different reasons."

"But isn't *defeated* the operative word?"

Grace loses track of the discussion as she struggles to uncap a bottle of aspirins. Roguishly, Iroquois Jefferson taps her from one row behind. "Aspirins before lunch? Does this mean you aren't enjoying the show?" Before Grace can fashion her response, Iroquois bemoans. "Yet another year and no comprehensive legislation. No wonder my canary refuses to sing. I see Senator Mungus found his way to work again. We are partly to blame. Government reforms went too far. Should never have cut their wages. They warned us, said we'd end up with raving idiots if we refused to pay the price. You get what you pay for."

Nosily, Iroquois extracts Grace's wallet from her unclasped purse, then sifts through her personal photos for something incriminating. "Ah ha! So here's the culprit. Just as I thought. He's bald. You married a bald man."

As Grace snatches back her pilfered wallet and photos, she protests. "He isn't bald. He shaved his head."

"Why? Is he a closet monk? How kinky. Or perhaps he has a skin condition. My sympathies."

"Not that it is any of your business but Aaron is very practical and not the least vain. Whenever his hair grew too long, he cut it off, cut it all off. Might as well start from scratch, he'd say."

"So what's his present condition?" Iroquois flaunts his dashing mane. "Can I interest you in a lock or two?"

"Needless to say, he doesn't do it anymore."

"Part of the conjugal contract, I suppose. Got him wrapped up in prenuptial agreements, in do's, and do-not do's."

"No, I simply asked him, and he simply did. The advantage of true love. You just have to say 'please'."

"Ah, if life were only so simple. Speaking of simple, the single-cell Mungus just ceded the floor to that lichen Krommueller. What happened to those fire ants we planted in his toupee? Didn't they take?"

While readjusting his golf cap, the maligned Senator Krommueller confusedly sifts through his reports. "This— this study here says an increasing level of certain atmospheric components is triggering an ice age, but this other study says an increasing level of carbons is causing global warming, so I say: let them fight it out." Shuffling the pages of the two reports together, Senator Krommueller delightedly notes. "The ice age will be tempered by global warming and everything will balance out. Besides, I wouldn't mind a little more warmth in my part of the country. Frankly, Hollow Hole is too damn cold."

The newly sworn in Dr. Carboni explains. "But if it gets too cold in an area where plants and wildlife have adapted to a temperate climate, those plants and animals will freeze. They cannot opt to buy mink coats. They rely on gradual mutations over many generations. On the other hand, if it gets too warm in an area where plants and wildlife have adapted to the cold, those plants and animals will wilt. Meanwhile, the temperate loving plants and animals won't know to migrate to this newly temperate haven. You will end up with deserts everywhere. You cannot redecorate the planet. It is not like moving couches."

Senator Grady is nodding vigorously. "And hasn't it been suggested that global warming can change the migration pattern of animals and insects, enabling them to transport viruses to regions of non-vaccinated populations?"

Senator Krommueller again readjusts his golf cap as he waves a page from his scattered reports. "But, but, but this study here indicates the increased nitrogen oxides of acid rain actually add nutrients to the soil, causing trees to grow faster. I'm sure I read it right. Yes, I did. It says right here: the increased nitrogen oxides of acid rain add..."

Dr. Carboni elucidates. "Initially, but soils can only neutralize a limited amount. Eventually, so much acid accumulates..."

Senator Krommueller waves another page from another report. "But this study on atmospheric gases intimates the increase in this, added to the decrease in that, uphold the chemical balance and therefore cancel each other out. Cancel! Cancel! So what's the problem?"

"If this were a bank statement, the gross numerics might balance. In actuality, there will be more ozone in the lower atmosphere due to increased methane, but less ozone in the upper atmosphere due to increased chlorine. That kind of redistribution will alter the temperature in the stratosphere, which will alter the circulation patterns which — well frankly, we don't know."

"Oh, so now you don't know." Senator Krommueller brutally chides. "But didn't someone from your institute prophesy that smoke from the oil explosions in that war we kind of won would trigger a disastrous drought? You calculated the smoke would penetrate the troposphere, eventually blanket the hemisphere, alleged this veil of smoke would cool the Betan plateau, preventing the seasonal updrafts which precipitate the harvest rains. You declared there would be a devastating drought, predicted millions of people would slowly starve to death. But that never happened. You got everyone overexcited for nothing."

Dr. Carboni coldly notes into the microphone. "No, that never happened, or rather — that is not what happened. Instead, the rains fell, and fell. Relentlessly as I recall. And no, the seeds did not shrivel. Instead, they washed away in torrential flood waters, and rather than millions slowly starving, hundreds of thousands drowned in a hysterical instant as freak cyclones engulfed..."

Senator Krommueller is not interested in the bottom line. "Whatever. The point is: you were wrong."

"About the triggering event, not the tragic..."

Senator Krommueller mindlessly maintains. "But technically, you were wrong. I could prove it in a court of law.

Senator Mungus, wasn't she technically wrong?" As Senator Mungus obligingly nods, Senator Krommueller persists. "She was wrong, wrong, wrong, so I say, let's beat up Mother Nature at her own game. I know a microbiologist who claims he can subtract some of that carbon from the atmosphere by dumping tons of iron into the ocean; this will cause plankton to multiply out of all proportion, and suck up the carbon dioxide. Happily, the plankton die and sink to the bottom of the ocean, never to be seen again, thus diminishing the greenhouse effect."

Dr. Carboni waves her hand cautiously. "But dump a little too much iron, draw out a little too much carbon, and you may plunge us into an ice age."

Senator Mungus shivers at the notion. "Like I said: tricky, tricky stuff. Well, I've done some research myself. Took a hands-on attitude. Trying to face this with my nose to the hot plate. Got one staffer measuring the sea level on the east coast; another measuring the sea level on the west coast. One tells me the sea level is rising; the other tells me the sea level is falling. On the rising side, the ice caps are shrinking as they melt into the ocean; on the falling side, the ice caps are growing as warm water evaporates and falls onto the ice sheets as snow. It's weird. Too weird."

Senator Seerington leans over his table defensively. "Dr. Carboni, this governing body is doing its best under the circumstances. Last month, we agreed that emissions of greenhouse gasses need to be curbed."

"But you instituted no mandatory steps."

"We tried. We legislated cleaner fuel to reduce carbon emissions; unfortunately, our good citizens proved unwilling to pay the price at the tank."

Dr. Carboni repudiates this version. "It wasn't the added cents to the gallon, Senator, but the poisonous additives in that debatably cleaner fuel which soured our good citizens at the emergency wards. That particular formulation leached toxic compounds like formaldehyde. Have you forgotten? Thousands of people became seriously ill. The intention was good but the solution was a crapshoot."

"Exactly. So these days we are more cautious. And apparently, it is the thought alone which counts. Look at the latest data. Global temperatures have stabilized without us lifting a legislative finger."

Exasperated, Dr. Carboni notes. "Because Wallatoba volcano exploded, sending millions of tons of pulverized rock and gas into the stratosphere. The resultant haze triggered a cooling effect. This is temporarily countering, skewing global warming statistics. Needless to say, we cannot rely on Wallatoba erupting on a timely basis."

"That's it!" Having confiscated Senator Grady's gavel, Senator Krommueller maniacally declares. "I move we act on this absolutely brilliant suggestion. See what happens when we work as a team, mash our collective minds together. We simply need to design magic bullets to initiate volcanic eruptions whenever the temperature rises above the designated norm. We're half there; we simply need to adapt those killer-bee bullets we've been debating. So what if they rip to shreds a handful of police officers and purportedly innocent bystanders. Look what they can do if we allow them to evolve into their most dreadful potential. One bullet point blank can set off volcanic eruptions. Think of the business uses as well; we can gouge out oil wells, puncture massive foundations for mile-high skyscrapers, all without slave labor or the minimum wage. Think of the structures we can erect if we strike deeper and deeper to build higher and higher. Why, we will be able to defy gravity, transgress the very heavens. From this vantage, we can literally vacuum chlorofluorocarbons from the sky."

Confined to her observer status, Grace laments. "Poor Webster, what have I gotten her into?"

Iroquois loyally bolsters. "Hey, that's not the Ivanosky I know, love, and mercilessly badger. In times like these, we peanuts can shed our shackling shells, rise from our hindsight gallery, and do something! This is not like watching television. We can switch them off. Gracie, Gracie, Gracie, you used to be so undomesticated. What happened to all those wonderful waves we used to generate? So what if we knocked a few boats from their moorings; they were going nowhere. What happened to your rampaging ardor? What's with all this work, work, work and no payoff. Don't you get tired? Frustrated? Pissed?"

Though inwardly wondering if her balancing act is merely a posture of defeat, Grace nevertheless defends. "During my lifetime, I chose from the list of options, then moved on. Since the world is not flat, I can't simply walk off the chessboard. Sooner or later I'm going to trip over those carelessly laid eggs. It doesn't much matter who laid them, so, no matter how I add, subtract or subdivide, the bottom line is still negotiation, compromise, consensus."

Forgetting his higher purpose, Iroquois perks mischievously. "Oh, I'm all for consensus, for consenting adults, so how about you and I skip the elective foreplay and go straight to— After all, you're a woman, and I'm a man. I'm lonely; you're not. The important thing is, we have a past. While you may prefer to forget it, and while I may embellish it beyond recognition, neither of us can undo the damage. I admit, I can't offer fidelity but I can spring for a knish."

Grace remains unwooed. Iroquois whimpers. "This isn't working. Why aren't you collapsing at my feet, writhing in carnal ecstasy, conceding the Cliff of Ancients back to the Qwaquiwei, and most importantly, admitting you adore me?"

"Because Sadu Qwa isn't suing, and this oxford can do some serious damage to your family jewels."

"Ah, the consummate romantic — but what do you mean, Sadu Qwa isn't suing? Doesn't she realize the value— Surely she wants— Don't tell me she's not interested in— Well, screw Sadu Qwa. Steeped in the mystical dogma part, she fails to realize the book value of that property. Luckily, I don't need her. I know tribal chiefs who value financial assets more than prayer sticks, who are willing to trade their enchanted stones for..." Iroquois is rudely derailed as a gawky galosh from an irate constituent spears the base of his skull.

"Hey! Re-read the shoe rules! This section is zoned for soft-soled moccasins. A boot this size can take a man's head off, cause a concussion — Now, there's a thought. What do you think, Ivanosky? Think I can take out Krommueller from this distance?" Always the cocky optimist, Iroquois leans over the balcony in order to more favorably position himself. Though the forewarning galosh lands within inches of the prating Krommueller, it fails to impact the debate.

If anything, Krommueller becomes more embedded in his point of view. "Well, halleluia! Did you get that, folks? The esteemed Professor Lannahan is bearing good news at last. So, to recap Professor Lannahan, we are releasing eight billion tons of carbon dioxide into the atmosphere every year. However, only four billion tons end up anywhere. The remaining billions and billions conveniently disappear."

Professor Lannahan leafs through his hasty calculations. "No, no, that is not what I said, Senator Krommueller."

"Did too."

Jabbing his pointer finger into his open notebook, the Professor corrects. "No. I said billions of tons are unaccounted for. That means billions and billions of tons of CO_2 are still somewhere, temporarily. If the missing mass is in the deep ocean, it will eventually leach back into the atmosphere. If the missing mass is in the forests, it will be released into the atmosphere when those forests die which, unfortunately, is occurring at an ever increasing rate. It is possible we will soon awaken to the full brunt— and I hope you realize when I say billions of tons each year go unaccounted for, that means, at this point in time, we are missing over one hundred billion tons of CO_2. So the question is: when will the ghosts of our past come back to haunt us. So far, global warming is going better than expected. That's bad news. It means we cannot predict when the planet will run out of hiding places, when CO_2 molecules will fall where they may. If you think the Pompousians were surprised when miles of volcanic ash entombed their civilization for our archeological perusal, well, suffice to say, we may find ourselves buried in the metaphorical ash of our carbon makings."

Senator Mungus raises his hand as he interrupts. "Professor Lannahan, that's a very interesting story but hard to believe you can hide one hundred billion tons of anything without someone, somewhere finding out. I mean, even the most innocent flirtation ends up on video tape and photocopied out of all proportion. So we're missing a little CO_2. It could have floated away on the solar wind, or slipped into a parallel universe — or been mined by space aliens."

Senator Mungus boldly rails at the snickering senate body. "Yes, space aliens. I'm man enough to say it. Hey, more people have seen intergalactic subspecies than CO_2 molecules. I myself have hypnotic recalls featuring miniature green women with miniature green breasts. They have purportedly been coming to this planet for eons. For all we know, one of their prime missions is to lug our excess CO_2 to some trash galaxy light years from here. Or maybe they process the CO_2 into hyper-fuel. I bet that's how they get around, on CO_2 hyper-fuel." Senator Mungus confidently summarizes. "So you see, it serves both our needs. What would happen if we stopped producing excess CO_2? Those enterprising aliens would bypass this planet. Those little green women will take their little green breasts elsewhere."

Turned off by the mounting inanity of the proceedings, Iroquois tries to interest Grace in more pressing passions. "Speaking of subspecies and little green breasts, are you absolutely sure you don't want to check out my glutial biceps, or triglyceral strapnoids, or any of my other subterranean sinews? Been working out for the past three months, but nobody wants to see me naked. What a waste of testosterone when here you are, so close, and you smell so good."

Grace convulsively recoils. "And you smell like..."

Skunk. The tangy stench chafes the contentious air. Lights go out. Lights flash on. Mysteriously materialized skunks rampage the Senate floor like crazed lemmings. Pandemonium strikes as the disoriented creatures scatter senators and spectators into manifold directions — down the aisles, up the aisles, over desks, under desks. Within minutes, the halls are cleared. Tables have been overturned. Chairs have been jolted from their orderly rows. Unflung shoes lay abandoned. The invading skunks have successfully preempted the proceedings, constitutionally indicated their malodorous distaste for all involved.

FALLING SATELLITES

All is well at the Cachoo Cafe as the clock strikes eleven. Old Man Jones has gone to bed. Aaron eases towards Rom on the sagging back porch. The day had redeeming moments. Reem was able to rig a contraption to carbonate the distilled water. Rom was allowed to concoct drinks for unsuspecting customers. Despite these concessions, the twins will not forgive the inclusion of antiantnoids in the blueberry pie. Consequently, they refuse to consume anything whose component ingredients cannot be authenticated. Aaron was able to scrounge enough corn kernels which Reem meticulously scrutinized for suspect particles. Instead of regaling the twins with an organic feast, Aaron is reduced to carbonated water and popcorn. Once again, they have run out of Munchies. As Rom shakes more salt into the bowl, Reem inquires from behind the screen door. "What are those things glaring at us?"

Aaron assures, "They won't bite. They're flowers. Their petals appear luminous under the moonlight. Their fragrance, so overpowering, is only released in the evenings. You'll hardly notice them come daylight. See what you're missing?"

"If you are trying to say they smell funny, well yeah." Reem ventures from behind the screen door. "What about that eerie sound? Vampire bats?" Reem protectively yanks the hood of his sweat shirt over his head as he creeps towards the popcorn bowl. "I hear they rip out head-hair to make nests for their blood-sucking young."

Rom further embellishes. "Then drill holes into the back of your neck so they can tap into your spinal fluid."

"No, no." Aaron resoundingly corrects these bizarre notions. "The majority of bats are innocuous little creatures. Mostly, they eat insects, nest high in the tree tops or deep inside caves, avoiding people whenever, wherever. In any case, those aren't bats. They're clickadees. A kind of grasshopper."

Reem remains unsatisfied. "What about those tinkling drums? Perhaps we are surrounded by cannibals performing pagan tribal rituals involving disemboweled goats or something."

Rom corrects Reem. "There are no such things as cannibals. However, it could be their long lost ghosts, or alien spirits trapped in another dimension, trying to manifest at some lower periodic pulsation."

Aaron dauntlessly explains. "I do hate to disappoint but those are frogs, croaking their songs of love. It's the mating season."

Rom and Reem don't get it as they ponder in unison: "Where did they get the drums?"

Aaron winces. "Uh, exactly what do they teach at this Gifted Institute you attend?"

Reem shrugs. "Well, certainly when it comes to frogs and slimy salamanders, they don't go into unnecessary details. By the time we're your age, all those squiggly things will be extinct, so why bother."

"Isn't that the point? Educating you to their plight?"

Inadvertently sputtering corn kernels, Rom defiantly declares. "Our economics teacher insists that's histrionic propaganda, put out by nature worshipers. Always touting those obscure creatures who can change sex, metamorphose into flying objects, hibernate for months or suspend their animation. The objective is to make us appear inferior in comparison, or somehow dependent on the fortunes and misfortunes of what amounts to pond goo."

Reem assents. "Yes, Mr. Middlerose assures us these biologic small fry, these sensational aberrants, are nonessential life forms, quite unnecessary to the balance of power. Whatever it is they do can be simulated if necessary. Our major concern is to maintain the sophisticated computers managing our economy. Before we graduate, we will need to perceive events in four, five, possibly six dimensions. You see, according to our assigned counselor, humankind is evolving into rows and rows of swollen brain pods — like fields of lettuce heads."

Emotionally ruffled by this dismaying vision, Rom stoically stiffens. "Not a pretty picture, but we must prepare for that eventuality. Already our teeth are shrinking, our hair is falling out, our muscles atrophying. Soon, we'll need to inject sperm via data download. Course, that part doesn't bother me, but I'll miss my teeth."

Faced with such techno-centric odds, Aaron gingerly proposes. "Then hold onto what you hold dear for as long as you can. Maybe nature devotees are fighting the inevitable technologic ground swell. Maybe there'll be no one left to remember that once upon a time flowers blanketed these meadows, trees thickly lined the horizon, creatures of unparalleled strangeness cast shadows from the sky. Mystics call it the face of God. However, with each extinction, another feature becomes inaccessible, meaning you are planning your fragile futures on flawed computer models. Doesn't it frighten you that the clues that guide us are being destroyed generation after generation?"

Aaron pauses to assess the impact of his words. Rom is yawning. Reem is casting reconnaissance pebbles into the luminous flowers. In light of this, Aaron suffices to say, "In any case, there's no sense debating the eventuality of brain pods some million years hence. Might as well chew this popcorn while our teeth are still in place, and of course, enjoy the full moon. Unless the Gifted Institute has some prohibition against moon gazing?"

The twins parrot in unison. "Just that it's space rubble."

Aaron inadvertently tips the bowl of popcorn. "Space rubble! That— That glorious, glittering goddess of the tides? You can't be— Well, look for yourselves. It's spellbinding. Not a meteorite fragment or chunk of kryptonite. Why, that damn thing is two thousand miles across, one quarter the size of this planet. Maybe in kindergarten, you drew a dimensionless circle on a piece of construction paper, then crayoned it white but now, you must understand it is *embodied*. It has weight, gravity. If it were any less distant, it would devour us and yet — it is close enough to touch." As if to reveal the moon dust of which he speaks, Aaron tenders his fingers for examination.

"When you think of the daunting light years between us and almost everything else, the presence of a companion planet merely hundreds of thousands of miles from our doorstep is miraculous, absolutely miraculous. Why, I can climb into a rocket and be there in a matter of hours. I could be standing there at this very moment, peering down at you and calling you space rubble!"

Reem tries to assuage his would-be parent. "Really Mr. Mushkin, don't make such a fuss. After all, it is just the moon. It is supposed to be there."

Aaron widens his eyes mischievously. "But it isn't. What we know indicates it is not supposed to be there. The theory that it is a sister planet, accreted from the same matter that created this planet, doesn't hold because its chemical composition and geologic construction are too dissimilar. The theory it was a wandering asteroid, subsequently captured, is implausible because asteroids bolt violently. This little planet with its paltry gravitational influence could never have lassoed something that big, moving that fast. Another theory, romantically fantastic, suggests an asteroid smashed into our burgeoning world with such ferocity, it ripped out part of us, literally ripped out our soul. There it hovers, awaiting our contemplation, forever reminding us what we are, where we are. Behold our awakening mirror. Can you imagine the night without the moon? The universe without stars? Don't you wonder why things are the way they are, or more importantly — aren't?"

Instead of wondering, Reem accuses, "So that's it! You brought us here to perform rites of manhood rituals. Having intoxicated us with carbonated rain water, you will make us wish and wish upon a star like wild wolves."

"Sometimes better to wish upon those stars than study them to death. You learn more about the outside, inside."

Expressing more disappointment than arrogance, Rom notifies. "Frankly, we considered that line of reasoning. Unfortunately, when you cut through the delicate skin, all you find is gunk and more gunk. We take anatomy to witness first hand there are no angels, or aliens, or talking potato heads.

All these centuries, people expecting something spectacular. How many times have children been told to locate the North Star at the stroke of midnight, to wish a wish on each stroke. And for all that wishing, has anything really changed?"

Rom checks his wristwatch then turns to Reem. Reem checks his wristwatch then turns to Aaron. "Perhaps this is the time and setting to tell you: we don't believe in gift-bearing fat men, or tooth fairies, or talking bananas. After all—" Rom confesses a burning conundrum, "why would a tooth fairy leave one lousy quarter?"

Reem elaborates. "Yes, Mr. Mushkin. A quarter seems a rather paltry sum coming from a fairy, don't you think? According to the literature, fairies have pockets filled with gold dust. Wouldn't a fairy more likely leave a chest filled with semi-precious stones, or a blank check?"

Rom offers a more credible solution. "A goblin might toss a piddling quarter. Goblins are notorious for scratchy pennies in slippers and bricks inside sweat socks. If we were told that the measly quarter came from the miserly tooth goblin, we might have considered the possibility. Now it's too late, now that we are old enough to have children of our own."

Aaron ruefully considers the children too tarnished by time and space to wish in innocence on a star. Sympathetic to Aaron's step-fatherly plight, Rom politely queries as his watch approaches midnight. "Is that the North Star over there, Mr. Mushkin?"

Aaron reluctantly divulges, "No, that's a weather satellite: space rubble."

Reem in turn makes his selection. "What about that one! It's so bright, it must be..."

"A military probe: more space rubble, falling out of orbit. That's why it's so brilliant. It's breaking up, burning out, about to smash someone's roof in. No, the North Star is — there!"

Rom expresses his disbelief. "Are you sure? Looks kind of dull for a famous star."

Before Aaron can assure its identity, Reem suddenly confesses. "Now I remember. How could we have forgotten,

Rom? It got us into such trouble the first time. Our mother's second husband, our biological father, took us to a planetarium when we were six. Remember Rom? He tested us and we failed. We correctly named the cloud formations but we couldn't locate the North Star. We couldn't tell Venus from Vegas from Jupiter so he wouldn't give us the purple lollipops. He couldn't eat them himself so he flicked them into the trash bin. Purple lollipops with spiced cinnamon eyes and lemon wedge smiles, remember? Mom got especially mad."

Rom belligerently denies remembrance. Reem prods, "Yes, this was the day our father, the biological one, told us about the modular people." Reem turns to Aaron and edifies. "He pulled them out of his shirt pocket. They weren't actual people. They were only blueprints at the time. I remember the sketches, the elaborate micro-circuitry, the endless lectures about humans not keeping pace, not taking advantage of their own technologic breakthroughs. He proposed we replace the four-chambered heart with a more reliable device, then network everyone's brains so humans could act more cohesively. He postulated civilizations would last longer if individuals didn't vary so much. His first proposal was to deactivate our taste buds. He reasoned we would waste less time designing salad dressings and conjuring special sauces for our Burger Blasters. It was shortly after that outing, he divorced mother, or rather she divorced him. On the other hand, we never heard from him again, or his dependable modular people."

Reluctantly, Reem further confesses. "I dreamed of him once. I dreamed he had a baby, created from items in his golf cart. He seemed very pleased with the final product, but to me, it looked like an erector set with no movable parts. Rom dreams about him often and it is often the same dream. In Rom's dream, our father has a dog but he cuts off the head, doesn't he Rom?"

Rom nods dejectedly. "Yes, Reem. Happily I forgot, but again you have reminded me. Yes, in it, he is a swollen brain pod and he cuts off the head of a small white puppy and he puts it on his disembodied, floating hand and he plays it like a puppet. It shouldn't frighten me. After all, it is only a dream."

Turning to Reem, Rom snipes, "A dream I do hate to recall. Why do you keep finding it, Reem?"

Reem cites his extenuating circumstance: "This time it wasn't my fault. It was Mr. Mushkin and his North Stars — that are really falling satellites. I didn't want to come here, either."

As the clock inside strikes twelve, Rom briefly considers the North Star before solemnly setting his watch one minute past midnight.

VISION QUEST

The next morning, Aaron's car won't start. Stuck in a dust bowl of cranking windmills and clanking clickadees, the twins grumble and gripe. Desperately, they attempt to find the Holy Lantern before their batteries run dead. Old Jones and Aaron tinker under the front hood, misconnecting wires, ritually tightening joints, sprinkling a dab of oil here, then a drop of water there. Yet another dirty rag is tossed onto the rag-littered roof. Still, the car won't start.

Old Jones grimaces. "Well, don't know, don't know, but this here hose is cracked. Could be this hose. Got any tape?"

"I'll check my trunk."

As Aaron backtracks towards his truck, Reem and Rom eye each other knowingly. Aaron's trunk is filled to the brim with scraps of lumber, fragments of metal, deformed plastic tops, cracked glass bottoms embedded in a medley of smashed odds, broken ends, and damaged what-nots. Jones is staggered by the sheer variety of stuff. "What is this junk?"

The twins confirm. "Junk. Our dad collects it." In this case, "our dad" is meant in the derogatory. Clearly, there can be no genetic claim between such a man and themselves.

Reem alleges, "That's why he drives so slowly. He received a ticket recently for driving dangerously under speed. Isn't that right, Rom?"

"Oh, yes, but he has to drive under speed so he won't miss the road kill and fresh litter. This trip we picked up three hub caps, one toilet seat, and we buried a muskrat."

"He says he can recycle it all."

"In the meantime, our basement fills with more and more junk. I think once, he used a strip of rope."

"No, Rom. It broke, remember? He had to throw it out."

"I stand corrected. However, I doubt he actually threw it out, Reem. I think it is still in the basement next to that orange refrigerator door with the chipped, chocolate-chip magnet."

Aaron is not the least insulted. Nothing Rom or Reem has said is the least untrue. If only he can scrounge a few inches of tape to justify his recycling efforts. Happily, something catches Jones's attention. "Whoa! Look at this aero-dynamic gem! Would make a perfect windmill blade. However many you've got, I'll take them all."

Aaron perks. "Well, I only have that one."

Jones abruptly loses interest. "Hell, one's no damn good. Got to have a balanced pair. One's just junk." As Jones tosses the scrap metal back into the trunk, Aaron worries what little bond he was able to create with Rom and Reem will quickly unglue if he keeps them here one moment longer. Jones has a suggestion.

"No local service stations, but we've got one great mechanic. Unfortunately, she's visiting her parents. Won't be back till Monday. Quince has got a wagon. Why not have him drop you at the Splitsville railway station? When Manigan returns, she'll set this back in motion. I'll drive it back myself. Got some business your way. Would love to meet Grace so it all works out. Quince won't mind. He's been on his way to Qwaquiwei territory for three days now. Splitsville's not more than twenty miles west of there. Just make sure you drive. Hey, Quincy!"

Jones makes the necessary arrangements. Within the hour, Aaron is behind the wheel of Quincy's dilapidated wagon. Rom and Reem sniff suspiciously before settling into the tattered back seats. Luckily, their batteries are still ticking. Almost immediately, they forget their bleak accommodations as they become absorbed in the pursuit of the Holy Lantern. Unfortunately, the front passenger seat is broken. Quincy necessarily seats himself between Rom and Reem. Without asking, Quincy snatches the electronic game, then proceeds to randomly press buttons. The Wizard is not amused. Eerie noises sputter from the device. Rom tries to repossess it, but not before Quincy hits another fatal button, invoking another fateful wail. Angrily retaking the device, Reem reproves. "Look what you've done! You stepped onto an instant death grenade in the goblin's hospitality suite. Didn't you see it coming?"

Unperturbed by his calamitous gaffe, Quincy studies Rom, Reem respectively. "Hey, which one of you is identical?"

Rom sardonically retaliates. "We're twins."

"Yes, but which one is the identical one?"

Refusing to succumb to the ploy, Reem asserts. "We are both identical. We are identical to each other."

Quincy squalls at such a preposterous notion. "You can be a mirror image of the image in the mirror but you cannot be a reflection of the reflection. One of you is lying." Quincy further tests the boys. Extending his left pointer finger from his bulbous fist, he pricks Rom. "You see this finger?" Reluctantly Rom nods. Turning to Reem, Quincy repeats, "You? You see this finger?" Though suspecting some artful dodge, Reem, in turn, nods. Assured they have attested to the finger, Quincy plunges his hands behind his back, jiggles his body as if shuffling a deck of cards, then thrusts his hands forward with his ten fingers defiantly flared. After burping a bit of Bourbon, he mischievously taunts. "Okay. Only the half of you that's real will be able to pick it out."

Unable to deduce whether he is being very zen or just insulting, the twins opt to nap. Rom tries to find a portion of window against which to rest his head. Tentatively, he runs his finger down the glass. It is layered in grime. Meanwhile, Reem tries to tuck his scrawny legs into a pensive yoga posture. Unfortunately, Quincy's bumptious torso cramps Reem's workable space. To make matters worse, the vehicle begins to wheeze. Rom nervously analyzes the commotion. "Sounds like the engine is stalling. Are we about to blow up?"

Aaron attentively fiddles with the fuel pedal. Reem strains forward, hoping to estimate the pending detonation. The noises grow increasingly bizarre. Notes, attenuated like violin strings dolorously stretched then twisted, reverberate through the vehicle. Rom surreptitiously assesses Quincy. Perhaps the rumblings are man-made. Perhaps certain bodily fluids are taking a decidedly wrong turn. Inching away from Quincy, Rom insistently tugs at Aaron's sleeve. "What's that gurgling noise? Doesn't sound healthy. Perhaps we should wait for this Manigan lady. Or maybe we can walk. Just how far is Qwaquiwei?"

Aaron chuckles in disbelief. "You can't be serious. This is a tape recording. Haven't you ever heard humpback whales? Jones thought we'd find the accompaniment contemplative, diverting."

The twins brighten. "A tape recording? A tape recorder! We could use the batteries."

"No batteries. This is a wind-up."

"A wind-up? You mean, you have to apply physical forces? How primitive. And, are you sure these are whales? A little off-key. Where's their background guitar, the jazzy piccolo to adjust for all those sour notes?"

"No guitar smoke screen, no intrusive instrumentation. Just raw whale melodies. Haunting, riveting, don't you think? Can't you just hear these titanic creatures caroling to each other across the ocean?"

Reem left-handedly agrees. "Exactly! What a racket! Who can sleep? They sound like asthmatic cows."

Rom appends, "Rasping, gasping crows, spasmodically hiccuping; warthogs regurgitating rotting rats."

Reem summarizes, "Clearly something dying or in disrepair. Hardly contemplative."

"Yes, hardly."

Having prevailed in their devastating critique, the twins roll their eyes into the back of their heads for the duration.

In contrast, in spite, Quincy refuses to doze. Each time Aaron checks his rear mirror, he confronts Quincy's gloating gaze. In defense, Aaron contemplates the road, dotted with dusty towns and burger concessions. The route brings back memories. Not far from here, Aaron ranged an open plain speckled with joshua trees and jojo bushes. It was an easy watch, managed by a resourceful clan of prairie dogs. Unfortunately, it was removed from the government protection program. Shortly afterward, it was delivered to developers for dissection. The prairie dogs were ground into dog food. The joshuas and jojos were bulldozed under parking lots. Despite this seeming glaze of civilization, few people inhabit the all too desiccate environment.

Hours pass. Aaron tries to count in reverse to stay awake. He keeps losing his place. Was he at two-hundred and eighty-one, or eight-hundred and twenty-one? Aaron surrenders to counting forward. He runs into the same problem. Was he at six hundred and forty-nine, or four hundred and sixty-nine? Eventually, he gets to nine-hundred and fifty-eight. At nine-hundred and fifty-nine, Aaron buckles forward.

Thinking he has blown a tire, Aaron precipitously slows. Again, his seat buckles forward as Quincy adjusts the seat to relieve his cramping legs. They are almost due west of Splitsville. Aaron wants to head directly to the railway station. Stubbornly, Quincy insists upon refreshing himself at the Qwaquiwei reservation. Aaron does not argue. Technically, he is Quincy's passenger. Besides, the remote mesa is a refreshing contrast to the compressive metropolis. Aaron recalls his original crayon rendition: zigzags of rust red, splotches of forest greens, and waves of popsicle purple on a strip of pink construction paper. Aaron's childhood paraphrase was prompted by his grandfather's account that a rainbow, lingering past the mist, had melted onto a mountain. Aaron continues to conjure memories as the mythical cliff comes breathtakingly into view.

No picture can capture the impression: a vast expanse of sky the intensity of sapphire — mountains like sand sculptures in colonnades of crimson and ocher — aromatic traces from blossoming wild flowers, and burning sage from distant ceremonies — a waterfall cascading into kaleidoscopic eddies — a jauntily tacking stream twisting tendrils of weeping fruit palms into capering maypoles — the desert scrub dappling the mystically spare plain — adobe huts like baking mushrooms in the whiffling dust.

Aaron places the car into park, then turns off the ignition. Cautiously, Quincy places his feet on his native ground. His typically rancid persona seems to soften. He appears more diffident, conciliatory as he comes to rest in his home sweet home.

A Qwaquiwei is hauling water from a well. Another mends his mud hut while children race by, chasing pine cones with hickory branches. Fires brew pots of savory stews. A woman tosses a few more sprigs into her cauldron. A man delivers blankets to a row of huts. A toddler chases a rooster past an old man playing a flute. On the distant cliff, circles of tribes people tom-tom their bare feet and chant "qwaquiwei, qwaquiwei, qwaquiwei."

Sadu Qwa rushes to greet Quincy. Aaron is surprised to see the legendary Qwaquiwei shaman hugging the infamous Qwaquiwei drunk with such seeming fondness.

"What brings the Raccoon back to the reservation?" Smelling the bourbon on Quincy's breath, Sadu Qwa astutely sobers. "Perhaps you hear God when you drink, Quincy, but know you can only obey the devil. Have you come to make peace with the Lord Mother? And who are these?" As Sadu Qwa affectionately strokes Aaron's hair, Quincy relates their unfortunate happenstance. Sadu Qwa half-listens as if she has already heard. "I recognize this Spirit. I often see him in the beaver pond." As the twins sheepishly adjust their glasses, Sadu Qwa inquires, "Is this your father?"

Reem hastens to correct, "Step-father."

Sadu Qwa ingenuously nods. "A *step* father? No doubt meaning one who steps before, making the way clear for those who follow." The twins suspect they are being obscurely reprimanded as Sadu Qwa continues. "We call him Beaver Spirit. He takes care of his forest the way the beaver takes care of his pond. With a beaver in the pond, everyone prospers. A beaver will deepen the waters so fish may flourish, so gulls may feast on the thickening flicker flies, and frogs delight on their lily pads. A beaver mates for life, brings bouquets of clover to his nesting lady, conceives one child so he may teach it well. I married a raccoon. A raccoon mates one evening, then abandons his victim lady. She is left to rear a litter of sucklings. Raccoon never knows his own children. He will mate with his own daughter, eat his own young. He will steal a squirrel's hard-earned stash of nuts. He is a scamp and a scoundrel." Aaron suspects a former intimacy as Sadu Qwa compassionately concludes. "But we cannot judge them. They are *step* fathers too. A step is a step whether it is brought forward, or left behind."

Sadu Qwa approaches the twins. "May I put these young men to use? I am on a vision quest — for rock demons."

Rom and Reem perk in their defense. "Uh, no thank you."

"No, no thank you. We're still searching for the key to the Secret Cavern."

"Trying to find it before these batteries run dead."

Sadu Qwa aligns her spine in commiserate reverence. "So you are also on a vision quest."

"Yes, in search of the Holy Lantern."

"I see. And why do you seek this lantern?"

Having never contemplated the goal, Rom looks to Reem. Reem whimsically responds. "It is the object of the game. If you find the Holy Lantern, you win."

"What?"

Thinking Sadu Qwa is slow to comprehend, Reem trudgingly repeats. "The object — of the game — is to find — the Holy Lantern. If you find — the Holy Lantern — you win."

Realizing that Reem is slow to comprehend, Sadu Qwa returns, "What? What — do — you — win?"

As Reem is driven silent, Rom giggles self-consciously. "Oh! Well, for one thing, you beat Cindy Jacobs at something. She already has the key."

Hastily, Reem defends, "Because she purchased her game an entire month before we purchased ours. We had to wait for a back order. According to the manufacturer, Socrates Software, only thirty-four of twenty thousand licensed players have reached the Wizard's Castle. You see, each time you complete a trial or tribulation, you have to upload your solution for inspection; if it passes, you may proceed in your mission, download the next segment of game code, that is, the next trial or tribulation. So far, only a handful of players have obtained the final code-set, the one containing the key to the Secret Cavern."

Rom proudly bubbles, "And no one, no one has submitted the encrypted win-message so, to date, no one has found the coveted Lantern. You have to be able to figure very sophisticated calculations in order to map out the underlying matrix, and you only get a certain number of chances in the form of seven wands. Once you use up your magic wands, the game is programmed to self-destruct. You can't purchase another copy because it is licensed according to thumb print. It was designed by Socrates Software to teach— teach—"

Rom defers to Reem, who reflects with certitude. "Well, clearly something of great importance because everyone who completes the game is granted an internship in their Creative Games Division."

Quincy gleams, "So how many points did I get?"

Rom explodes. "None! Not only that, you cost us one wand."

Sadu Qwa chides Quincy. "Raccoons always stealing."

Reem defensively boasts. "But of course, we're not worried."

Rom corroborates. "No, not worried. We're already inside the Wizard's Castle."

"So it is just a matter of time until we secure the key to the Cavern."

"Then find the Lantern. And we still have six wands left."

Sadu Qwa seems impressed. "Six wands left and one stolen: according to my calculations, that makes you virgins. I need virgins." Sadu Qwa commands Aaron. "Beaver Spirit, join the dancers on the setting Cliff. Before the corn is dry, the fire is cold, join your Qwaquiwei blood. Quincy must rest before he can drive you to the station."

Partly honored, partly curious, Aaron does not argue. Qwaquiwei rarely allow outsiders into their territorial circles. Aaron assures the twins that it won't be much longer. Sadu Qwa offers her additional assurance. "Not too long. Raccoons hardly sleep. Too busy doing mischief."

Troubled by a deeper mischief, Aaron lingers. "It is not my place or business, but the sacred Cliff of Ancients has been sold to Deloy Enterprises. The sacred Cliff? How could Qwaquiwei have let that happen?"

Indeed, without sky-scrapers or totems, the cliff, with its sedimentary gashes of red and ocher and reflecting flecks of mica, is the defining signet of the Qwaquiwei people. They have asked for so little for so long. This wounding incision upon their heritage could mangle their culture beyond repair. To Aaron, this seems a form of suicide. Dutifully, he informs, "If there was misrepresentation, a misunderstanding, you have the option to sue. You can..."

Sadu Qwa sternly avers, "It will be what it will be if it is the will of the Ancients. Perhaps they grow tired of our callused feet waking them from their blissful dreams with our worldly troubles. Perhaps this is the release we have been seeking: a transfer of guardianship. This coming Eve of Inner Lightning, Qwaquiwei may at last shed this dusty husk, evaporate into the wider vapors. In that case, we will need no cliff of clay to weight our mist spirits."

Aaron is about to say, "But you don't seriously believe?" when he realizes she seriously does. It is a discomforting thought. There will be no one to bear the burden of the righteous way. Humankind will nibble themselves into oblivion, grind the planet into its primordial dust, gnaw at their very tails, never connecting the insufferable pain with their own handiwork. Aaron may be among the last to dance around the fire of Qwa. His Qwaquiwei blood mysteriously awakened, Aaron proceeds to his commanded destination.

Abandoned to their fate, the twins resignedly scan for rocks. After tripping over a troublesome stone, Reem angrily offers it to Sadu Qwa.

Sadu Qwa gravely probes, "What is this?"

Reem notes the obvious. "A rock. Didn't you say..."

"Did it speak to you?"

Reem again notes the obvious. "Of course not."

Tossing the mute offering over her shoulder, Sadu Qwa instructs Reem. "The rock must speak to you." Overhearing this constrictive specification, observing the rejected rock smash to bits, Rom jettisons his fistful of equally reticent stones.

Meanwhile, Aaron scales the imposing Cliff of Ancients. With each body length forward, the rarefied air seems to further distill. By the time Aaron reaches the summit, the course molecules of oxygen have alchemized into a transcendent ether.

Aaron leerily pauses. The fire of Qwa seems to be raging out of control. Adults appear unconcerned as small children gambol within inches of the blistering flames. Fire tenders steadfastly sustain the engulfing ferocity with unwieldy chunks of wood and bundles of sage. A giggling toddler rushes dangerously close to the unpredictable flames in order to pitch her twig offering. Dancers, on some seeming cue, fling their anointed corn husks. Like fire crackers, the sweet kernels crackle and burst. All the while drums and sticks beat unwaveringly to the subtly deafening chant: "qwaquiwei, qwiquawei, quiweiqwa, weiqwaqui, weiquiqwa, qweiwaqui, eiqwaqwui, eiqwuiqwa, waqweiqui, waqquiwei, weqwiiqua, weqquawii." Each phrase is a variation on qwaquiwei; each orbit of dancers maintains a particular chant string so that one orbit of chanting dancers echoes another orbit of chanting dancers, ring within ring, echo within echo.

A young girl coaxes Aaron to remove his shirt so she can insulate his upper body with moistened mud. A young boy hands Aaron an ear of corn from a pile of decorated husks. Starting at the outermost orbit around the fire, Aaron takes his first tentative steps. Upon chanting 'qwaquiwei,' Aaron hears the echoing *qwiquawei*, then *quiweiqwa*, then *weiquaqui*, then *weiquiqwa*. The hypnotic variations, with their interleaving vibrations, perforate his skin, resonate within his long sleeping soul.

After completing several cycles, Aaron finds himself stepping sideways into the next inner ring. Effortlessly he pivots into its opposite direction where he takes up his new chant string. The movements seem automatic, but not automated. He feels possessed, or rather empowered by a hitherto unrevealed self. His body undulates. His head swirls.

His mind cautions him to remain at a calm, collected distance. All the while his impulse is to merge with the mastering salvation of Qwa, to dissolve unconditionally into the blazing, magnetic center.

Again Aaron steps sideways into the next inner ring. Cycle after cycle, ring after ring, Aaron chants "qwaquiwei, qwiquawei, quiweiqwa, weiqwaqui, weiquiqwa, qweiwaqui, eiqwaqwui, eiqwuiqwa, waqweiqui, waqquiwei, weqwiiqua, weqquawii." As the sun begins the set, Aaron finds himself one fragile body length from the feverishly ascending fire of Qwa. Images flash at the back of his head like visual expletives. He sees himself flickering in the distant darkness like a firefly, swept like a leaf into the ocean. Precariously he drifts. At any moment the merest wave can drown him. The ground palpably quivers as Aaron enters the innermost circle. This last time, Aaron sees himself for the first time: a flickering fire fly, on a crumbling leaf, on a fracturing eggshell. All his life, he has been asleep to the smoldering yolk beneath. At any moment this incubating planet may...

A flame strikes into the dancers, dislodging Aaron from his orbit. Dizzily, he spills into the outer corn husk heap. The unaffected dancers take no note, continue to dance, continue to chant. Slowly, Aaron regains his senses. Slowly, he shifts. As he attempts to rise, his elbow accidentally strikes a fallen fellow — Quincy, eyes closed, flat on his back, rapturously chanting "qwaquiwei, qwiquawei, weiqwaqui, weiquiqwa."

Aaron shakes Quincy from his trance. "I thought you were resting."

"Am resting, sobering from the intemperateness of civilization."

Fresh from his altered state of consciousness, Aaron senses a lying dog. "It was you! You sold the Cliff of Ancients to Deloy Enterprises. You had the authority. How could you? How could you betray your people, betray Sadu Qwa? How could you single-handedly destroy, ruin— Don't you realize what you've done, you— you—" As Aaron struggles to smite Quincy with a rending epithet, Quincy, confiding no remorse, remarks bitterly.

"What do you know? Your doting Almighty lets you into heaven on the flimsiest of moral details. Qwaquiwei must oblige a planet Queen who gives us no more credit than lice. I have tried so hard, so long. Well, I'm tired, tired of waiting for Lord Mother to fulfill her promise to the Qwaquiwei nation. We do not belong here, among the struggling seeds and toiling worms and peoples like you. Curse our ancestors for sinning, for having us banished to this compost heap. What chance have we to redeem ourselves now that your kind have salted this planet with your poisonous refinements. We are damned for all eternity."

Plucking pebbles from his mud-stuccoed chest hairs, Aaron chastises. "A fine one to talk. What about people like Old Man Jones, people genuinely making a difference? Why not work with them?"

"Too little, too late."

"Meaning you'd rather give up, let the blood be on someone else's hands."

Quincy smears a smile. "That's one strategy."

Aaron observes an evident flaw. "Then why are you here? Atoning?"

For a moment, Quincy seems to ponder the paradox. "Raccoons always driven by hunger. Not always in the belly, though. After feasting and drinking and drugging myself into oblivion, I remain maddeningly unsatiated, maddeningly awake. You don't know how it is, how it was. I once shared a life with Sadu Qwa. As a man, I shared her bed. As a shaman, I shared her soul. We were united in our vision quests. It seemed to me what happened, happened all of a sudden. It seemed to me that one day I woke to find myself deaf, dumb, and blinded. It must have been happening, happening. We presume if we live long enough, we will incrementally grow wise. But this state of knowing is like the state of health: one can simply grow sicker. Perhaps I am just growing old, willing to forfeit my body as it militates against me. What use are the mating songs of the daydream warbler or the amorous fragrance of the rolling rose? As the supple body hardens, as the feet conform to the grave-ground, the seeker loses hope.

Having failed to find the inward path to heaven, I have surrendered to the downward path to hell. If I cannot win the Lord Mother's grace, I will provoke her wrath. I don't care how she comes, whether she comes to bestow her blessings — or strike us dead, so long as she finally gets here."

From the towering Cliff of Ancients, Quincy gazes down at Sadu Qwa as she carefully positions another rock.

Her circle is nearly complete. No thanks to Reem who continues to protest her story. "Let me get this straight: if you married a raccoon, how could you have produced a normal child? It's not genetically possible. If you married a raccoon, which you couldn't have unless, unless that is why your son died. He was a mutant? Like those evolutionists, like that man in that horror movie who garbled half his body, metamorphosed into half a fruit fly, but that— well, that was purely for entertainment purposes, so you must be speaking metaphorically. This is some kind of tribal jargon, isn't it?"

Sadu Qwa nods pensively. "With intelligence comes the sheerest stupidity."

Reem grows exasperated. "There you go again. Trying to rile me with these quaint but annoying, counter-intuitive declarations of yours. Well, forget it. I'm very well-educated, therefore immune to these..."

"I thought to educate meant to enlighten, not to immune. If one is ever to imbibe wisdom, one must become susceptible."

Reem refuses to be bested. "You're doing it again. If I wanted, I could conjure my own nonsensical..."

"Then I would have to strike you."

"You would — hit me?" Reem is devastated by this proposition.

"To keep you from falling hopelessly out of reach, I would cut off your legs. Yes, such is a mother's love." Sadu Qwa kneels to readjust a rock, then proceeds down the spiral chanting "qwaquiwei" for each rock, each time stepping to the opposite side of the succeeding rock, entering deeper and deeper into the circle.

Horrified at the thought of losing his legs, Reem nervously equivocates. "I think I'm leaving you with the wrong impression. I get what you're getting at, kind of. You're the environmental type. I'm more or less on your side. After all, I was born into this age of diminishing resources. This planet is going to run out of oxygen before my sixteenth birthday, but I'm making the best of it. My social science class has generously adopted a tribe in Zambambulia. We're getting extra credit for building them a septic tank and Burger Blaster concession. Since Zambambulia has no grazing land, we replaced the beef with yakakee meat. It's a little tougher but we've customized the special sauce so you hardly notice. And since they can't afford the price of fossil fuel, we're employing solar technology. So far, we've solicited enough donations to purchase the requisite aluminum panels and photo voltaic cells. We just finished modifying the electric sensor to guide the panels. As soon as the collector tank arrives, those Zambambulians are in business."

Sadu Qwa pauses, unimpressed. "Don't need no panels, no copper tubing, no pumps, no tanks. Just put in a damn window and let in the light. Don't need no anemometers, no aerodynamic blades. Just open the damn door and let the breeze pass."

Reem decides not to press his case. Reluctantly, he resumes his rock search. Occasionally, he kicks over a stone to ascertain if a scorpion is lurking beneath. He is certain there are no talking rocks.

His brother refuses to give up. Every so often, Rom selects a prospective candidate and holds it to his ear. He hears the wind through the leaves, the birds in the sky, the coyotes in the hills, the crickets in the grass. He hears the water tumultuously cascading down the cliff wall, but the rocks remain obdurately silent. Carefully, Rom observes Sadu Qwa performing her private dance along the spiraling circle. Emboldened by curiosity, Rom ventures. "How did you get to be a witch doctor? I mean, medicine man. Were you born this way? Do you see spirits, hear voices? Can you hypnotize snakes?"

Persevering in her ritual steps, Sadu Qwa answers unreservedly. "I was born knowing. We are all born knowing. That is why we come into this world kicking, screaming. Too soon we are lulled into the waking dream by brightly rattling gourds, sweet corn laced with sweeter honey. Just like this planet, our molten blood convects within, enslaving our attentions; we cannot help but suffocate within the smothering layers of sinew and bone. Still, I was not distracted. I refused to release my golden thread, the umbilical cord which leads back to the wombs of heaven. While my friends played run-around-the-pine-cone, learned their graded lessons, I re-ascended the cord, escaped the body just in time. You see, at nine, ten, eleven years of age, the skull shuts close, the cord gets severed, the inner eye plunges into darkness. In this way, the mind sets, the heart hardens, the experience becomes memory — the memory dies. One becomes a ghost in one's own lifetime."

Rom perplexes. "But if you escaped, why are you still here?"

"I am here, but not here. It is a shaman's blessing and curse to serve the drowning. Often, I must descend the cord, re-enter the body to nourish the needful heart, calm the turbulent blood, inflate the dispirited lungs, embolden the collapsing gut, tidy the entangled mind, guide the seminal flux. Even as the body ruptures and rots, I must remain its loyal keeper."

Unable to decipher the metaphors, Rom distractedly taps at his unresponding console. Sadu Qwa speculates. "And you? You masquerade as this Wizard hoping to secure his Lantern. I see no golden thread tied to your thumb. You think you can re-ascend given enough wands and the correct algorithm?"

Rom does not like playing disciple. Defiantly he challenges. "And you? You get to where you get by laying down rocks? Is that what I'm supposed to believe? Exactly — exactly what are you doing here?"

Sadu Qwa playfully demurs. "Trying to coax out the demons." Sensing Rom's consternation, Sadu Qwa assures. "Not like your demons, so ugly and ill-mannered. We seek to make peace with our demons. They are the children we have born out of wedlock, or disowned, or failed to give proper birth. Often they bear a gift: a gift too great to bear. One may easily be crushed by truth. We call it a dark dream because we are blinded by its almighty light."

Rom brightens. At last, something to which he can relate. "Oh, oh! So that's their story. What a relief. I have dark dreams. Never seem to have much of a plot, just murky images, disquieting feelings. I once ran them through my Dr. Diagnose program. It indicated a lack of folic carbonate to the medulla oblongata. I'm overdue for an upgrade. Perhaps the new version includes this almighty-light scenario. Why, just last night I dreamed— Course, it seems so silly now. Would you believe, I was attacked by a pack of cottonwoods? After surrounding me, the very largest insisted she was my mother. She tried to pry off my shoes with her wizeny branches so my toes could root. Imagine being a tree for the rest of your life. So unbearably, unbearably boring."

Sadu Qwa commiserates. "Hard for us: we who chase the wind, though never, never catching it, never catching on. In contrast, how patiently the trees bear witness. See that whisperwill? Three thousand years old. She can reveal things long past, moments scrolled out of view, rolled into her recorded rings like sepulchered heirlooms. Look at them." Sadu Qwa indicates the various clutches of whisperwills, cottonwoods, honeysaps. "Surrounding us as you dreamed. What if they yanked out their roots to join our frenzied dance? What if they bloomed and died in one hasty season? It would be like a civilization lost."

As Rom suspiciously counts the pack of cottonwoods, Sadu Qwa unburdens her own darker dream. "You and I may appear separate blades of grass: you flowing right, I flowing left, but the tree beholds a single field of green, undulating to the same doleful tune. Last night, I found myself ascending the Cliff of Ancients. In my haste to reach the top, to petition the Lord Mother, I carelessly clutched a young sprig growing from the cliff face. My aged weight was more than the new growth could bear. I ripped it out. In turn, an unseen force ripped me out, plunged me into a raging whirlpool below. I struggled, struggled until I wakened. But I did not *awaken,* so I have recreated my dream here, hoping to knead the tumultuous whirlpool into a delivering womb. I require one last rock."

Reluctantly, Rom presents his concealed offering: a small, pock-marked lava stone. However, before he can justify his selection, he is distracted by his brother's distant screams. Reflexively dropping his rock, Rom races towards Reem.

Having given up on talking rocks, Reem went looking for lizards. They were more easily sighted than caught. Nevertheless, his forbearance paid off. Reem hovers over a fledgling eagle, newly fallen from its nest. One wing appears broken. Aaron and Quincy stand on either side in rapt attendance. Crouching solicitously beside the injured creature, Reem indicates to Aaron. "It's just a baby. Shouldn't we put it back in its nest?"

Quincy responds autocratically. "Can't you see, it has fallen? Like humpty dumpty, it cannot be put back. It must die. Nature has decided."

As the fire dancers descend the Cliff, a curious crowd gathers. Reem implores, "But surely someone can scale the cliff, return the eagle to its nest?"

Aaron tries to explain nature's harsh strategy. "It would be no use, Reem. Eagles often lay two eggs. If one hatches then dies, there is the chance the second will hatch, will survive. If both hatch and thrive, invariably one will be more mature and stronger. The older eaglet instinctively defends its territory, competes for the food its mother..."

Quincy dishes the more grizzly details. "In other words, the second is just a back-up. The stronger will hack the weaker with its sharp, deadly beak. I have seen hatchlings with their stomachs shredded. Mercilessly harassed from the nest, many plunge to their deaths. It is a wonder this one was not immediately killed."

Reem is undeterred. "Then I will take it home, care for it myself."

"You will take nothing that is not yours. This is Qwaquiwei territory. Here, you follow Qwaquiwei law."

"But you'll just let it die."

"I will do as I must do. I am Qwaquiwei. This is Qwaquiwei land. This is Qwaquiwei law."

Sadu Qwa approaches Quincy scathingly. "If you lived the law so well as you quote it. How can we dispute the boy's claim?"

Reddening, Quincy quibbles. "He cannot partake of this eagle. Its spirit was clearly meant to anoint this ground. This ground must need anointing. The boy is here by chance, in error. Besides, he is not Qwaquiwei. He cannot partake."

"Is not his father Qwaquiwei? Do we not recognize the merest shadow of qwa? And did you not bring him here? Against his will? Were you perhaps following a higher will?"

"These boys are step-children, Sadu Qwa. Mushkin is not their biological father. He is not even married to their mother so they cannot..."

Snatching a child from her parent, Sadu Qwa displays the little girl to the crowd. Innocently she giggles, despite the griping gravity with which Sadu Qwa maintains her hold. "When a baby is born, we perform a ritual. It is called the Embracing." Sadu Qwa sovereignly bristles at Quincy. "Do you not remember?"

Quincy winces at this reference to their dead son. Sadu Qwa continues. "The Embracing cautions the woman who carried, the man who conveyed, that mere intermingling of body fluids did not cause their child to be. A child is a gift from the Lord Mother, like the garden Earth was a gift to Qwaquiwei. Let no one imagine the divine qwa drips from the body like hemoglobin from a slaughtered cow. No, the qwa flutters from the heart like a wave passes upon the ocean."

Gently, Sadu Qwa releases the child. She toddles towards the fallen eagle which Reem so diligently defends. In the tranquil hush, Sadu Qwa pronounces. "This man calls these boys his children. These children call this man their father. I heard this child say 'father'."

Quincy counters, "He was being sarcastic."

Sadu Qwa insists, "Only after the word comes the revelation. I will not dispute the boy's claim. Neither shall you."

Reem cannot contain his joy. "So? I can keep the eagle?"

This time Aaron objects. "Not actually keep it. After all, it's not a gerbil. However, we can donate it to the avian specialists at the Animal Research Center. They have the facilities and expertise to..."

Sadu Qwa overrides his good intentions. "No. Neither you nor I, nor the Lord herself can condition or undo their covenant."

AN EAGLE IN THE HOUSE

"A live eagle?" As Grace considers the bird of prey inside her drawer, she cannot help but note to Aaron with some rancor. "When I bought goldfish for our backyard pond, you protested the introduction of wilderness critters into a domesticated setting, so please explain this predatory beast with its malevolent talons and razor sharp beak — inside my silk kimono and bath oil beads."

"Oh. I thought those were jelly beans." At a loss to explain, Aaron hedges. "Personally, I disapprove but what could I do, Grace? Sadu Qwa gave it to him."

"Remind me to thank her for not giving him a bush bear, or does Rom have one stuffed inside his knapsack? We haven't finished unpacking."

Before Aaron can assure Grace of no such stowaway, Rom prods his mother. "Look! Look what Sadu Qwa gave me."

Grace cautiously supposes, "A tarantula egg?"

"Don't be silly, Mother. It's a talking rock." As Rom extends the object for examination, he is thrown from his feet by his enthused sibling. Dangling bloodsucker worms from his fingers, Reem devotedly feeds his ravenous pet. Incredulous, Grace turns to Aaron.

"What is he doing? This can't be Reem. Not the boy who refuses to walk barefoot least microscopic dust mites traverse his talcum protected toes?" Perplexed, Grace pokes Reem in the back. "Reem? Did those native shamans slip you some peyote? Can't you see that those are mealy, mucky ickymacallits? All over my silk kimono!"

"Well, I couldn't find any mice. With all our strange contracts with ants and spiders, didn't we make any deals with nice juicy rodents? What a weekend! Did Dad tell you we ate bugs?"

Grace smiles an anemic smile as she contemplates the mounting misdeeds. "You fed them bugs?"

Fearing much too much is being left to the imagination, Aaron squiggles nervously. "Not exactly. They were antiantnoids, and they were an incidental ingredient. Perhaps I should explain."

Grace furrows her brow as she grouses. "To say the least. Unfortunately, I'm late. Expected you guys back yesterday. Expected to find Rom and Reem out of Munchies, out of batteries, and out of patience. Wasn't expecting souvenirs: no live eagles or tarantula eggs."

Rom interrupts to correct. "It's not a tarantula egg. It's a talking..."

Grace swings Webster into Aaron's arms as she summarily contends. "Whatever. I have to meet with Senator Seerington. There was a minor crisis last evening. Rom and Reem need to come with me. I made an appointment with their optometrist. I won't have time to return them, so they'll spend the day with me. Hear that, boys? Go pack some Munchies; I'm all out of bugs. As for you, Aaron? It's unlikely we'll be home for supper, so you and Webby make do."

Loath to separate from his coveted pet, Reem pleads. "Can I bring my eagle?"

"Absolutely not!"

"What about my talking rock?"

Cursorily assessing Rom's seemingly benign object, Grace relents. "All right, but it has to keep its mouth shut."

Left on his own, Aaron forlornly avers, "Missed you." To further amend, Aaron snuggles, then sniffs. "Interesting scent. Kind of musky and raw."

Wryly, Grace explains. "It's skunk."

Fortunately, Grace was one balcony up-wind from critical impact. Her dosage was mild compared to the unfortunate senators now sequestered at the request of unaffected members. The twenty-two offending skunks were rounded up and questioned. While none could be tied to members of SOIL, several belonged to a research scientist in sympathy with extremist elements.

Grace tries to maintain her composure while an aide smashes a fresh tomato atop Senator Seerington's head. Seeds dribble down his sideburns. The critically injured: Senators Seerington, Grady, Mungus, Fingerstein, Krommueller, and Dr. Vanetsky have been confined to the back room jacuzzi to conduct business. Aides enter and exit, pouring cans of tomato juice into the overflowing tub. Gloppy red bubbles burst and splatter as jet streams wriggle through the increasingly viscous liquid. Senator Krommueller is unusually silent as he glumly soaks his toupee. A few feet to his left, Senator Fingerstein tries to wipe the tomato juice from his glasses while a visiting dignitary distressfully observes his white robes become spattered with amorphous red globules. He seems genuinely mystified by the peculiar parliamentary ritual of naked, tomato-soaked senators.

Grace wonders why she has been summoned as she stands between the unknown dignitary and a somber Qwaquiwei tribesman, who surreptitiously winks at Rom, then Reem. Quietly, they sit in a corner licking their cocoa pops, refusing to acknowledge the pestering Quincy Qwa. Rom has neglected to pull the price tag off his new prescriptions.

Belligerently, Senator Seerington splashes Dr. Vanetsky. "How come we are still de-skunking the old-fashioned way? We can capture neutrinos, take shuttles to the moon, make decaffeinated tea taste like caffeinated coffee, but we have yet to develop some kind of masking ointment or convenient antidote to that malodorous vermin. Why can't we simply breed skunks not to stink? Why do they have to stink? How does that benefit society?"

Senator Mungus takes up the cause. "Yes, and why do piranhas have such vicious teeth? I saw them eat a cow on a nature documentary. Hear they also ate the cameraman. Now, I'm afraid to go fishing. What good is life if you can't go fishing? What's their story anyway? Do we look like flounders? We can't taste any good. We certainly can't be healthy. I thought dumb animals were supposed to be smarter than us in that respect.

How can I go fishing, knowing I may capsize, inhibited by the thought that a grazing piranha may munch my balls off?"

Senator Grady furiously hurls a pitcher of tomato juice at Senator Mungus. "Keep those private parts to yourself." The small jacuzzi is making strained bedfellows.

"Pardon me. I wasn't— Just trying to ascertain why we're always fighting the elements. Why can't we create a perfect bubble to live happily ever after in?"

"Why create what has been created?" The twins instinctively recoil as the wrathful Quincy Qwa enunciates. "It is called Earth: a big, blue bubble upon which you maggots prey."

Senator Seerington challenges. "Give it up, Quincy. We suspect you were one of the culprits. Kind of suspicious there were exactly twenty-two skunks. That's the number of years between Inner Lightnings, isn't it? Perhaps you planted those skunks to make some tribal point. We could have you hanged."

Still trying to wipe tomato juice from his glasses, Senator Fingerstein disputes. "No, no, we no longer hang Qwaquiweis. Not in keeping with our democratic notions. Besides, he has an alibi. He was at the Qwaquiwei reservation until this morning."

"Who will bear witness? Fellow Qwaquiwei don't count." Thinking they may be called upon to defend the unsavory Qwa, Rom and Reem plug their mouths with their cocoa pops. Fortunately, Quincy Qwa shows as little interest in protesting his innocence as Senator Seerington shows in seeking corroborating witnesses. Instead, Senator Seerington clamors, "Ivanosky! Is she here?"

Grace steps forward. "Yes, Senator."

"Ivanosky, they say you are a voice of reason, willing to see both sides. More importantly, you know a lot of people. Perhaps you can make a few calls, trade tit for tat, find out who was involved so we can string them— I mean, discuss the disparities in our viewpoints. Let's try to avoid another war. Just because one smarmy guy turned out not to be the messiah, do we all have to go to hell? Just because we can't pinpoint exactly where heaven begins and ends, doesn't mean there aren't other suitable stepping stones."

Grace circumspectly queries. "You want me to reconnoiter for possible paradises? A little out of my league."

Excusing his disdainful overtones, Seerington clarifies. "Pardon a portly, old man. I just don't understand. For a while, it seemed to be working. One continent, one government, more or less; a few ethnic, cultural renegades like Azukaway, Zambambulia, Qwaquiwei, and of course French Canada, but otherwise this great land of ours seemed to have tumbled onto the same bandwagon."

Senator Grady testily interjects. "You're making a speech Seerington. We agreed: no speech making, no farting, no exposed arm pits."

Seerington raises a sopping sponge over his head, defiantly displaying his tomato stained underarms. "Hey, I'm polling a fellow citizen. Need to know what's going on. Why the discontent? Most people are employed. Everyone has coats and shoes and library cards. No one is starving. Granted, few get rich and famous, but I thought that was understood. The reason behind free therapy: to help those less fortunate learn to live with the short end of the stick."

Pointing an accusatory finger at Rom and Reem, Senator Seerington bemoans. "Too many people addicted to fairytales, expecting frogs to turn into princes. When is it going to sink in? We aren't what we think we are. We are what we think other people are. We've got to stop looking in the mirror and start looking at the mothers who bore us, the sons we engendered. Too many..."

Senator Grady scoffs, "Big fat senators going bla, bla."

Undeterred, Seerington turns to a nearby page. "Take a memo, boy! Too many heroes walking into the sunset unscathed. Need to get out a public service announcement, remind our listening audience that in the real world, the frog gets eaten by the toad, the swan princess runs off with the butcher, and the hero dies. Too many would-be saviors expecting to get out alive. Not to implicate anyone but—" Senator Seerington waves towards Grace, "bet that Iroquois

Jefferson and those Soilists had a part in this skunk caper. Still trying to overthrow this government. What an incredibly meaningless act. Our good citizens will replace it with one just as maladaptive. Civilizations inevitably grow old and die. Not a single one transforms itself. Driven to mutation or extinction, they die ignoble deaths or barely survive, only to repeat the sins of their predecessors over and over ad nauseam. I've accepted it. Why the discussion?"

"Speaking of the sins of father—", Senator Fingerstein interjects, "we should consider mutant evolutionists. They could be involved. Not that I blame them. We kind of screwed them over, not intentionally, but we did create those toxic waste ghettos. People there suffer disproportional cancer rates, curious neurological disorders, and now this ASD scourge. The majority of mutant evolutionists come from those neighborhoods. That's one reason they avoid daylight. Their skin is usually sensitive. We should..."

"Round them up and bury them. Learn from our failures and move on. Cut the losers off at the pass. That's where you come in, Ivanosky. You have a reputation. You— you and that Jefferson guy go way back. You must— well, keep in touch, eh?"

Grace surmises she has not been summoned because of her reputation but because of "a" reputation, a rumor of a past liaison with Iroquois Jefferson. The esteemed subcommittee is not interested in bringing the disparate elements to the negotiating table. They simply want to wall off the encroaching floodwaters until after their re-elections. Grace is too angry to answer. Luckily, Senator Mungus takes center stage. An aide has cut too big a hole in a gallon tin of tomato juice. While the apologetic aide wipes the cascading liquid from Senator Mungus' eyes, the Senator whines. "Glory be! Now I'm seeing double. A little boy, holding an insinuating microphone, replicating himself as we speak."

Grace hastens to explain. "Those are my twin sons, Senator."

Mungus peers more closely. "If they're such twins, why are they out of sync?" Rom and Reem are licking their cocoa pops at different tempos, like a pair of pistons alternately engaging and disengaging. Used to the queer effect twins seem to have on non-twins, they obligingly re-synchronize, lick their pops in mesmerizing consonance. Grace smiles imperceptibly. Her children have learned the art of beguilement. Taking their cue, Grace renders a response more diplomatic than the one originally come to mind.

"You're only partly correct, Senator Seerington. Yes, I know a lot of people, unfortunately, all of them law-abiding citizens. And you have been misinformed. Iroquois Jefferson and I do not *keep in touch*. Needless to say, I am more than happy to arbitrate on your command. However, if you have nothing further to request, I shall excuse myself. I have an appointment with an important client."

Senator Seerington conjectures, "Deloy Enterprises? They're after him too. Trying to get back that ancestral land. Any excuse for mischief." Sensing he is not intimidating in the least degree, Senator Seerington roguishly forewarns. "In this world, it's who you know. Do you know who you know, Ivanosky, meaning — just who will be after you next?"

A PLAGUE ON PHARAOH

When Grace arrives at Deloy's electrostatic archway, she finds the doors splayed open. Several yards down the hall, Deloy's office, or rather its remains, continue to eject dust as uniformed and plainclothes police scour through the debris. Connery is visibly shaken. The ceiling over his desk has collapsed, destroying Tootsie, mangled beyond all recognition.

Connery maniacally paces back and forth. "I want her murderers found. I want..."

Wielding one of Tootsie's severed electronic limbs, a uniformed officer explains a fine point of law. "But sir, we can not consider it murder. Tootsie, if that is what you called it, was not an actual life form."

Connery halts, appalled by such provincial logic. "Not actual! She was more intelligent, more efficient, more charismatic than you'll ever be."

The scorned officer deferentially shrugs. "May well be the case, but she was not 'biological' according to prevailing definitions. If it is any consolation, sentences for destruction of property run harsher than for waylaying a life. Can afford to lose people; they routinely die, whereas valuable property is, well, valuable."

Connery is not listening. Instead, his eyes glower at the streets below where members of SOIL and activist Qwaquiwei threaten their respective vengeances. Waving a sheet of paper in the air, a plainclothesman tries to gain Connery's attention. "Exactly when did you receive this letter?"

After sheltering the twins in a corner, Grace solicitously petitions. "What's going on? What happened to your ceiling, Connery? What letter?"

Deloy remains fixated on the streets below, compelling the plainclothesman to acquaint Grace with the dire details. "This ceiling collapse does not appear accidental, especially in light of this letter. These past months, many political and industrial leaders have received threatening plague-on-pharaoh letters prior to some malicious mischief. Started with Pietri Numetri, the playboy tycoon. Woke one morning to find his hundred-foot swimming pool filled with dead fish and grape juice. What a mess. Grape stained his expensive ceramic tiles; rotting fish drove his bathing beauties into the whitecaps of other men. Co-interestingly, environment groups were accusing Numetri Juice Works of polluting the local lake. His plague letter predicted his river would fill with the blood of his deeds. Turns out, more glucose than hemoglobin.

"Then there was that incident with Elaina Bluebonnet of SweetCheeks Cosmetics. Animal rights groups were faulting her for using rabbits as guinea pigs, alleged the rabbits suffered unspeakable unpleasantries at the hands of her researchers. Bluebonnet defends her experiments. Hasn't quite found a cure for cancer, but she has ascertained that certain dyes can dissolve a rabbit's cornea, canker a cat's meow. Her plague-on-pharaoh letter cursed her with boils. Shortly thereafter, she developed mysterious eruptions on her— well, not polite to say, but no wonder. We turned up traces of itchymichticktahide, a bothersome skin irritant, on her office sofa."

Grace stalls his drift. "So what are you saying? There is some kind of plot?"

While fiddling with Connery's laser fly zapper, the plainclothesman speculates. "Let's just say some one, or some group is trying to make some kind of point. Why, just last week we had to rescue the well-known mountain developer Frederick Hisenbocker." After the plainclothesman heedlessly presses an on-off switch, a miniature beam darts across the room; the same moment, a uniformed policewomen yelps as her left sunglass mysteriously vaporizes. Precipitously dropping the firearm, the sharp-shooter accuses. "Hey, hey, hey! Is this Deloy fellah some kind of weapons dealer? This thing should be locked..."

Grace re-threads his thought. "What about Hisenbocker?"

"The mountain developer? Well, the week after he was threatened with hail, a suspicious avalanche struck his mountain resort. Had to yank arthritic Fred out an attic vent. Broke his collar bone. Extraordinarily, the houses on either side were not the least effected. Qwaquiwei, dislocated as a result his controversial development, proclaimed it an act of Lord Mother Earth." The officer cunningly winks. "Not quite. Found bulldozer tracks everywhere. Determined the snow was created artificially so we have cleared Mother Earth of any wrongdoing. By the way — who are you? Got clearance?"

Grace belatedly introduces herself. "I'm Mr. Deloy's lawyer, Grace Ivanosky."

"Of course. Thought you looked familiar. Wouldn't find me rattling on and on to nobody. Saw you once on *Meet the Powers Behind the Powers That Be*. You're kind of influential."

"Not really. I've prosecuted, defended some defining cases, arbitrated several—" Realizing she is resumizing, Grace discontinues mid-sentence. The plainclothesman takes up the slack.

"Yes, yes; you yourself were victim to one of those plague letters."

Grace confusedly counters, "No, I never..."

"One of the early ones as I recall, so I don't have to tell you. And of course, just prior to this Deloy assault, there was that skunk escapade on the Senate floor. What you don't know is that subcommittee was threatened with a swarm of *something*, that something to be determined by the pestilence at hand. To date, the department hasn't been overly concerned. However, this ceiling collapse is a more serious matter. Mr. Deloy was threatened with the last and most deadly plague: a curse on his firstborn."

Connery motions despairingly to the dismembered ruins. "Tootsie was manufactured from circuitry developed by my very first venture. All subsequent products evolved from that seed chip so, in a sense, she was..."

Grace takes up his defense. "This is more than malicious harassment. What is national enforcement doing to..."

"Well, as you know, Ms. Ivanosky, most of these letters are merely pranks, like that one you received."

Grace peevishly repeats, "I told you. I never..."

The officer blithely continues. "Never gave it a second thought. Just as well. Probably one of many crank letters you received for defending that textile mill. Lot of anti-industrialist sentiment out there. Most of these curses never come to pass. This one had a fatal flaw. It almost killed a man. Happily, we have a prime suspect. A known agitator, Iroquois Jefferson, was seen leaving these premises. Already got him under lock and key. Claims he merely rewired Tootsie to append 'big fat jerk' after Mr. Deloy's signature. How convenient the robot is no longer functioning to testify in his defense."

Connery storms towards the door. "I have to get out of here."

Bluntly collecting the twins, Grace hastens after. "Wait! There are contracts we have to discuss, papers you need to— I realize this must be unsettling, but don't let it derail you. That's how they win."

"I know that. Of course, I know that. Still, I can't stay here. Not with her lying— I have an apartment a few blocks upwind. Let's reconvene there. I can make dinner. You can..."

Connery steps back warily. Rom and Reem stand on either side like toy tin soldiers. "What— what are these? Security clones? Who's controlling them?"

Grace corrects, "These are my sons."

"You have clones for sons?"

"They're not clones; they're identical twins."

Disappointed by their lackluster origin, Connery bemoans. "Oh. Well, hope they like hot dogs."

In fact, Rom and Reem are delighted. Deloy's apartment is a high-tech zoo. Lights switch on and off automatically as the twins gallivant in and out rooms, up and down staircases. At every nook and cranny, robotic devices follow like pestering flies offering trays of refreshments, extra seat cushions, and investment tips. Grace finds them unnerving. Wherever she turns, she is accosted by some digital life form. When she attempts to kick a knee high model out of her way, it misinterprets her gesture. Instead of desisting, it obligingly buffs her shoe. A casual examination of a trinket on a coffee table triggers a sell transaction. The object offers itself at a ten percent discount. Though she declines, it continues to bid, offering deepening discounts with each refusal.

Grace escapes to the toilet, hoping for a moment of privacy. The lights do not switch on. Hesitantly, Grace turns a dial. The room illuminates. The compartment is surprisingly spacious and seemingly devoid of robotic contraptions. Even the techno-crazed Deloy must realize certain amenities are best left in the backwaters. Leisurely, Grace inspects the sanctum of marble tiles, crystal fixtures, velvet towels, and mosaic murals. The antique, footed tub is molded from an unusual, translucent substance. Embedded in its synthetic lagoon are tropical reeds, exotic corals, and flamboyantly colored fish. Grace bends to examine the exquisite replicas in more detail. Inadvertently, she triggers the automated shower head.

Grace enters the kitchen, wringing her wet hair. As Connery struggles to uncork a bottle of wine, Grace sniffs cheerily. "Something smells tempting."

"Honey-roasted duck, au-gratin potatoes, and julienne vegetables in a ginger-tamari marinade."

"What happened to the hot dogs?"

"Grocer delivered the health food version by mistake. Like anyone these days has time to boil water." Instead, Connery peals aluminum foil from several frozen mounds. Promptly popping them into the microwave, he presses three buttons, then counts to six. Dinner is done. Robots have already set the table.

Grace sits across from Connery, passing him papers which he obligingly initials between bites. The twins fidget on either side. They each have their own media monitor. In mock protest, Grace has placed a napkin over her screen. While Connery keeps one watchful eye on the scrolling commodities, the twins rat-a-tat from channel to channel as they guzzle their respective milks. While swallowing the last drops, they excuse themselves by way of hand signals. Via counter hand signals, Connery indignantly indicates their virtually untouched meals. Grace apologetically discloses. "They rarely consume anything that has to be chewed. Wastes too much time. They've promised to progress to solid food once they've located the Holy Lantern. In the meantime, I give them multi-vitamins. So far, they seem none the worse for wear."

In contrast, Connery devours his food morsel by morsel. Grace picks at each item curiously, wondering what strange by-products fabricate the moulage. When Connery coaxes her to partake of a bowl of multi-colored wafers, she politely declines.

Connery bargains. "Just one. It's my next sure thing. A wafer that tastes sweet or fried or salty depending upon your mood. The ultimate pacifier, made from a staple called mazing. Fills you up without fattening you out. I'm marketing it as a miracle diet..."

Grace inauspiciously sneezes. Before Connery can utter 'bless-you', the robot clearing the table offers a napkin from its dirty dish tray. Not to be out-computed, the robot serving the wine offers a handkerchief from its tuxedo pocket. Tugging at her skirt, the pygmy shoe shiner offers its shine cloth. Overwhelmed, Grace implores. "Is there a way to turn this apartment off? Shift to manual? I'm getting really tense."

Against his better judgment, Connery flips a switch. The three proffered cloths fall simultaneously. A honey silence replaces the abrasive buzzing. In gratitude, Grace extends her hand into the bowl of neon wafers. Compliantly, she crunches a green wafer. Pleasantly surprised, she takes a second bite from an orange one.

"Actually, these are pretty damn good."

Connery preens, "Amazing. Sent barges of seedlings to the drought stricken plains of Azukaway. They've already seen a second harvest. One ounce of mazing provides the same energy as a pound of beef, yet you can grow it without fertilizers, grow it on rocky soil or clay ground, and you only need a drop of water. One single drop of water. The salvation for starving nations. Subsidized the entire relief effort. Not to wax political but, what are members of SOIL doing? And Qwaquiwei aren't interested in anything but that desiccate Cliff."

Grace hesitantly ventures. "I know your good intentions, Connery. You are a man of vision. Unfortunately, you are one too many light years ahead of everyone else. Would you consider not developing the Cliff of Ancients?"

Connery lowers his forkful of julienne vegetables. "Has Sadu Qwa been bugging you? I already committed to holding off construction until after the eve of that lightning stuff. What more..."

"I don't mean waiting until next year or even the year after. I mean waiting until the Cliff and its people evolve in their own way, in their own time."

Connery shieldingly hoists his hand. "Hey, I know what I am doing: turning ceremonial pomp into cash you can count on. Not just for me, but for the emerging generation of Qwaquiwei. I want to bring them into the current century."

Grace breaches professional etiquette. "Maybe they don't belong in the current century. Maybe we don't belong." Momentarily penitent, Grace pushes away her glass of wine, but she cannot retract her statement or inhibit her nagging thoughts. "Haven't you noticed that the world is becoming less compatible? Who would you guess is out of sync? Remember your ancient history? Civilization is flourishing until one day the emperor makes a big mistake; he chooses the colorful lead plate with the naked Nubians over his mother's well-worn china. Next thing we know, we're dodging rats, succumbing to deadly microorganisms, having a really bad millennium. Inch by inch, we made our way back to the promised land, but once again, we're wearing out our welcome.

"The good news is: we're smart. The bad news is: we're never smart enough. We go about inventing doohickeys we don't really need and jumping onto band wagons headed for who knows where. When our house of cards starts to crumble, we patch it with just enough tape to get us out the front door, but not enough to keep the roof from collapsing onto the incoming tenant. I don't get a good feeling. To date, we've only seen a few warning sparks, but something potentially devastating is underfoot." Mindful she has been ministering without a license, Grace smiles self-consciously.

Connery compassionately sighs. "Like most common creatures, Ivanosky, you suffer the onus of—" Connery gropes for the appropriate words, "being related: the problem with offspring burdened by parental guidance. They never get the opportunity to start from scratch. Me? I'm an orphan, raised in an orphanage: ideal environment for an aspiring entrepreneur. Lots of kids to play with, each with grand schemes to spare. Other children get stuck with one family's interpretation. Not me 'cause I invented mine. Created an astronaut dad named Henry Higgs Deloy. When I was three years old, he got marooned on Saturn. And my mother? My mother was a mermaid who had to return to the ocean to rescue the whales. With such parental backing, I was destined for greatness. Course, my real father was probably a hallucinogen addict or unskilled laborer. My mom? No doubt single, uneducated. If I knew them, I would have become just like them. As an orphan, I was free from that original sin, free from my ethnic heritage, from the religion of my ancestors, the opinions of Aunt Harriet, the superstitions of Uncle Moe.

"People always, always telling me, 'But don't you know that can't be done?' I don't, because I am free from that pre-emptive knowledge. That's why I cannot accept Qwaquiwei being Qwaquiwei as inviolable fact. They are Qwaquiwei only because Aunt Harriet says so. It's easy enough to prove. Take an infant sea turtle from its home in the Barogo Islands, then deposit it in downtown Splitsville. Sure enough, it will return to Barogo, because it is indeed a sea turtle, but take a Qwaquiwei infant and deposit it in Hoboken, I guarantee it will be selling pretzels at subway stations and be none the wiser or worse off."

Grace stubbornly sharpens her point. "I'm not defending the sins of the father. I am just questioning whether we can escape them. After all, the father got it from his father; his father got it from his father. How can you be so different? It's just your say so. Like each of us, you have your one piece of puzzle. I suspect it is designed that way, to ensure no individual gets too far ahead of the pack. Some kind of shrewd trick to encourage us to work together."

Connery dangles a strand of honey roasted duck from his fork. "You're just envious of my unmitigated nerve."

"Perhaps. Don't love myself the way you do so love yourself. When I see how I am, I say, 'Oh no, that can't be me'. But then how did that who, who I see as not being me, get inside to be me? I'm less the naked ape than the consensus ant — so insignificant in and of themselves, although *en masse*, they are capable of quite remarkable things. Like the pot calling the kettle black, we dismiss their seeming brotherhood. We say: but see how they hypnotically follow the rampaging streams, leaving their dead to bury themselves." Grace peers into her soul with mounting anguish. "Well, how many stranded cars have you passed on the highway? How many old men did you leave wrestling their deflated tires? How many women, their back seats filled with mewling children tried to flag you down with their last diaper? Look at your life? Can you count all the people you overlooked? Not the people you loved, not the people you bested or sent to an early grave — just those countless, countless people you obliviously bypassed as you held to your rampaging stream."

Grace chomps another wafer. This one is much less sweet. "Don't take this personally, but does the world really need another panacea? And why an ounce worth one calorie? Why not an ounce worth a thousand calories?" Grace crumbles the remaining wafer into her plate. "What do you make of the parable of the obese Benedicts? We all read the study. Why are the Benedicts so fat, fat, fat. Turns out they have Qwaquiwei blood. Like their ancestors, they are genetically able to cope with harsh environments, missed harvests. Their metabolisms are supra-efficient; they require less food than normal to survive. If they were a kind of rodent, we would be marveling at such evolutionary accommodation. Too bad they are people; we can only see them as fat, fat, fat. Rather than duplicating a genetic masterpiece, we devise ways to eliminate it, to convert miraculously blooming cactuses into garbage gobbling weeds — on purpose. Seems to me we're flushing our pearls down the toilet, biting the hand that feeds."

Crunch.

Grace turns. Rom is quietly munching on a handful of blue mazing wafers. Without his mirror image, he looks oddly out of place. Grace questions, "Where's Reem?"

"He has a stomach ache."

Grace knits her brows incredulously. "From what? He didn't eat anything." More curious than concerned, Grace hastens upstairs to find Reem snuggled in an over-stuffed easy chair. He appears pale as he doggedly recalculates his next equation in pursuit of the elusive lantern. Grace presses her hand to his forehead. "You feel a bit warm. Guess you ate too many bugs, huh? Maybe I should call the doctor."

"No, just fresh batteries, and maybe some water."

Grace dutifully administers two aspirins, then calls her doctor from the hall phone. Briefly, she explains. "I took his temperature. It's slightly elevated. He's had a rough few days. Probably just exhausted. However, he did cross the border, ate some local pie, drank the water. I'm sure it's just—" Grace abruptly sets down the phone. Someone is crying.

Grace returns to Connery's guest room to investigate. There, she finds Reem peacefully napping. Rom has taken control of the Wizard. Clutching it in his whitening hands, he contemplates it blankly. Grace questions what's wrong as she tests Reem's forehead. This time it is cool. She proceeds to breathe a sigh of relief, when suddenly — she cannot exhale, then she cannot inhale as she wakens to the horrifying realization — her son is dead.

AND THEN, THERE WAS ONE

At the hospital, Reem's prognosis improves. The intern on duty assures Grace, it is just a coma. Reem only seems to be dead. On subsequent examination, a neuro-surgeon declares all life signs have ceased. Her son has indeed died. Grace stares uncomprehending, then summons the original intern for a recount. At last resort, Grace refuses to shift, refuses to blink, hoping to invoke quantum law. If she doesn't move too many frames from the longitude and latitude of the present moment, perhaps when no one is looking, she can re-cast the dice. Certainly, one waking nightmare can be downgraded to a disquieting dream without destroying the reigning causal universe.

An hour passes. The nurse begs Grace to concede. They need the medical equipment. The doctor prods her to sign papers, to print her name on page one, initial page two, sign page three, then enclose a check for two thousand dollars. On repeated pretexts, Connery ushers the dogged doctor outside. Time after time, the doctor returns, obsessively etching signatures in the air as if to mime Grace into compliance.

Rom, quietly crying, lays curled inside Aaron's lap. Distractedly plucking Rom's untied shoe lace, Aaron softly pronounces, "He won't be waking up; he won't be coming home; it's time for us to leave." Grace doesn't budge. Again, Aaron repeats. "He won't be waking up; he won't be coming home; it's time for us to leave." Despite his own declarations, Aaron makes no motion to move. He is regurgitating familiar words from long sunken memories, words spoken by Aaron's mother, in reference to his gherkin grouse. Aaron was eleven. Gerkin, the grouse, was twelve. She had developed massive tumors, become blind and partially paralyzed. Night after day, she remained coiled in on herself, powerless to digest the pain. Finally, they consulted the veterinarian. Aaron expected a miracle. His mother, herself dying of cancer, knew better. Aaron was advised to let go, to accept the compassionate solution: the injection of a fluid that would put Gerkin to sleep. Mentally adjusting to the idea, Aaron bowed to bid his pet ado. However, the moment he touched Gerkin's wavering wings, still pulsing with life, he started to hysterically wail. His own living molecules, vibrating in harmony with the grouse's living molecules, convulsed at the notion that a substance, so awesome as life, could be flipped like a switch. Aaron anguished: not even God should have such power. Now, playing his own necessary parent, Aaron obligingly counsels, "He won't be waking up; he won't be coming home; it's time for us to leave."

At last, Grace flinches. Grimly she drags the bed sheet over Reem's lifeless body. Intuitively, Rom scurries to secure his mother's outstretched hand. As Aaron clears his throat, Grace fends off the rankling words of consolation. "You can leave Webster with Matilda for the night. I'll pick her up tomorrow. Tell Matilda..."

"That isn't necessary. I can—" But he can't. Aaron sees in Grace's eyes that he can't, that it's over.

"Why? Why didn't you show me that letter, Aaron? Of course, I'm not blaming you." But she is; Aaron sees that too.

"It seemed of no consequence." Aaron again explains what he could not explain an hour ago. "I meant to tell you, thought I did tell you. You have been so preoccupied. After the sheriff reviewed the letter, he said not to worry. We— We need to discuss this. Once we are home, we can..."

Grace pushes him away. "You're not coming home. We have no home, no happy family, no..."

Aaron persists. "Grace, the letter threatened 'a plague of frogs on your vegetable garden'. Not this. Certainly not this. I can't understand how you can—" But he can, can understand how a woman who has just lost her child can fail to hear mere words being said.

Grace turns to Deloy. "Didn't think someone's bad karma could leak out like toxic waste and kill an innocent bystander. I'm suing. I'm sure that cyber-nasty hovel of yours is radiating fatal doses of— everything." It is apparent from the flatness in Grace's voice that she has no intention of suing, that she is retaliating at no one in particular, and anyone in sight. Turning to the pen pressuring doctor, Grace pleads. "How do I get him home?"

Momentarily considering Rom, the doctor nods towards Reem. "The dead one? No, no; you know how it works. Lots of unexplained epidemics. Without a cause of death, we'll have to take him apart to ascertain—" Lowering his eyes, the doctor wearisomely sighs. "You know the rules. Hospital owns him now. We'll get back to you when we can."

Grace has no energy to argue. The reigning casual universe has spoken.

In the cab home, Rom repeatedly ponders. "Where's Reem? Where's Reem?" He echoes it to pacify himself, to ride out the waves of grief. In turn, Grace twirls a lock of his hair over and over until her finger tangles to a stop. Grimly, Grace relives the sins of her mother.

Madora Ivanosky married seven times, then committed suicide on her thirty-eighth birthday. She had been a soldier in the Boetian war. She could have left her two children in the care of their grandfather, a solicitous wood carver whose only vice was too much clove in his streusel. Instead, Grace's mother, neurotically independent, dragged her children behind enemy lines. Grace remembers the nightly bombings and a baby brother with sea-foam eyes. One evening, he crawled into a back alley to retrieve a toy truck. It exploded the moment he gripped it to his mouth. Grace can not remember if he had a name. Now, almost a lifetime later, she is retracing those steps. For the past several years, being pro or con anything has proved a dangerous occupation. A number of colleagues recently expired under suspicious circumstances. Some had defended industrialists. Some had defended environmentalists. The contagion leaked both ways. Grace had refused to consider the possibilities. Belatedly, she considers them. When the cab passes the police station detaining Iroquois Jefferson, Grace convulsively commands, "Stop!" Grace directs Rom to remain in the cab. He is reluctant to let go her hand. After whispering her assurances, she kisses Rom on the forehead.

Grace has trouble ascending the precinct steps. A recent rain has left a mucky film. An officer stands outside, smoking her cigarette. Another sits behind the night desk picking pieces of donut out of his cooling coffee. Neither questions Grace's business. She looks so much the lawyer, her purpose is presumed.

Grace immediately sights Iroquois. Duly processed, he sits hunched inside a small cage, ready for transport. Misconstruing her intentions, Iroquois exuberantly ushers Grace. "At last, my lawyer has arrived to bail me out. I knew you would come to defend me, Ivanosky. You know I didn't do it."

Ashen and seemingly anesthetized, Grace advances clockwise around his cage. "I want you to listen to me very carefully. Earlier this evening, I was at Deloy's apartment."

As he awkwardly twists to keep pace, Iroquois corrects. "His office. I didn't do it. You know I didn't do it."

Grace accusingly reemphasizes, "His apartment. But of course, you knew I was there, you and your cohorts from SOIL. Well, Reem is dead. Murdered. If that was the intention, then you will be pleased to know your mission has been accomplished."

Iroquois resists comprehending. "What are you talking about. Who's Reem?"

Fighting the blinding tears, Grace threateningly rattles his gilded cage. Iroquois topples back reflexively as Grace rails, "My dead, murdered son! Don't pretend you don't know. My first born!" Grace's heart seems to be rupturing inside her chest. Apprehensively, she turns towards the night desk where the night officer surveys the commotion. Momentarily suppressing her rage, Grace demands. "For the record, I want to know — was the intended victim Deloy? Was my son a mistake, or does it even matter? Any means to an end, eh? But why? What flimsy reason? And how? Was it gas? Was it poison? In the milk? Through the vents?"

"Are you out of your mind? I would never. You know I would never. Is this a joke? Your son?"

"You tried to kill Connery. Having failed, you killed Reem. I know how you think. You don't." As Grace cycles more quickly around the cage, Iroquois swivels in defense.

"Hey, hey, I reprogrammed Connery Deloy's robot, that is all. Kill your son? How could you possibly think— Grace, for all it's worth, I still care for you. I could never— I don't do violence. I'm not that quick on my feet."

Grace petulantly cites. "You've pledged to overthrow the government."

"Oh come on, these days, everyone pledges to overthrow the government. It's a mark of good citizenship. So, maybe, maybe I threw in a few skunks but I would never— Someone is setting me up. You, of all people, should know how it works. You attend the pertinent bull sessions, know the cloak and dagger antics industrialists employ to protect their big fat profits. They spend millions discrediting groups like SOIL. They killed native activists in the Mozon jungle. They kill; they steal; they falsify evidence, poison ground waters, adulterate baby food. A little more rope and they'll hang us all. That recent archaeological dig in Bindustan proved what we long suspected. There was a highly developed civilization before ours. What happened to it could happen to us. If..."

Tired of the polemics, Grace snaps, "I don't want to hear this. I'm going home now, but don't you sleep. I'm not finished with you. I'm not finished with anyone."

Grace ascends her front porch broken into too many pieces to ever set right. Rom, asleep in her arms, is almost too heavy to carry. Grace dares not waken him. She cannot deaden his pain for one moment, let alone for the rest of his life. Grace swings open the front door. The full moon outside makes the darkness inside conspicuous. Grace becomes disquietingly aware of the many walls in the three bedroom dwelling. There are walls in the kitchen and walls in the den; there are walls on the ceiling and walls on the floor; there are even walls on the windows and closets and doors.

Grace tucks Rom into the double bed where he and his brother always slept side by side. She considers caulking up the void, crawling in beside him. But how would that seem? When he wakens, he will clearly see the error of her being there. Reluctantly, Grace retreats to her chamber. The moment she sits on the edge of her mattress, she senses her unbalancing weight, like a child alone on a seesaw. Exhausted, she crumples onto her back. Again, she counts the walls. When she comes across the corner colony of spiders, cozily spinning their webs, she angrily snatches Aaron's pillow, then pitches it at the complacent arachnids. There is a chilling cry.

Belatedly Grace considers the eagle fledgling inside her drawer — hungry and cold and crying for Reem. Grace bursts into tears. Rom appears at her door, wavering sheepishly. This time, he does not ask about his brother, having wakened to the realization: "Is this what it is to be lonely?"

FLICKING CHANNELS

The reporter grips her microphone at so dramatic an allegation. "You can't be serious. A tragedy, yes, but certainly not murder."

The man in the surgical coat points insistently at the dissection table. "See for yourself. They ripped those swimmers to absolute shreds."

Despite these charges, the reporter dispassionately summarizes. "But sharks are predators by nature. They have no hidden agenda. To a shark, a swimmer is just another flavor sea urchin. Not to minimize the misfortune, but you can't accuse a dumb animal of malicious intent."

Agitatedly, the man in the white surgical coat raises his bloody scalpel. "Haven't you been listening? Those sharks did not *consume* the swimmers." Using his surgical instruments to spoon mime-full mouthfuls, he contends. "Those sharks were already feeding at Lester's Wharf, gorging themselves on leftover fish parts. According to witnesses, those sharks interrupted their feeding, then headed towards the shallow bay where they maliciously attacked, *attacked* those swimmers. One young man was dragged down and drowned. Intentionally drowned then left floating on the waters without a toe being taken. It was murder by any definition of the word. This culprit here. Can't you see? Not a scrap of a swimmer in its stomach."

Peakishly peering into the intestinal remains, the reporter signs off. "Well folks, that's our human interest story for the evening. Back to you, Fred."

Fred Fooey fidgets nervously behind his anchor desk. "On a lighter note, Popco Industries, a division of Deloy Enterprises, claims to have solved an age-old problem: how to eat as much as you like, whenever you like, and never gain an ounce. They call it Mazing Wafer." Fred Fooey takes a crunch from the seemingly inedible snack. "It may look suspect but it tastes a little sweet, or is it salty? It's designed to read your mind, or rather taste buds. As for its purported effects? What do you think, Hillary? Do I appear any thinner?" Co-anchor Hillary refrains from answering the corpulent Fooey. Instead, she proceeds to forecast rain.

Flick! Aaron changes channels to no avail. WDBS, NBCC and TTS unanimously forecast rain. It has rained every day for the past two weeks in keeping with the rainy season. In times gone by, he and Grace would snuggle by the fireplace, making chewy-chuckles while drinking mozulberry wine. Aaron latches onto a photograph of himself, a pregnant Grace, and the twins picking chunks of chocolate out of the chewy-chuckle batter. Months have passed and still Grace has not called.

Grace slams shut the window. The persistent rains have thoroughly soaked her garlic cloves. For three weeks, dusky clouds have remained mistily suspended. In keeping with the somber mood, Grace has taken to knitting. So far, she has knitted the same scarf several times. Invariably one row is too loose, another too tight. Over and over she wrestles with the wily wool. When she determines to make the rows taut, her mind surreptitiously strays, and a loose row, like a savage weed, unravels the orderly compaction. When she reconciles to loose rows, her fingers subconsciously tense, injecting an apprehensive snag. In the meantime, her fleurs-de-lilies have all but washed away.

Old Man Jones offers Aaron a slice of blueberry pie. Aaron refuses, busily flicking from channel to channel in search of good news.

Flick! Flick! Flick! "A tidal wave has hit the resort community of Paisley. Thirty-eight vacationers are reported missing."

Flick! "A tornado has struck the Piedpont nuclear power plant triggering a meltdown alert. Plant supervisors insist there is no immediate danger. However..."

Flick! Flick! "Three hours into the four-day summit, five agricultural consortiums declared trade wars; another three walked out, upon noting their brand of jelly not represented at the breakfast bar. Officials of the summit..."

Flick! "...must now decide if the Environmental Safekeeping Agency carried out an unlawful sting. The defendant, who admitted skinning the endangered digerie bear, insists he was unfairly lured by relentless promises of wealth. After being repeatedly badgered with enlarging sums of money, he eventually succumbed to the proposal. The ESA insists they were trying to ferret out the evil lurking in the minds of men. The jury will attempt to decide which mind, which men, threw the felonious stone."

Flick! Flick! Flick! "They are calling it the 'exploding cow' phenomenon. Somehow, the anaerobic bacteria which break down cellulose in bovine stomachs are being destroyed. Unable to digest their grass dinners, the animals essentially detonate. While a vaccine is being worked on, affected cows are being injected with cultured bacteria to alleviate the..."

Flick! Flick! "...naturally occurring phyto-estrogens in plants have been known to disrupt animal reproduction. It is a defense on the part of the plant, a way to eliminate the predator by reducing its grazing offspring. For reasons not yet understood, produce grown in the Cornerstone region is registering excessive amounts of phyto-estrogen. Its pervasive presence came to light as the result of a study commissioned by Cornerstone communities suffering extincting birth rates. Initial targets of the study were local industries and their by-products: heavy metals, pesticides, synthetic chemicals. Though phyto-estrogen is natural, this massive overdose is not. Since man-made contaminants have been implicated in past genetic breakdowns..."

Flick! A sun, orange and luminous as polished amber, sets behind a distant range. High above, a blue-tail hawk sails across the teal-gray sky. Pensively, a reporter indicates, "Upon that distant cliff, the Qwaquiwei nation is preparing for the Eve of Inner Lightning. This ceremony transpires every 22 years, lasts 22 days then culminates with a flash of lightning, sacred lightning, directing the Qwaquiwei to continue their terrestrial lives. According to tradition, Qwaquiwei are descended from gods and, one day, will return to that divinity from which they came. It remains to be seen if this upcoming Eve is that fateful eve. It will, unfortunately, be the final one. Deloy Enterprises now owns the sacred Cliff on which this ceremony is performed.

"Some suggest: relocate the ceremony; what's in a cliff? Indeed. According to Qwaquiwei, the sacred cliff itself performs the ceremony. The whispers of their dead ancestors condense upon the living like anointing dew. Without the quixotic Cliff to drum their footsteps, guide the dance, there can be no delivering vision.

"This leads one to wonder if Qwaquiwei culture will collapse without this defining stone face and the buried bones of their instructing forefathers. In honor, in memory, we will share some of the curious Inner Lightning rituals with our viewing audience. Needless to say, we cannot witness the events first hand, we outside the circle, as Qwaquiwei would say. However, joining us this evening is noted Qwaquiwei authority, Obigeewan Cohen."

Deferentially turning to the diminutive woman, the reporter cites her credentials. "Obigeewan Cohen has Qwaquiwei ancestors, Qwaquiwei blood, the authenticating qwa. She herself has participated in two Inner Lightnings. You were thirteen for the first ceremony, thirty-five by the next. You have not participated since, is that correct?"

The softly smiling woman nods. "I started my own business. Since Qwaquiwei cannot own things, I stepped outside the circle. A few of my relatives are practicing, fully practicing. That's kind of how it works. You are Qwaquiwei so long as you *are* Qwaquiwei, and yes, have the authenticating qwa, some distant, however distant bloodline. Nevertheless, I remain philosophically Qwaquiwei. After all, my ritual role for both ceremonies was the fire squash watch."

Leafing through his crumpled papers, the reporter raises his voice incredulously. "Yes, in this fire squash watch you observe the fire squash turn from its budding yellow to its ripening red for 22 days. Why? Everyone knows it eventually turns red — or rots. Perhaps you are looking for some defining moment, some metaphorical metamorphosis?"

The softly smiling woman gently flourishes her hand like a dusting windshield wiper. "No, no. The feeling behind the fire squash watch, the intended sentiment is the inevitability of Lord Mother's will. You say 'A watched pot never boils'. We say 'It boils but you never catch the kindling bubble'. Things are born and die, slip out of oblivion then back in, without revealing the routing portal. The ritual of the fire squash watch makes one keenly aware that life changes by such imperceptible degrees, one can never really know."

Disquieted by this sleight of hand, the reporter frowns. "One can never really know *what*?"

"One can never really *know*. For instance, today we encounter 1, so we expect 1 tomorrow. When tomorrow brings 2, we switch our expectation to 2. However, the next day brings 3. We believe we have finally caught on, so we cleverly project 4 in anticipation. Instead, we waken to 9, proving the effort is constant, the results unpredictable. There can be no blinking, and there follows no certainty. We will invariably miss a frame as the story flashes by us. The fire squash watch helps us accept the nature of our nature, the nature without, and the nature within."

"Uh, not quite following how this fire squash gets you from here to there?"

"Well, it's subtle, very subtle. During the fire squash watch, one day will be dry. The squash will wither. The next day it rains. The squash perks. Should it continue to rain, the squash may drown. Should the sun return, the squash will turn golden. Should it shine, shine, shine, the fire squash will mature into its supreme crimson. By the Eve of Inner Lightning, one is left marveling how it came to be."

The reporter distastefully notes. "Sounds kind of zen."

Enthusiastically confirming, the diminutive woman proffers the golden squash. "It makes a great meditation tool. I often advise friends, in distressed states, to keep vigil with a fire squash for however long they can. It has a calming effect. I knew a man, very troubled by the hole in the ozone. After spending some time with a slowly ripening squash, he confidently asserted, 'There are no holes in God's story, no gaps in the equation. If you find the rightful angle, you will see perfection.' Isn't that beautiful?"

The reporter crisscrosses his eyes in beleaguered analysis. "Meaning there isn't really a hole in the ozone?"

Obigeewan shields the misquoted squash to her bosom. "No, no. The point is not to refute ozone depletion; the point is: he was able to go beyond..."

"Oh, the beyond thing. Yeah well—" Unable to follow the circuitous crypticism, the reporter tunes his ear-mike to more saucy news. "This just in! JJ Cranberry, video-game maven, was found innocent — yes, innocent of hacking to pieces his wife and three children. Those pictures in a moment. Apparently, the jury did not dispute his evident guilt but sided with forensic experts who speculated a poppy seed stuck between his back molars constricted his medusal-cystic nerve ending, numbing him to the grievous consequences of his hatchet. As you can see from this gruesome re-enactment..."

Flick! Flick! Flick! Flick! "They say thunderbolts don't strike the same place twice. Today, Frugen's Fine Furs factory was struck by lightning the ninety-seventh time this month. Building inspectors speculate a design flaw has created some kind of charged magnetic field. However, sources close to the company suspect excessed workers..."

Flick! Flick! "...were taking bribes. If this is the case..."

Flick! "...the incumbent candidate has lost by a landslide. The opposition party has been..."

Flick! "... purchased at the RevRover dealership for..."

Flick! "...another thirty-six pounds. Yes, thirty-six." Old Man Jones excitedly snatches the controls. As Jones turns up the volume, Fred Fooey effusively exclaims. "Yes, folks, it's me, Fred Fooey, anchorman for channel 73. Never thought I'd be doing a sleazy commercial, but I just had to go public about Mazing Wafers. Did the initial report myself over a month ago. I am now thirty-six pounds lighter. I still have some pounds to go but so far, I don't feel hungry, and I have more energy than when I was fat and ugly. The very best part? I don't have to exercise. All I have to do is eat." In demonstration, Fred crunches once from a purple wafer in his right hand, then twice from an orange wafer in his left hand. Aaron doesn't wait for him to swallow. *Click!* Aaron manually powers off the television.

Undiscouraged, Old Man Jones brags. "Told you that mazing stuff was amazing. See how it's taken off? Why don't you join my operation, Aaron? Get away from this political mayhem and memories of— You, you could have rangered any forest or park. You chose a vanishing suburban woods just to be close to..."

Wistfully, Aaron explains. "You're talking to me, Jones. Don't you remember? Always chasing frogs in the pond. Never caught any. You would give me one from your bucket. As you roasted yours, I played with mine. If I squeezed it, I could get it to croak. I would feel its little neck puffing against my palm. Then it would jump away. I wanted a collie. Grandfather wouldn't allow it, remember? Said dogs were really wolves, and wolves were really spirits of ancient warriors. He sent me into the forest to talk to the trees. I poured out my heart to them, but they only waved in the wind. They weren't even waving at me, weren't the least bit aware of my presence, even when, in exasperation, I plucked their buds. When I met Grace — it was like falling into a well but finding myself at the top of that mountain I had been trying to ascend my whole life. I'm a grown man, Jones. How can you not understand? I cannot go back to chasing frogs."

Jones dips his finger in his oozing blueberry pie. "Fine, but find another well. Forget her, Aaron, and forget this town, mismanaged by politicians, abused by the rich, infested by people who don't give a damn. Take back your life. Don't think. Don't breathe. Just pack your bags and..."

Quietly, Aaron takes a seat on the sofa. "No. I have to wait here. She's going to call. I know she is going to call." To indicate his absolute certainty, Aaron places the phone on his lap.

Graces dials, then hangs up, then re-dials, then hangs up, then dials again. Anxiously, she demands. "Why haven't you called — Well, how much longer? Dr. Overton diagnosed an

131

asthmatic seizure. Dr. Leitz implied a spinal tumor. Dr. Dayletter indicated a virus. Reem was south of the border the day before— Perhaps a bacteria from the water or a parasite. There are swarms of pogowillies in those swamps — Well, when will you know? It's been too long — Yes, I know the rules, know the cryogenic catacombs that— I don't care. I want to—"

Bury him. Grace cannot utter the word. Instead, she cries, envisioning her son on an icy slab like something unidentified, mysteriously washed ashore. Don't they realize she bore that child, felt his awakening pulse inside her womb. Grace tries to explain. "I know Reem. I'm still his mother and I'm telling you: he just wants to come home."

Unshaven, Aaron seditiously digs into a box of Captain Munchies as he flicks from channel to channel.

Flick! "Just this month, on this lonesome stretch, forty-nine drivers were killed by deer. Crash-crossing of car and deer, while not unusual, should not be commonplace. Survivors from the car side of the equation insist the deer intentionally spring into their paths. Residents are anxious to ascertain what is prompting this kamikaze behavior. A local biologist suggests the deer, disoriented by solar flares, are trying to mate with the oncoming traffic. This morning, a deer, amorous in the extreme, jumped from an overpass, landing on these railroad tracks seconds before a train loaded with frozen turkey-dogs..."

Flick! Flick! Flick "Termite mounds are mysteriously disappearing. The queen termite is increasingly unable to reproduce. Environmentalists blame it on the deteriorating quality of air, water and soil. Not everyone shares their lament, considering the millions spent each year to exterminate the voracious..."

Flick! "Asthmatics, anyone with allergic tendencies or chemical sensitivities migrate to this desert haven where planting flowers is illegal, hanging mistletoe a punishable offense. A visitor will notice no florists, or arboretums, or tree lined streets in Drydunes. On Sweetheart's Day, no one sends flowers, not even plastic ones, since polymer molecules are banned as well. Consequently, a visitor will notice no car washes, no beauty parlors, no gas stations, no smoking sections. Anyone caught wearing perfume, after-shave lotion or even talcum powder can be evicted. As you can imagine, this town doesn't get many visitors. Even native scrub has been fumigated from the landscape. So how very ironic that clouds of pestering puffballs have targeted Drydunes. Spores from the airborne fungus are precipitating onto the helpless inhabitants like acid rain. Many have been forced to abandon their homes, their businesses. Those remaining must don cumbersome masks to filter..."

Flick! Flick! Flick! "...the drizzling rain, mixed with local pollutants, is making a slippery slick. Vehicles, caught off guard by the seemingly innocuous sprinkle, literally spin off the road, plummet into a precipitous ditch with fatal consequences. When the road was temporarily closed, bicyclists and hikers reported no such problem. During this period, the rainfall was tested. The problem had mysteriously evaporated. However, when the roads again re-opened, the treacherous rains returned; so did those fatal consequences. Needless to say..."

Flick! Flick! "...decided not to extend unemployment benefits. They have, however, allocated fifty billion to establish a research facility on Titan. Meanwhile..."

Flick! "Fred Fooey has lost another twenty-seven pounds."

Grace carefully hand-feeds Reem's eagle. Rom carefully pours milk into Webster's bowl of cereal at the same time he balances his homework on his lap. Unlike Webster, the eagle is prepared to take flight. For the moment, its wings remain clipped. In addition, it wears mock rubber feet to safeguard furniture and family members from its razor-sharp talons. The eagle does not seem to mind. It flops around the kitchen table like a gangly toddler in search of food.

Webster now walks and speaks one-word sentences. Mostly she repeats "bubanah". Clumsily, she cups her hand to scoop out a few puffs of cereal. Milk splatters over the table. Webster points to the banana that Rom has just peeled.

"Bubanah!" Obligingly, Rom separates one from the bunch. As he hands it to Webster, she tugs at his glossy red pencil. While wrestling it back, Rom implores. "Mom? This problem is harder than I thought. Can you help me with the math? I'm supposed to calculate the ideal rate of decay for a typical society."

Grace holds a chicken wing in place as the eagle rips out choice pieces. "Rate of decay? As in nuclear particles and rotting apples?"

"No, decay for an economy. For instance, what impact, what economic impact will doubling CO_2 concentrations have on our economy, the part of it that's in our economic range. Can we reduce carbon emissions to ten percent and still produce the optimal levels of pollution verses production?"

Grace rotates the chicken wing as the eagle becomes less choosy, methodically picking it clean. "Optimal levels of pollution? Ten percent? Are these real numbers? To prevent global warming you would have to..."

"Well, the idea is not to *prevent* global warming. This isn't my social science class. This is economics, cost analysis, so we don't have to factor in human health, biological diversity, or the quality of life. We just need to calculate a workable rate of decay. According to my numbers..."

Grace cannot get past the premise. "A *workable* rate of decay? Meaning eventually the civilization dies?"

Rom shrugs, "Well, yeah. You can't factor in forever. Forever would require tremendous overhead. You only need to factor the foreseeable future, within our economic range. According to chapter fourteen, you have to decide how many generations to take into consideration. I mean, do you really care about your children's children's children? By then, your genes and culture have been diluted past recognition. There has to be some perimeter on accountability."

"Are you speaking for yourself, your personal accountability, your children's children's children?"

Rom lifts his text book defensively. "This is my homework, Mother, not real life. Perhaps if you heard the scenario. You see, Mr. Pointer wants to build a golf course. He calculates he can generate a million dollars a year and employ

45 people. However, he is prevented from doing so because the pied-peeper crow nests in the obstructing woodlands which would have to be bulldozed. This pied-peeper crow neither toils nor weaves. It just sits on the willow maple and crows. For all we know, it isn't even happy."

Grace puts down the chicken bone. The eagle gnaws at the marrow. "I see, but then does the world really need another golf course?"

Rom groans. His mother is being unnecessarily argumentative. "This isn't my opinion, Mother. It's the scenario that has to be worked out. I get graded on this, so please listen. According to the scenario, Mr. Pointer can pump a million dollars into the economy, heating it up, growing it, you know. He employs people so they can reap, multiply and bake their own bread. Meanwhile, there's this pied-peeper who doesn't employ anyone. So what if it becomes extinct."

Grace compulsively disputes. "Okay, but by the same argument, do we really need this Pointer man? Does he toil or weave? I'm sure his workers do, but does he? And how long before he automates his operation, lays off those toiling workers? Does the economy really need to grow, heat up? Sounds like economic warming, a lot of hot air so Mr. Pointer can purchase a RevRover, or cabin cruiser, to greatly improve *his* quality of life, his fatty esteem. It's cost effective for him in his self-contained lunch box, but what about everyone outside his economic range. Is it also cost effective for them? Are you willing to bulldoze a woodlands that will take centuries to regrow, kill off a pied-peeper who may have held the key to..."

Rom does not appreciate his mother's helpful hinting. Lowering his voice, he withdraws into his workbook. "Uh, thanks Mom, but I don't think that's the answer I'm supposed to be going for." In the middle of his calculation, Webster plucks the pencil from his hand. Rather than wrestling the pencil as before, Rom negotiates an exchange.

Recalling Aaron's prophetic nubs, Rom wields a golden banana. "Look Webby! Did you know bananas can talk?"

"Bubanah!" Webster anxiously gropes for the withheld treat while Rom clarifies.

"But they only answer 'yes' or 'no'. Since you're not proficient at constructing coherent sentences, perhaps Mom will formulate one on your behalf." Rom flags his mother with the stripped banana peels. "Mom, it isn't ethical for the banana cutter to pose the question. Could you..."

Grace proceeds towards the kitchen sink to wash the chicken drippings from her fingers. As she opens the faucet, she realizes it has finally stopped raining. She contemplates the cascading tap water. Momentarily mesmerized, Grace turns the faucet off, then on, then off, then on. Focused on the miraculous stream of water at her command, she is slow to respond to Rom's prodding. "Actually, I was wondering if the fleurs-de-lilies will bloom." Satisfied with the question, Rom cuts into the fruit oracle, melodramatically appending 'abracadabra'. This time, the banana says 'no'. Unimpressed, Webster slurps her spilt milk from the table.

Rom anticipates his mother's disappointment. "Sorry, Mom. Did you see that, Webby? That splotch means 'no'."

Grace fastens shut the faucet. Of course, she planted too late.

Still in pajamas, Aaron samples a green Mazing Wafer. As he methodically chews, he flicks, flicks, flicks.

Flick! Flick! Flick! "The man who launched a thousand satellites has been struck dead. Dr. Kugel-Nicklous was conducting his annual satellite camp-out with local boy scouts when a fragment from his original satellite came crashing through his nylon tent, dismembering..."

Aaron defensively flicks. Though safe from the maiming satellite, he finds himself in "the amusement park from hell" where a short, lightweight reporter prudently clutches a bent pole. His thinning hair further attenuates in the snarling winds. His voice fades in and out as his microphone struggles to pick up his besieged vibrations. "In its initial months, this amusement facility functioned nicely, entertaining mommies and daddies and kiddies with its ferris-wheels, and carousels, and cotton candy. Then, the seasonal Santa Una winds changed course, vented into this upper valley. Now the ferris-wheel goes round and round, all on its own. Horses and ostriches have been flung from their bolted carousel course. The space-coaster momentarily took flight before crash landing on the twirl-a-whirl, putting it out of its clockwise-counterclockwise misery."

The camera pans wide as the reporter points rearward. "Behind me, the arcade trees have been stripped of their ruby blossoms and lemon leaves. Their pared, peeling branches hideously whip in these infernal winds. Santa Una should have died down weeks ago. Extraordinarily, this demonic updraft stubbornly stays its course, maintains its hundred mile an hour rage, day after day after..."

Several flicks forward, the news is no better as the bleary-eyed Tim Tinkerton laments from the Balboa coast. "Not merely tragic. Inconceivable. Health organizations are baffled by the decimating plague. After decades of drought, the long starving Azukaway people were coming back to life. The introduction of mazing grain single-handedly turned desiccate hills into productive farm lands. Not long ago, you would have found emaciated women giving birth to stillborn, gaunt men slumped against dilapidated buildings, skeletons shaped like children, huddled in piles like discarded soup bones. In contrast, last week women bartered bangles in thriving markets, men carted wagons filled with ripe produce, children romped merrily beside their decorated donkeys, but today — not a single Azukawayan is left to enjoy the harvest."

Flick! Flick! Flick! "President Stomp has been voted out of office. Newly elected President Linkyn has vowed to take the country out of its economic depression, moral morass and bad karma. As importantly..."

Flick! Flick! Flick! Flick! Flick! Flick! "Fred Fooey has lost another thirteen pounds."

Rom places plastic fleurs-de-lilies on Reem's grave. In turn, Grace places Reem's electronic Wizard device into Rom's palm. He refuses. Grace presses, "But, honey, this belonged to you and Reem. You should..."

"I can't."

Rearranging the fleurs-de-lilies, Grace insists. "It's time, Rom. We have to continue our lives."

Rom kicks the dusty dirt under which Reem lays. "Did they have to take him apart? Did they have to seal him into little boxes? He wasn't a contraption, wasn't something you ordered by mail, then put together. Why..."

Though inwardly at odds with her words, Grace responds, almost bitingly. "As I explained, Rom, they don't know why Reem— They are still examining his data. Don't you learn this in school? There have been too many inexplicable viruses, cancers, tumors. Too many mysterious ailments. When someone dies unexpectedly— It's a health regulation, a law enforced for our benefit. Years ago, we accepted that life began at conception, ended at death. To gain rights over the living, we released rights to the dead. As Reem stands now, he is no longer my child, no longer your—"

Discerning his mother's inner anguish, Rom crouches beside her. In sympathy, he picks up a plastic fleurs-de-lily. Accidentally, he plucks a plastic petal from its socket. While trying to twist it back, Rom proposes. "Maybe we could bring him to the Qwaquiwei reservation. Cindy Jacobs says Qwaquiwei don't actually die. They just teleport to an invisible world. That's because the dead are given over to the hawks and wolves and worms who eat away the flesh, remove the crust of death, release the immortal qwa. Qwaquiwei say even non-Qwaquiwei have qwa, can become whole again, alive in spirit. Wouldn't that be better for Reem? I think he would like that, unless—" Rom's eyes swell with tears as he considers, "they didn't give everything back. He may not be all here. Perhaps this Qwaquiwei stuff won't work if we are missing..."

Grace snuggles Rom to her chest. "Oh, honey, he's already in that invisible world, happy and whole. Don't ever think he cannot hear you, that he isn't listening." Again Grace presses Reem's electronic Wizard device into Rom's palm. Again, he refuses. Grace strokes his hair assuringly. "Okay, you let me know when..."

Angrily, Rom rips away. "Don't your understand? Not now, not ever. I—" Rom's voice cracks, "I don't know how."

"What are you talking about, Rom? You and Reem played this game sunup to sundown. You..."

"I could manipulate the trigger to ward off the random ricochet attacks. I have quick reflexes, but I could never predict where the Wizard would be in the castle. I never understood the underlying matrix. Reem tried to explain it to me, but I could never figure the mathematics." Rom balefully contemplates the electronic interloper. "I hate this game. I only played it because Reem played it and now—" Rom falls painfully silent.

Grace relieves Rom of the galling gizmo. After placing it on Reem's grave, she turns to Rom. She gave him life. He has lived with her these thirteen years. After all this time, Grace wonders who he is.

Except for a pair of pilling socks, Aaron lays on the couch stark naked. Staring at the wall with little enthusiasm, he flicks from channel to channel munching green Mazing Wafer after green Mazing Wafer. The wafers, wavering between salty, sweet and mildly intoxicating, have a hallucinatory effect. Seemingly out of nowhere, a life-size reporter materializes in the middle of Aaron's living room. Dutifully, he broadcasts. "So far, he has predicted three disasters. His name is Casey Watts. He insists he is neither psychic nor psychotic, leading many to wonder, 'How?' How have you been able to predict these events?"

The reporter extends his microphone to another life size materialization. This one looms to Aaron's left. The uninvited specters neither notice nor mind Aaron as he nakedly observes them from his potato-couchdom. The Casey Watts phantasm fidgets inside his flannel shirt as he plainly explains. "I'm a retired general, trained to analyze strategies. It is clear to me that many of these attacks have been purposeful, predictable."

"Attacks?" The reporter paranoiacally spies over his shoulder. "But these are natural catastrophes, are they not?"

Aaron gingerly props himself up, self-consciously plunking a pillow over his private parts as he nervously assents, "Yes".

Casey challenges. "Oh really? Then why did that tidal wave impact that resort community? There were seventeen points where that wave could have impacted, but it impacted where it did the most damage and—" Casey Watts plucks the channel changer from Aaron as he alleges, "where coincidentally, members of SOIL were protesting the introduction of power boats. Why did that tornado hit that nuclear facility?"

This time Aaron has no response, leaving Casey free to postulate that the tornado "literally jumped over the Sierra Bambinos." Using the channel changer, Casey flicks to the scenes of suspicion. "Didn't hit the pasta restaurant one hundred feet to the left." Each scene appears on the television screen as he accusingly narrates. "Didn't hit the abandoned flax mill fifty feet to the right. No, it hit the nuclear facility, coincidentally being picketed by Qwaquiwei militants. And that possessed ferris-wheel? Mutant evolutionists dousing the site for subterraneous waters located mythical energy generators called pyramids, or so they say.

"I can cite other examples. They all follow the same suspicious logic. So I did some research." Upon handing Aaron a crumpled map with circles and crisscrosses, Casey officiously reports. "Marked all the people and places being harassed by malcontent elements. For instance, I knew members of SOIL were protesting the Amy Apple Orchards. They claim the preservative injected into the apples causes flatulence or some such nonsense."

The interviewer corrects. "Fetal brain damage."

"Whatever! That apple orchard is in the flood zone, so I predicted the Amy Apple Orchard would be flooded. And it was." As the reporter absorbs this prophesy fulfilled, Casey Watts derisively sniffs Aaron's wafer. Making clear he has no intention of ingesting the questionable delicacy, he cockily proceeds. "Then the Chauncey Golf Club — being sued for using insecticides which injured local avian pests, as if we need more pigeons."

Aaron tries to snatch back his channel changer. His hand goes through Casey Watts' hologram body. Unable to provide screen proof, Aaron flings open his birder's guide to display the rare blue heron. Still in possession of the channel changer, Casey triple flicks, unleashing a flock of mocking pigeons. As they descend upon the arguing twosome, the interviewer sneaks a piece of Aaron's Mazing Wafer. Nodding approvingly to Aaron, he amends. "I believe the primary concern was not the beleaguered blue heron, but the growing incidences of respiratory failure suffered by landscapers handling the hazardous..."

"Whatever! The club lies on an earthquake fault so I predicted that a quake, small enough to destroy the club but not severe enough to topple the adjacent natural museum, would occur, and one did — and it didn't. I can go on and on and on. That mud slide that destroyed the genetic engineering clinic. That carbon dioxide cloud that leaked into that factory farm. Those bird droppings that besmeared the annual flag ceremony. That..."

Hastening to move the allegations to a headline conclusion, the reporter leans over the couch and whispers. "If I am following you, Mr. Watts, you are alleging that someone or some group is playing a very dangerous game."

As Aaron strains to catch their covert interchange, Casey Watts dramatically escalates. "Game? Outright war! Waged by those back-to-the-soil fanatics and Mother Earth heathens. Well, I have one word for them." Casey flails his righteous right arm like a jutting bayonet, causing Aaron to tumble from his couch onto his channel changer.

Flick! Flick! Flick! Flick! Flick! Flick! Flick! The apparitions precipitously vaporize. Aaron finds himself alone with his pilling socks and TV set to Channel 21. There, a two-dimensional, three-inch talking head lugubriously informs: "At seven forty-seven this morning, Fred Fooey, beloved anchorman for Channel 73, was found dead."

DINOSAURS IN OUR BED

President Linkyn summons a nationwide meeting to address the mounting oracles of doom. Pounding rains have swelled rivers, forcing them to overflow their protective levies. Harvests and towns have washed away. Rising sea levels wage bloodless battles. After futile defiance, coastal residents concede their cobblestones to the invading tides. Meanwhile, the ozone hole mushrooms ominously outwards like a tumorous cloud. Old people die younger. Young people die young. Expectant fetuses shrivel inside insupportable wombs. Some say, these are the lucky ones as water becomes increasingly unfit to drink, air increasingly unfit to breathe, food increasingly unfit to eat, and life — increasingly less tenantable.

President Linkyn paces back and forth as senators and constituents collide *en route* to solutions. For the past three days, citizens from all walks of life and fields of endeavor have voiced their soulful sentiments and concoctive schemes. Microphones are strung up and down the Senate aisles like holiday lights, in order to tap the collective intellect. No idea is considered too absurd, no measure judged too small. The result is pandemonium.

"Whole damn mess stems from decades of fiscal mismanagement..."

"... from disintegration of family values!"

"... compounded by government fraud!"

"... and corporate misconduct!"

"... not to mention scientific incompetence!"

"... apathetic citizenry!"

"... increasingly unskilled work-force!"

"... rising illiteracy!"

"... and misapplied technology!"

"Can all be traced to lead in the drinking water..."

"... pesticides on our produce!"

"... antibiotics in our bloodstream!"

"... insidious electromagnetic waves!"

"... refined sugars and nutritionless fillers!"

"It's time we overcome our addiction to caffeine..."

"... enslavement to television!"

"... video games!"

"... stick-on shoe laces!"

"If only we increase the number of garden worms..."

"... prisons!"

"... retirement age!"

"If only we decrease the extent of regulation..."

"... work week!"

"... pollen count!"

"... taxes!"

"All the fault of political lobbyists..."

"... satanic cults!"

"... extra-terrestrial life forms!"

"... inbreeding!"

On this note, Senator Grady tries to re-focus the conversations. "Yes, well, the good-old days are clearly gone, so let us proceed under the assumption that this planet can be repaired, though not restored to its pristine splendor. The economy can be stabilized, even grow, but profits will be lean and daily life lacking certain frills. Everyone will have to compromise. We can survive, even progress if we approach these problems constructively."

A heavyset man grips the microphone with callused palms. "Let's not duke it out. If the logging industry won't back down, won't accept retraining, won't consider retooling, want to be buried in the nest that hatched them, let them hack down the trees. Every last one. Like a man yanking out his own teeth for the lousy quarter the tooth fairy will bring — when they find themselves sucking on their bleeding gums, they'll realize their folly."

The heavyset man waves his hand full-knowingly. "I know, I know. By then it's too late. Seems to me, we always come through. Like when lung disease threatened smokers and non-smokers alike. Air quality got so bad, everyone contracted lung disorders. When we couldn't sufficiently improve the air, we perfected lung replacements. Today 70 percent of people over 65 have artificial respiratory systems. Technology is so cocksure, professional athletes opt for replacements just to enhance their oxygen capacity. Like having a tummy tuck. No big deal, so by the time we've run out of trees, we'll have found some suitable substitute. Worse comes to worse, we can embed umbrellas, string laundry lines like vines. Granted, it won't have the aesthetic appeal, but umbrellas can keep out the sun, and laundry lines can provide structural webbing necessary for perching birds and swinging monkeys. As for paper? We got all them cutesy cards that capture every occasion, every emotion, every silly thought we think. What else is left to say?"

President Linkyn abruptly stops pacing. This was not the quality of solution so fondly anticipated. Perhaps there is too much lead in the drinking water. President Linkyn gazes out a window. On the dying grasses, hundreds of tribes people chant "qwaquiwei, qwaquiwei" in cryptic protest. Turning to a nearby page, the President notes with rancor. "They refuse to come inside, refuse to participate. They object to our laws, but they won't vote against them. They contend their feet leave no imprints, but I see no wings to support their claims. They want no ownership lest they be made to live in the house they built. Meanwhile they complain about the drafty halls, peeling wallpaper, and noisome neighbors. They won't get away with this. When I die, I will inform their Almighty that they did not vote, that they did not participate — that it wasn't fair."

The page politely nods. President Linkyn resumes her pacing as a crinkled man marshals, "Let's declare war!"

Rows of adherents cheer in support. Senator Grady gently hushes the crowd and demands, "Against whom?"

Before the crinkled man can name his enemy, a lanky fellow snatches an opposing microphone. "Not again! Didn't work too well the last time. Look at me! I'm barely ticking. Eyes can't focus. Toes don't face the same direction. Considering how everything stinks, what would we be fighting for? Been digging a well in my back yard for years. No matter how deep I dig, contaminants persist. Seems to me, we should forfeit this damn planet to whoever still wants it. We can colonize Venus or Mars, or put together a space city, can't we? Didn't scientists discover an atmosphere on Venus, essential elements on Mars, something somewhere? What happened to those micro-organisms we seeded across the solar system? They were supposed to photosynthesize, pump oxygen into the atmosphere, leach out enough carbon to cool the surfaces and precipitate rain, lay the stepping stones for intergalactic travel."

As new rows cheer in support, Senator Grady disputes his calculations. "In another trillion years, perhaps. At the moment, those microorganisms are too lowdown on the evolutionary scale to sponsor our migration. Certainly, this planet has as much potential. Certainly, we can come up with solutions more practical and close to home?"

A woman ominously dangles an empty key ring from her key chain. "We can hang Connery Deloy. His venture into biogenetic engineering is responsible for the deaths of those hapless dieters following that fool anchorman. How many have succumbed so far? Hundreds? Not counting the entire population of Azukaway. Deloy Enterprises sabotaged their harvests, proffered those engineered seedlings like poisoned apples. Part of a plot to buy up the land. I hear he has already purchased thousands of acres. I hear he and a consortium of industrialists are out to monopolize the remaining resources of this planet. They will squeeze us everyday citizens out of our piece of the pie crust. I hear rumors of plots to sterilize babies born to politically unacceptable parents, to turn citizens into docile zombies. Isn't that what happened to Tootsie Rustbottom?" To support her claims, she waves a tawdry tabloid. "When she refused to toe the line, Connery transformed her, his own daughter, into a clanktankerous android. They say he replaced her pulsing heart with a ticking microchip. They say..."

Senator Grady slams down her gavel. "Since Mr. Deloy is not present to defend himself..."

Rows of disgruntled listeners cast their ballots of boos. Someone angrily shouts. "Does this mean you are not pursuing the Mazing Wafer scandal?"

Senator Seerington quickly interjects. "We are investigating Popco Industries and Mr. Deloy with respect to the unfortunate effects of Mazing Wafers. However, until all the facts have been..."

"Government cover-up!"

"Corporate misconduct!"

"Mutant evolutionist!"

"Witch!"

Autocratically stomping his foot, Senator Seerington reminds. "Hey, this is a democracy, which wasn't my first choice but if I have to live with it, you have to live with it. So as per our constitution, cut us some slack. I'll grant you, preliminary research seems to indicate the main component, mazing grain, has minimal nutritional value. Consequently, anyone consuming massive doses of a product containing mazing grain may succumb to malnutrition, ironically starve to death in the mind-set of plenty."

Consulting her fellow senators posthaste, Senator Grady offers. "While we were not prepared to discuss this matter, considering the misinformation currently in circulation, I will allow Dr. Blending to report her findings to date. Let me stress: these findings require additional analysis. Dr. Blending?"

Uncomfortable about the sudden change of venue, Dr. Blending inaudibly recounts. "Ahum. With regard to— to the allegation of biogenetic tampering..."

"We can't hear you!"

"Speak louder!"

After a page adjusts Dr. Blending's microphone, her faint "ahums" deafeningly reverberate through the hall. Taken aback by her new found volume, Dr. Blending shyly stutters. "We— cannot determine— have not yet determined — myself and my fellow researchers, whether the grain has been genetically engineered."

Someone snatches a microphone in protest. "Oh, come on. It had to be engineered. Nature would not conjure anything so devious: something that hypes you up, calms you down, satisfies every gastrointestinal whim without providing a single nutritional calorie. What is it? Some kind of fly trap?"

Repeatedly sipping from a glass of water, Dr. Blending strains to enunciate. "Contrary to initial analysis, mazing grain has a caloric content, albeit minimal nutritional value. For this reason, many mazing consumers — including the unfortunate people of Azukaway, essentially starved to death. Interestingly, the plebeian moss mite — an insect which often feeds on Azukawayan crops, did not die out, even though the plebeian moss mite, like the Azukawayan people, fed exclusively on mazing grain. Interestingly, the plebeian moss mite ate ten times the amount of grain it traditionally consumed. In other words, if the plebeian moss mite traditionally consumed an ounce of lentil beans or an ounce of rice, it instead consumed ten ounces of mazing as if instinctively aware of the reduced nutritional value. In contrast, the parasitic stickler worm, not equally apprised, ate its usual portion of porridge — and subsequently died."

"Exactly!" A man in a trim suit slaps his hands climatically as he commandeers a microphone. "Those people, those idiot dieters were not supposed to subsist solely on the wafer. They resorted to the product like a drug. I have no sympathy for them. They should have been eating a balanced diet. They ignored their bodies when their bodies cried out to them with the warning signs of starvation. People that stupid are better off dead."

Senator Seerington sneeringly concurs. "Hear that! You citizens are too dependent upon government. How many labels can one person read in a day? We're not your Lord Mother, you know. Can't tell you what cereal to eat, what shampoo to wallow in. If you don't know *not* to put your finger into an electric socket, or jump off a bridge, we are better off without you. It's time we wean you overgrown sapiens off the government tit. You're supposed to be intelligent life forms. When are you going to use some of those excess brain cells?"

Senator Seerington grows increasingly caustic. "Speaking of excess brain cells, did my honorable colleagues read the latest report by our esteemed atmospheric chemists?

You know, the report explaining that ozone, itself a greenhouse gas, is turning the absorbed ultra violet energy into heat, contributing to global warming." The Senator dramatically pauses. "Let me repeat. Ozone, the stuff leaking out the hole, is itself a greenhouse gas, is itself turning the absorbed ultra violet energy into heat, contributing to global warming. But that's not the nifty part. The nifty part is their indecent suggestion to puncture a hole in the ozone layer — in order to release some of the accumulating hot air." As his fellow Senators puzzle, Seerington recapitulates. "You heard me right. Our esteemed atmospheric chemists are suggesting we *puncture a hole* in the ozone layer, you know, that thing with the *hole* in it, the *hole* we have been trying to patch up for the past ten years. Apparently, the reputable institute that told us to stitch the hole closed is now telling us to slit its seams, as if this planet were a garment we could tailor to our gruntings. Needless to say, after re-reading this report to ensure I was not suffering from hypoglycemic confusion, I asked: What the hell is this? Some kind of zen koan? A fucking joke!"

After a strained, cogitating silence, a petite man anxiously jiggles his microphone. "Isn't anyone going to mention the dark star? Not to dismiss the issue at hand but frankly, that ozone hole is a pin-prick in the face of the dark star, the impending doom. These strange happenings are the consequence of the gravitational distortion of that massive planet of death. We all know the theory: every so many years, the tenth planet comes into play. Its cycle is so prohibitively long, most civilizations are unaware of its existence. Unfortunately, those who witness it are doomed to die. It passes with catastrophic results. We have geologic evidence of this inauspicious event, don't we? Wouldn't it explain Bindustan?"

Dr. Vanetsky raises his qualifying hand as he approaches a nearby microphone. "The dark star, or a tenth planet, is an interesting but debatable theory, based on the observation by certain scientists that there are cycles of extinction. However, these cycles are not exactly cyclical, and the cited extinctions are not always massive. There may indeed be a tenth planet or a companion star to the sun. These bodies may disturb distant comets, send them careening into the inner solar system. But even if true, we are not due for an encounter for hundreds of thousands of years, meaning the problem lies elsewhere."

The petite man anxiously questions. "Then why did Channel 73 report a shift in our orbit?"

"An amateur astronomy group reported an infinitesimal shift. Infinitesimal." To exhibit this infinitesimal measure, Dr. Vanetsky pinches his thumb and pointer finger tightly together.

"Well, isn't that all it takes?"

"Without getting too technical, let me just say, no one takes their measurements seriously."

Senator Mungus rises to his feet. "You heard the man. It is all a mistake so everyone go home. There's no problem. We're just having a bad year."

"It's not a mistake." A man wearing a striped bow-tie unzips his left tie pocket to display his laminated credentials. "I am a professor at the university. I have a Ph.D. in mathematics and astrophysics and I can verify those findings. There has indeed been an infinitesimal shift in our orbit. However, it is not due to an outside contaminant. In my estimation, the likely cause is not enough Chaos."

Senator Seerington scoffs, "Not enough chaos? You have got to be kidding. In another minute, we'll be giving out straight jackets."

A handful of popcorn rains down on the straight-laced bow-tie man. Dusting a kernel from his jacket shoulder, he qualifies. "I am speaking mathematically. Chaos is a theory which suggests that all systems, no matter how complex, are ruled by underlying patterns. Take the stock market. According to traditional theory, the stock market is driven by speculation about a company's future performance based on its internal management structure, its level of research and development, its assets and liabilities, the economy, the political environment and all the rational etceteras. However, despite the best calculations of cautious investors and portfolio experts, the market invariably seems to rise and fall against predictions. Traditional theory asserts this happens because not all factors have been taken into account. Then came automated trading. Using the most sophisticated computers and sophisticated minds, we programmed all those conceivable etceteras. For a while, the market inched steadily but slowly upward; everyone profited, though not by much. The random pattern had been seemingly exorcised — until that fateful Monday when the market crashed with such force, it shattered the reputation of many market gurus. Turns out, we had only momentarily suppressed the natural direction of the stock market, like a raging river, but when the rains proved too much, the underlying pattern reasserted itself. Sometimes, it only takes a single, unexpected straw.

"In other words, the system, whatever the system, is far too complex for the human mind to—" When more protest popcorn besieges the professor's head, he patiently concedes. "Perhaps a more comprehensible illustration. Tuna salad. Remember when your mother deposited a can of tuna into a salad bowl, minced in celery, onion and mayo, then mushed the ingredients into a creamy spread? Remember how she peeled off the crust before dissecting the unwieldy sandwich into four little squares that perfectly fitted your diminutive hands? Have you tried making tuna salad lately? No matter how long you work the mixture, you end up with clumps of onions, strings of celery, globs of mayonnaise. It refuses to magically mush, as if..."

Stunned by the introduction of tuna salad into the debate, Senator Seerington cantankerously counsels. "Oh, get a life! Switch to spam. What's your point?"

"That, that the more we control, the more we subvert natural forces — but never for long. I suspect that is what is happening. Over the past many centuries, we have manipulated the biosphere, altered the chemistry of this planet and ourselves. Unfortunately, we can't perceive the underlying pattern. We end up putting in a little too much sugar, and not enough spice. We suppress certain forces, driving them underground. Eventually, they vent in mysterious ways. I suspect this orbital shift is such a venting. The more factors we control, the more unbalanced, unstable the pattern becomes

— and the more likely an unexpected flint in the haystack will burn down the house. So what we have to do is: stop; stop doing. Shut ourselves off. Let the planet heal itself."

Seerington suspiciously accuses. "Sounds like Qwaquiwei thinking."

Old Man Jones reluctantly approaches a microphone. "Maybe Qwaquiwei are right about Mother Earth." As grumbling mumbles sputter around the hall, Jones clarifies. "I don't mean the angel-stardust stuff, but perhaps there is a core of truth. After all, this planet did create us, has sustained us, so in a sense, it is our omniscient mother."

Senator Seerington heatedly interrupts. "The planet is a planet, not a sapient life form. You can't..."

Old Man Jones reasons. "This planet created us conscious life forms. How can inert matter give birth to conscious being. It must itself be conscious. Or do you suggest we are bastards from another galaxy? That's Qwaquiwei thinking. Look, every folklore germinates from a kernel of truth. This romantic notion of Lord Mother Earth, of a planet as a living, breathing, intentional force, may stem from an innate understanding that this planet has weathered many civilizations, like seasons. As we come and go like its leaves, this planet remains an ever deepening root. Maybe we should listen. Maybe an overly technologic route is not the most effective. Maybe it goes against planet physiology. I'm not saying we should discard our thingamajigs, but maybe we should reassess the way we 'evolve'. Maybe we should revisit the myths of Atlantis and..."

Senator Seerington raps a shoe against his head in absolute frustration. "And levitating crystals, and psychotic ghosts, and telepathic cats, and time warps, and worm holes, and dark stars lurking in the outer orbits, and missing links trying to reinsert themselves, and amazing wafers you can eat and eat and never grow fat — except you drop dead and die!" In his self-flagellating zeal, the Senator nearly knocks himself unconscious. He needs a moment to compose himself before pronouncing: "That's what becomes of fantastic thinking!"

Old Man Jones protests this ridicule. "Hey, I'm a gravity and potatoes man myself, but there is some funny shit going down, or haven't you noticed? What about that archeological dig in Bindustan?"

"It was proven a fraud."

Senator Fingerstein corrects Senator Seerington. "It was discredited, for no scientific reason. The evidence at the Bindustan dig is as valid as the evidence at the Clover dig. We've long accepted the Clover dig, the Clover people, so why not accept..."

"Because the Clover people make sense. They fit into the scheme of things, explain current glitches: Qwaquiwei, mutant evolutionists. The Clover people were an agrarian culture, shamanic in the extreme. They painted their penises green, hoping to propitiate the deities of spring. They worshipped forest sprites, consumed massive quantities of alcohol to induce alternate states of consciousness in which they traversed rainbows to procure golden pots of grain to feed their hungry clans. Much like Qwaquiwei shamans today. The Clover people had a sense of evolution, of natural mutation. They pasted a fourth leaf onto a three leaf clover, possibly to bewitch the goddess of transformation. Unlike those misguided evolutionists, the Clover people only symbolically pasted the fourth leaf onto the clover, then dutifully waited their turn to mutate. Aside from excessive alcohol consumption, there's no indication these Clover clans did anything untoward with their body parts, and no indication they were technologically proficient. In contrast, this Bindustan dig suggests you can have it all — then lose it. I accept civilizations come and go, but they don't outright disappear. This Bindustan dig is heresy. A hoax! It implies vast, highly civilized societies..."

"Exactly why it is so unsettling. No one wants to believe it, myself included. Imagine a civilization called Atlantis, succeeded by a civilization called Earth, and who knows how many before them, in between, or thereafter."

"But the Clover people were primitives. How could they have coexisted with these sophisticated Earthlings?"

"The Clover people may not have been so primitive. Just because two guys painted their penises green. Most of them simply wore garish ties."

"Ties which served no purpose. At least our ties turn into phones, hold lunch money, house keys, cold lozenges. Their ties were purely symbolic, typical of pagan peoples."

"Granted, but what we found may not have been the best representation of the Clover people. In any case, the evidence from Bindustan is genuine. It too explains some mythology. There really was a Kansas, and there may indeed have been dinosaurs."

Senator Seerington agitatedly points towards the lobby. "Oy! Do we have to go through this again? Every one back onto the couch while Dr. Sigmund repeats how we are suffering panic anxiety. One of the delusions of panic anxiety is that once upon a time there was a land of Oz and a wise old Wizard who, to this day, protects humankind, like a fairy godmother. After Dr. Sigmund explains this archetypal fantasy, he will give us a lesson on subconscious fears manifesting as dragons and dinosaurs: humongous creatures which represent our feelings of being overpowered, overwhelmed..."

"You can't dismiss dinosaurs."

"You can't be serious, Senator Fingerstein. Creatures one hundred feet long, weighing more than two herds of unicorns? Creatures the size of airplanes flying over oceans filled with creatures the size of lakes? It boggles the mind to imagine. Such creatures would collapse from their own weight. If they were so damn colossal, we'd be falling over their skeletons to this day."

Senator Fingerstein insists, "It's not so preposterous. Two hundred years ago, we scoffed at the idea of unicorns until we uncovered those fossils. Maybe, the same geologic event that wiped out all traces of billions of Earthlings, wiped out all traces of dinosaurs."

"Billions of Earthlings?" Senator Seerington clamps his hands over his ears. "I can't believe you believe— Billions of Earthlings are even more inconceivable than hundred foot dragons. Planet Epsilon is at capacity at five hundred million.

How could this continent ever have supported a population in the billions, unless Earthlings were as small as dinosaurs were large, and lived in the clouds like the sea swallows."

Dr. Vanetsky astutely apprises. "Supposedly there were other continents which became submerged when polar ice caps melted."

"Polar ice caps couldn't fill my jacuzzi, let alone submerge a continent." Senator Seerington exaggerates for effect, and for the lauding laughs of his loyal disbelievers.

After the sniggering subsides, Dr. Vanetsky patiently contends. "A hundred thousand years ago, polar ice caps were more vast and extensive."

Senator Seerington yanks a cigar from his tie pocket, then challenges. "Just what are you alleging Dr. Vanetsky, Senator Fingerstein and Mr. Gravity and Potatoes man? That we are at war with Lord Mother Earth? That she repeatedly destroys hard-working humans? What is she? Some kind of subterranean force field? A mischievous forest sprite? Do we placate her by propitiating ourselves at the fire of Qwa?"

Dr. Vanetsky answers for the maligned threesome. "I am not offering a solution, Senator. I am merely..."

Agitatedly gnawing one end of his unlit cigar, Senator Seerington reproaches. "But of course not. You only came to fan the fires of discontent. Who the hell publicized this event? Did people think we were giving out free beer?"

Jones despairingly throws up his hands as he struggles to articulate. "We— we can't offer a solution because we have yet to consider — what we have yet to consider. Nobody knows exactly what to do, but we better be facing the right direction when the final warning hits. Evidence from the Bindustan digs indicate Earth suffered climatic changes, drastic warmings, inexplicable ice phases. Northern continents became colder, desiccate. There is mention of a nation of men: males. A billion of them. Perhaps the result of genetic tampering, disease, mutation. Whatever, this male-tilted nation invaded the lower continents. Great wars ensued. While we horde a handful of nuclear devices to counter stray comets, these Earth nations mindlessly stockpiled nuclear and chemical weapons. If we are interpreting their number system correctly, they had more explosives than they could reasonably use. No wonder we have no evidence of this Earth era."

After adjusting his golf cap and failing, Senator Krommueller raises a puzzled hand. "So let me get this clear. Are we saying that once upon a time there were people, half angel, half dragon, only male, with green penises, who lived on clouds? Is that how Qwaquiwei came to be misfit angels, or are they really birdlike Aliens?"

Senator Mungus anxiously interrupts. "More importantly, did they lay eggs? I myself do not understand the significance of this question, but they always ask on those nature shows, 'Was the species an egg-laying species or did it give birth to live young?' Perhaps because some species eat their live young. It is documented that during the great plague, infected citizens were bricked up, right there in their houses, then left to die. During the famine of '29, executed prisoners were supposedly ground into muesli. I find it hard to believe we could do such a thing. After all, we are more or less friends. I hope so because as it happens, I ran out of chips." Senator Mungus giggles nervously as he pulls apart his empty bag of Cracker Wackers. "Frankly, I don't think well when I'm hungry. If my esteemed colleges wouldn't mind, I'd like to excuse myself so I can..."

President Linkyn petulantly snatches the fresh bag of chips Senator Krommueller attempts to pass to Senator Mungus. "No senator leaves this floor. No citizen leaves this hall. No future civilization is going to find the remains of the last, and apparently least of the civilizations of Epsilon. Do you hear what I am saying? We have no evidence — of anything. How did we come to such a state of ignorance? We do not see the wall that is there, yet there must be a wall because we can't get through. I suspect this is where those disappearing civilizations most likely disappeared, so please pay attention. We don't know who, what the enemy is. It may be disgruntled environment groups. It may be conspiring politicos. It may be conniving industrialists or militant native factions. It might indeed be alien life forms, newly unleashed force fields, mutant viruses — or just us chickens. The key point is: we have no evidence, so don't anyone close their eyes for a single second. Do you hear what I am saying? I don't want to wake up tomorrow with a dinosaur in my bed."

SCHRODINGER'S CAT

It has been six months since Reem's death. Doctors from various specialties failed to pinpoint the cause. Grace buried Reem, not knowing why she buried him. Not having died of something leaves the semantic argument that Reem still operates in some gambit dimension like the proverbial quantum mechanical cat — who exists both alive and dead while unobserved inside a hypothetical box, where a hypothetical vial of cyanide remains both broken and unbroken. Should someone explicitly open the box, the vial must settle upon an outcome; the vial may break, causing the hypothetical cat to die. Unobserved, the cat remains both alive and dead as it pleases.

Envisioning Reem in a similarly paradoxical state, Grace hesitates outside Dr. Mandarin's office. Turning the door handle will compel Reem's amorphous box to collapse into its unresurrectable coffin. It was easier to lay Reem's body into the ground than to now face the fatal error that put him there. Perhaps Reem had not been well, but Grace had failed to notice. As his duly appointed mother, she should have insisted he ingest more cruciferous vegetables. Perhaps he was deficient in iron or selenium or chromium picolinate. Perhaps there was something in the air that day, some windblown contaminant she should have plucked particle by particle from the ethers. When was the last time she scrutinized Reem's eyes for suspicious sun spots or scoured the scruff of his neck in search of subterraneous ticks. Dr. Mandarin takes no note of Grace's inner hauntings, nor does he offer any consoling salutations. Evasively sifting through his expandable folder swollen with quizzical footnotes, illegibly titled charts, and magnetic ray images, he waits for Grace to pose her burning questions.

"Did it have anything to do with the microwave emissions saturating Mr. Deloy's apartment?"

Dr. Mandarin waves his hand assuringly. "On a long-term basis, microwave leakage poses health risks, but in Reem's case, there was not enough..."

"His excursion south of the border? The water? The pollen? He was slightly asthmatic. Perhaps he..."

Dr. Mandarin discounts, "Not a virus or bacterium, not a parasite or asthmatic attack."

Grace quivers as she enunciates the unthinkable. "Was he poisoned?"

Doctor Mandarin raises an eyebrow as he painstakingly explains. "I see we left this much too long, but a boy dropping dead that young? Had to make sure it wasn't the tip of a bubonic iceberg. We suspected many things but weren't absolutely sure. If you hadn't petitioned he be buried, we might still be testing, testing. The problem with modern medicine. In some respects, we know too much. According to my notations, you made a request concerning his body parts. Why? Were you missing something? I mean, did you take some kind of inventory? As far as I know, everything that could be forwarded was forwarded. We—" Dr. Mandarin opens his empty palms to attest. "We don't save things."

Unwilling, unable to explain, Grace trails her voice despairingly. "So what's the bottom line? What should I have done? Or do you still have no idea?"

"Oh, we have reached consensus. It is our opinion, Grace, that your son suffered an atria-ventricle-node impasse, meaning the conducting tissue through which electrical impulses travel stopped conducting. These electric impulses stimulate the heart to contract, to beat. We don't fully understand the mechanism that caused the fatal outage, though we have implicated the gene. A transplant could have done no good, like putting a new engine into a car that has no gas. His heart failure precipitated his death, but it was not his heart that failed. Something outside delivered the fatal message to stop. It occurs in an instant and without warning. I suppose that's the good news: there was nothing anyone could have done."

Grace is stricken with a terrible realization. "Rom is his twin. Are you telling me Rom will..."

"No. We examined Rom. He does not suffer the same genetic sequence."

"But Reem and Rom are—" Grace pauses but does not correct her tense as she perplexes, "identical."

Dr. Mandarin submits Rom and Reem's genetic prints for comparison. "In fact, no identical twins are actually identical."

Grace ponders this counter-intuitive statement with its residue of relief. Probing the cryptic genetic codes with her fingers, Grace searches for life after ashes have turned to ashes.

SETTLING SCORES

Iroquois races down the court halls as an angered chihuahua chomps at his heels. The distempered chihuahua was one of many distempered mongrels at Judge Corbin's stray puppy reunion. When the uninvited Iroquois interrupted their heated feeding frenzy, three chihuahuas, still awaiting bones, attacked. Iroquois escaped, without pleading his case, and without his accompanying court guard. Unfortunately, one rabid chihuahua snaps and snarls Jefferson into a corner, forcing him to take refuge in Judge Rollands' courtroom.

Iroquois had hoped Judge Corbin could hear his case. To her, justice is less an accounting than an art form. Unfortunately, she remains on temporary leave for keeping garter snakes inside her desk draw. The censure was not for harboring garter snakes, but for failing to inform the unsuspecting cleaning crew. Without Judge Corbin overlooking the objections, he has no chance. Although the hearings are still preliminary, Iroquois can feel the odds stacking against him.

As Iroquois falters, gulping for air, Judge Rollands craggily reprimands, "You're late. And where is your court guard? And why is a big rat gnawing on your pant cuff?"

"Told you I had connections. My fairy godmother turned that snippy court guard into a dirty dog, so watch your step." Recalling his circumstances, Jefferson politely appends, "your Honor."

Judge Rollands cautions. "Not only do you need a good lawyer, you could use a new fairy godmother. Would court security please remove the afflicted court guard. Perhaps we can provide some ChowChewies until the spell wears off. As for you, Jefferson..."

"What do you mean, I need a good lawyer? Who has been assigned to represent me? Caselli? Papdopoulos? Morris? Gunter? Needleman? Franco? Hashimoto?" As Judge Rollands continues to blink 'no', Iroquois quips. "Running out of layers here. What's the deal?"

"Fact is, no lawyer wants to take your case. Some fear for their lives. Most refuse on the grounds they will unlikely be paid. We can't force them you know. Not like in the old days."

"I see. Well then, I'll just defend myself. I'm a lawyer, you know."

Wearily, the judge notes. "A disbarred lawyer."

"Merely suspended!"

Again, the judge wearily notes. "Either way, you lost fourteen out of your last sixteen cases. Not an inspiring record. Look, I could get my nephew. Boy could use the experience. Fresh out of law school but eager, eager, eager. If you want someone more seasoned, I could get Fenster. New medication seems to be working. He rarely hears the voices and when he does, they give surprisingly good advice."

"Uh, thanks, but I'll defend myself."

"I'm warning you, Jefferson; you can't plead insanity later. Are you sure, absolutely sure, you want to defend yourself?"

"No!" Grace slaps down her briefcase.

Iroquois is noticeably baffled. "Where did you come from? More importantly, what are you doing here?"

Grace sportively teases. "I drew the shortest straw. Besides, if you defend yourself, you will probably be hanged. If I defend you, I will make certain of it."

Iroquois nervously inches away. "I could get a restraining order. You wouldn't want to create a scene."

"It was a joke, Iroquois. Lighten up. I—" Grace wants to apologize. Iroquois was a memorable lover, a sometime friend, an unnerving colleague — and the man she unjustly accused of murdering her son. She should say something to that effect. Instead she shrugs. "Whatever our past differences, you deserve a fair defense."

Discomforted by this cavalier quip, Iroquois testily insists. "I am not guilty! I tampered with that computer creature, yes, but I had nothing to do with that ceiling collapse, and I had nothing to do with— what happened to your son. I—

I am not guilty. I may have had something to do with the skunks. I am not admitting that I did, but I may have."

Grace assures him. "You did; you already told me you did."

Iroquois tries to re-sort his facts. "Well, what do you expect? I'm dedicated to fighting polluting industries, corrupt politicians, ineffective bureaucracies — jackasses, because someone has to stand for something. We used to be a continent of diversity, used to believe in a pantheon of gods, danced to divergent drumbeats. Now, everyone is as unvarying as clumpy white rice."

"Not to nit-pick but you left out the part where we waged wars, leveled entire cities to determine which drumbeat got played at the opening ball game, then whose God ended up on the official stamp. We didn't mind anyone who was different for as long as we didn't mind. The moment we did, we hanged them, then fed them to the wilderbeasties, until all the wilderbeasties died. Too much human excrement in their diet, as I recall."

Iroquois again grows testy. "Why do you always pretend not to know what I mean. You know what I'm talking about: the transforming ideas, the driving passions. Doesn't it bother you that we're evolving into artificial life-forms? Trying to circumvent evolution, fast-forward without decaying between lifetimes. Everyone waiting for some grand unified theory to tie up the loose ends, plug up those embarrassing oral-anal interfaces. Wake up and smell the rigor mortis! We didn't come out of a box of Cracker Wackers. At least, I didn't. No one appreciates what I am trying to do."

Belatedly, Grace voices her concern. "Iroquois, are you okay?"

"No, I am not okay. I have been dungeoned, like a dirty dog, in a lime-green cell, for months. No one was willing to defend me; no one brought me vitamin supplements. The media was too busy reporting on missing sugar packets from the Senate cafeteria to bother about my unprecedented detention. All I had to occupy my intellect was a fraying poster of the pogowilly pond at the Fairweather Golf Haven. Some kind of mind-bending plot. Everyone knows how I feel about golf courses. Now, night after night, I am plagued with recurring dreams where I am chained to a lawn mower, a lime-green lawn mower, on a lime-green lawn. Lichen grows on the clouds; clot-moss tangles the noon-day rays. Beneath, in the twilight darkness, the lime-green tuffs glow like irradiated waste as I am doomed to mow, mow, mow. The grass runs on relentlessly, without a single relieving weed, or reprieving gradient. If that weren't haunting enough, I am pestered by the ghosts of poisoned gofers. Their portly little bodies are tied into lugubrious chains, depravedly hitched to my demon juggernaut. As I mow, this chain of ghostly gofers grows longer. It takes increasing effort to push forward. All the while, the gofers woefully wail, accuse me of not representing them, of catering to the high-class minks, the amusing otters, the well-connected eagles. They blame me for their excruciating deaths in their subterraneous hovels. I'm not getting any sleep; this mowing, mowing, mowing is wearing me down. Meanwhile, each night the chain of gofers is ever longer. If I don't escape that lime-green cell soon, they'll yank me to my subterraneous death. I will have died, having been falsely accused — by everyone!"

Iroquois directs this accusation at Grace as he boldly embarks. "And for the record, I did catch a fish. I distinctively remember having blackened catfish for your birthday. I reeled it from the muddy bottom with my own two hands. Don't you remember? You complained about the pepper. Too much pepper and not enough lemon, you said."

Grace gawks at Iroquois. "What?"

The judge is equally confused. "Yes, what?"

Increasingly flushed, Iroquois confronts Grace. "You said 'We never did have fish for dinner' but we did. On your birthday. I distinctly re..."

Grace lowers her voice as she cautions. "Iroquois, I'll get you moved to less lime-green quarters, get you some multiple vitamins. However, this is not the place to revive..."

"Fine for you, but I had invaluable time, time, time to contemplate in my claustrophobic lockup. I thought about us. It wasn't so bad. I may not have been the perfect man, but it was hardly hell. You exaggerate the minor kinks in our relationship. It could have worked. After all, I did bring home that catfish."

"Since we are speaking for the record, it was tofu." Grace sorts and resorts a stack of papers while bluntly challenging. "You blackened a wedge of tofu. For the record, I didn't mind it being tofu. For the record, I let you think I thought it was catfish, but it wasn't catfish, was it? And you didn't catch it, did you? And *you*!" Grace raps Iroquois with the now rolled up papers as she emphatically maintains. "You complained about the pepper."

"I complained about *your* pepper. My *catfish* was already blackened. Had blue and blackened it with my own two hands. Went through all that effort trying to save you some trouble, but you had to go and add more seasoning."

"Because the *tofu* started to show through. I was trying to save your face, as I am trying — unsuccessfully, to do now." Grace again raps Iroquois with the rolled up papers as Judge Rollands appeals.

"Ms. Ivanosky? Mr. Jefferson? Could one of you please..."

Grace isn't finished with Iroquois. "But as usual, you are making it very difficult. *Difficult* is your middle name."

"That may well be, but at least, at last, you admit to putting on that pepper."

Grace cannot let sleeping catfish lie. "Because *you* mislabeled the cayenne as chili. I thought I was adding chili but it was cayenne so of course it was too hot. You only ever add a pinch of cayenne." Grace petitions Judge Rollands. "Your honor, I smeared an entire plunk. Like dissolving a pound of sugar into a teaspoon of tea. That was how our relationship ended: with a lethal dose of cayenne on one bitsy wedge of tofu. Of course it was hot." Turning to Iroquois for her final summation, Grace blusters. "It was too damn hot! I still have scars in my tracheal lining to prove it, so exactly what is your point, Jefferson?"

Yanking back his shoulders, Iroquois plaintively puffs. "That I am not guilty. I just want you to know, to believe — I am not that kind of man."

Grace contritely bows her head. "I know, Iroquois. I know you are not guilty."

At last satisfied, Iroquois motions to the Judge. "As it turns out, your honor, I plead innocent to the charges and Grace Ivanosky will be representing me — and will protest the conditions of my internment."

Caught off guard, Grace reluctantly nods. Taking this as his cue to make matters worse, Iroquois hastens to add, "As well as the shameless delay in my case being heard, along with the glaring irregularities of these proceedings."

Grace narrows her eyes. Taking this as his cue to litigate full swing, Iroquois spumes. "Prompted by political pressure, corporate payoffs and..."

Grace cuts Iroquois off at the pass. "And your honor, my client has nothing further to say!"

Having made her peace with Iroquois, Grace hopes to lessen the rift with Connery Deloy. She is partly responsible for his troubles. It was unprofessional to forsake him. His replacement lawyers did not counsel well. As a result, he has been judged without jury. Grace surveys Deloy's renovated office. This time, there is no gregarious robot to greet her, only a pallid human secretary named Wayne who officiously informs: "Mr. Deloy is not in, nor is he expected anytime soon. This nasty scandal over Mazing Wafers has compelled him to retreat to his country estate. I'm here to collect messages." Popping his gum, he solicits, "Got any?"

Grace inquires, "Does he often call in?"

"Once a week, to ask how many messages I have taken. But he doesn't want to know who they are from, and he doesn't want to know what they have to say."

Grace is oddly relieved. Connery has not traumatically changed. "Mind if I use your phone?" Wayne shrugs 'no' as he returns to his romance novel and bag of Cracker Wackers.

On the seventh ring, Connery flicks a button, triggering his prerecorded message. "I may or may not be here. I am incommunicado. Anyone wishing to harass me, should contact my well-paid lawyers, area-code..." Thus shielded, Connery retreats to the sanctity of his bathroom. After exiting the bedroom, the lights switch off. Upon entering the bathroom, the lights switch on. When he sits on the toilet, a dispenser obligingly dispenses eight sheets. When he commands, "More", the dispenser obligingly dispenses another five. Before and after, things activate and deactivate: the toilet flushes; the faucet anoints his hands with soap and lukewarm water; a gust of hot air expeditiously dries his dripping fingers. Satisfied, Connery smiles at himself in the mirror. The mirror doesn't smile back. Failing to notice, he mechanically commands, "Teeth." An electric toothbrush thrusts from the medicine cabinet. Placing it against his teeth, he commands, "Brush." Industriously, the toothbrush brushes up and down, then side to side, spraying water and toothpaste into his orifice crannies, pausing briefly to note, "Cavity in molar BL2." Connery groans, his mouth filled with paste suds. Meanwhile, a glass has filled with water. He rinses. This time, the mirror registers a dot of toothpaste at the corner of his mouth. After duly rectifying this blotch, he re-enters the bedroom. Once again, the lights switch on.

He continues through rooms, triggering off, triggering on light switches. Eventually, he retires to his auditorium. In lieu of rows of theater seats is a single, sofa chair. Musty velvet curtains from a by-gone age shroud the semi-circular stage. As Connery snuggles into his conventionally plump sofa, a solicitous device arranges a tray stacked with pancakes, strawberries, and a pot of piping hot coffee. After sipping a sip of his cinnamon-spiced brew, Connery pronounces with great relish, "Jungle John."

The heavy, velvet curtains slowly open, revealing a prop-less stage. A flick-flick later, multiple projectors activate, filling the awaiting space with holographic images from Connery's favorite Jungle John movie. The plot revolves around a baby boy left to die on a jungle island. Remarkably, he survives, abetted by nurturing wolves. Years later, an extraordinarily beautiful princess is shipwrecked on this same jungle island. Despite the fact that he is a grunting ape man, and she, an articulate blue-blood, as the incredible story goes: they live happily ever after.

When the reel starts to roll, Weston Finley, the famous Jungle John actor, hurdles from a cliff. Moments later, he splashes into an emerald green lagoon. By pressing an option on his remote control, Connery superimposes his own face onto Weston's burly, bronzed body. While Connery's jelly-belly torso jiggles inside his pink-flowered boxer shorts, and his knobby knees knock open his frayed terry robe, and his bunion-studded feet wriggle inside his worn, blue slippers, and his flat rump cowers into his plush sofa, his technicolor rendition swings through the jungle with the greatest of ease, making love to a brainy redhead—

No. Playback. Superimpose. Swings through the jungle with the greatest of ease making love to a buxom blond—

No. Playback. Superimpose. Makes love to a brassy brunette—

Pause. This is where the plot tends to slow down. Connery has settled upon the perfect ending, but he cannot settle upon his supporting woman. Once, he attempted to painstakingly piece her pixel by pixel, but no matter how he mixed and matched her component parts, he could not get her right. Despite his database of happy endings, despite his archives of bathing beauties and homecoming queens, Connery never manages to fall in love. To compensate, he relies heavily on special effects. He can dispatch tornadoes with a simple click, trigger earthquakes, precipitate fire, brimstone and hail. He can toggle between soft summer breezes and raging cyclones. He can drench the room with the scent of gardenias, conjure screeching monkeys, stampeding buffalo, enticing redheads—

Stop! Rewind. Make that: stalking cheetahs and a puckering blond, leaning her buxom—

Stop! Rewind. Make that: projecting her long, lean legs from her half slit skirt as she demurely caresses—

Stop! Rewind. Make that: as she bewitchingly slips her hand under his—

Stop! Rewind. Make that: insistently slips her hand under his— Yes! Rewind. Replay: under his— Oh yes, yes.

Damn! Tape snag. A robot wheels to the rescue. It yanks, it tugs to no avail. Conceding the movie over, Connery returns to the bathroom. After commanding, "Teeth," the medicine cabinet thrusts the electric toothbrush forward. Connery places it against his teeth, then commands, "Brush." After dutifully depositing water and toothpaste, the toothbrush brushes up and down, side to side — then stops. Brandishing it threateningly, he repeats more loudly, "Brush." It remains motionless, deaf. Connery insistently demands, "Brush! Brush!" In obliging response, the lights go out.

Connery exits the bathroom. However, when he enters the bedroom, the lights in the bedroom do not switch on, then the lights in the bathroom do not switch off. Instead, the lights in the den switch on. When he enters the den, the lights in the bedroom switch on, then the lights in the den switch off. He re-enters the bedroom. The lights switch off.

Connery surmises something is wrong. Clutching his non-functioning toothbrush, he proceeds to the backup generator outside. Oblivious to a misting rain, he tramps forward, muttering fuse curses. The moment he converts to the backup generator, all the lights in the house switch on. Connery stops cursing. Perhaps back-up generators, like understudies, must have their day. He is pleased with his best-laid plan. However, as he starts back towards the house, every device connected to an electric outlet begins to execute its given function. Like a house possessed, the steel burglary gates slam down on all the windows, all the doors, including the garage with his brand new jeep-jet sealed safely inside. A moment later, the deafening hum falls silent — as the entire house ominously fades to black.

His mouth filled with paste suds, Connery returns to the generator where he belligerently flips switches up and down, on and off, side to side, over, over, and over. He continues this ritual for some time, unable to accept the unthinkable: that he is locked outside, lost in the woods.

LOST IN THE WOODS

Like a dog put out for the night, Connery waits by his front door hoping to be let inside. He waits all afternoon. He waits all evening. The next morning, cold and ravenous, he tries to pry open doors designed to withstand a nuclear blast — with his electric toothbrush.

Connery considers the facts: no phone, no car, no crackers in his pocket. The meter reader won't make her round for another three weeks. His secretary does not expect a call for another five days. Since Connery prepaid him until the end of month, five days could easily stretch into seventeen. Wayne will unlikely attempt to ascertain his benefactor's whereabouts, until those benefacts run out.

He considers the options. The paved road leads nowhere long before somewhere comes into view. Due east is the sprawling metropolis. Unfortunately, due west of due east is a forest. The answer seems semi-clear; he can't sit still until he starves to death. Reluctantly, Connery hazards the woods in his royal blue slippers. Unlike Jungle John, his pace is painstakingly slow. His slippers keep slipping off. Eventually, they vanish beneath a bog. The more fervently he strides, the more deeply his heels sink into the accommodating mud. Moments after impact, his prints dissolve into the gulping ground.

Hour after hour, Connery climbs over felled trees, rips through creeping vines, ducks under pinioning branches, snags on holly prickles. Twice he tries to build a fire, hoping to get warm, or attract attention. Carefully, he selects the driest leaves, the smallest twigs, then flints two stones over and over until his fingers bleed blisters. He considers turning back. Clearly, he has underestimated this patch of green on his mental map, and conversely, overestimated his boyscout readiness. Occasionally his right hand clutches for the remote control, awakening him to the material difference between reality and its virtual version. In this reality version, there is no one to bring him a pitcher of water. In this reality version, there is no water. Initially, Connery prospects for a stream. He knows for a fact there are no lakes, but there must be a stream. As the day draws to an end, Connery concedes there need not be a stream. Perhaps there is only the rain. Wistfully combing for clouds in the cloudless sky, Connery crashes to the forest floor; his slipperless foot has snagged on a tangle of ground vines. Cursing, he rubs his scraped elbow, then wipes his face where wet leaves gunkily adhere—

Wet leaves? Connery dangles a damp frond before tentatively licking. At first, he presses clusters to his thirsting tongue hoping to quench himself by numbers. Unfortunately, the least efficient proves the most effective. Connery resigns himself to the gritty, sweet mizzle of leaf by leaf. The process is time consuming, but the passing insects entertain him. Eventually, the tormenting parchedness abates. Occasionally, an industrious ant ambles by with a juicy berry. In the long run, the berries come few and far between, compelling Connery to press onward. He reasons, if there is one berry, there must be others clinging to a berry bush. He tries to sniff them out.

Unlike his crass special effects of ode-de-wintergreen, the scents of the forest run more complex. A light breeze carries the scent of wild lavender; a sudden gust bears the aroma of burning pine sap; a blustery undercurrent mingles the potpourri of decomposing leaves with the germinating fragrance of rambling mosses, budding mushrooms. These luring scents aggravate Connery's hunger, weary his efforts. The air begins to smell like wine. Serendipitously, he comes upon a clutch of eggs. Suspecting a forest mirage, he crouches to examine the dainty white orbs twinkling in their nebular nests like newly exposed stars. Gently, he addles one; it butts its comrade, creating a hairline crack. Instinctively salivating, he contemplates them scrambled and smothered in mushrooms. Driven by this gourmet vision, Connery maniacally excavates for truffles. As he mentally whisks his savory fungi into his yolk batter, something rustles him to attention.

"Cheep, cheep." Inside the nest, a newborn morning dove has hatched. Connery will have to settle for a side-order, over-easy. Perhaps, he will be lucky and find a tuber or... "Cheep, cheep." The second egg begins to break apart, shattering his culinary delusions. As the incipient dove makes its way into the world one chip at a time, Connery despairingly observes. "Don't expect me to regurgitate a mouthful of worms into your bellies. On second thought—", he licks his lips experimentally, "a bird is not unlike a chicken. Why can't I marinate you guys in some tangy tree sap, then fry— Of course, what will I use for oil? And what will I do for a pan?" Connery reconsiders the gamy appetizer. "And who the hell am I kidding? The thought of ingesting grungy, mite infested, barbing bones, gunky gizzards and slimy— is nauseating, gross beyond all— Let's face it, you're no chicken nuggets, and I'm no Jungle John. I'm exhausted, hungry, cold — and doomed."

Stoically collapsing his spine into the rippled bark of an ancient redwood, Connery yanks his cocklebur-studded terry tightly around his body, then sinks to the ground where quietly, very quietly, he begins to cry. His life is ending so absurdly. The morning doves cheep in consolation, or perhaps self-pity for their own unhappy plight. Connery pats one gently on its stubby, stubbled head. "If your mother doesn't return, guess you'll die too, or grow up orphans. I'm an orphan. Kind of. My mother is a mermaid. Had to abandon me to save the whales. I know — whales are now extinct. So much for good intentions. The upside is: one day I'll inherit her ocean dominion. With one flick of her wand, my mother the mermaid will transform me into a porpoise. Imagine floating effortlessly and unbound inside the amniotic elixir of that fathomless womb. I would choose never to be born again into a world so oppressed by gravity and dryness."

Connery responds to the chirping birds in mock protest. "Why so surprised? Opting for whales over widgets? He must be delirious. Hey, if I knew how to make a whale, I'd make a whale. Don't believe my critics. They say I'm trying to construct machines that think like humans when the correct approach is humans who think like machines. You know: logical, rational, even-handed. My covert intention is to plant robots in every home, every government backroom, every corporate closet. Humans, being such mindless mimics, will pick up the noble qualities of their digital nursemaids. Machines have no hidden agenda. Well, I don't have to tell you. Of course, you shouldn't take our actions personally. It is our nature, our genetic tragedy.

"Speaking of genetic tragedies, my father, the sperm keeper, was a paper boy. Really. He turned up unexpectedly, unwantedly years too late. What a letdown. Had convinced myself he was an astronaut. Turns out, he was a space cadet." Connery swirls his hand derisively to indicate. "A little slow in the head, if you know what I mean. He contacted me because he had contracted a fatal case of tripoli after being bitten by a rabid tsetse fly. He warned me to get vaccinated, then stay out of Hoolungadin. He thought getting bitten by a tsetse fly and ending up in Hoolungadin was hereditary. I think he was a little nuts. I thanked him. He left. Never saw him again.

"One of the many reasons I denounce people. They are so inferior to — themselves. Problem is not competing with the guy next door, but the guy inside. I'll let you in on a deep, dark secret. I often experience supreme notions, but when I look in the mirror, all that reflects back is a naked ape. Why is that? Why can I debate like a well-versed professor, but invariably argue like a chimpanzee? Instead of presenting the overwhelming facts, I end up throwing the nearest stone. I can seduce like a romeo, but I screw like a wild dingo dog. I can spend hours stoking the fires, arranging the kindling, but once that fire starts to rage, I become consumed, promise her anything, forfeit everything I believe. When I have the mind to, I can prepare a banquet feast like a fastidious epicurean with a quarter teaspoon of this and a pinch of that. I can simmer the sauce, sauté the scallions, layer the noodles so they perfectly perpendicularly intersect, but once I start to salivate, it's chomp, chomp, chomp like a frenzied hyena. I can tell you every last ingredient that went into the dish but, to save my life, I cannot tell you what it tasted like, because I can act out supreme notions like a very well-trained seal, but can only react like an orangutan.

"Is it the same for you? Do you harbor supreme notions, wonder why you glide like an eagle but cower like a morning dove? Perhaps not. Perhaps your place in the biologic hierarchy has made you humble. Humans have no natural enemies to keep them honest, no comparable creature to challenge their point of view. We get to destroy everything. We invent gods who threaten retribution, but they are only for show. None has ever called our bluff. Sometimes, I wonder if we misbehave on purpose, like a child testing its mother. If she comes, it means we are not the forsaken bastards we so evidently seem."

As if on cue, mother dove returns to the nest, her beak brimming with mealy worms. Growing increasingly feverish, Connery anemically smiles. "Guess you guys won't be orphans after all. Hi, mother dove. Didn't by any chance bring me a beetle to gnaw on? Don't strain for a resemblance. I take after dad."

With heavy heart, Connery confesses. "Vowed never to seek her out, you know, but I was driven by a supreme notion — or was it idle curiosity? Whatever, I hired detectives to locate my mother, the mermaid. After the whales expired, I expected her to return home. Instead, I had to track her down — to a faded photograph. She had died years earlier, having boozed herself into oblivion. Had a bald spot on the top of her head. Rest was painted orange like a harvest squash."

Connery's tears ooze like pus. "My mother, the harvest squash, never said she loved me, never heard me say how I loved her. How I loved her. How so illogical. The bitch abandoned me, expelled me from her womb like a common twitch-tick. All my life, I have been trying to construct a surrogate, hoping to crawl back in, make my peace. The age-old story: looking for love, looking to love. You can't escape the impulse. Exactly what is it? Some kind of tenacious microbe, I suspect. You find them in the most barren dessert, most frigid arctic, most far-flung, extinguished moon: things too microscopic to mention, thriving despite such hostile odds. When complex organisms crumble, unable to agree on the supporting details, these nearly negligible life-forms, these very lowest common denominators persist. You can bulldoze your way out of anything given enough dynamite, but there's no escaping something that perniciously small."

Overwhelmed by the scope of his contemplation, Connery succumbs to sleep. Hours later, he wakens ravenous, thirsty, and sore.

"Ouch!" A squirrel, high in the tree-top, is using Connery's head for target practice. Attempting to defend himself, he retrieves the assaulting projectile, then aims at the jesting sniper. Just before unleashing his cracked nugget, he pauses to assess — the cracked, edible nugget, along with the mounds of similar nuts now littering the forest bed. He does not debate their nutritive value. Voraciously, he scoops, chews and spits, scoops, chews and spits, while the administering squirrel drops nut after nut for good measure. Connery sputters his gratitude, his cheeks stuffed like a chipmunk's.

"Can't tell you how I appreciate your hospitality. I was starving. Stomach got so tight thought it might actually digest itself. Kept dreaming about barbecued pigeons smothered in mushrooms, but after picking out all the annoying bones, there was nothing left to swallow. By the end of the dream, I was as hungry as when it began."

Connery crams the nuts into his mouth almost continuously, lest some mangy ground scavenger plunder a portion. In between bites, he rhapsodizes. "These acorns are delicious. Nice chewy texture. A few rot spots, but I suppose that makes them organic. Could use a roasting and pinch of salt. Not that these aren't perfectly perfect, but if you glaze them with honey— I could market them for you. Under an assumed name. Deloy Enterprises is having some minor perception problems with the consumer public. Why are you helping me? I'm not one of those environmental types. God knows, I'm not here for the fresh air."

Refreshed and hopeful, Connery begins his trek anew. The squirrel, whimsically christened Paper Boy, follows from tree to tree, directing Connery towards pools of ground water, patches of mushrooms, and bushes of mozulberries. Two days later, like Jungle John, Connery is almost enjoying himself. He brushes the dirt off a tuber while Paper Boy perches on his shoulder crunching a tree fruit. After dinner, Paper Boy naps on his lap leaving Connery to peruse the rationale driving his life.

"Kind of nice out here in the woods with the clicking crickets, and hooting owls, and croaking frogs. Of course, years and years ago, before my time, before my father's father's father's time, wild animals: lions, elephants, those grizzly beasts from oft-told fairy tales roamed this continent. Nature types blame the onslaught of human progress for their demise, but lions and elephants were just as wanton in their own space and time. We don't speak blue jay and we don't speak bush bear, so we can't hear how half the time they are calling each other 'stupid.' Ultimately, if there is a God, it's his fault, but there's the rub. How can you blame the only one who can save you from the maelstrom for sticking you in the faulty dinghy that got you there. So we blame each other, point our fingers in the mirror, and chase our own tails.

"Guess we all have our day. My theory is the universe is just experimenting, trying to determine which products work, which products don't. We assume the universe should know, but like us, it's probably new here itself. Didn't exist before the big bang, so how is it supposed to know how all those spewed out ingredients are going to interact.

"When humans die off, this land will be up for grabs again. I suspect it will take too long for a cricket to evolve into a creature capable of manufacturing a self-cleaning oven. The next best hope is the porpoise. Not to put down squirrels, but porpoises are remarkably intelligent. In fact, we had a trade war with them some years ago. When we started seriously polluting the seas, over-fishing the coastlines, porpoises revolted, routed fishes from our fishing areas, nearly killed the industry. We were forced to negotiate, shut down some off-shore facilities. The incident was kept secret. Humans, always harboring romantic notions, would attribute magical talents to this noteworthy but hardly exceptional creature. I was brought in to analyze their electromagnetic faculties. Thought I could learn some neat trick, but after studying porpoises point for point for point, aside from being technically mammals, they are just another flavor fish. Traded a lot of beach balls for tuna, though.

"Dolphins were more promising but also more susceptible; they died *en masse* of a mysterious disorder. That's because everything on this planet is so biodegradable. Supreme notions never get a chance to entrench themselves. Just when a species is on a roll, it becomes extinct. Can you blame us for trying to etch our names on distant stars? Can you fault us for creating plastic? Make something out of plastic and your handiwork remains for all to see, forever and ever." As if to disprove this notion, Connery picks up a discarded plastic article. Sardonically, he concedes, "Like this lovely tampon dispenser."

Bang! Bang! Bang!

Spasmodically waking, Paper Boy bolts from Connery's lap. Connery crumples to his side, dodging another several shots. Cautiously, he rises to trace the assaulting echoes. On the positive side, shots means guns; guns mean hunters, fellow sapiens, and most importantly — jeeps!

Paper Boy does not keep pace. Instead, he screens himself behind a fallen branch, nervously twitching the tip of his tail. Connery surmises. "Not quite relieved as I am, being considered mere game in this neck of the woods. Guess this is where we part ways." Folding his hands, one palm over the other, Paper Boy gazes forlornly. Connery protests, "Hey, don't expect me to say good-bye, to say — you know. I'd invite you home but I'm afraid I'd end up treating you like a pet." Realizing there is nothing more to say, Connery digs into his pockets to extract his remaining nuts. He deposits them on the ground, in farewell parting.

The hunters are just ahead. They welcome Connery with open arms, offer more suitable clothes, then press him with tin after tin of beer. As he sips his third BrewBanger, finishing his tale, the hunters grunt their amazement.

"No food?"

"No flea cap?"

"Wet leaves? Man, I could never. Maybe a day, given enough beef jerky and gin."

"You were going in circles. Didn't you realize that? Didn't you pack a compass? Oh, but of course, you was lost, so I guess..."

"Those acorns probably had worms. You're gonna need shots."

"Why didn't you use your tie-phone? Man like you must have a tie-phone. Oh, but of course, you was nearly naked: boxer shorts and terry robe and shoeless."

"Bet the squirrel had ticks. Lots of twitch-ticks in these woods. Better get tested."

"Couldn't you crawl down the roof vent? Man like you must have a roof vent. Course, you'd need a ladder, which now that I'm thinkin' was probably locked in the garage with the jeep-jet."

"Sorry tah be vulgar but, what'd you use tah wipe your asshole?"

"And how could you sleep without a flea net? Must be bit black and blue. Need some dermocalm lotion?" While the dermocalm dappled hunter offers ooze from his tube, the designated chef advises. "Forget the dermocalm. Man must be fuckin' famished, protein depressed. Needs a slab of this!"

Connery takes another quenching sip from his fermented beverage as a bloody steak is flung onto the hibachi. Suddenly, his perception shifts. The site of the festering meat nearly causes him to vomit. The romantic notion of finding fellow humans is spoiled by their jarring presence. His angelic rescuers seem slovenly and drunk. Their camp is more refuse than refuge. Hacked cartons, cigarette butts, and empty beer tins litter the ground like spit.

Bang! Bang! Bang!

Connery spirals one-hundred-eighty degrees as two hunters start shooting at fire flies. In their zeal to down one, they nearly blow each other's heads off. Connery concludes he is having a delirious seizure. Too many unroasted nuts contending with cheep beer have hyperbolized his sensibilities. However, as one hunter gnaws on a barely cooked piece of meat, as another tears at a bag of chips with his rot-grouted teeth, as others alternately guzzle beer, convulse on thickening cigar exhaust, and scratch themselves, the scene insinuates something ominously familiar. Connery panics as he recalls a recent docu-drama where a picnicking family get captured by a troop of survivalists — then eaten alive. Hoping to dispel this fear, Connery scans the camp site for assuring fish bones from a fishing excursion, or binoculars for birding, or cameras for photographic journals, or dead deer. Instead, he spies charcoal and beer, charcoal and beer, charcoal, and charcoal — and beer. Perhaps the meat is poisoned. Perhaps the beer is drugged. As the hunter-cook flips the sizzling meat, Connery sniffs for closet cannibals, men gone wild in the woods. Without substantiating evidence, he surreptitiously backs into the forest. He backs up farther and farther. Finally, he turns to run. Almost immediately, he trips and bashes his head against the stony ground.

Connery lays unconscious for half a day. Only after the chips have been digested, the alcohol drained from his system, does he waken to his mistake. Connery retraces his steps. Unfortunately, the jeeps have packed and gone. He scrounges a scrap of bacon from the cold ash, finds one glove, puts it on, then follows the tire treads as far as they will take him. This time, there is no Paper Boy to guide him. Occasionally he finds some berries to eat, but day-in, day-out, he grows weaker. By chance, by grace, limping and starved, he comes upon a cabin. The occupant, a little old man with three gold teeth and a telephone, offers the contents of his cupboard, along with one local call.

While Connery peruses the pantry for something to his liking, the gold-toothed man surmises, "You're that there Deloy culprit, aren't yuh? Seen your face on the news. Cops been looking for yuh. Figured yuh for dead. Busted a bunch of radicals who tried tah burn your house down on account of those Mazing Wafers. Courts ruled in your favor, yuh know. Police came tah defend yuh from the rioting rabble. When they got tah your country estate, all they found was your slippers. Suspected foul play. Got a bunch of radicals in jail for alleged kidnapping and murder. So what happened? Did yuh escape? Don't look like they fed yuh much."

Despite Connery's gaunt condition, he bypasses boxes of Captain Munchies, bags of Cracker Wackers, and microwavable Burger Blasters. Spying a bouquet of flowers on the kitchen table, Connery starts to pluck petals. He plucks three rose petals, four white daisy petals, then tears off a lily leaf. As he rolls the petals into the leaf sandwich, he notes a jar packed with seeds, nuts, and dried berries. Gratefully, Connery pours the mixture into a handy vase, dribbles a few tablespoons of honey on top, then scoops a palm full with his bare hands. The little old man with the three gold teeth apprehensively indicates a parrot on a nearby perch. "Uh, you is eating the bird food, fellah."

Connery apologetically nods, prompting the gold-toothed man to return to his freezer to extract a suitable substitute. While Connery compliantly scoops some of his honey-coated concoction into the bird dish, the old man seasons a frozen burger with sassy sauce. Oblivious to the burger thawing on the cast-iron skillet, Connery returns to his seat with the remaining portion of seeds, nuts and berries. Perched like a pampered parrot, he dines, with joyous abandon, on the great outdoors.

SYMMETRIC TERMITES

A sudden heat wave has caught the building crew off guard. Grace removes her jacket, then unties her collar bow, acknowledging the air conditioner has died for the duration. As the jurors grow sleepy, the prosecuting attorney testily curdles. "If it walks like a duck and it talks like a duck, I can only deduce that the man is a skunk! So as not to further taint the good citizens of Epsilon, he should be quarantined along with his radical ideological stench."

As the prosecuting attorney points a snarling finger at the defendant, Grace solicits, "Your honor, Mr. Jefferson is entitled to due process. I insist Mr. Kruger refrain from these incendiary allegations, these reckless proclamations issued solely to prejudice the jury."

The prosecuting attorney lowers his voice to accentuate his practiced glower. "With all due respect, Ms. Ivanosky, I am merely informing the jury of the man's record. He cannot name a single satisfied client. He has no knack for normalcy, no bank account to substantiate his good standing. He is an acknowledged member of that extremist group SOIL, a melange of miscreants who indiscriminately resort to mischief and mayhem of the most reprehensible sort. The man is without conscience, without..."

Grace belligerently approaches the bench. "Your honor, please advise Mr. Kruger to stick to facts. Mr. Kruger is no more privy to Mr. Jefferson's conscience, than I am privy to Mr. Kruger's sperm count. My client admittedly tampered with Mr. Deloy's robotic device."

The prosecuting attorney dramatizes. "He killed her."

"He reprogrammed a robotic device. At most, that is a misdemeanor."

"He sabotaged Mr. Deloy's ceiling, nearly costing Mr. Deloy his life. At least, that is attempted murder."

Grace grows increasing hoarse as she defends. "Mr. Jefferson had nothing to do with that ceiling collapse. It was the work of..."

"Termites!" The prosecuting attorney derisively rolls his eyes. "Yes, we heard your fantastic evidence to that effect. Termites, methodically eating away a perfectly round circle. Since when are creepy crawlers so artistically inclined? I am disappointed to find an attorney of your caliber presenting such absurd arguments."

Iroquois's defense is not going well. A key piece of evidence, termites in Deloy's ceiling, has been dismissed. To make matters worse, Iroquois insisted upon taking the stand. From that vantage, he alienated the one sympathetic juror. The prosecutor had only to fuel the fire, brand Iroquois an environmental terrorist, intent upon egging the faithfully revolving Epsilon into a mutinous outer orbit. According to the prosecuting attorney and his expert witnesses, Iroquois and his radical ilk will set the planet adrift in the subzero vacuum of space. There, the good citizens of Epsilon will be tormented by antimatter, corrupted by missing mass, fettered by dark stars, ambushed by hidden worm holes, then regurgitated into rogue dimensions. Rather than disputing these paranoiac auguries, Grace decides to play her last hand. She motions the court clerk to extract her next witness from a bulky black box punctured with air holes. Mr. Kruger is not amused.

"A skunk, your honor?"

Grace counters, "You've been invoking them throughout the trial, Mr. Kruger. It's time one speaks in its defense. Besides, Mr. Skinks can shed critical light on the character of Mr. Jefferson. Unfortunately, Mr. Skinks speaks no Epsilonite, so I must translate for the court."

Grace's esteemed colleague snipes. "Fine, but I will be able to cross examine this witness in due turn?"

"Of course. However, for the record, Mr. Skinks has been granted immunity in exchange for his testimony."

Luckily for Grace, Judge Corbin's senility hearing has been postponed. Judge Corbin conspiratorially winks to Grace as she confidently leans towards the witness chair. "Mr. Skinks, please inform the court how you came to know Mr. Jefferson." After pondering the nuances of skunk dialect, Grace discloses to the jury. "Mr. Skinks alleges that Mr. Jefferson represented himself as a film producer in search of stunt animals. When they stormed the sub-committee on Environmental Trends, Mr. Skinks and company assumed they were merely acting in a nature documentary."

Grace proceeds to badger her own witness. "But there wasn't a camera in sight, Mr. Skinks. Skunks cannot be that naive. Remember, you have immunity, so please inform the court exactly how Mr. Jefferson induced you into such an act of terrorism."

Concerned over this dubious line of defense, Iroquois raises a puzzled hand. "Your honor, could I please consult with my attorney?" Judge Corbin fails to take note. Grace fails to respond. Mr. Kruger objects.

"Really, Judge Corbin, this is highly irregular. Who signed off on this witness? To my knowledge, Ivanosky doesn't speak skunk. I know for a fact that she failed French, so how could she possibly have mastered Skunk."

"Oh look, look, look!" Judge Corbin excitedly points to the mangy witness. "He's scratching his nose."

The jurors simultaneously rise and coo. Mr. Kruger sarcastically chimes, "Yeah, yeah. With one little claw. How adorable."

Grace sighs despairingly. "Unfortunately, a claw to the nose indicates the defendant, Mr. Jefferson, not only planned the skunk raid but threatened to overthrow the government and assassinate..."

"I object!" Iroquois bolts from his chair. As court security re-seats him, Iroquois agitatedly declares. "Perhaps this would be a good time to throw myself on the mercy of the court, have my lawyer declared insane, out to get me, in the throes of some manic, menstrual contraction. So it wasn't catfish. Tofu is better for your health. But I could get you catfish if you still want the damn catfish."

Grace pays Iroquois no mind as she checks her watch, then paces right. "As I was saying, Mr. Jefferson has threatened to — and I quote — assassinate the asshole who puts one more tree into a museum."

Several jurors moan their approval. Grace paces left. "Industrialists will tell you, we have too much plant variety as is. They argue: how many vegetables can you fit on your plate. They say: no one is starving. They say: look at all the fat people. We must be doing well."

Grace pauses bodefully. "Others say that looks are deceiving, that people are only fat on the outside. If we gaze for one steady moment into each other's eyes, we will see our hearts are empty."

Divining a method behind her madness, Iroquois settles back as Grace checks her watch, then paces right. "Mr. Jefferson has also vowed to assassinate the asshole who spills one more oil tanker into the ocean."

Computing their tax burden for these corporate failings, jurors angrily mutter. Grace paces left. "Industrialists will tell you that crude oil contains trace minerals which actually nourish porpoises. They will say this with a straight face. However, as more and more oil tankers spill into the ocean, more and more porpoises wash up dead."

"Judge Corbin?" Mr. Kruger points an accusatory finger at the testifying skunk. "Mr. Skinks is not even moving his lips, so how can Ms. Ivanosky be translating?"

Judge Corbin shushes him like a pestering gnat as Grace sustains her thought. "Mr. Jefferson has vowed as well to assassinate the asshole who defeats the dreaded, dreaded cockroach." The entire courtroom adversarially boos. Grace checks her watch before conceding. "I understand the revulsion. Who, in their right mind, would accommodate a cockroach?" To demonstrate, Grace plucks one from her bowtie pocket, then flicks it into the jury box. The skittish jurors scatter as Grace rails. "These Soilists are clearly fanatics. Roaches are hard enough to exterminate. You spray them with an array of fiendish poisons, and like demons, they come out dancing." As the jurors tiptoe around their seats for fear of encountering the dreaded vermin, Grace poses her disquieting question. "So what can it mean when we wake one morning to find them dead?

"Remember the winter of '84? Flicker flies awoke from their frozen sleep, ascended from their ice ponds, not in droves, but one by one like samurai soldiers. We tried to tempt them with our honey traps, but they remained adamantly at our sides, day-in, day-out, mysteriously semaphoring their wings. At night, they hovered over our beds, buzzing into our ears: buzzing, buzzing. What were they trying to say? What could a vagrant fly possibly say to a savvy sapien? When they returned to our discarded hot dogs, we returned to our untroubled sleep.

"And now, according to insect watchers, the dreaded cockroach is conveniently retreating, without a shot being fired. Are we thinking: how lucky? They have plagued this planet for eons, defied our maniacal recipes to destroy them. Millennium after millennium, they remained unchanged, unbowed."

Retrieving the lifeless cockroach from the floor, Grace places it on the jury pew for review. The jurors crowd in curiously as Grace opines. "So what can it mean when we wake one morning to find them dead? As the miners asked the canaries, we should ask what is wrong with our water, our air, our life styles, our attitude? Has the nose we've long spited finally renounced our face?"

As the jurors reflect upon this troubling truth, Grace again checks her watch. In turn, Mr. Kruger again objects. "Ivanosky, you're not even pretending to be talking to Mr. Skinks." Mr. Kruger approaches the bench with this insinuating evidence. "Your honor, the woman is not even pretending to be talking to the skunk. I know this is not the time to argue the merits and demerits of recent torte reforms, but for the record, I don't believe the article stating lawyers could paraphrase for inarticulate witnesses meant they could channel testimony for dumb-struck animals. However, in keeping with the judicial experiment, I am willing to play so long as we play fair. As professional courtesy, I expect at least the pretense of..."

Grace boldly proclaims. "But as you can clearly see I am no longer talking for Mr. Skinks."

"I thought you were translating for him?"

Grace shamelessly exposes. "Frankly, he is just a prop, so I can mince words as I please."

"Judge, did you hear that? The woman has admitted to undermining due process, to fabricating— Did I— Did I miss something? Ms. Ivanosky, have you started your summation?"

Graces anxiously scrutinizes her watch. "Oh, no, no. I'm not ready for summation. For the moment, I am merely philosophizing with the jury."

"Philosophizing with the jury? You can't—Judge Corbin, she cannot philosophize. This is a court of law, not a tea party."

Judge Corbin defensively slams down her gavel. "Well, of course, of course, I know this is not a tea party. You think I'm senile? Think I see dancing teaspoons and crooning tea kettles? As for you? Can't you see this cuddly skunk is trying to tell us something, so sit down and stay down, Mr. Kruger!"

"But, your honor?"

Judge Corbin aims her gavel as she hisses her final warning. "Sit, so Ms. Ivanosky can finish her train of thought, so she can get to her summation, so I can take this adorable little critter into my chambers and feed him some Cracker Wackers." Turning to the thoroughly mystified mammal, Judge Corbin coos, "Oh look, look; he's winking at me."

Grace props her chin ponderously. "Meaning we are missing his point. Instead of asking if this insignificant Mr. Jefferson is responsible for some meaningless action on some trifling time scale, we should be asking, asking and ever asking: for what purpose does any one of us exist?"

Mr. Kruger dramatically falls to his knees and groans. "Oh, no. We're not going to argue the existence thing. We'll be here all night. I move we break for drinks."

As Grace passes the genuflected Kruger, she absolvingly pats him on his head. "I sympathize with Mr. Kruger. How can we ask the unanswerable? We do not know definitively how or why we came to be, yet we race about as if we know where we are going. We make stuff, stuff and more stuff, populate every nook and cranny of this continent, drive fellow species to extinction to get — where? Is our mission to populate to the point of collapse in order to serve ourselves up as fossil fuel for future generations? How very noble if that is our intention; otherwise, we've simply screwed ourselves.

"We tried to expand into the ocean, but our underwater cities kept perishing. Some suspect porpoises sabotaged our endeavors in an effort to keep us at bay. Purportedly, they are evolving superior features. Having retained their fins, their vestige angel wings, they will beat us to heaven's gate. According to Qwaquiwei, we lost our wings. According to Qwaquiwei, we came from a more fashionable part of the galaxy. Unfortunately, we failed to appreciate our assignment in the great master plan, deserted our designated rudder to man the more glamorous helm. Unable to steer, we ended up crashing our metaphorical ship on this forsaken planet where we remain marooned. Is that why, year after year, we send probes into outer space? Trying to find our way back home like the stranded sculptors of Easter Island? Clearly, we haven't managed to voyage far or capture the attention of the intergalactic cavalry. To date, we have a concession on the moon manned by a few research scientists, and tourist trappers who persistently complain about the solar glare and glazing silence. Ironically, the moment they touchdown, place their wobbly legs on their native soil, they begin to plan their next excursion elsewhere, always elsewhere.

"Some say we are reincarnations of previous civilizations, holdouts from Atlantis, hand-me-downs from Earth, reborn to redeem past sins. There are those who don't want to reflect past this moment, who steal from today to live for tomorrow. What happens when tomorrow actually comes? There are those who resist changing a single straw in the haystack when Nature, herself the supreme destroyer, keeps evolving, keeps changing her mind. Is that the primal fear: eventually she may change her mind about us?

"We defensively argue: we had to do this to get that, ended up here because of there, choose us over them. Had to. But those million riddled reasons, in retrospect, in light of a later day, buried in the rubble of our consequences..."

Cree-eak. Cree-eee-eak.

Grace crosses her fingers as creak becomes crunch, becomes crunch-crunch — crash! At last, Mr. Kruger plunges to the floor. All four legs on his chair have mysteriously snapped. Grace hastens towards the stunned and stuttering prosecutor.

Thinking she has come to assist him, he extends his arm. Instead, Grace collects three of the four severed chair legs.

"Your honor, I can now submit my final evidence." Grace places the first chair leg on the Judge's desk, then hands the second leg to the foreman of the jury. The third chair leg, she wields like a conquering sword. "You dismissed my termite eggs. You doubted termites could munch a perfect circle. I suspected this would be the case so, at the start of this trial, I had termites applied to various sites on Mr. Kruger's chair. No one tampered with the chair after that first seeding. However, as you can see, the termites made their way to the same position on all four legs, then ate away at perfectly level angles. This is a repeatable phenomenon. I have affidavits from corroborating researchers with analogous results. Admittedly, they are baffled. They are hypothesizing some kind of geotropism, geomagnetic perturbation, geo 'logical' something. Whatever the reason, termites everywhere are suddenly gobbling in very symmetric patterns, as if driven by some higher mind. Perhaps they simply want to point out that we are not the only ones passing *Go* on the game board."

Furnishing her leg for comparison, Grace directs the jurors. "The more immediate point is: that leg looks sawed off but it isn't. It wasn't. And this leg has been severed at the exact same position."

Judge Corbin offers further evidence. "Oh look. You can actually see little termites scampering about. How very darling."

"Yes, it's a mystery, but it's a fact. And just as it happened today in this courtroom, it happened that day in Mr. Deloy's office. Now, for my summation—

"Iroquois Jefferson did organize the skunk raid on the sub-committee for Environmental Trends. It was unbecoming a lawyer and not very effective politically. However, it was neither traitorous nor life threatening. Iroquois Jefferson did tamper with Mr. Deloy's robot. He has engaged in questionable ploys to convey his ideological notions. If you must know, he has fathered several children, defaulted on a car loan, thrown spit balls at logger lobbyists. He is flamboyant, opinionated, uncompromising, forever deviating from the norm but—", Grace singles out one juror, "if your boss fired you because you refused to perform a task you deemed inappropriate, you would have no case. You are under legal obligation to your employer to execute the tasks for which you are paid. No lawyer will take your case. No lawyer, except Iroquois Jefferson. He won't take the case because *he* thinks you are right; he will take your case because *you* think you are right.

"Mr. Jefferson struggled through law school. Not because he wasn't smart but because he was stubborn. He insisted a lawyer practice justice, when we all know that lawyers only practice law, the way hula-hoopers practice hula routines. That's why Mr. Jefferson doesn't have a bank account. You know how he pays his rent? He teaches at night school. You know what this subversive radical teaches?"

Iroquois hides his face in chagrin as Grace reveals his mortifying secret. "This odious threat to our established government teaches audit-fearing citizens how to complete their income-tax forms — by the book. So no, Iroquois Jefferson is not a successful lawyer, but Iroquois Jefferson is a good man who, if justice is served, will be found innocent."

The moment the verdict "not guilty" is read, reporters surround Iroquois, eager to grill him on his clandestine tax class activities. Grace tries to suppress a smile as she overhears Iroquois at a loss for words.

Snapping shut her briefcase, Grace heads for a phone booth nestled in a quiet alcove outside. Before lifting the receiver, she takes three deep breaths. It has been so long. The question is: has it been too long? Nervously, Grace dials. Perhaps, no one is home. Perhaps, it is too late. Perhaps— Someone lifts the receiver. Grace falters, "It's me — Yes, but— Well not back together, like a shattered plate you glue then re-shine. Everyone knows it is never the same. Things will have to be different. I will have to be different. And you? Will you marry me, Aaron?"

GIVING UP THE DEAD

Aaron wakens at 5:07, just as the sun begins to rise. After brewing a cup of tea, he griddles a stack of granola patties, then takes two bites before driving to the marriage bureau. Aaron taps his watch. Though the bureau is not yet open and Grace not due for several hours, Aaron rests assured he has staked his place at so critical a moment in time. Without complaint, he sits on the marble bench in the outdoor foyer as a gentle drizzle falls. Hours later, his tuxedo has rumpled and his firmly clutched fleurs-de-lilies have shut their blooms. Grace is not due for two more hours.

A fellow groom anxiously peers through the bureau window before joining Aaron on the marble bench. Dressed in overalls and clutching two king-size pillows, the fellow groom nervously prods, "Getting married? Me too. Mostly for economic reasons. Not that Julie and me don't care for each other. Course, we care. Just wasn't on our list of things to do this weekend. But we was watching the news and we got to thinking. If you are married, they allow you to be buried in the same grave. Been living in her van for some time, so why not make it official, get some perks for our trouble. Got these pillows from Aunt Trudy. Now, all we need is a mattress and place to settle down. My brother, Harry, says come north."

The fellow groom compulsively bites his fingernails as he debates. "Julie says it's too damn cold, especially now: ice storms trampled by accumulations of three, four feet of snow. Flew up to see for myself. Harry tried to show me the sights. Didn't see much. Actually, didn't see anything. Got pelted with hail, snow, sleet, fog, and icy rain. That was day one. People spend their waking hours shoveling. Half the time they never make it to work. Other half time, they never make it home, so we sure as hell won't be heading north. Not in my body.

"Julie's sister says come south. No way, I says. Too wet. Rains every damn day. Every damn day. Your roof leaks; your basement floods; worms take refuge in your shoes. Streets remain under water months on end. I'd have to trade my four wheel for a paddle boat. Out west is too humid, like being in a steam bath. Hear some people walk around naked. Can you imagine? Mold grows on your ceiling; mushrooms sprout from your walls. If you don't continuously suck ice cubes, your brain melts. Can't do any complex calculations, and can't keep popsicles on their sticks."

Pausing briefly to gnaw on a peeling cuticle, the groom confesses. "Had planned to settle in Lotus Ridge."

Aaron enthusiastically observes, "Lotus Ridge is nice."

"Yeah, had me a stretch of farmland till the encroaching permafrost literally froze my assets. Now, can't plant crops, can't dig a foundation. What's left? Northwest has got them rattler earthquakes. Southeast has got them swarms of pogowillies. Hear the weather's nice in Piccolo, except the bombs keep you indoors and up all night. Yesterday, they blew up the main library. People just going crazy. So, marrying seems like a good idea. These days, man shouldn't wait too long."

Aaron nods politely as the expectant groom notes glumly. "Now that our penises are shrinking — well, I don't have to tell you. Got major scientific types testing this stuff. They're getting smaller and smaller and smaller — and smaller."

Aaron protectively crosses his legs as the chatty groom continues this discourteous topic of conversation. "Ovaries too: shriveling, shriveling. Ironic huh? Always worried about what's going to kill us, assuming we get here in the first place. If things continue to— well, there will be fewer and fewer—", the groom pauses to discount Aaron, "and fewer of us to wonder. Partridge-pigeons will gather on street corners to comment on our decreasing numbers. So, marrying seems the way to go. Worse comes to worse, we can be buried in the same grave."

Examining a hangnail, the fellow groom perks. "Wouldn't mind flying north for the reception. Just for the day.

From a purely artistic perspective, it's— well, look at these photographs from this honeymoon brochure. Granted, it's no place to live, but, according to the Arcadia Hilton, it's a—", the groom scrupulously quotes, "nuptial dreamscape, a wonderland of shimmering frost flakes on glistening branches, bush-berries cocooned in— in—"

Aaron obligingly pronounces, "pell·u·cid pods".

"Yeah, and 'icicles trickling into crys·ta·lline tresses, and snow drifts like dunes of diamond dust'. Dunes of diamond dust. Dunes, dunes of diamond dust. So romantic. Have to pucker just to say it. Course, with my luck, I'll book the Wonderland Suite during a sudden thaw. Like the day I left. The snow began to melt an inch an hour. There I was on Harry's porch sipping my hot cocoa while the corpse of a deer rose from the icy ashes inch by inch." The gregarious groom slips into an alternate persona as he dismally concludes. "Hour after hour, it's rotting body bared its bleak presence beneath the seemingly flawless snow, like a precursor of the coming doom." Stuck in the dark-side ditch of his soul, he blankly footnotes. "Naturally, they don't mention that in these here brochures."

Confronted with such ill tidings, Aaron wistfully checks his watch. Only 9:10. Grace will not arrive to rescue him for another hour and twenty minutes.

Grace wakens at 9:11. In due time, she perks a pot of coffee, then drinks three cups while toasting slice after slice of bread. Each slice is more burnt than the preceding one. Finally, Grace runs out of slices. To appease her gnawing stomach, she munches a palm full of Cracker Wackers while waiting for her cab. She arrives at the marriage bureau at 10:37 with a melted chocolate cherub for her blushing beau.

The ceremony is short and simple. Aaron and Grace whisper their vows, then sign their names one upon the other, as is custom, to signify their entwining lives. The reception at the local beach is attended by a few close relatives, namely, Rom and Webster. The banquet is casual: a handful of breadsticks and a few wedges of bean cheese. In keeping with the humble repast, the musical accompaniment consists of random notes from a harmonica as Webster tries to blow bubbles through the apertures. It is family life as usual. Rom gets his pant legs wet while trying to snatch guppies in the shallows. After losing her harmonica, Webster chases sandpipers along the swash. Aaron pockets crushed beer cans and discarded candy wrappers while Grace repeatedly tests. "Did I tell you I love you?"

Aaron faithfully affirms. "You did, and didn't I swear to cherish you now and forever, until our death, amen? Well, I will go one further. I will pledge my heart in this, and every subsequent incarnation."

"How will you know who is me?"

"I will mark you with a tracer tag, like they do migrating pigeons, only I will attach my tag to your soul. So even if you aren't tall, and aren't blond, and aren't..."

"Female? Human?"

Aaron dismisses this possibility. "No, no. I am sure we will be compatible, complementary. I am sure we will return along the lines of opposite-sexed frogs, in the same lily pond, on the same lily pad, where we can revel once again in each other's arms, or legs — or tubule protuberances."

Wincing at the imagined erotica of amorous protuberances, Grace grills. "Ah, and will we have equally stupid conversations to authenticate our consuming attachment?"

"Oh yes. Invariably, whatever the fated organism, the blood, or plasmatic solution which propels our limbs, or hairy cilia will drain from our logic circuits as we gratify our animal magnetism. Very likely, we will be eaten while in the carnal throes of..."

As they kiss, cuddle, and coo, they trip over a space probe. Aaron tumbles onto his back. Grace tumbles onto Aaron. Rom, logic circuitry intact, attentively inspects the grounded satellite. Ever astute, Webster vigilantly points to the commotion one hundred feet ahead.

A newscaster, one foot in the wafting waters, microphone in hand, describes the indescribable to his remote viewing audience. He describes what he cannot explain: an eight-story, three-thousand foot ocean vessel submerged in the deep ocean for hundreds of years, now washed upon this beach, along with satellites, planes, boats, tires by the hundreds, beach chairs by the thousands, and mounds of miscellaneous refuse from centuries of invention. One snarled pile contains a computer keyboard, a pressure pot top, a mattress, a hula hoop, a tread mill, a dog house, a bird cage, a can opener, a bicycle wheel, a stereo speaker, barbed wire, bubble wrap, three boots, seven wine bottles, a clock without hands, a camera with no lens, a book with no pages.

Grace and Aaron catch the newscaster's closing words. "As if the seas decided to clean house, cast out garbage long littered there. This floating monstrosity sank two-hundred years ago. It weighs ten million tons. No known power could have raised this craft. In other words, this is no mere prank. On the contrary, this is really, really weird."

Along with the inquiring crowds, Aaron and Grace survey the historic vessel. Hundreds of years ago, the people of Epsilon tried to construct a ship as large as a city, a floating city in effect, to extend the domain of ever populating humans. Unfortunately, prototype after prototype sank. The endeavor was abandoned in favor of population control. This particular model, the Ark Angel, was the last and largest ever constructed. It tragically sank three days after launching. Seventeen thousand people perished.

Silently, the wedding party surveys the surreal diorama, a civilization's worth of discontinued technological triumphs. The litter seems purposely concentrated, as if for effect. Fifteen feet away, another newscaster records a local man's horror.

"And then—", the frantic man snatches his ears, as if to hold his rattled head in place, "the toilet backed up, spilling foul smelling ooze all over my carpet. It— It chased me down the stairs, literally evicted me from my apartment. Me and everyone else in the complex. Pursued us down the street. Had to evacuate the vicinity as this creeping ooze, oozing creepily, made its way door to door like the malevolent blob in that horror movie. But this was worse. It was permeated with the most vile kinds of refuse. Some people say they saw body parts. I myself saw an eyeball. Had an oddly idle stare. Not vacant like the dead but idle, like it wasn't seeing me, like— like I wasn't, in actuality, here."

Grace hastens her children from the visual commotion while Aaron hesitantly explains to Rom how, over time, these objects naturally drifted to the same deep ocean pocket. Aaron reticently proposes that a torrential underwater storm propelled them into the same jet stream. Aaron tenuously muses that a sudden tidal swell unexpectedly heaved them ashore. Rom obligingly considers these explanations, implausible in the extreme.

Half an hour passes. The beach is once again empty and warm with sand, the ocean, again blue and pulsing with white caps. Everyone resumes their ritual behaviors. Each time Webster stuffs a clam shell into her mouth, Grace pries it out. Each time a waves wets Rom's pants leg, he rolls it up another fold. Occasionally he chances upon a curious bone. As he offers one to Aaron for identification, he innocently erupts, "I like this being married thing. I mean, you being married, mother being married, you and her married together. I don't remember what it was like before, with that other man, that other father. We never really knew him. We—" Rom wistfully remembers Reem, then precautiously adds, "How long do you think you'll stay married?"

Embracing Rom, Aaron pledges. "Your mother and I took 'uddup' vows. We wouldn't settle for the good neighbor clause. You see, most couples who marry commit to being good neighbors only. They promise to respect each other's spiritual paths, safeguard each other's property, share household expenses, tolerate each other's relatives. Nevertheless, they can dissolve their marriage at any moment. Certainly, not without consequences. There are legal agreements to divide bank accounts, share custody of children, but couples are essentially free to go their separate ways. They remain good neighbors. They just don't remain in love. Your mother and I felt so strongly, we decided to take 'uddup' vows."

"Like in the olden days? Like the religious zealots?"

Aaron annotates. "Centuries ago, couples married before God, married 'until death do us part'. Unfortunately, couples divorced despite the presence of that divine witness. However, should your mother and I part ways, we break a mortal law, very real and very binding. Instead of dividing our bank account, we forfeit it to the government. We lose our home, our pensions. We could never remarry or even cohabit with another person. And we risk custody of our children."

Seeing Rom's bewilderment, Grace edifies. "The option was put into place after organized religions were outlawed. Religions that started as enlightened insights invariably ended— Suffice to say, exasperated and war weary, the peoples of Epsilon determined religious practices, like seamy thoughts, had to be kept in one's private closet for the public good. This 'uddup' thing was enacted as a concession to religious factions — a dare. The government allows you to publicly summon God on your behalf in this instance only. However, to ensure you don't swear in vain, the government punishes on God's behalf should you fail to honor your sacred promise. It is really a lovely notion — which cannot be taken lightly."

Concerned that Rom may fret the consequences, Aaron guarantees. "On paper, we risk custody of our children, but the way I love your mother, the way she loves me, that can never happen."

Despite the potential consequences, Rom hoists a curious bone into the glittering sunlight. "Good, because I like being married. And wouldn't it be something if this bone came from an extinct whale? Wouldn't that make this day completely incredible?"

Aaron anatomically speculates, "You never know, though this doesn't look— although it's quite strange. I would guess— but the size is completely out of proportion, completely..."

Grace traces the trajectory of Aaron's startled gaze. At the same moment, Rom squeals in boyish delight, then races towards the spectacle skeleton, one hundred feet long and sixty feet high, tangled in seaweed, with teeth as sharp as scimitars, as long as sabers — dinosaur !

AT WAR WITH ONESELF

When unicorn fossils were first uncovered, they caused a palpable stir, but nothing on the scale of this. When public opinion is pricked to ascertain why, the consensus is simply: dinosaurs are so damn big. How could such colossal creatures go so long unrecorded? It seems to defy the sacred law that matter is neither created nor destroyed. While neither created nor destroyed, it can be twisted to reveal a fatal flaw. Matter can easily and often change — or worse: it can be forgotten.

In defiance or defense, there is a rash of name carvings on boulders and trees. Memorabilia burials prove a boon for funeral parlors, often outnumbering actual corpses. Survival in mind, body or spirit has become the order of the day. Academic types settle for nicknames on distant stars. The lunatic fringe are not so easily assuaged. They refuse to be taken alive.

"Remember, fellow warriors: we have to live like foraging animals." Since foraging animals do not wear steel helmets and carry rifles, President Linkyn has declared a state of emergency. Rifles are legal, but bullets are not, as stupidity runs rampant. A case in point: Casey Watts, retired general, now paranoiac insurgent, does nothing to alleviate the tension as he stomps back and forth on his portable card table outside the Senate hearings. Around him, women, men, and children congregate, outfitted in layers of mismatched clothing, knapsacks and canteens, their pockets provisionally stuffed with beef jerkys.

Periodically gnashing his teeth, Casey Watts asserts. "There will be little left when it is all over. Not enough to sustain the current population. You can starve, be killed — or take the first shot. I was right before so don't question me now. I said we were under attack. I suspected the Soilists, the Qwaquiwei. There is yet another culprit. Through some demon witchery, Qwaquiwei have tapped into a warped planet energy called Mother Earth. Abetted by the Soilists, they are conspiring to misdirect this energy to destroy civilization. They want to return this planet to its primordial soup. Well, we refuse to sip softly after having partaken of the fatted cowburger. We will fight the Soilists, fight the Qwaquiwei, fight this Mother Earth to the death."

"But—" a young man diligently maintains, "isn't this Mother Earth, in essence, this planet? How can we combat our own planet?"

"We can blow up her mountains, burn her forests, salt her rivers, mine her oceans, sterilize..."

Again, the young man maintains, "But, if we destroy the very land we are standing on, won't we be destroying ourselves?"

There is a sudden silence as Casey Watts wavers back and forth on his rickety table. His loyal contingent await his rebuttal with baited breath. With seeming forethought, Casey divulges, "In the short run, yes."

The young man perseveres. "But isn't the short run pretty much it? I mean, there will be no long-run after the short-run runs out."

This provokes a second wave of silence as Casey Watts wavers between irreconcilable thoughts. "Well, you know what the Good Book says: better to reign over spilt milk than hatch another man's eggs." Enchanted by the metrical poesy, the crowd cheers. No one questions the confucius content or raging bonfire upwind, where repentants burn books, films, birth certificates, anything, everything, hoping to propitiate — whom?

Epsilonians, frightened and confused, call upon a pantheon of gods, seek fairies in the meadows, wizards, witches and exorcists. Readily they ingest bitter herbs, utter tongue-twisting affirmations, soak in tubs of mud, balance crystals on their heads, masticate seaweed. Unquestioningly, they place pyramids under their pillows, anoint themselves with aromatic oils, swallow mega-doses of vitamins, subject themselves to enemas and chiropractic adjustments. Deeming anything worth a try, they walk on coals, glue magnets to their temples, reorient their mattresses to face north. Some have taken vows of celibacy. Others regress to former lifetimes, astral project to distant stars. Members of a stray cat cult leave offerings of baked tuna in back alleys along with catnip balls and cashmere socks, hoping to placate Mother Earth by showering their affectations on this token creature. Believing Mother Earth has chosen Qwaquiwei to be the surviving tribe of Epsilon, they are attempting to imitate the Qwaquiwei low-impact way — with as little impact to their actual lifestyles. They speculate: a self-initiated initiation into Qwa will protect them from extermination. It is a curious fact that no Qwaquiwei has fallen victim to the wrath of Mother Earth.

Statisticians explain Qwaquiwei constitute a small percent of the population and reside on an inland desert. There are no flash floods because there are no sudden downpours. There are no fires because there is scant timberland. There are no volcanic eruptions because there are no volcanoes. There are no earthquakes because there are no subterraneous fissures or faults. Others argue, there are no faults because there is no blame.

Qwaquiwei have long honored the planet, behaving like grateful guests. They live in harmony with the seasons, accept gentle rains and harsh winds with equal favor. Qwaquiwei build their houses out of straw and mud, their utensils out of stone, their weapons out of words. When the sun bakes the air, Qwaquiwei perspire, then stroll more slowly. When the winds blow cold, Qwaquiwei shiver, then pace more quickly. When the clouds burst open, Qwaquiwei remove their shoes. When snow laces the cliffs, Qwaquiwei pause, first to look, then to listen, then to pray. Unlike traditional prayer, they pray in praise. Whether a baby is born or dies, Qwaquiwei venerate life's blessings and mysteries. Whether lovers marry or friends depart, whether cupboards are bare or harvests are plenty, whether hearts dissolve into joy, or cramp with pain, whenever they inhale, whenever they exhale, for better, for worse, Qwaquiwei accept the kaleidoscoping fates.

Epsilonians, unable to accept their fortunes with commensurate equipoise, flee for Qwaquiwei cover. Having renounced their accursed parents, they offer themselves for adoption. Unscrupulous Qwaquiwei perform the sacred Embracing for the asking — and for an untraditional fee. Hoping to shield themselves from the wrath of Lord Mother, gullible Epsilonians purchase Qwaquiwei blood rights. Despite warnings by legitimate elders that such adoptions are fraudulent, Epsilonians continue to submit on the chance the redeeming fire of Qwa will shelter them from the coming storm.

Once adopted, puzzled converts realize it is easier to become Qwaquiwei than to be Qwaquiwei. Though Qwaquiwei seem bound by traditions, in actuality, they have no transcribed rules. There are no Qwaquiwei scriptures; there is no Qwaquiwei constitution. Qwaquiwei live by example. Since written words can been misinterpreted and spoken words misconstrued, Qwaquiwei rely predominately on observable moments. What man is blind to an act of kindness? What woman is deaf to a righteous plea?

Not everyone is enamored of tribal ways. A Casey Watts adherent throws a stink bomb into the Qwaquiwei adoption proceedings. Another group accuses Qwaquiwei of being extraterrestrial progeny, controlled by an extraterrestrial ship, code named Mother Earth. They allege Earth aliens have been experimenting on Epsilon humans for generations. After cross-breeding, inter-splicing their genes with human genes, they have achieved their desired genetic configuration in the Qwaquiwei tribe. Only Qwaquiwei will be allowed to propagate. All others will be exterminated, eliminated from the gene pool. The more terrestrial minded argue the problem lies closer to home, postulate Mother Earth represents the life-force of the planet. Epsilon is simply protecting itself from a dangerous infestation. Qwaquiwei have proven benign so they have not been targeted. Meanwhile, the rest of humankind is being pruned like a harmful strain of weed.

Theories abound, punctuated by more questions than answers, leading thousands of Epsilonians to line the streets divesting themselves of their suspected sins. Unable to locate the cause of the contagion, they burn their clothes, curse their parents, swear off cigarettes, booze, and money. Left destitute, they go begging in the streets for food, clothing, cigarettes and money.

In the Senate, theories run no less rampant or rational. President Linkyn solemnly sets the scene. "Friday the thirteenth, 10 children were electrocuted when lightning struck a playground in Everly. I mention it, because it was the only bolt recorded the entire day, along the entire continent. Ten days later, 100 people perished when mud slides buried the historic town of Arkin. Ten days after that, 1000 people—" President Linkyn convulsively inhales before detailing, "were consumed by fire when a meteorite fragment set off a gas tank in the city of Rolensky. Hundreds fled to the rivers. Those who remained submerged, drowned. Those who ascended for air, ignited like kindling. Yet another ten days passed when an earthquake violently rent the metropolis of Tunis. There were no other quakes anywhere but in the densely populated metropolis of Tunis where 10,000 people lay sleeping—" President Linkyn pauses as her fellow citizens slowly calculate, "where now 10,000 people lay dead. This morning, a mere ten days after this horrific catastrophe, the peninsula of Holio—" the President's voice cracks, "the peninsula of Holio sank. The peninsula of Holio was inhabited by an estimated 100,000 people."

As a collective sigh begins to swell, Dr. Vanetsky addresses the hall. "Esteemed President, Senators, and Citizens of Epsilon: we have been called to attention, asked to gather our thoughts and courage to address this assault upon our survival. Consequently, top secrets have been revealed. I can now speak in unveiled terms about the Bindustan findings, as well as the confirmed intelligence of the Porpoise species. Previously, only top government service persons, noted scientists and key technocrats have been privy to the extraordinary faculties of these amazing sea creatures, or rather, sea beings. We are inclined to recognize porpoises as intelligent life-forms. We hope we can work with them, they with us, to shed light on..."

Dr. Vanetsky is interrupted by a teenage girl pronouncing loudly, unrecognized, and out-of-turn. "Excuse me, excuse me, Esteemed President and the lot of you, my name is Foster Midgely." Standing on her petite tip toes, Midgely vociferates into a suspended microphone. Her voice is attenuated and tense, her posture anchored as she counsels. "I represent the Porpoise community of Orbit Ocean, as they, as porpoises, more rightly call this planet. They have asked me to speak on their beleaguered behalf. For this reason, I object, object to the atrocities that have been committed against them, and to Dr. Vanetsky's human hubris. Do not compare porpoises to sapiens. While they prize wisdom, they do not rate intelligence so highly as we do. In fact, they consider the brain an organ of the lower function."

Dr. Vanetsky is genuinely enticed by this revelation. "Really? I had heard their higher centers lie elsewhere. How intriguing. Could you tell me..."

Foster Midgely self-consciously sighs. "I— I can't. I don't know. Porpoises contend humans are incapable, quite incapable of comprehending..."

Senator Seerington bellows his indigence. "Ah ha! You can't say because they *won't* say because they have devised a secret weapon to manipulate natural forces and direct these forces against us. I suspect they have subterraneous machines churning out counter-currents, screwing up ocean jet steams, making it impossible for us to navigate our ships, harvest fish. I'll grant you they are intelligent, meaning they can't be trusted. They deliberately sabotaged our underwater cities so we could not monitor their perfidy, witness how they were developing the means to eliminate us."

Senator Grady roundly disputes this statement. "Senator Seerington, porpoises have lost thousands of their own kind in freak sea disasters. They are not immune to this planetary tumult. In fact, it was the Porpoise community who contacted us, concerned over the growing number of ASD victims. Apparently this auto-immune shutdown is affecting their population as well."

Senator Seerington remains uncompassionate. "As I've been telling those mutant evolutionists, not enough sunshine in their diet. Tell them to spend more time at the sunny surface and less time at the muddy bottom, being covert and cunning."

Trying to wrench the dangling microphone closer, Foster Midgely counters. "Not the lack of sunshine. Rather, the degradation of ozone, increased UV rays, acid rain, fetid fecal matter we dump into their living spaces."

A gaunt man jams his mouth to a microphone. His dark skin is ironically as pale as ash. His lips are bloodless, his eyes distant and unfocused. "Some parting words of wisdom from an extincting fellow. ASD was a test. A test! And you fucking failed it! This impulse called life is ever selecting and re-selecting. ASD was a litmus to see— see—", he gasps for breath as he struggles to be audible, "if humans would hold together, help each other out. Instead, you looked at us, then put down your thumbs, little realizing you were passing an extinction sentence on yourselves. Before you take me out and shoot me, let me remind you, that you, *you* dumped all those toxic ingredients into our neighborhoods. Thought you could get away with it. Thought worse comes to worse, some politically disenfranchised, some economically depressed people would develop cancer and die. Well, we did develop cancer, and suffer neurological impairments, and tumors and skin lesions, and we wobble when we walk, but we hold the payback card. Our loss is a parasite's gain, a parasite which would not have taken hold if you had not set the stage — engendered us with your crippling cruelty. As we die off, the parasite moves on, having gained insight into the human host. We are living toxic waste, the apocalyptic plague that will bring down the bastard overloads. Didn't you realize that humans are ninety-eight percent identical to baboons, so how different can I be from you? Try to distance yourselves; you won't get far enough. Knot on life jackets till you choke. That anchor tied to your ankle is going to take you down— down—" he pauses several seconds to recapture his breath before denouncing, "with the stinking, sinking ship."

Senator Seerington motions to the security guards. "I thought they couldn't talk. Throw that man overboard!

Disinfect that microphone! Who let that mutant in here? Spouting such absolute nonsense!"

As scampering security guards drive the objecting evolutionist off the premises, Senator Krommueller furtively tugs Seerington's coat-tail. "Psst, psst, psst." Krommueller is deaf to his words reverberating over the loudspeakers. "Seerington? This auto-immune shutdown syndrome is a ploy. I've received communications from covert sources alleging these mutant evolutionists are only pretending to die out, to keep us off guard. Why put up an expensive force field when you can simply cry 'leper'. Can't you see what they are up to? For years, they've tampered with their bodies, hoping to trigger the next evolutionary advance. Well, what if they succeeded? Decoded all those ancient mysteries? While we were thinking the obvious: some extraterrestrial alien race, the ground beneath our feet was breeding mutant evolutionists."

"Oh, I agree ASD is a ploy, but porpoises clearly engendered this virus. They started with our weakest link, those mangy mutants; now, like dominoes we will all fall down."

Hearing her clients so unreservedly maligned, the feisty Foster Midgely contends. "If porpoises were out to get us, why, why do they save human lives? Why do they swim hundreds of miles out of their way, hundreds and hundreds of miles just to return castaway humans to shore? Why do they confront sharks at great risk to themselves to prevent humans from being harmed?"

Senator Mungus vigorously raises his hand. "Oh, I know, I know! Call on me. I can tell you!" President Linkyn nods to indicate that she will not recognize Senator Mungus. Unfortunately, Senator Mungus pays no mind to rules as he frenetically reveals. "They save humans but only in handfuls, for public relations porpoises. I mean purposes, purposes! You see! They are already altering our mind waves. I hear they can do that. Part of a nefarious plot to take over our bodies. They can't get far on land until they can turn their flippers in for toes. They may save a handful of humans, but what happens to the remaining hundreds lost at sea? I'll tell you what happens. They are abducted by mad porpoise scientists, dissected, then frozen inside icebergs until their DNA can be injected into porpoise fetuses. That's how they evolved so swiftly. They are part human."

Someone stalks from behind a crowd. "Part us, but not part human. Part us as we are part of that larger something else. Human nature is not the master print. Just one resultant squiggle. When will you realize: we didn't get here first, and we didn't get here alone."

As Quincy Qwa quivers angrily, Senator Seerington rudely points out. "A Qwaquiwei? In the Senate Body! Who's letting these subverts in here?"

President Linkyn temperately pounds her gavel in melodic phrases, like a tribal drum, to appease the combating factions. Graciously, she receives Quincy into the fold. "Fellow citizen of Epsilon, we are pleased and honored by your presence."

Unimpressed by a Qwaquiwei in the Senate Hall, a testy woman raps a nearby microphone to ensure its working order. "Yeah, yeah, welcome to the promised land. Now let me second Senator Mungus; he's on the right track. Read the writing on the bones, guys. No one I know had a dinosaurus for dinner, so if it wasn't us, it must be them scheming porpoises. Who else? Don't believe those humans returned to shore. They've been tampered with by mad porpoise scientists. Their memory banks have been altered to reflect the Porpoise line."

Reveling in his new-found contingent, Senator Mungus elaborates. "Yes, yes! And in some cases, they aren't really humans. They are actually porpoise spies sporting severed human limbs. With a bit of cosmetic surgery, they can infiltrate our society. There could be one among us at this very moment. I've heard those sharks that attacked those swimmers at Lester's Wharf were really porpoises disguised as sharks."

Dr. Vanetsky rips at his head hair in despair. "I have never heard anything so outrageous. Those sharks were autopsied. I myself autopsied— We've been through this. Those sharks were sharks behaving like sharks. They killed those swimmers for the same reason lions often kill lion cubs. In a world of diminishing resources, even one's own young represent future competition. Apparently, life is getting a littler rougher on the high seas. Humans, being fishermen, are now considered competitors. The species separation we've enjoyed to date seems to be breaking down. We are no longer the invisible, inviolable man."

Senator Mungus notes suspiciously. "That seeps of Porpoise propaganda. When were you last at sea?"

A harried Dr. Vanetsky incredulously rails. "You think I could be— Well, yes, yes. You found me out. I'm a porpoise spy! I have gills under my armpits and— and— and these insane allegations have prompted crazed citizens like yourself to slaughter thousands and thousands of innocent porpoises. We are not at war with the Porpoise community. We have no right to round them up and massacre them. What are we coming to? This is a witch hunt. We should be ashamed."

Ever unblushing, Senator Mungus bolts from his seat. "But porpoises have been abducting humans for eons. People under hypnotic trances have revealed how they were taken off cruise ships by pirate porpoises, then brought to subterraneous caverns to perform erotic mating rituals with lecherously pulsating eels and ogling octopussies. I myself have recalled pornographic interludes with nymphomaniac sea slugs inserting their slimy, sensuous— Suffice to say: we have to do something. Perhaps, poison the ocean. We don't need the ocean. We can't drink salt water. If we can have farm factories, we can have fish factories. We can..."

President Linkyn crashes her gavel through a side window. "Isn't anyone listening?" The remonstrating voices outside resound through the embattled halls as President Linkyn flares. "Next Wednesday, ten days from today, is the next day of woe. Am I the only one who hears the echo ten times ten. I repeat: this morning, the peninsula of Holio sank. An estimated one hundred thousand people— not widgets— people, as in flat-assed men and fat-assed women, cranky children and nursing mothers, apple-baking aunts, tall-tale-telling uncles, doting grandfathers and beloved friends. All those blushing girls with golden laces, those bashful boys who never kissed them, washed away on the same silencing wave. According to my abacus, next Wednesday, ten times ten times ten times ten times ten times ten." President Linkyn's bellowing voice trickles to a rasping whisper as she sums, "One million people are going to die."

There is a brooding silence as those present resist comprehending. After moments straining his mental faculties, Senator Mungus becomes startlingly lucid. "Now I get it. The encroaching dark star. A tenth planet would explain the significance of ten times— What else could do such damage? The gravitational havoc of such a large body could surely— and wasn't it some kind of astronomic calamity that devastated the lost Earth civilization?"

Dr. Vanetsky recounts. "We considered the theory but it doesn't fit. For decades, we have been scouring the solar vicinity for such a doomsday planet or star. The latest data from our deep space satellites indicate a ring of asteroids and some planetary debris but no massive orb of death. I feel confident in affirming there is no tenth planet. As for the lost Earth civilization, well, it's not clear what did them in. We suspect a climatic trigger. Seems there were massive, massive ice caps compared to what we have today. These melting ice caps flooded land masses. Numerous Earth cultures disappeared. To make matters worse, since there was less ice to reflect sunlight, the planet grew even warmer, then the increased ocean surface with its absorbing blue waters captured more heat, making the planet warmer still. Ironically, luckily, the forests receded, turned into deserts. With less forestation, less heat was absorbed; the planet grew cooler, and coincidentally, the glare of the bare deserts acted like the missing ice caps to reflect sunlight, cooling, cooling the planet. By some quirk, we canceled out the problem."

Seerington performs an explanatory jig. "Landed feet first. So now we know these global warmings come and go. Granted there are trade-offs, sacrifices, a little rack and ruin but that comes with an expanding universe. There's an age old saying: change is good."

Quincy stealthily taps the spouting Senator from behind. "You think so, you and your fellow Earthlings? From what I understand of the Bindustan digs, Earth convulsively plunged into climatic doom. Humans found themselves confined to one continent. Once confined, everything conveniently snapped back in place. Odd, don't you think? Less like a what, than a who — than a *she*. Lord Mother Earth tripped the fateful wire, routed humans to a manageable reserve. Only now, we are getting on her nerves again. The question is: where is left to go?"

Having distastefully removed Quincy's impertinent fingers from his shoulder, Senator Seerington hisses. "Pagan nonsense! I for one am not disquieted by the consequence of my presence. You and your tread-lightly polemics! Expect me to turn off my air conditioner, accept that sweat is good for the soul. Well I'm not afraid to discomfort the grass beneath my feet."

Senator Seerington turns towards the crowded hall. "How quickly we forget." Snapping his fingers, he bellows. "Who can name the worst pollutant in recorded history? Anyone? Of course, we're talking billions of years. Take a guess. Anyone? Someone? No? Onk! Time's up. The answer is oxygen. Yes, oxygen. It wasn't here when here began. It oozed out of rogue bacteria, propelling atmospheric percentages from less than one to twenty-one. This toxic overdose poisoned the flourishing microbial life, made way for *us* oxygen synthesizing mutations." Senator Seerington fingers himself lovingly.

"As for this persistent tenth planet fable, these suspicious disruptions along our weary path to paradise? Well, perhaps this tenth planet isn't a planet subject to ellipses and cycles and such. Perhaps this goblin planet is an automated cosmic probe controlled by big-brained beings who periodically patrol our galaxy, then flip our magnetic poles to intentionally turn us on our heads. Perhaps they introduced this mortal oxygen, just to see what they might see. And now they are back, tinkering, toying, to see what else. I hate to scare the shit out of everyone, but since we are such seekers of wisdom and truth, we should consider the geologic record of recurrent, catastrophic events. However, there doesn't have to be an astronomic force behind the trigger, and certainly no maniacal mother. Perhaps Epsilon is a test site. Considering how many barren planets litter the universe, isn't it curious that this one has been host to so many fantastic creatures? We are at once unusually lucky — then unlucky as species come and go, and come and go.

"Hell, maybe we were manufactured like monkey wrenches. Maybe all the creatures on this planet have been deliberately engineered. Prototypes which pass their specifications get exported to fertile planets to multiply and prosper. Perhaps that's where Qwaquiwei got their crazy notion about ascending to the clouds after having perfected their sacred soul. Only it is not their soul, but their genetic sequences which need to qualify. Now, for the discomforting question: what happens to the losers? If this tenth planet is a cosmic clean-up squad, I suspect the rejects get reconstituted into their proverbial pounds of clay. If indeed there were billions and billions and billions of Earthlings — there aren't now. Perhaps they didn't make the cut, were intentionally drowned in their own bathtub."

Senator Seerington seems to be reading from inside his mind like a man possessed. "Where does that leave us? Does it really matter if we are creations of God, or manipulations of fallen angels, or accidents of nature? So what if we are patched from this and spliced from that? It doesn't make us monsters, doesn't make us potato heads, doesn't mean we have to get off the stage because some off-site project manager needs a new storyline. I for one am not finished living my fragile life. I don't believe our foreparents were thrown out of Eden. I believe they clawed their way out, out of the test tube, out of the gilded cage.

"No one ever said we had to face judgment day without a fight. Maybe we should take a second look at those heavens from which we fell — and start readying our missiles."

DAY OF WOE

By 4:00 a.m., Wednesday morning, day of woe, the roads are impassable. Cars jammed tightly with residents of prime target cities flee to less populated regions.

At 5:00 a.m., an ice storm hits Dunnigan Falls. One person is injured. Meanwhile, high-rises are emptying like punctured bean bags. Stadiums are shunned like leper colonies. Department stores and corporate headquarters are eerily deserted. No one loiters on corners engaging in conversations with friends. People heading uptown sift past people heading downtown like oil and vinegar. The thinking is: there is safety in singularity.

At 9:00 a.m., a tidal wave hits the coastal city of Torenzo. Three yachts are capsized and two hotels are seriously damaged. Miraculously, no one is injured. Miraculously, because Torenzo is at season's peak — or should be. After calculating ten times ten, many vacationers decided to curtail their stay. Ironically, Torenzo, at its peak, barely tops twenty thousand. However, Epsilonians are not taking chances. The merest perception of a crowd, like the cry of fire, sends people scattering. Unfortunately, for every person subtracted from point Alpha, an arriving person from point Beta needs to be added. At the end of the day, the names on the mail boxes have changed but the numbers remain the same.

There is a sudden exodus to Limburger, a dreary landfill of no economic or aesthetic consequence. Initially, only a handful of people can be counted squatting in makeshift tents on the methane smoking mounds of decaying garbage. As word of the peculiar haven spreads, nine becomes ninety, becomes nine hundred, becomes nine thousand. By 11 a.m. Wednesday, nearly one million people are huddling in Limburger like sitting ducks. No one undertakes to decide who will leave, who will stay. There is no time for undertakings. Instead, cars packed with human lemmings take to the highways once more.

At 1:00 p.m., a grease fire destroys a local pub. Three people suffer smoke inhalation.

At 3:00 p.m., four people are killed after being run off the road by a driver desperate to disassociate himself from the geometrically increasing crowds. The surviving injured are taken to a nearby hospital where two nurses and a janitor do what they can. Doctors did not show up for work, as doctors avoid hospitals, teachers avoid schools, actors avoid theaters — people avoid people like the plague. Railroads and restaurants, supermarkets and factories, amusement parks and parking lots are considered ripe for ambush. Like nomads, people drift from site to site dodging probability bullets. Occasionally, one wandering clan will embrace another wandering clan without taking into account their precipitating numbers. For some, dying seems better than surviving at all costs.

At 6:00 p.m., a volcano erupts. One hundred people are left homeless. Grace notes, "At least, they are alive." Aaron clicks off the television, mistakenly switched on by Webster as she curiously clutches the remote control. The family has made a pact to live the day as usual. When Aaron began to whisk together his holiday raisin scones, Grace insisted they exhume their traditional mid-week fare. The only permitted special event is Rom's first romantic interlude. Grace fiddles with Rom's necktie while Aaron gently goads. "Now will you tell me who the young lady is? I would like to know the identity of the person you and I have been conspiring to woo."

Reluctantly, Rom confesses, "Cindy Jacobs."

Grace abruptly stops fashioning Rom's tie. "You have a date with Cindy Jacobs?"

Aaron is equally amazed. "You had the nerve— I mean, how wonderful. After all, you and Cindy have so much in common. You're both—" Aaron gropes for the common denominator, "budding adults. In the same home room. From the same home town." Still stuttering, Aaron sights a safer subject. "Hey, didn't Cindy Jacobs win..."

Grace pokes Rom excitedly. "She did! I read about it in the local edition. Cindy located the Holy Lantern. Guess she'll be getting that internship with Socrates Software."

As Rom murmurs, "Not exactly", Aaron interrupts to ascertain. "So which particular subterfuge did the trick?"

"I told her how smart she was, then I told her how pretty, in a good way, in a smart way, and of course, how tall, how agile, how..."

Aaron nods in sober approval. "Ah, you resorted to the subterfuge of last resort: the humiliating truth."

Grace defends, "Oh, I don't know. I think Rom is just as pretty. But what do mean 'Not exactly'? Did Socrates Software renege? I'll take those liars to court. I'll..."

"No, no, Cindy turned down the apprenticeship. She says it's just a public relations scheme to obscure the fact the game doesn't teach anything really useful. Cindy thinks kids — I mean, budding adults, should spend more time in sports-related activities. That's why she's taking me hiking."

"Hiking? Rom, I just dressed you in your starchy, concert suit."

"Well, I wouldn't know. I've never gone on a date-hike."

Grace yanks at Rom's securely fastened necktie. "Aaron, get this thing off while I dig out his rag pants."

As Aaron tries to unknot the tie, Rom anxiously probes. "So — do you think the world is going to end?"

"Rom, you know what we decided."

"I know. I just meant: should I try to kiss her?"

Aaron momentarily gropes. "Well, it's not a matter of should you kiss her or not kiss her. Kissing her is not the point."

Rom grimaces incredulously. "It is in every movie I've ever seen. And I haven't seen the adult versions. I can just imagine."

Before Rom can elaborate, Aaron argues. "Well, in the movies, of course. Movies do the kiss routine for symbolic closure, because a two dimensional vehicle cannot effectively convey feelings. In actuality, love doesn't always begin or end with a kiss. It could happen with a glance, or when you squeeze her hand, or smell the mocha oil in her hair."

"My friend Doogie kissed a girl. He said it tasted like apple jelly. Best of all, it made his body fizzle like a swizzle pop."

Aaron wisely instructs. "I know you'll think I'm saying this because I'm your—" Aaron hesitates assuming his paternal title, "I'm a grown-up but, don't ruin a longing glance by suffocating it with a kiss. If—" Having conceded potential doom, Aaron nevertheless maintains, "Well even if— you can't make today tomorrow. Tonight, you and Cindy be yourselves and honor the moment. If a kiss happens, it happens. In the meantime, enjoy the hike."

Grace scurries down the stairs, solicitously waving Rom's rag pants. "Correct me if I'm wrong, but the sun is down, way down. Where can you and Cindy be trekking to at this hour? Exactly where is this moonlight romp?"

"Some cave, I think. She's been there before."

Tugging Aaron, Grace whispers her misgivings. "Perhaps I should give Malcome Jacobs a call. Cindy may be savvy enough to traipse through a wizard's castle looking for holy lanterns unchaperoned, but my son is too young to go hiking — in a cave."

Aaron seizes her hand assuringly. A car beeps. The door bell rings. Wistfully brushing back Rom's bangs, Grace hesitantly lets go. Rom doesn't introduce Cindy as he slams shut the door in his concert suit and tangled tie. '

At 8:00 p.m., Grace puts Webster to bed while Aaron builds a fire. They spend the remainder of the evening toasting marshmallows from shades of ginger to shades of chestnut. Neither Grace nor Aaron eat the smoldering confections. Instead, they set their burnt offerings one atop the other in mindful meditation. Hours pass; no one speaks. Finally, Grace discloses. "For years, I had a recurring dream. Something to the effect of Rom and Reem, and later Webster, on an exploding island. I try to save them but in the end, I can't. Since Reem's death, I don't dream. They say you continue to dream, you just don't remember. I tried coping by playing the switch game. When I would see Rom, sometimes I would pretend he was Reem. They used to play the switch on me. Rom would be

Reem. Reem would be Rom. So why not trick myself. It didn't work. Rom failed to include those telltale things that Reem used to say. I never realized Reem used to say them — until I heard them not being said. Like hearing half a beat. You keep waiting for the resolution.

"Unable to reach Reem in life, I try to imagine myself dead. What could be more simple? Dead is dead. But I can't. Why is that? I can imagine times long past, and times to come. I can imagine making love to Jungle John on a bulavine, or being lead guitarist of the Trade Warriors, or President of a united Epsilon. I can imagine being old and sick, a dervish dancing on a distant moon, but I can't, can't imagine being dead. I suffer Reem's death. I suffer his death intensely, almost unbearably, over and over. Sometimes, at night, I envision you dearly-departed, even as you lay breathing beside me. But for myself, death seems inconceivable. Is this delusion? Or is death illusion? That would be comforting — but which would be real? And why can't I, so immortal in my own mind, bring everyone out there, into the seeming safety of my imagined continuum?"

At 10:00 p.m., Rom returns from his date-hike. Smiling enigmatically, he kisses his mother, then hugs his father good night.

11:00 p.m., Grace switches off the lights. The moon shines through the diaphanous curtains as Grace and Aaron ebb into each other's arms. Contemplating midnight, Grace muses. "How does that theory go? The one where you set out from point G in quest of point Z without ever arriving?"

Aaron scrunches his brows. "Mathematical infinity?"

"Yeah, that arithmetic trickery where you divide a conceptual line between point A and point Z, creating point N, then divide the line between A and N creating point G..."

Aaron carries out the computation, "then divide the line between A and G, creating point D. Yes, you can go on ad infinitum, theoretically. The conceptual line can be divided into smaller and smaller, and always smaller segments. If you look down, it may appear an immeasurable speck, incapable of supporting your advancing mass. Confused by the optical illusion of a dead ending, many mistakenly conclude their quest. However, the odyssey only seems to be over. In actuality, it continues as long as you journey halfway between 1 and 2, then halfway between 1.5 and 1, then 1 and 1.25, then 1.125 and 1, then 1 and 1.0625, then 1.03125 and 1, then...

THE INNER LIGHTNING

In the end, Wednesday, day of woe, passes without event. Days dissolve into weeks, weeks into months. The unhappy string of disasters has apparently run its course, like the incoherent grumblings of a feverish dream. In retrospect, geologists explain: the magnetic orientation of the planet's core materials shifted, not dramatically enough to swap magnetic poles, just a momentary two-step, enough to convulse the molten flow. Consequently, the outer mantle buckled, causing the sea floor to shift, causing sea levels to rise, fall, and trigger tidal waves. The tectonic underpinnings of the continent unpinned, precipitating volcanic eruptions and earthquakes. As the ash from these eruptions drifted into global air currents, local weather systems backfired. Hurricanes descended upon deserts; hail pummeled tropical resorts; electric storms hurled lightning bolts like angered ancient gods in seeming tantrums. Animals, sensitive to subtle vibrations, reacted instinctively. Deer fled blindly while termites suspended construction of high-rise mud dwellings. As one forecaster explained to a class of first graders, there were ten little Indians sitting in the bed when the littlest Indian said "roll over". Unfortunately, when they all rolled over, one fell out. From a planetary point of view, it was a minor chiropractic adjustment. Epsilonians are satisfied with the explanations though unsettled by the facts. It happened, no matter the reason, and now that it has happened — can't it happen again?

Grace readies for work wondering when the other shoe will drop. Each morning becomes an act of faith. After zipping shut her briefcase, she stops by the kitchen for a spare apple. Instead, Grace finds Aaron knee-deep in a culinary misadventure. Dozens upon dozens of banana peels lay in disorderly piles on the table and floor. Seeking an explanation for the mounds of mutilated fruit, Grace picks up the food timer, then forcefully triggers the alarm.

Aaron abruptly stops slicing. Noting her presence, Aaron distraughtfully declares, "Grace! You won't believe! Webster wanted a 'yes' banana but when I de-nubed one for her, it said O meaning 'no'. She started to cry, so I cut the nubs off several others. I failed to produce a single Y. Webster started to scream, so I cut into yet another bunch but would you believe: only O after O after O."

Grace surveys the piles of peels, then nods despairingly. "We need to discuss some rules of parenting. This is not the way to handle a tantrum. In any case, Webster is no longer crying so why are you still cutting bananas? And why are you bothering to peel them? Who are you peeling them for?"

"Aren't you puzzled over the mystery of the missing Y's? I considered the possibility of a mutant batch, purchased dozens, dozens more. Not quite through but so far, not a single Y. Grace, this goes against chance and — as to why we are peeling them, well, that is clearly an error. The point is: this is extraordinarily, extraordinarily suspect."

"Extraordinarily, extraordinarily yes." Grace is not referring to the missing Y's as she surveys Webster steeped in mashed bananas. While Aaron and Rom continue to amputate, Webster snatches the mounting rejects. Clumsily, she directs them towards her mouth, mushing them inside her grappling fingers. As the decapitated top topples to the floor, the severed bottom plops into her lap. Reflexively, Webster wipes her hands in her hair before grasping another banana. Dutifully retrieving the multiplying lap bananas, Grace offers a second opinion. "Perhaps these bananas are simply unripe. In any case, after this little research project is over, what do you intend to do with all these bananas, honey?" Grace appends 'honey' on a decidedly tart note. Assessing the extent of his banana empire, Aaron lamely suggests. "We can bake a banana bread. You like banana bread."

Grace obligingly sets aside the three bananas required in the recipe. Fortuitously, the phone rings. Aaron is spared the final calculation. Momentarily checked, Grace politely queries, "Hello? — Sadu Qwa?" Since there are no phones at the Qwaquiwei reservation, Grace flashes the receiver by Aaron's ear for confirmation. "Sadu Qwa? I, I can hardly hear— Where are you calling— A tie-phone from a refugee. Yes, very convenient. Isn't, isn't this the week of Inner Lightning? Aren't you— No, we are just having breakfast." Assuming Sadu Qwa wishes to converse with her compatriot Beaver Spirit, Grace offers, "Aaron is right here. If you hold, I'll put— Me? Ah, well, if this relates to the Cliff of Ancients, I no longer represent Connery Deloy. However, I can refer you— But how can I— Yes, but—"

Sadu Qwa has hung-up the tie-phone, having peremptorily summoned Grace to the Qwaquiwei reservation to partake in a sacred Qwaquiwei ritual. Grace feels compelled to comply. Cryptically, she confesses, "Dry thunder." Aaron fails to intuit. Grace elaborates. "There has been no lightning at the Qwaquiwei reservation. It keeps thundering, thundering, but there has been no lightning at the Inner Lightning. At least, that is what I heard, what they are reporting. According to weather records, this has never happened, or rather has never *not* happened. On the other hand, I've started dreaming again, but I keep dreaming about lightning. Find myself walking down the street on a bright, sunny day when suddenly something is struck by lightning. Sometimes it's a vehicle, sometimes a stray dog. No one else seems to notice. Without corroborating thunder, people continue to turn corners, count change, compare remaining minutes on parking meters. Meanwhile, I can actually smell its sizzling vapors, but I never hear the warning thunder, and I never feel the healing rain. I hardly sleep wondering why no lightning at the Inner Lightning, why no thunder in my dreams."

Aaron drives the dreary hours to their destination as Grace sits contemplatively beside him. Seemingly sensing her unease, Reem's eagle thrashes inside its protective cage. It was Rom's idea to return the eagle to its birth place. Rom steadies the bulky box containing a creature whose unwelcoming talons he can never embrace. There can be no physical bond. There can only be the letting go.

When they reach the Qwaquiwei reservation, the drums are drumming. The atmosphere is charged with the scent of burning sage. Daily life has been suspended as the focus shifts within. There is quiet desperation as Qwaquiwei try to fathom the incessantly rumbling thunder. Occasionally there a punctuating blast, a conclusive detonation, but not a single bolt of lightning, not the faintest flash. Whatever is Lord Mother trying to say? Clearly, something has been missed in the prophesies.

Aaron is directed to a tent filled with men smoking disorienting herbs. Webster is taken into the arms of a nurturing midwife. Rom is surrounded by a ring of curious children who tap at his curious box and puzzle him with Qwaquiwei phrases. Meanwhile, Grace is readied for the ceremony.

She is brought to a small hut where her clothes are removed and burned. Naked in the enfolding darkness, she waits and wonders. She dares not demand an explanation lest her ignorance despair the spells so faithfully tendered. Meanwhile, three old women huddle in a corner, humming. A flickering flame from a solitary candle struggles to articulate the disarranging shadows. Over and over the women chant "aah·umm". It is barely audible. "Aah·umm." Their fingers rest upon their hearts. "Aah·umm." Their arms extend, then lower; as their fingers graze the ground, they repeat "aah·umm". Grace is drawn to the chant. Mentally she imitates ah·um — no, aah·uum — no, no. There's a third syllable: aah·aah·umm. The first and second "aah" are chanted in the same key for the same duration, barely separated one from the other; the "umm" syllable is lower, but longer. Over and over the orchestrating fingers rap the heart "aah·aah·umm", then tap the ground "aah·aah·umm" as if fine-tuning the strings of two instruments in an attempt to harmonize their melodies. Boldly, Grace creates her own circle, commands her own corner and chants "aah·aah·umm." She actually feels the "aah·aah·umm" reverberating inside her chest, then tingling up her arms when she connects with the powder-clay floor.

Meanwhile, Sadu Qwa is circling the center of the hut, arranging bones and lighting candles and splashing ritual oils. Grace curiously observes Sadu Qwa cradling bones to her chest before mindfully placing them. Occasionally, she converses with them. As she sets each bone down, she recalls a name. Grace realizes these are the hallowed Ancients, or rather their vestiges retrieved from the vultures, the cherished qwa of the Qwaquiwei lineage. Each bone remnant has its own embroidered pouch. Sometimes Sadu Qwa opens a pouch, then re-closes it without disturbing its occupant. As Sadu Qwa lays down bone after bone after bone, Grace begins to sense the pains and passions that once encrusted these ritual wands. At first, the arrangement seems random; in time, they take shape. A circle. A star. The human body.

Grace is asked to lay within this figurative skeleton, in essence, to take on the hand of Cheechawei, the arm of Yahnoah, the thigh of Kakirtu, the knee of Mogawah, the hip of Heehotuck, the neck of Anishwak, the spine of Potea, the foot of Sumati. Grace must be reborn, must replace her particular bones with the aggregate body of Qwaquiwei wisdom. At first, Grace feels only the cold. From the corner of her eye, she contemplates what appears to be a forelimb, dark and crushed. In life or death? Uneasily, Grace turns to a smooth, porcelain fragment glistening beneath a steady candle. This congenial relic looks more like milky quartz than once living matter. Perhaps, this person died in sleep, and remains forever dreaming. Grace finds herself musing upon the lives behind these bones gone dry.

Too long quiescent, her arm reflexively twitches. Accidentally, she disrupts a small wrist bone. By some bewitching alchemy, the wrist bone's original manifestation re-weaves itself. The wrist bone become a wrist; the wrist extenuates into an arm; the skeleton grows skin; the stillborn stare ignites with consciousness. Grace finds herself clutching the diminutive hand of Sadu Qwa's deceased son. She cannot know it is him, but she does. The boy gazes at her with Reem's

227

eyes. Compassionately, he squeezes her hand before collapsing into his remnant wrist bone.

Hoping to recreate this magic child, Grace intentionally reaches for the wrist bone. Unfortunately, she has slipped out of body. The bones beneath appear smaller and smaller as she ascends higher and higher. She begins to forget who she is, then she begins to forget what she is — until she simply is. Adrift in the inscrutable void, Grace unravels her life, from its coarse cloth into its tensile threads. Thread after thread after thread — until something snags. Only now does Grace notice her golden cord. It begins to reel her in, reel her down, re-weave her, return her to the clutches of gravity, to the optical chicanery of flesh and pain and bone. And so the ceremony ends.

The bones are reverently returned to their embroidered pouches. The candles are extinguished. The chanters dress Grace for the fabled circles of Inner Lightning. She is dressed in a worn tunic decorated with a circle of yellow light representing the sun. Inside the circle of yellow light is a circle of green light representing the continent. Inside the circle of green light is a circle of blue light representing the ocean. Inside the circle of blue light is a molten red flame representing the smoldering heart of Lord Mother Earth. Sadu Qwa explains.

"I wore this vestment on the Eve of Inner Lightning. It has been passed down century to century, shaman to shaman. It is your shield. You will be entering the sacred circles, the circles of Inner Lightning. You will be entering as my shadow. I returned from my quest with the threads of a dream I cannot unknot. I cannot return to the circles, not for 22 years, but we cannot wait if what I fear is true. If what I fear is true, you must act as my shadow."

Sadu Qwa bends her head in silent shame as she confesses. "In recorded memory, no shaman needed shadow self. Always there was lightning to illumine the way. This time, there was neither the grace to continue — nor the blessing to leave. Qwaquiwei have been left in shadow, so you must go as shadow into the circles. Find my reflection; fixate on the unblinking eye. It will reveal what I saw, what I so feared to remember, what you must not forget."

Distracted by her own concerns, Grace does not catch every word. Besides looking for the consort thunder to her lightning, Grace hopes to find Reem. It is rumored that Qwaquiwei encounter the souls of their Ancients, of their departed, within the sacred circles. Self-consciously, Grace confesses, "I have heard one can communicate..."

Sadu Qwa nods acquiescently. "Do what you need to do for yourself. That is always the way. You will also do as the Ancients bid. In the twilight we call waking, we dabble at the surface, but in the blinding awareness of Inner Lightning—" Sadu Qwa cuts to the essential. "Do you understand what you are undertaking?" Grace nods yes, and yes. She came not knowing why. She will not leave that way.

After being purified with burning sage and anointed with patchouli oil, Grace is blindfolded, then led into the circles by a single silk thread. Initially, she is led into the circle of rocks, circling the circle. The drums are drumming. She is then led into the circle of nuts and berries, circling the circle. The drums keep drumming. Next, she enters the circle of feathers and bones, circling the circle, always circling the circle. Lastly, Grace enters the sacred circle of Inner Lightning. The drums stop.

A few haunting notes waft from a wooden flute before the drums begin again. Sadu Qwa takes off the blindfold, then knots the silk thread around Grace's neck. After directing Grace to sit cross legged on a nest of sage, Sadu Qwa withdraws to the outer circle of feathers and bones. The women in the sacred circles begin to chant "qwaquiwei, qwaquiwei, qwaquiwei". Those outside the sacred circles chant the enchanting variations, "qwaquiwei, quiqwawei, weiqwaqui, weiquiqwa, quiweiqwa." Occasionally, a gathering spontaneously clap their hands, beat their sacred sticks and sway rapturously as "qwaquiwei" reels into "waqweiqui, waqquiwei, quiweiwaq." Meanwhile, the women within the sacred circles keep a constant vigil, a tempered tempo, focusing exclusively on the divine sound, the unifying pulse "qwaquiwei, qwaquiwei, qwaquiwei".

As the night grows thick with stars, Aaron begins to fear for Grace. "She must be thirsty. She must be tired. She isn't Qwaquiwei. Why did Sadu Qwa insist my Grace..."

Quincy pats Aaron assuringly. Still puffing on his pungent pipe, he explains. "Your wife may drink if she wishes. She does not wish. She does not need. The circle sustains them. Only we, outside the circle, need drink, need eat; within the circle, the circle sustains." This does not answer Aaron's real question: why Grace? Quincy smiles smugly.

"Is the Beaver jealous? His wife has no qwa in her bloodline, yet she enters the sacred circle before him. It is uncustomary. I can only tell you Sadu Qwa heard something on the Eve of Inner Lightning. Hours, she was lost in trance. For once, tears bled from her eyes. How hard for a woman as hard as stone. How they must have burned."

Aaron narrows his eyes in judgment. "Why do you exaggerate her fierceness? Why would she not feel pain?" Aaron inadvertently scrapes a long cankering wound. Quincy backfires.

"You must know our son died. He was eight years old. Too young. Too, too young. I cried. I cursed. I drank. Sadu Qwa said nothing. When I demanded an accounting, all she would say was, 'Within the year, your molecules, your cells, your body will have replaced itself. Will that make you dead? Will that make you reborn? Who are you now that you are not what you once were? The man I married no longer exists. The son I bore died seven times before today. You did not notice. Why notice now?'

"Not one trickle of blood did she release from her heart. Just words in codes I could not understand, like this beast Mother Earth who churns from moment to moment without pausing to concede the pain of passage. How can I have been born of such a demon? I feel only the loneliness of the eons grinding mountains down to dust."

The drums grow distant as Grace's mind transcends her body, as her spirit transcends her mind. The silk thread around her throat seems to pulsate with energy, acting like an intravenous worm hole, nourishing her subtle body with the elixir of enlightenment from hitherto inaccessible dimensions. Afloat in a cerulean expanse, Grace feels like an incubating kernel inside a burgeoning seed. Atom by atom, she merges into the absorbent blueness, losing all sense of self, of separateness. She remains suspended in this ocean of bliss for seeming hours, or is it days? Perhaps entire lifetimes are passing.

Remembering her mission, Grace curiously approaches an ecstatic being; from the back, it appears to be Sadu Qwa. Beads of precious stones ignite the flowing fringes of her swirling robe. Strands of black and silver hair palpate as if plugged into the electric blueness. Remembering her directive, Grace tugs at Sadu Qwa's sleeve, intent upon confronting the unblinking eye. The being turns. In place of Sadu Qwa's unblinking eye, Grace confronts her own wide-eye wonderment. When Grace points at her image in confusion, her image points back. Taking advantage of her inertia, the mischievous mirror sprite sprints away.

Grace pursues this counterfeit self into a thicket. As she sifts through branches dense with leaves, she unexpectedly comes upon herself in the arms of her first husband. He is eleven years old and he is demonstrating the willow-waltz. He was older and wiser for a time. Grace remembers how much she loved him. Had he only been able to leave his child self behind. Each time they spin, Grace grows taller and older. Her first husband refuses to release the moment nor hazard wider steps. They grow increasingly out of sync. When they were children together, Grace could see herself in his eyes. When she became a woman, he could not offer an equal measure of man.

Farther down the path, Grace comes upon a beach laced with pink sea shells, blue-toed sandpipers, and Iroquois Jefferson making passionate love to his latest *coup d'état*. Grace hardly recognizes herself: a mistaken, romantic notion of what a woman should be. Ultimately her mannequin self shatters, leaving poor Iroquois thrashing in the tidal pools, alone.

231

Grace comes upon the head of her second husband in a rock quarry. When Grace could not find the perfect man, she settled for one perfect part. After skewing her life to fit one facet on one grain of sand, she came to see her anorexic reflection, the other parts of her being atrophied from disuse. They say you marry your self-image, but how few know their own selves, let alone another. Perhaps that's why Rom and Reem fascinated Grace. They weren't compelled to look elsewhere, see themselves distorted in the carnival mirror of another's wishing-well.

Grace wonders if this contemplation will conjure up Reem and Rom battling the Wizard for his Holy Lantern. Instead, Grace comes upon cardboard cutouts of her sons propped inside a crib filled with nesting material. Talking doll cords are attached to their backs. When she pulls one, it testifies, "Hi, I'm Rom." When she pulls the other, it swears, "No, I'm Rom." When she pulls the first again, it quips, "That's right, I'm Reem." When she pulls the second again, it taunts, "That's wrong. I'm Reem. Try again."

Seeing her pained confusion, her mischievous twins ripen into real little boys. Before Grace can embrace Reem, he metamorphoses into a butterfly, then flies away. Grace calls after, as he obliviously flutters higher and higher, dissolving into a pinprick of light. While pursuing the diminishing glimmer, Grace again encounters Sadu Qwa. This time, she finds herself lilliputian in comparison. Sadu Qwa looms sixty feet high. At first she seems two dimensional, then holographic, then sculptured by the desert windstorms, ever drifting and shifting along the mesmerizing dunes. Remembering her mission, Grace dutifully scales Sadu Qwa's braided hair in order to peer into the oracle eye. There, Grace beholds a lighted candle. As she contemplates the flame, she perceives butterfly wings, rapidly fluttering. Grace surmises that Reem is safe and in his heaven. That is what she will report to Sadu Qwa. The point is clear. All is well. The light is lit and Reem rests safely...

Belatedly, Grace notices her nightmare island trembling beneath Reem's fluttering flame. As the fated island begins to crumble, Reem's fluttering flame goes out. Grace beats her fists against the unblinking portal. Perhaps she can retrieve the candle and re-light the flame. Before she can act on this intention, the eyeball starts to orbit within its socket. The extinguished candle and the sinking island rotate out of view. Meanwhile, frame by frame, the eyeball morphs into planet Epsilon.

Grace can make no sense of what is happening. As she anxiously ponders the eerily spinning orb, blackened clouds ominously spew from the cavernous nostrils. Suddenly, the bridge of the nose collapses like a mountain caving in on itself. Puffs of smoldering smoke sputter out the darkened shaft. Grace clutches the silver stands of hair as the allegorical body breaks apart. The mouth tears across the cheek like a rifting plain. Teeth topple from their decaying gum ranges. Lava spews from beneath the fingernails. Veins burst, spewing rivers of crimson into tumultuous tornadoes. Grace loses ground as the locks she clutches sprout thorns, then shrivel like withered grasses. The exposed skull starts to fragment, then separate like drifting oceanic plates. Grace assures her pounding, pounding heart that it is only, only a dream. The moment she applies this cushioning thought, blood admonishingly trickles from beneath her own fingernails. Her lungs refuse to aspirate. Her neck begins to snap. Grace realizes she cannot differentiate between metaphor and madness.

Desperately, Grace scans for Reem. The more deeply she digs her fingernails into the eroding flesh, the more rapidly the flesh turns to sand. Eventually, only the mammoth skeleton remains. Grace strains to scale the widely spaced ribs. Tremors from mounting aftershocks travel up, down the decalcifying spine. As the precarious beams slow-motionly collapse, Grace spies a prick of light, of life, ripening from a glimmering yellow seed, to a golden blossom, to a crimson human heart.

Suddenly, the moment freezes. Grace finds herself, outside looking in, on an arrested frame of time. Delivered from the gurgling maelstrom, Grace scrutinizes her surroundings. In a corner of the frame, she again spies that prick of light she knows to be Reem. Unfortunately, he cannot be peeled from the clutches of the arrested backdrop. Realizing she has to move forward, Grace re-enters the inevitable frame. Immediately, the heart begins to pulse, to throb, to tick, tick, tick like a teasing time bomb. The next moment, the heart fatally ruptures. Knowing exactly where to find Reem, Grace hurls herself towards his flickering essence. As she cups his dwindling light inside her palms, the skeleton flies apart like nebula debris, propelling Grace to the dabbling surface.

Grace finds herself afloat in a dead calm. It is a welcome respite. She can feel Reem pulsing inside her grasp, pulsing assuringly. For a long time, she holds him to her heart. She hesitates uncupping her hands lest...

Abruptly, the drums stop drumming. Grace appears to be paralyzed. Sadu Qwa approaches cautiously. "What is it, Grace?"

Grace tries to answer. "I— I cannot inhale. I cannot exhale."

Sadu Qwa strokes Grace tenderly. "Then come back to the ground, Grace. Come into your body. Feel your breath. Summon your breath."

Grace stutters as she struggles for air. "It was Reem. Here— Here on my face. I could feel his breath. Here in my hands, I could— could feel his rapping fingers, then suddenly silence, so numbing, even now, I have to struggle not to suffocate."

Sadu Qwa tightens her arms around her chest, visibly chilled. "Then you heard it too. I had to be sure. So long Qwaquiwei have waited to hear Lord Mother breathe her spirit into our souls. We thought: if she breathes her breath into us, we can stop inhaling with such effort, exhaling with such anguish. Now I see, all along, that effort, that anguish was Lord Mother breathing in, breathing out. She has been beating in such perfect harmony with our pulse, we did not notice she was there. Like a subtle undercurrent, like a background breeze, she was coursing through our bloodstream. Now, she has ceased to flow. That is what you heard: the silence between breaths, the Lord Mother not breathing — *not* breathing. She did not come this time. However, this time she left. You too lost a child. I knew you would recognize..."

Before Sadu Qwa can speculate, she is interrupted by Rom's rending cries. He was preparing to release Reem's eagle. For its own safety, one of the eagle's legs had been tethered to the wooden transport box. While Aaron and Quincy were debating the best way to encourage the domesticated creature to take flight, the eagle took the initiative. Its clipped wings, now fully grown, seized a passing updraft's promise of deliverance. Unfortunately, the eagle's leg is still tethered to the box.

Desperately, the eagle beats its wings, struggling for altitude despite its anchor. On first attempt, the eagle struggles along twenty feet before collapsing. Rom barely reaches the eagle when it again takes flight. Each time the eagle reaches sufficient momentum to lift the box from the ground, the weight of the box tightens the tether. After several failed launches, the tightening tether cuts into the eagle's ankle; it begins to bleed. Rom valiantly gives chase in order to untether the eagle's leg. With each attempted rescue, the wildly resisting creature claws Rom's arms. Blood seeps through Rom's flannel sleeves and trickles down his fingers. Aaron races to assist. Rom screams. The eagle shrieks. Quincy shouts for a knife. Fearing the eagle will fracture its leg, Rom shields his eyes and boldly snatches the fastenings. At last, he loosens the tether.

The eagle takes to the sky with wanton zeal. After reaching a safe elevation, it proceeds to circle. It circles as if following a protocol. Suddenly, a deafening stroke of thunder punctures the sky, followed by lightning — lingering lightning. While the children cheer the counterfeit flashes, Aaron uneasily supposes, "Comets?" As he counts "Two? Five? Seven?", Quincy tremulously refutes, "No! Lightning, stuck in the sky! A little unusual, but not comets, not those agitators. I didn't send for them. Who would be so crazy?"

Grace solicits, "I take it, they're not a good sign."

Aaron fixates on the puzzling streaks. "Depends how close. Depends what they are spewing our way. Depends what triggered them. No, not a good sign."

As if on cue, a pregnant cat crosses their path. Abruptly, it gives birth to two kittens. It does not stop to nurse or nurture.

A few steps later, three more kittens gush from its womb, crash to the ground in a rude awakening. Again, the cat takes no notice, continuing in the direction it was headed, seemingly with no destination in mind.

Grace is horrified. "What's wrong with her? Is she dazed?"

Quincy sneers, "The bitch! Like, like she just took a shit."

Sadu Qwa nods somberly. "Don't you see? Mother Earth is leaving us to our own devices, expelling us from her womb. An injured or threatened mother will often desert her young to protect her own life."

"Evicting us from the Garden yet once again?"

"Or herding us back, like rioting goats. We, who were never in control, have been discharged from our honorarium positions. She will fix what we have broken, reclaim the talents we failed to nourish. As for us? How long can we survive in that abyss between breaths?"

EBB TIDE

When children question why is the sky blue, does the sun set, do summer leaves turn red with autumn rust, do robins fly — they are invariably told how. No one really knows why. Over time, in place of answers, adequate responses accumulate, enough complete sentences to tangle those nuisance neural tendrils ever seeking the unanswerable.

In Chantilly, cows no longer give milk. Veterinarians say: not enough zinc in the marrow. Exactly what happened to the zinc in the marrow, no one knows. In Mabamba, trees no longer bear fruit. In Tralink, hens lay hollow eggs, and all along the Touche coast, tides are ebbing inch by inch with no sign of returning. Fishermen report the disappearance of sargasso weed from the Logo Bay. Huachuca farmers complain the binga birds no longer eat the fudoo ants. Allowed to run rampant, the voracious fudoos devour the harvest. Ironically, the feted fudoos burst when their distended bellies rupture. In Grindale, a cat reportedly tried to mate with a muskrat. In Kayoto, frogs drown in their ponds. In Frakenstat, clouds swell with rain, grow ominously black, then descend like tormented spirits. Weather forecasters daily predict rain, but the bloated clouds, unable to unleash their troubles, defy meteorologist logic. In Tampatown, daffodahlias no longer produce pollen, which is just as well because bees won't leave their hives. In Sillsbury, grass gulls try to hatch golf balls. In Merlington, turtles struggle to scale trees, flip topside down and die. Meanwhile, in Peching, rats refuse to eat the mounting carrion.

From his roving helicopter, Tim Tinkerton reports. "From my aerial vantage, it looks like ash, the aftermath of a volcanic blowout, but it's a teeny-weeny worm, or more correctly, teensy-weensy worms in the nightmarish zillions. Omwell is now buried in them. Until last week, no one knew what midgedomites were. Apparently, they have been here all along, kept conveniently in check — until now. The corrosive excretions from their exponentially increasing numbers are dissolving stone buildings, stripping skyscrapers to their steel frames. While we have the means to exterminate, we cannot outpace them as they unremittingly replicate..."

Grace switches off the radio. Connery does not protest. Indeed, he fails to notice. His back remains to the door as he contemplates pigmy blackbirds perched outside his window. Defiantly, they huddle on bare branches as numbing winds rustle their stiffening feathers.

"They said I would find you here, said you're back in business, up to your old tricks." What Grace actually heard was: Connery had blown his marbles. Since his incident in the woods, he has been behaving like a man unpossessed, given up all claims to the Cliff of Ancients, halted all projects, divested himself of chairmanships, switched to manual. Despite being cleared of wrongdoing in the Mazing Wafer scandal, Deloy Enterprises settled all suits. Riveted to the distressed blackbirds, Connery poses.

"Why don't they fly south? Why isn't anything working? Perhaps you were right about ants, about us. While lost in the woods, I realized civilizations come in all different sizes, careen into opposite directions, come to contradictory conclusions, go backward, forward, then backward again. We rhapsodize about parallel universes undiscovered, oblivious to the parallel universes at hand. Why, there are ecosystems high in the tree tops and ecosystems on precipitous escarpments; there are organisms huddling under frozen ice caps, boiling inside lava flows, languishing on decomposing corpses, clinging to streaking asteroids. There are creatures whose aspirations we cannot fathom basking beneath our toenails. So what's so special about us?"

Grace disquietingly counters. "You can't think like that. After all, I was hoping you..."

Plagued by his own agenda, Connery beseechingly interrupts. "Like when a scrubgrub suddenly grows wings: there it is, a scrambling scrubgrub, sliming along the gritty ground when suddenly, serendipitous wings appear. Without evolutionary scales to gauge its relative ascension into heaven, it quite naturally believes itself an angel — until that fateful day it chances upon a shattered mirror, a hologram fragment from the proverbial big bang-up. In one ego wounding moment, it sees the bigger picture, realizes its fragile, flotsam nature. Lost in the woods, I realized I could neither save the world, nor put it out of its misery. In fact, a pond three inches by three inches by three inches has more magic, more mayhem than I can ever—"

Connery retrieves a globe paperweight from a bottom shelf. Contemplatively, he turns it upside down, then right-side up. Confetti snowflakes obscure the miniature skyline. Solemnly, Connery grumbles. "There in the woods, I realized we're only a point on the cosmic thread. There in the woods, the moment the sun rose, it filtered through my eyelids, pulled me open like a morning glory. I was so absolutely tired but she tapped into my spinal column, drew me upwards like a vine. I wanted to curl close and die, but she tugged here, then prodded there, compelled me onward. You can build walls to shut her out, turn night into day against her wishes, but she controls the umbilical reigns. We imagine the cord gets severed in one mortal snip, but that's just the metaphor for the simulated birth. The connecting umbilical loosens momentarily, allowing us to display our potential properties, perform our brief dance on the cutting floor. If we please the Lord Mother, the cord loosens, permitting us to embellish our dance further. If we screw up, she reels us in, kneads us back into the starter batter for some later baking."

Unused to hearing the invincible Deloy prattle so dishearteningly, Grace assuringly bolsters. "You can't think like that. Just as children conjure winged dragons to save them from the cave demons, we must sometimes shrink the universe to more comprehensible dimensions, confine it to a four inch screen, which we can switch on and off as necessary. Sometimes, you have to look at the bigger picture one frame at a time."

"Always right of left and left of right. Unfortunately, you were correct the first time. We are just a bunch of worker bees following the rules of the hive — until someone huffs, puffs, and blows off our rose tinted shutters."

"I was hoping the inimitable Deloy would offer a more silver lining, implicate solar flares or something. That is what you do. Now is not the time to stop doing it. Exactly what is — and isn't going on? This morning, I saw a falcon fall from the sky. It wasn't injured. It simply stopped flapping its wings as if suddenly, in mid-stroke, it forgot how. Some days, I lose contact with my feet as if I'm losing gravity."

Connery momentarily lightens. "Well, we're all losing gravity. You lose gravity with age, don't you?"

Welcoming his musing smile, Grace reports. "I left Rom at the Qwaquiwei reservation with his father. They are performing rituals. As effective as what I've been doing: trying to get the government to do something. I was hoping you would work with me to convince politicians, industrialists, the lunatic fringe to— Not exactly sure. The first hurdle is prying them from their disaster shelters. After publishing a thousand page document signifying nothing, the reigning powers announced via electronic mail: *Environmental trends not good. Everyone get out of the boat.* So, that's the second hurdle: they've lost their minds."

Dutifully performing his secretarial duties, Wayne enters the room, mildly flustered. "What— what were those files you wanted? The something or other?"

Wearily, Connery repeats. "This morning's calculations from the Asteroid Belt Society, and last week's journals from the Bindustan digs." After Wayne leaves, Connery bewails. "I told him that fifteen minutes ago, then fifteen minutes before that. He's been asking that same question every fifteen minutes for the past three hours."

TO ASHES

Rom and Sadu Qwa sprinkle sage ashes into their ritual circles. Several weeks after the Inner Lightning, the Qwaquiwei continue to chant, continue to pray. Not a single Qwaquiwei has died, proving in the minds of many that Mother Earth safeguards her chosen people. Consequently, frightened citizens of Epsilon continue to pilgrimage to the Qwaquiwei reservation. Like refugees from war torn lands, they huddle along the riverbanks and sacred Cliff seeking protection.

Sadu Qwa hands Rom a bare plume to place amidst the sage ashes. Sadly, she notes, "If they come to save their souls, I rejoice, but they come to save their skins. How soon their skins will blow away, leaving them naked in their nightmare."

Several hundred yards away, Aaron and Quincy carefully balance themselves on a splintered wooden fence. Quincy hands Aaron another smoldering pipe. They are already drunk on cinogen tea. Pointing to the most recent influx of Epsilonians, Aaron laments. "Being Qwaquiwei won't save them. Don't they understand: termite mounds are disappearing. Doesn't that tell them something? Termite mounds produce methane. Among other things, the planet is trying to reduce methane in an effort to repair the chemistry of the atmosphere. The planet isn't out to exterminate termites, or us. It is simply following its own path to survival — and we are coincidentally in the way. I don't take it personally. I could be just as happy as a holly bee, or a porpoise, or a binga bird. I see that now." Taking another puff on his cinogen leaves, Aaron declares. "Yes, I now see the entire schematic. I see the world though a puff of smoke and it is not all that complicated."

Quincy is not so easily placated. "Turns my stomach. So many generations, Qwaquiwei have been branded a silly people, a pagan people. Now, our detractors drop like repentant flies at our feet."

Aaron picks at a cinogen leaf stuck to his tongue. "Ah, yes, the doctors of today are proven witch doctors tomorrow; the witch doctors of yesterday are our reigning wisdom teachers. So it goes."

Quincy continues his lament. "Went walking by the stream last evening, on my way to the depository, when an Epsilonian, drunk with beer—", Quincy hiccups, then swigs on his fermented kanuk-kanuk, "suggested we sacrifice the 'problem' people: prominent industrialists, politicians, a musical group called the Migraines. Wanted me to scalp them. Can you imagine anything so gross? Were these people raised in a barn?

"Of course, when it came to putting his money where he shits, he suggested we install port-o-toilets. What is it with you people? So consummately selfish, you won't part with your own feces. Mother Earth gives you to eat. What you don't utilize, she expects back. Instead, you wrap it like feast stuffing, then bury it like nuclear waste. And you call me barbarian?"

Completely missing this cultural exchange, Aaron anxiously sucks on his extinguished cinogen pipe. "What's happening? I'm coming down — down, down. Has my cinogen lost its hallucinogenic bite? Perhaps I have misplaced my qwa. In that case, can I borrow a pinch of yours, just to tide me over? Only a moment ago, I was a carefree binga bird feasting on fudoo ants. Now I see the oracle swirls in the pond scum are taking a decidedly negative stance. Worse, I think I am going to vomit." Aaron begins to fall from his perch.

Quincy leaps to catch him. "No, no, no, no, no! We must make a circle. Do some chanting. Get some spirit input."

"I thought men couldn't make circles."

"What do you mean: men can't make circles?" Quincy pounds his chest vaingloriously. "Why, I have been making circles since I was a boy. I can make circles. I can make squares. I can even make an isosceles triangle."

Aaron waves his hand apologetically. "No, I mean men aren't ordained to make ritual circles, or sit in them, or something. Isn't that why Sadu Qwa sent for Grace and not me, when I'm just as good a mother, just as good a wife. What's more, I'm a dedicated forest ranger, friend to the bush bear, squish berries, and muck beetle. Why is Mother Earth rejecting me? Am I not just as biodegradable as the next creature? So why can't I make circles? Why can't I..."

Quincy shakes Aaron from his cinogen stupor. "Get a grip Mushkin! During the Inner Lightning, men traditionally don't make circles. Now, next to anything goes. No time to stand on ceremony, no time for pride. Get down on your knees while I beg, remind the Lord Mother: we are her children." In defiance, in defense, Quincy tries to stare down the sun.

SHATTERED WINDOWS

While Grace and Connery continue to ponder the reams of data, Wayne continues to confound himself. "Excuse me, Mr. Deloy. Did you say the Atlantis Mint factory, Atlanta Mining company or was it..." Having heard the question seven times before, Grace directs him to the Atlantis Myth cult.

Connery counters, "No. Go home, Wayne."

Grace concurs, "Yes, Wayne; go home."

After Wayne has left, Grace gently interrogates. "Some people— some reputable people are saying—" Grace hesitates to say what even reputable people say. "Sounds preposterous but, do you believe an extraterrestrial race has been tampering with us, is now preparing to re-inject an updated version, that this is what the turmoil's all about?"

Connery does not immediately answer. "Ever been to the moon?"

Grace blushes as she puckishly divulges. "Years and years ago, with Iroquois. We were young, enamored, and as I recall, spent most of the time inside the anti-gravity suite perfecting kama sutra positions. Never got to see the green cheese. Did I miss something?"

Connery suppresses a smile. "Well, of course it's all a matter of priorities, but if you know where to look, who to pay off, you can explore the outposts of several extraterrestrial species. Nothing has ever been officially admitted because there is nothing now to tell. Governments like to pretend some looming invader lurks in the outfield in order to keep the incorrigible players on base. Actual evidence indicates these observatories were abandoned thousands and thousands of years ago. People always talking about the Alien Coming, when the reality is ancient history. Who knows where they were from, what they were like, what they intended. Evidence does indicate they tried to breed Sapiens to specification. The demise of many predecessor civilizations may not have been accidental. Wouldn't be too hard to concoct a decimating virus, leak lethal gas into the atmosphere."

"Meaning they laid us eggs, then left?"

"I suspect humans kept retrograding — stayed human. When these extraterrestrial engineers realized their enhancements weren't taking, they gave up. Another possibility is they succeeded. If their final brood was too distinct to blend with the native sheep, perhaps they decided, instead of destroying us once again, to graze their prize herd elsewhere. Maybe they began to suspect some kind of planet consciousness directs the destinies of its creatures. Their foreign transplants were recognized, targeted, and ejected from the native kingdom."

"So you're saying that these super beings were ultimately defeated by Lord Mother Earth?"

"I suspect, as advanced as they were, they were just another flavor of dominant species. Unfortunately, we may never evolve to say 'I told you so'."

Grace squints at the disheartening data. "This asteroid belt is thickening. Its gravitational tug may have triggered those explosions in the planet's core. If the asteroid belt is thickening, the likelihood of being hit by some astral projectile increases. This Earth document records a crater 190 miles across caused by an asteroid only 5 miles wide. It suggests the impact of the encounter precipitated the demise of those dinosaurs. Like seasonal flowers, we seem to bloom and die. Makes perfect sense. It's the way everything else operates. Whatever made us think we existed outside the regulation paradigm?"

Grace crinkles the reams of paper as she waveringly proposes. "What— what if the asteroid isn't here on its own volition? What if it was purposely invited? They say if you tamper with a fledgling in its nest, its mother will abandon it. Even if those extraterrestrial enhancements didn't take, we might have been damaged in the process. If so, our own Mother Earth could be mistaking us for extraterrestrial weeds. Rather than a work in progress, we may be the wreckage of a failed dream. Did some foster overlord stuff too many brain cells into our pudding heads, shove too many circuits onto the motherboard? Have we become misfits, outcasts belonging nowhere? Is this planet intentionally wobbling to set itself up — to set us up?"

Indicating the asteroid data, Grace theorizes. "And now comes the magic bullet: an asteroid that will put the fatal hole through our heads. Tell me I'm paranoid. Tell me I'm crazy. Perhaps, we just broke the damn thing. Now, it can't maintain a steady orbit. We'll end up crashing into Mars, become asteroids in our own right, another has-been Jupiter moon.

"Everyone expects to die. It happens sooner or later. You have to give up your carbon kingdom for the transcendent grail. For the most part, we go gracefully, assured our human nature survives in our children's children's children. There is the presumption, sins get averaged out, added and subtracted from the billions and billions of past and future culprits but, like musical chairs, what happens to those left standing when the music stops? What happens to those left last on line? Are they held accountable for the final reckoning? It's one thing for a pigmy blackbird to say, 'I ate, mated and died', it's quite another for Grace Ivanosky— Looking at the name on a mail box, the code on a tax form, I think I did okay, but looking at the human being, the relic of the human age, I can't help thinking — I was supposed to be better."

Connery defends his life. "I for one did what I could with the tools at my disposal. If we behave like humans, it's because we are humans. If humans seem half-animal, it's because we are half-animal. If life seems odd the way it is, it's because life is odd. Perhaps Lord Mother Earth is not the one calling us back as prophesied. That feeling: your feeling you should have been better? Maybe that's the problem. We're missing something we ourselves can't do without. It is we who have turned ourselves in, admitted failure."

Connery turns towards the pigmy blackbirds. "Look at them, sitting there day after day, freezing to death. Day after day after day. Are they mocking us, or are they just stupid?" Angrily, Connery pries open his window. The bitter winds tangle his tie as he hurls his coffee mug at a blackbird burdened bough. Three birds fall off. Two were already dead. The third topples to the ground where it wobbles dazedly. Not one of the remaining birds on the remaining branches flinches or attempts to alter its position.

Shaken, Connery discloses. "Last night, I thought I was awake but I must have been dreaming. A pigmy blackbird, the size of a colossalsaur, shattered my bedroom window. It asked me what I was doing. I said I was trying to sleep. It told me to put on my running shoes — and get the hell out of Kansas."

THE VORTEX

Aaron and Quincy have made a rather distorted circle. Chewing on a handful of cinogen leaves, Aaron traces the circle around and around before noting. "It feels more like a spiral than an isosceles triangle."

Quincy defensively shouts. "Well of course. It's a vortex. I made a vortex. Can't you tell?"

"Was that wise? Won't a vortex suck us in? Now we will need to dig a hole to take shelter from this vortex."

Fearing his vortex has hidden convolutions in mind, Quincy concedes, "I see your point. Be careful what you pray for, eh? After all, I have been trying to sabotage nuclear power plants, induce riots. I have been saying: if you want to cross the river, first tear down the bridge; otherwise, when you get to the other side, the grass is no more, no less green than the grass from which you came. I have been saying the only way to start over is to have no reference point. I was talking loud, thinking Lord Mother was deaf to my pleas. What if she heard me all along — so now she is thinking what I'm thinking: turn on the vortex. Get rid of them all — only sure way to eliminate the contagion. From the perspective of Lord Mother Earth, we must look like an infestation of aphids. Ever try to pluck one aphid at a time off a sticky bush? Much easier to hack down that troublesome tree. So, yes, yes, we must dig a hole to escape the consequences of our actions. We must build this hole so deep, when the vortex comes after us, it will be swallowed and expelled into a parallel universe. Eventually, that parallel universe will catch up. Eventually, we all end up on the same thin line, but if we dig deep enough, we can buy time, enough to die like a man, not die out, like a strain of streptococci." As an afterthought, Quincy spits out his cinogen leaves. "For this, we better get sober."

SHOOT THE MOON

Grace lags behind the stampeding Senators Seerington, Grady, and Mungus as they march towards Deloy's office. "Mr. Deloy will never promote such a mindless endeavor. I can't believe you still seriously consider shooting the damn thing down with a mega missile."

Senator Seerington balks, "You have a better idea?"

"No, but considering the last mega missile veered off course, ended up destroying the city of Bengala..."

"Small price to pay. We should have done this long ago instead of giving into bleeding hearts, listening to consensus nonsense. I always said democracy was a damn fool idea. You can't listen to all people at all times without everyone succumbing to that one rotten apple. Those relief efforts got us nowhere. We spent all our resources helping babies out of burning buildings when we should have been blitzing the sky with mega-maniac shells. I say: go for the calculated risks."

Grace sorts through her jacket pockets for clipped news articles, pages from computer reports, personal notes. Referring to them, she edifies. "According to the scientific community, it would be more than a calculated risk. This planet is wobbling in its orbit. It is already unstable. The reactions to the actions of mega missiles could warp our trajectory even further. We might end up catapulting outside our solar system."

Senator Grady snatches one of Grace's articles. "You don't mean the same scientific community that failed to predict these cataclysms we are encountering? You can't mean those assholes. Besides, at last count, you conceded to a proactive approach."

"To do *something*, not *anything*. We tried the missile. It backfired. No point trying it again — or playing into citizen fear. People are burning mutant evolutionists at the stake. I missed how we jumped to that solution. Why aren't you stopping them?"

Senator Seerington belligerently asserts. "People need to feel empowered. What are we supposed to tell them: hold your breaths and pray?"

"But what can Deloy do? He doesn't stockpile mega missiles."

"He has financial connections, gadgets, thingamajigs. Perhaps..."

Grace cogently reminds. "Senators, aren't you listening? No one can predict where this planet will be with respect to the asteroid at any given moment. It's not like in the movies. We don't have nifty asteroid zappers, and we don't know what we're doing. If we shoot and miss, we could blow up the moon."

Senator Mungus ingenuously simpers. "So, who needs the moon? It just gets in the way of the sun. I wouldn't mind if it remained daylight 24 hours on end. I wouldn't mind not having to go to bed or take another morning shower. And if we do get catapulted into wherever, well, why remain in this solar system any longer than we have to? There's no life on the other planets. We can't vacation on Venus and we can't mine Pluto. It's really a very depressed region of the universe. It's time we moved on, go where no duly elected official has gone before."

Grace can no longer bear the strain of dispassion. After removing her left shoe, she hurls it at Mungus. "How did this man get into office? How can he govern year after year without benefit of a single working brain cell? Am I alone on this? The man is an idiot! A criminally insane idiot making decisions that affect millions, and millions, and millions of human beings." Calculating the extent of his insidious, legislative reign, Grace stomps on his fleeing feet with her right heel, citing, "He should be put to sleep, incinerated. His ashes should be treated like infectious detritus."

As Mungus 'ouches' and 'ooos', Seerington laments. "What happened to you, Ivanosky? Used to be a stand-up kind of guy: savvy, sensible, understood the material difference between a dollar and dime. Thankfully, Deloy does not share your raw emotions. He knows when to be necessarily cruel." On this sourly sarcastic note, the Senator rams open Connery's door.

In lieu of the hoped-for gadgets and thingamajigs, piles of seeds and soy lecithin granules litter the rug. Pigmy blackbirds amble on tops of desks, under chairs, on shelves, in wastebaskets, inside coffee mugs. One pecks curiously in Connery's disheveled hair. Another tries to traverse Wayne's hunched shoulders as he huddles over a nest of fledglings, eye-dropping glutinous globules into their peeping mouths. Like a harried chef, Connery scoops portions of sesame seeds and vegetarian burger mix into a coffee grinder. After grinding to an espresso consistency, he conscientiously taste-tests.

The Senators are dumb struck. As they silently mourn the loss of yet another stand-up act, Connery and Wayne argue over the nutritional value of the various ingredients. While they argue, painstakingly fine-tune their batters, additional boxes of pigmy birds are delivered by special courier.

END TO A COVENANT

Aaron and Quincy are exhausted but satisfied. After laboring for several days, they have constructed a sturdy underground shelter.

Quincy proclaims, "It's solid."

Aaron pronounces, "It's deep."

Quincy inhales. "I feel good about this."

Aaron exhales. "Good to feel good about something — and my headache's gone."

"Whatever will we do with it?"

"I don't know. Why did we dig it?"

"Don't know. Getting more and more forgetful. Don't know last time I ate. Am I even hungry."

Aaron uneasily reveals, "Strange, strange happenings. They say: not a single person was born yesterday. They say, doctors who induced labor reported mother, child — and father died. Not a single person being born?"

Quincy avoids commenting. Instead, he considers their curious burrow. "This hole looks dangerous. You should never have dug it."

"Dug it? I thought we were filling it in?"

"Well, yes, of course; otherwise someone could stumble and break their neck."

Still clutching their shovels, they pause to rest. Their respite is brief. A thundering rumble ripples across the unmarred plain as a segment of the Cliff of Ancients unexpectedly collapses. Tons of avalanching stones reverberate through the reservation. Hundreds plunge to their death; hundreds more are crushed beneath the rubble. Many are Epsilonians who sought refuge. Many more are Qwaquiwei.

Mothers frantically attempt to loosen mangled children from the settling stones. Youngsters struggle to free pinioned guardians. A toddler with bleeding hands tugs her father's pant

255

leg. A teenager pounds his palms against a massive boulder as he shrieks his companion's name. A dog anxiously claws his old master, interred in the resultant mud-slide. With bleeding, crippled legs, he paws his captured keeper.

Bitterly, Aaron and Quincy survey their implicit tomb, dug just in time to bury the dead.

AFTERSHOCKS

The collapse of the Cliff of Ancients confirmed in the minds of many that there is no one to whom to appeal for salvation — and therefore no salvation. Planet Epsilon, alias Earth, is an expendable leaven in the ceaselessly churning cosmic soup. At any moment, the fragile curio may shatter, and never be missed amidst billions of more resplendent stars.

Having buried the dead and attended the injured, Aaron and Rom leave the Qwaquiwei to their pain and prayers. They rejoin Grace and Webster, as the proverbial other shoe continues its fatal free fall.

Aaron switches on the radio. Unlike every day before, the announcer refuses to apprise his listening audience of the encroaching distance of the assassin asteroid. It is now too close, too menacing to mention. This sudden evasion of facts should have alerted Aaron that it was no time to be putting out fires on distant hills. Considering how few citizens were reporting to work in the face of extinction, Aaron was taking his responsibilities too seriously. While Grace encourages Aaron to attend to business, she doesn't mean it. Aaron knows she doesn't mean it — so why is he putting on his hat and coat to leave? Perhaps, it is a pretense for the children.

As Grace tucks a pair of gloves into Aaron's overcoat, he, in turn, clips a metallic bracelet around her wrist. Grace examines the brassy bangle curiously. Somberly Aaron explains. "A tracer. Not the one I vowed to attach to your soul, but it will do for now. It will let me know just where you are should—", Aaron abruptly encodes, "you travel to buy a loaf of bread."

Deciphering his meaning, Grace kisses Aaron mindfully. Wishing to impart at least a ritual wand for protection, Grace extracts an umbrella from the hall rack. Solicitously, she nudges. "They are predicting rain."

This coming rain proves a gross miscalculation. It only briefly precedes the ferocious hail storm. Aaron curses as he tries to tune into Grace's bangle device. The distant fires were a cruel ruse. Before Aaron could reach their smoking embers, a blustering hail had put them out. This same hail now obstructs his return home. Aaron cannot see more than a few feet in any direction as ice chunks pummel the roof of his car. Eventually, his vehicle stalls. Unable to restart it, Aaron waits alone on a back road, in the pelting tempest, attended by the dolorous thought that he will never see Grace again. Though Grace and Aaron remain bodily separate, their minds at irreconcilable distances, their hearts have inextricably merged, surrendered themselves to an unaddressable space that cannot be accessed by one without the other. One heart beats; the other echoes. Neither can return to its original vacuum.

Aaron guns his engine, stomps his pedals over and over, all the while pleading with his indifferent vehicle. Eventually, his roof starts to leak. Trickles of freezing water drizzle down his face. Forlornly Aaron notes: many will die; souls will overrun the nether world. How will he find Grace amidst this din of spirits in quest of their respective heavens? Thunder cracks. Lightning scuds the sky. Icy droplets mediate Aaron's ardent tears as he bleeds to death inside.

Attempting to batten down the hatches, Grace hammers another plank of wood across the kitchen window. Too often, she misses the nails and further cracks the weakening wood. Webster whimpers. Rom gnaws his lower lip. To allay their intensifying doubts, Grace unconvincingly rasps, "I think we will be safe." Rom nods his agreement, though equally unconvinced. Seconds later, one end of the wooden board, loosened by the wailing winds, snaps off. The exposed nails strike Grace across the forehead. As blood seeps from the resultant gash, Rom tries not to cry lest he further distress Webster. Grace responds with instinctive assurance. "I'm all right, honey. It's just a scratch. Everything is going to be all right. It's— it's just a storm."

The service announcements statically contradict as the radio ricochets from station to station on a ripple of ill tidings: *A major quake has struck... Tidal waves are devouring... Communication lines down... 400 miles of coastline have been ripped... Mounting aftershocks... Entire cities buried... Hurricane winds... Volcanic eruptions... Scientists at a loss... Government dissolved... Aptly named killer asteroid is due to impact at...*

A rock smashes through a side window, crushing the electronic doomsdayer. Mud-soaked rain, squalling through the broken glass, splotches Rom and Webster with globules of grime. Grace pauses to wipe the affronting mud from their innocent faces. She labors in vain as the sullying rains, still blasting through the shattered window, splatter Rom and Webster with ever more rain and mud. Webster starts to shriek hysterically.

At a loss what to do, Grace desperately searches for something to seal shut the window. While debating the substantiveness of a recipe-studded bulletin board, a muddy surge ruptures the splintering window frame, plunging Grace into the rampaging sludge. The quicksand medium drags her along the living room floor. Fortuitously, she crashes into her couch. With decided difficulty, she claws into the fabric, scales the high back rest. Completely sheathed in mud, she convulsively spits out the intrusive grit.

From her precarious outpost, Grace fretfully observes that Rom has climbed from the rickety kitchen chair to the rickety kitchen table. He is clutching Webster, choking her to his shivering chest. Panicked, Webster grasps Rom's glasses as she slips down his mud-slicked shirt. As he cries for direction, Grace is again bulldozed into the deadly flow. This time, she crashes through the bay window.

Outside, Grace is exposed to the full brunt of the elements. As she sinks beneath the torrential runoff, she observes a portion of her roof collapse. Within seconds, she begins to drown. It does not seem possible. It is not yet noon.

She has not yet showered. Her children are not yet grown. Providentially, a garage door surges upwards, lifting her above the flood waters. Gasping for air, Grace feels the unsettling weight of mud and water inside her lungs and stomach. Grace reaches for a tree branch. With great effort, she pulls herself towards the massive trunk. It is a cursed respite, perforated with terrible thoughts.

The sky is drenched in a bewitched grayness. Grace cannot distinguish objects within the veiling vapors. Webster was surely wrenched from Rom's arms. Grace resolves to dive in after them. Extraordinarily, she cannot relax her grasp. Having found safe harbor, her arms will not let go. Momentarily disposed to survival, Grace tries to distance herself from the rising waters. Carefully testing the strength of each limb, she ascends to a seemingly secure net of branches. There, she cradles herself as she weeps inconsolably. Skimming the burning tears from her face, she envisions Webster swept into the murderous mud, then Rom blinking blindly as he thrashes within turbulent whirlpools.

Intermittently she hallucinates. During one delirious episode, Grace finds herself selling flowers on a street corner until suffocating ash from an exploded volcano engulfs her. She is excavated hundreds of centuries hence. Amazingly, her flowers are still intact. When her embedded ghost overhears a team of archaeologists discussing her preemptive demise, it occurs to Grace that this is how we all must die: wrenched from our body in one blinding moment. The neck snaps. The mind freezes on a worrisome thought. This is what we are left holding when we face our God.

Grace cannot estimate whether hours, or days, or only minutes have passed. The racking pangs have been replaced by an analgesic exhaustion. Is this the final grace? When everything has been lost, when all attachments have been severed, the burgeoning spirit begins to wriggle from its shackling husk. Abruptly, Grace's circulation returns, displacing the humane numbness with cramping pain. Cruelly awakened, Grace again remembers her children. She trembles with tears as she envisions Webster fractured by raging streams, envisions Rom face down in the splintered wreckage of their broken home. Grace tries to rhapsodize her children in happier moments: Webster, racing in resolute circles, chasing butterflies round and round the bayberry bush: Rom, making satellites out of cereal boxes, and volcanoes from pancake batters. Instead, she sees them as they surely are: dying, dying — then dead.

Their presence and absence constrain Grace from realizing her final peace. Futilely, she shrieks into the howling darkness. "Rom! Webster! Rom! Webster! Rom! Webster! Aaron? Oh Aaron, Aaron, Aaron!" Grace wonders why her heart does not burst inside her chest. Eventually, her voice gives out. She is no longer breathing involuntarily — an auspicious sign, assurance that the end is near, that it will soon be over.

THE AFTERLIFE

A burning light billows from a mystical darkness. Grace wonders where she is. Perhaps she is transcending the incarnate state. Certainly, she is not where she was. Perhaps they have buried her. That must be it. She must be dead.

Someone gently strokes her hair. Grace strains to open her eyes only to realize her eyes are open. A slowly solidifying image, a solicitous sentinel sent to guide her along the celestial way, takes familiar shape. In the billowing light, the guardian angel looks a bit like Aaron. Tenderly, he smiles. He is Aaron.

So Aaron must be dead too, meaning at any moment, Rom, Webster — and Reem will burst into this post-life antechamber. Neither Rom nor Webster could have survived the devastation, so there is good news after all: her family will be reunited. Webster will jump onto the bed, her cheeks caked with cooked cereal. Rom will bounce at the edge of the mattress while Reem interrogates, *Where is Webster? Where is Rom?*

Aaron does not verbalize the question. Grace reads his face — meaning she is not dead and he is no angel. Grace is neither grateful to be alive, nor relieved to see Aaron. Precipitously, she declares. "We need to find Rom's glasses." Aaron nods as if he understands, but he cannot understand what Grace does not herself understand. After easing Grace to her feet, Aaron leads her outside.

Stunned by the brunt of annihilation, she falters. Aaron explains. "If this planet had not wobbled in its orbit at just the right moment, the asteroid would have impacted. Unfortunately, that saving action caused devastating reactions." Aaron fumbles with Grace's tracer bracelet. "I was able to track you. Brought you to this abandoned kiln. You've been unconscious for days."

Grace surveys the local ruins: houses leveled, forests splintered, lakes where there were once ponds, mountains of mud where there was once a strip mall. Only the sky remains a tranquil turquoise. Again, Aaron explains. "A mile up the road—" Realizing there is no road, Aaron feebly points eastward. "Survivors have set up camp. A ham operator rigged a radio. According to whoever is broadcasting, everything is back to normal. Not back to what was, but our orbit has stabilized. Not everywhere looks as bad as here, though some places are worse. Hard to believe the birds are about making nests. Sadu Qwa says it's over. She put her heart to the ground and heard the pulse of her Lord Mother coursing through the mountains, streams, and trickle vines. The government has reconvened. Everyone is making promises, committing to all sorts of things. Qwaquiwei vow to become participating citizens. There will be a new world order." Aaron turns atypically acrid. "I suppose it is human nature to believe after worse comes better."

Belatedly Aaron perceives Grace's exhausted indifference. Distractedly she retrieves a Debbie Debutante doll from the loamy squalor. "I swore never to buy Webster a Debbie Debutante doll. Disapproved the brassy hair, and pouting lips, and gauzy gown, remember? Poor Webby, not even out of diapers and I was disputing her choice of dolls, determining her whole life. Could have saved myself the trouble."

Contemplatively, Grace pulls the loosened gauze from Debbie's gown. Aaron takes solace in her seeming acceptance, but there is no acceptance as her eyes again moisten. "I didn't say goodbye, didn't say 'I love you'. I kept trying to make breakfast. I burnt the pop-toast. Found a jar of peanut butter but I couldn't pry it open, and I didn't say good-bye, didn't get the chance to— I told them it was just a storm."

As Grace weeps silently, Aaron rests his head on her quivering backbone. Eventually, Grace straightens, and questions, "What's that?"

Aaron speculates. "A river dove. Or willow lark. I saw a pair beyond that ridge."

"It sounds like Webster."

Aaron insists it's just a willow lark. Grace again insists, "It's Webster."

Aaron urges. "Grace, look around you! Can't you guess? Millions—" His voice cracks. "Perhaps, hundreds of millions of people perished in a matter of days. Don't you think I..."

Though discerning his days of frantic searching, Grace nevertheless maintains, "I know it isn't probable but— during the Inner Lightning, I felt this Lord Mother presence. Maybe it was God. Maybe it was the universal life force, the ever-changing, or changeless. Whatever the mechanism, the overlord, it was real. She— she was real. I tell you: she cried for Reem as if she too had given birth to him, as if she too had buried him. She would not have taken Webster and Rom, having taken Reem. Not only would she not have taken them, she would have protected them. I know this sounds delusional but we— we had an agreement. It was necessary for me to understand her cycle of loss, but it would serve no purpose to leave me barren."

Aaron converts to a more comprehensible scale. "Grace, Iroquois Jefferson is dead. Old Man Jones is missing. Connery Deloy was executed. We've all been through a terrible, terrible upheaval. You need time to adjust, time to face the fact that our baby-sitter with the three pigtails is dead; our paper boy and his dalmatian dog are dead; the friends we entertained last New Year are gone, all gone. Don't you see? Days and days, I have been crying out to no one."

Grace glares wildly. "Don't *you* see! I will not adjust. I am not a river dove. I won't go make another nest. If the world I know is gone—" Grace considers her tremoring palm. "See these lines? Each passing pain, I mapped out the mystery. If the world I know is gone, these lines lead nowhere. I've come this far for nothing."

Hoping the truth will make her free, Aaron determines to lead Grace to the willow larks. After tracing the mercurial echoes to a grassy indentation, Aaron locates a tiny blue egg in a hastily patched nest. There, Grace concedes the sweet weedle-dee-dee, dee-dee-weedle of the lucky lark.

For several moments, Aaron contemplates her assuring inhale, exhale, inhale, exhale, inhale. Instinctively synchronizing his own breath to sustain the momentum, he finds himself hyperventilating. He finds himself inhaling, exhaling, inhaling, inhaling, inhaling. Something is throwing off his pace. Aaron turns to Grace. "That isn't you, is it?" For her part, Grace is no longer listening, no longer responding, leaving Aaron to deliriously douse for a direction.

"If it isn't you, then— Hear that? A kind of pulse? A kind of—" Flinging himself onto an undistinguished mound of mud, Aaron frantically begins to dig. Grace concludes he is having a breakdown, succumbing to her own desperate mind. Recalling Connery's persistent sun, she assists Aaron, determined to avoid any resurrection plot.

Things go as planned; for hours, their notch leads nowhere. They dig up the clink of kitchen utensils, the clank of rusted pipes, the body of a dead dog. The elusive inhale, exhale grows increasingly faint. However, the pretense of an impending miracle invigorates the moment. They will dig, dig until their fingers bleed, become infected, until their last drops of blood seep into the soil. No need to overstay one's turn around the wheel. In time, there comes the time to go.

The narrow entrance grows long and steep. Aaron wriggles through, then wriggles back with deposits of mud. Each cycle through the crawlway takes longer. Five minutes become ten, become fifteen. Peering into the gaping darkness, Grace gently calls, "Aaron?"

There is no response. Perhaps a section of the narrow entrance has collapsed. Faced with final abandonment, Grace screeches, "Aaron? Aaron!" All the while, the sun shines upon her, against her will. Angrily digging her nails into the hardened clay, Grace curses. "Let him go! You greedy bitch! Give him back to me. Please, please give him back." Her plaintive, blaspheming prayers do not go unrequited. Aaron returns — with Webster.

Overjoyed, Grace cradles her precious daughter, feverish but alive. A few minutes later, Aaron gingerly delivers Rom, his cheeks ashen, his leg broken. Shivering, and stuttering, Rom relates, "Mom! Dad! Mom! Dad! Webster and I— After you were swept away, Webster and I— and I— I don't know. It happened so fast. We ended up on a hill. The rain came beating down. I heard thunder and— thunder and things crashing and— I thought I heard you calling. Was sure I heard you calling from this cave. I followed but couldn't find you, then the water rose and— and rose and I couldn't crawl out and I thought— thought you were— then Webster threw up, and I started crying, and crying, and crying."

Aaron rocks Rom gently as Webster interjects "Dapplepums! Dapplepums!" Hungrily, Webster points to the ancient fruit tree that nestled in their backyard like a secreted elder. Miraculously, it still stands. Grace investigates the mirage. The old tree that continued to flower year after year with fewer and fewer blossoms had long ago stopped bearing fruit. A landscaper advised Grace to cut it down. It is now heavy with appleplums.

As Grace reverently plucks one, Aaron professorially puzzles. "I swear I passed this tree just yesterday. I would have noticed these fruit. Amazing. Never underestimate the instinct for survival. This planet must have a will of its own. If it were just a fomenting configuration of geologic forces, it would not have moved mountains to save itself. We have lost very many things, but still, how lucky."

Grace sees it differently. "Don't you understand? This planet would have survived the asteroid impact. It did not exert such effort for its own sake. It would not have been blasted from its cozy orbit. Only we would have been routed from our fragile niche. The aftermath of such an impact would have made this planet inhospitable to us. While I was unconscious— dead— adrift on some vision quest, I saw Reem, and Rom, and Webster, and you, along with many, many others embedded inside Earth, like embryos inside an incubating egg. Suddenly, the planet exploded. Naturally, I feared annihilation, surely annihilation. Instead, I felt myself soaring into an inner sanctum so far beyond that fabled rainbow— I can't explain except to say: one morning will come this day. Yesterday was not quite ripe. We would have spilled stillborn into the universe. If this planet had a will of its own, its will alone, it could exist as happily with dinosaurs as mites, prefer porpoises no more than viral fungi. What would it care, unless there really is a Lord Mother Earth, capable of compassion, made in our image. Perhaps we are her favored children, blossoming ever so slowly, in need of much protection — much forgiveness. If so, do you realize what we owe her, what she sacrificed to protect her prodigal sons and daughters? We aren't lucky, Aaron — we are blessed."

With this, Grace proffers the ripe and redolent fruit.